# The Boards Between Us

## Cassandra Moll

## Other Titles By Cassandra Moll

*To those currently feeling burned or jaded—*
*Love (& maybe even a hockey coach) are waiting to skate in*
*and tear down your walls.*

# The Boards Between Us

## Cassandra Moll

# 1
# Alex

"I owe you, girl. Seriously, thank you. Cooper would be so upset if he missed this." Peeking my head around the doorframe, I scan the living room for my twelve-year-old son. I find him on the couch, staring blankly at the TV, one arm elbow deep in a bag of Cool Ranch Doritos.

"You don't owe me anything but permission to punch Nick in the balls the next time I see him."

A chuckle escapes my lips as I duck back into the kitchen. "Brooke, don't do that," I say, readjusting the phone on my shoulder. "Go for the face. It's worth a lot more."

Brooke scoffs. "You're so right. What was I thinking?"

"My guess is you were looking for a challenge because his balls would be incredibly hard to find."

"Ha! Write about that one in your column."

"Oh yeah, I can see the title now. *Fist To Face or Knee To Balls? The Pros and Cons of Beating Your Ex.*" Brooke laughs on the other end of the line. "Hey, I have to run," I say. "But thanks again."

"Text me later?"

"Obviously." I press end on the call and slide the phone across the island.

Resting my elbows on the granite, I drop my head in my palms and take a deep breath. I knew this would happen. Work always comes first for Nick. I should have known better than to expect today to be any different, but I thought maybe he would prioritize his son over his job for once in his perfect little life. I was wrong. *Shocker.*

When I met Nick Mercer in college, he was totally different. He had just graduated, and I was starting my sophomore year. I was still naive enough to think that journalism was going to pay my bills one day, and he still believed he'd have a life outside of business. We met at a coffee shop while I was waiting by the pick-up counter for my mid-morning muffin. Standing there, in my North Face and Uggs, he walked in and took my breath away. He was tall and handsome in his dark navy suit, and he ordered his macchiato quickly and decisively like he had places to be. Coming from campus, where most guys wake and bake for their morning fix, seeing a man in pants without a drawstring ordering a *real* coffee was captivating. I was both impressed and intrigued as I drank him in.

*"You're staring," he said, snapping me out of my trance, now standing by me at the counter. He let out a chuckle that sounded like a goddamn symphony, and I suddenly struggled to breathe, let alone speak. "Is it the tie? I knew I should have gone with the blue." He ran his long fingers down the length of the fabric giving me time to gather myself.*

*I cleared my throat and spoke with false confidence. "No, the orange looks nice."*

*"My mom called it apricot." He raised one brow and the corner of his lips.*

*"Well, your mom sounds..."*

*"Like the back of a crayon box?"*

*I failed to smother a laugh, and my cheeks turned warm. "I was going to say creative."*

*He shifted closer to me with narrowing eyes, and my heart rate increased with each passing step. When he was close enough that I could count the blonde waves that framed his beautiful face, he parted his lips. As if he changed his mind, he closed them again and took a deep breath before actually speaking.*

*"Hi," he said simply.*

*"Hi."*

*"I'm Nick." He offered me his hand.*

*I placed mine in his and spoke in a shaky voice. "I'm—"*

*"Alex!" the barista called out. My lips curled up, and tilting my head sideways, I nodded toward the cup with my name written across the front. I dropped his hand and reached for my latte.*

*"It's nice to meet you, Alex."*

*I bit my bottom lip before smiling at him over the rim of my drink.*

*"Would you like to have that coffee with me?" he asked, piercing my soul with his hazel eyes. I took a second to pretend I was thinking before I spoke the phrase that would change my life.*

*"Let's do it," I said.*

*Famous last words.*

Nick and I became inseparable after that. We dated the rest of that year, which was his first in law school, spending every free second hanging out and hooking up. We had a plan—because those always pan out when you're young and in love. Nick would graduate at the top of his class, and I would get my journalism degree and find a job somewhere that mattered. He'd defend the country from its problems, and I'd write about them for all to read.

We were a match made in Heaven. A power couple. But that all changed over Christmas break my junior year.

There are a few three-word phrases that seem to rock people's worlds:

*"I love you."*

*"Now or never."*

*"Be the change."*

*"Live, laugh, love."*

But if you ask me, those all pale in comparison to the one I heard in Nick's apartment one random Friday night.

*"It says pregnant."*

That one sentence changed our lives forever—mine astronomically more than Nick's.

As soon as we found out, he panicked. I mean, we both did, but for someone whose future job was going to put him under extreme pressure, I had never seen him so flustered. Eventually, all we did was argue.

*"I had my life planned out, Lex. How am I supposed to finish school let alone land a job at a good firm when I'm up all night with a baby? What do you expect me to do? Walk in for interviews with spit up on my suit?"*

*"First of all, Nick, I thought it was our life that was planned out. And of course this wasn't part of it, but what are we supposed to do about it now?"*

*He paused, one eyebrow raised, until it clicked in my head. I knew what he was thinking.*

*"No," I said. "No. I'm not giving up our baby."*

*He came and sat next to me on the edge of his full-size bed. Putting his hand on my knee, he turned and looked at me sincerely. "I just think we need to think about things." He stroked my cheek, and I leaned into his touch. "Are we really ready for this?"*

*Looking down at my flat belly, I brought my palm to the area low on my torso. "Probably not," I said. Nick visibly relaxed, a slow smile growing on his face. "But that doesn't change that I'm having this baby."*

*Blowing out a heavy breath, Nick stared at the carpet under his feet for what felt like hours until he finally began to nod his head slowly. "Okay," he said, his voice barely above a whisper.*

*My head snapped up, and without a doubt, my eyes held hope behind the tears that were forming. "Okay?"*

*He nibbled on his bottom lip before speaking. "Okay," he repeated. "We'll adjust."*

We did not adjust much. I, however, adjusted enough for the both of us. For starters, I dropped out of school with only one year to go. That wasn't my intention. In fact, I was determined to finish my final semesters. But *morning* sickness? Never heard of it. I was sick constantly. All. Day. Long.

After a while, I missed so many classes that I had two options—fail or quit. I figured it would look better when I eventually went back if I explained to schools that I simply took a year off, rather than a transcript full of zeros and incompletes. *Poor naive Alex who thought going back to school would be that simple.*

Besides withdrawing from all of my classes, I also moved into Nick's one bedroom apartment. Not being a student anymore meant no more student housing, but I wanted to stay near him, so this was my only choice. I thought not much would change, but I was wrong again. They say moving in with a potential partner shows you their true colors no matter how much time you spent together before. Unfortunately... they were right.

With Nick finishing up his hardest year yet, already looking for jobs and swimming in student loan debt, and me sick as a dog and flat out broke, we were miserable. As the months passed, Nick grew distant. At first, he blamed it on the fact that he was up studying all hours of the night and any free time he had was spent working at a small firm downtown. He always said he didn't have time for *anything* besides work. *"It wasn't me."* But then the resentment set in. For both of us.

I stayed home all day, cooking and cleaning to try my best to prove that I was cut out to be the wife and mother I was now destined to become. And he never even noticed. He was always tired or busy and never wanted to talk about the baby or our future plans. It felt like I was trying to see the good in things and he was trying to avoid them.

I was lonely and swollen, and as my belly grew, so did my discontent for how he was acting. Eventually, I started hating him in general. He made a comment one night in the middle of an argument that he thought we were making a mistake. We were too young, and he was only years away from accomplishing his dream. *"Maybe we were wrong thinking we should keep the baby."* At that point, I didn't even have it in me to argue anymore. I moved out the next day and went to live with my mom an hour from the city.

It was always just my mom and me. She's the only one who raised me—my best friend—and she took me and my round belly in with no questions asked. Maybe it was the fact that she knew what I was going through. Or maybe it was a mother doing what was best for her child, which is exactly what I was doing. Either way I was grateful.

Nick played the role of heartbroken boyfriend for a little while, visiting me if not just for the sake of appearances. He even called me one night and asked if I thought maybe we should reconsider separating like this. But even that faded quickly, and those visits grew scarce.

When I went into labor, I called him, and to his credit, he came right away. He showed up to the hospital in his usual suit, once again, a complete contrast to my appearance. He wore a jacket versus my hospital gown. His hair was slicked back, a loose wave tucked casually behind his ear, and mine looked like I stood in a storm with a wire hanger. The only similarity between the two of us, in every sense of the word, was the sheen of sweat on our foreheads. Mine was from trying to push a cantaloupe out of a grape-sized hole, and his was from the fact that his entire life was about to change. Only it wasn't.

I always thought Nick and I were such a cute example of how opposites attract. I used to laugh off the contrasts between us—our wardrobes, our job choices, our family history. It was quirky—our thing. But that day, bringing our baby into the world, alone despite a room full of people, our differences were anything but cute.

Nick came around a few times a week after that, whenever it seemed to fit into his schedule. He was good with Cooper, and when he was around, there was no doubt in my mind that he loved our little boy. Nick has always just been selfish.

I didn't see it at first. I mean, I barely caught my breath from being with this man until I peed on a stick one night in his apartment. But that's the lawyer in him. He's a smooth talker, a convincing negotiator, and his pretty face only adds to his charm. Now, it's the same.

When he's with his son, there's no doubt that he cares, but unlike me, he only has to parent when he's around—when it's convenient for him. Since making partner, that's been even less than before, and Coop's getting to the age that it's harder to cover for him. Sure, he throws money his way for whatever he needs, but there isn't much quality time spent together.

He always has some excuse. There's a trial or a meeting or he's *just really slammed.* "So, when he told me two months ago that he'd go with our son to the NHL game that his peewee team planned, I figured this may happen. But it wasn't until this afternoon that I actually got the call.

*"I'm sorry, Lex. I thought this trial would have ended by now, but there's a recess every damn day. I can't be there tonight, but tell Coop that I'll take him to a game soon, just the two of us. Oh, and my assistant is dropping off a jersey right now. It's Anderson's. He'll love it."*

*I scoffed under my breath at the mention of her. "How is the PA you're banging, by the way?"*

*I knew it was petty, but I couldn't help myself. As much as Nick complains, he loves being the boss. He only ever dates people inferior to him in some way or another. It's why I'll never again date a guy in a suit. I'm convinced that he saw me that morning in the cafe—in my college girl uniform of a fleece jacket and furry boots—and somewhere deep down, he got off on the power trip. Even back then, it was built into him to think little of people "less successful" than he is. To Nick, money means success, success means power, and power means you can treat people however you want.*

*"Oh, grow up, Lex," he said in response.*

*I inhaled audibly. "You always did like them beneath you, Nick."* In more ways than one.

*"Just tell Cooper I'm sorry. I have to go."*

It's unbecoming, I know, to stoop down to that level, and honestly, it's very unlike me. But I've had it with Nick constantly letting us down. He thinks he can just cover up going back on his word by throwing a gift in Cooper's direction. I'm sick of it, and on top of it all, now I have to give up my best night at the restaurant for tips.

I take a deep breath, preparing myself to tell my son that he now has to drag his mom to the game. I exhale through pursed lips, then my next thought hits me.

*What the hell do I wear?*

# 2

# Levi

"Get your head out of your ass, Anderson," I yell to our star forward who looks like he woke up about five minutes before he got here. "We're here to work on our power play, not work off your hangover."

Drew Anderson drops his head in response and makes his way back to the neutral zone to run the drill again. I smack a puck to the empty corner where a group of players, including a dragging Anderson, are waiting by the net to put it into play. Crossing my arms over my chest, I stick my whistle in my mouth, looking at them like someone pissed in my cheerios.

I give these guys shit because it's my job, but let's be honest—I used to be them. I spent the majority of my time as a player pushing my body to every possible limit. It's what landed me on The Crossbar's Wall of Fame, with the record time for chugging a forty from a skate, and what gave me my career ending injury in the last game I ever played. I never settled for average. When I wasn't crushing beers at the bar or skulls on the ice, I was crushing PRs in the gym left and right—constantly putting myself through the ringer.

Puck drop isn't until 7:05pm. That gives these guys the majority of the day to recover from whatever they got into last night. At their ages, that's practically a lifetime. It's how I used to see it, and I know damn well it's how they see it now. In reality, maybe I'm a little jealous. I wish

I was that carefree again. I wish I had the best of both worlds—hockey and a life outside of it. Shit, I guess I should be happy they're even here at all.

The practices before games are always "optional." It's a time for injured players to work out some kinks and everyone else to work on areas of weakness and get themselves loose for the night's big game. Per their contract, they aren't required, and as such, I remind everyone before each one that they don't technically have to come. But they all know they're expected to be here. If they're not perfect on the ice, it'll be the first thing I comment on. And that's not usually a gamble they're willing to make.

I didn't become one of the youngest NHL coaches in history because of mediocre commitment or half-assed preparation. You join my team, you know what you're getting into—high potential and even higher expectations. Hell, it's often the reason players want to come to the Flames. They know that they're getting 110% from me and that I'll always push them to give me that back. For sixty minutes under the lights, I expect them to be exceptional—not good, not even great—and that starts with the practice time before.

I'm like that because I know what they're capable of and that they need someone to hold them accountable. Besides, I already lost entirely too much when it came to my time as a player. I refuse to be subpar as a coach.

Anderson is the first to touch the puck and put it into motion. Tapping it off of his stick, he slides it to Alexei Petrov, our Russian forward, who takes it behind the net. When he calls for it again at the point, Petrov swiftly passes it back to him. In his typical showman fashion, Drew plays with the puck a second too long, and our best defenseman, Brett "Burnsey" Burns, steals it away. Burns winds up and dumps it into the opposite zone, ending the drill and our forward's chances at capitalizing on the power play. Anderson throws his stick in Burnsey's direction, which is a little dramatic for losing the puck in a drill, but Burns laughs it off and kicks it back toward him as he skates to grab water.

Drew Anderson is hands down our best player. He's hit a bit of a rough patch recently, but he's quick and accurate and his knowledge of the game is unmatched on this team. But he's also a performer. He's the type who puck handles for the hell of it and whose celebration they show on TV the next day—always the latest dance move or current social media sensation. He's a huge personality on the team and an even bigger talent, but he and a few others occasionally forget that all of that comes second to their actual job.

Don't get me wrong, our guys are good. Our team is good. In fact, with only a few games under our belt, the Flames are already projected to make it to the Cup this season. But I know better than anyone that all kinds of plans can end in an instant, and just because something seems like it's going to work out, doesn't mean it won't end in the gutter. It's happened to me on more than one occasion—both on and off the ice. There is no way I'd let my team—or my life—be at the mercy of anyone but me again.

Shaking my head of my thoughts, I blow the whistle that hangs from my lips. "Run it again."

The boys skate back into position as Burns mumbles under his breath to Petrov who probably doesn't even understand him. I don't catch all of what he says, but there's no missing the "get laid" at the end of his statement. Burnsey tries to hide his amusement afterward, but I can see his goofy smile even from underneath his helmet.

I roll my eyes in their direction. These guys are on big screens a few nights a week and pictures of them literally hang on people's bedroom walls. That doesn't change the fact that most of them aren't even old enough to rent a car on their own.

It's locker room banter. They aren't stupid. They know that the idea of me not getting women is far from the truth. In fact, it's their go-to joke when they want to give me a hard time.

They never let me forget that, according to the papers, I'm one of Golden City's most eligible bachelors. The gossip magazines constantly take advantage of the fact that I'm not only one of the youngest coaches to join the roster, but that I'm also admittingly single.

*"Coach, is there a Mrs. we'll be seeing this season?" one reporter asked at my onboarding conference.*

*"No," I answered. "No Mrs., no girlfriend—nothing like that. The only ring I'm looking to get can't be bought."*

The press ate that up, of course. Every hockey channel or podcast commented on Golden City's committed coach, and bloggers and journalists spun it as a challenge for every available influencer in the sports' world. If you ask me, the fact that my relationship status is a conversation at all amongst these people is fucking stupid. That being said, it's become even more of a conversation recently now that Olivia's been around.

Liv is a model and an influencer—whatever that means. We met at an event a couple of weeks ago and ended up hooking up the same night. Of course, afterward, I explained to her that I don't do the couple thing. I told her not to expect anything from me except for what she got that first night we met—which was admittedly great sex. Apparently, she thought so too because she still texts me a few times a week to get together. The problem is, Liv leaves no mystery when it comes to her life online. Though she hasn't posted about me directly, people are starting to put two and two together.

If I'm honest, Olivia is a lot, much like the other women that keep coming around. They all talk about themselves more than I thought was possible, and more of their body is fake than not. Luckily, neither of these pose much of a problem for me—we don't talk much when we're together, and plastic surgery is sort of the norm in the sports world. The bottom line is, I may be single, but much to my big brother's dismay, there's no shortage of release.

Liam, the Gator's star shortstop, and leading pain in my ass, hates the fact that I won't settle down. In typical big brother fashion, he thinks he's protecting me by trying to tell me what I should and shouldn't do. But he was there when everything happened before. He knows the reason I don't even entertain the idea of love anymore. The problem is, he also has no issue reminding me that getting my dick wet a few times a week doesn't fix a broken heart. What I keep trying to tell him is that my heart *isn't* broken. Not anymore. I'm just making sure it stays that way.

Liam has a hard time with this concept because unlike me, he refuses to be with *anybody*. It's understandable considering what he's endured the last few years, but it's one area where we find it hard to relate to each other. He thinks I'm out sleeping around to hide the fact that I'm lonely and devastated, and I think he's hiding away for the same reason. I'm not sure what either of us are doing makes much sense, but *my* plan at least seems to be working for me.

My thoughts are interrupted by Burns' heinous, yet infamous, cackle. I look over only to see the group of boys quickly trying hard to cover their laughter, and I suck my teeth in response. They avoid eye contact as they scoot down the ice, but there's no hiding their shit-eating grins. For now, I choose to ignore them being that there's only two minutes left in practice, and I have more important things to get to. But that doesn't mean I won't happen to remember the next time either of them decides to run their mouths.

I toss a new puck into the zone and watch Petrov take it behind the net. He gives his teammates a chance to set up before skating up the boards. He moves around one defenseman and bounces off another before pulling back for a slapshot and ripping it toward the goal. Anderson sits near the crease, and just when our goalie leans to the right, he tips it in on the left-hand side—smooth, fluid, exactly what I'm looking for.

Pulling my hands behind my back, I nod toward the group of them now huddled together. "Showers," is all I say. "I'll see you tonight."

The boys tap sticks as they make their way to the bench. Reaching for my phone in my pocket, I pull up my calendar, the reminder for the facilities tour tonight for the Junior Rockets written at the top.

The community program I created called Spark the Flame was one of the first initiatives I set up as head coach. It gives the young teams in the area an inside look at the Flames and our arena. They get to tour the facilities, ask questions, get autographs, and take pictures, but if you ask me, it's mutually beneficial. Yes, through the program, the kids get the opportunity to see their heroes on the other side of the glass, but more importantly, the professionals get a chance to reconnect with their purpose.

It's so easy to get lost in the madness of this lifestyle. I know that better than anyone. My playing career and my job now mean everything to me, but to ten, eleven, twelve-year-old eyes, what we do isn't work—it's a superpower. Giving them an opportunity to see the locker room, the offices, and even the tunnel that leads out onto the ice is like watching them witness magic for the very first time. It's an experience of a lifetime for them, but for the team and me, it's a good reminder that this game is much bigger than us.

If there's one thing I have a soft spot for, it's kids. Ever since my niece was born, I've seen how incredible and resilient they can be. Honestly, I think they have more to offer us than we have to offer them sometimes. The young boys and girls who take part in this program think we hung the moon for wearing red and black. But what they don't realize, is we used to be them. Before we had all of this, hockey was just a dream. Sometimes we forget that too.

Exiting out of that reminder, the next one pops up—Ruthie's game. Perfect, I get to see my girl today. Ruthie's only ten, but she may be the funniest person I know. She's definitely the cutest and hands down has the biggest heart.

She's probably my favorite person in the entire world, and I like to think I'm at least tied for hers, despite the fact that she's almost at the age where she's too cool for me. Liam may be up there, but no one spoils her like Uncle Levi.

I shove my phone back into my warmup pants and hustle to the bench. If I hurry, I can finish up everything I have to do here, shower and change, and still have time to stop for coffee on the way.

# 3

# Alex

Pulling the hood of my sweatshirt from under my vest, I rush down the stairs. Stopping in front of the entryway mirror, I pause long enough to throw my loose waves into a messy ponytail before I'm off again.

I went with the bright red vest I bought at the beginning of Cooper's first season, simply because it matched the Junior Rocket's jerseys. A vest is often appropriate in New England weather, but I would have gone with one in a less aggressive shade if it wasn't meant to represent Coop's team. It didn't occur to me when I purchased it that unlike the Flames' temperature-controlled arena, his team plays in an actual ice rink where a vest just wouldn't cut it. That being said, the statement piece mostly collects dust in my closet because I don't often have opportunities where it's appropriate to wear a crimson puffer—until today.

I run into the kitchen, first poking my head into the living room to look for Cooper. When I see he isn't there, I head back to the island to look for my keys.

"Cooper!" I call, lifting yesterday's mail. I throw the bowl with my son's mushy, seven-hour-old cereal into the sink, then lean toward the junk drawer by the fridge.

I like to think I have my life together, but then something happens like Nick bailing last minute and the pivot completely throws me off. It's not like I'm a total mess, but at the end of the day, there's only one of me.

I'm sure every parent feels stressed and overstimulated the majority of the time. Raising kids without royally screwing them up is flat out hard. But it's even more difficult when there's no one else there to share the burden. No one to lighten the load or even sit and complain to at the end of an exceptionally hard day. Sometimes I feel like I'm barely keeping it together. Like if one more thing gets added to my pile, it may topple over and bury me completely. Add in losing my car keys, and those little fuckers may very well be my downfall.

"Coop, we have to get going!" I anxiously rummage through countless pens, loose coins, and one empty tape dispenser, before moving on to the next possible hiding place.

"It's four o'clock!" I yell, grabbing my belt bag from where it sits on the counter. I dump it out onto the granite and quickly scan its contents. A wad of cash, a pomegranate ChapStick, and a rogue hair tie now litter the space in front of me, but my keys are nowhere to be found.

"We're seriously going to be late!" I scream to apparently no one that's listening as I throw everything back in. Tossing the strap over my shoulder, I walk to the front door to check if I once again left the keys in the lock. I throw it open and look down at the keyless knob before letting out a frustrated groan. As if this day wasn't a mess already, now I have to worry about being late to the arena and having my kid resent me for the rest of his life. *Excellent.*

I run my hand down my face, careful to avoid the only makeup I applied to my lashes. I shoot my head back up. "Cooper I—"

Mid-sentence, I look outside and see my son sitting shotgun in a parked car. *My* parked car. He's wearing his new Flames jersey that Nick's PA did in fact drop off and his worn Junior Rockets beanie. Waving at me frantically, I see him mouth the word *hurry* through the window. I laugh either *to* myself or *at* myself, my mood instantly lifted. Sometimes this kid drives me absolutely crazy, but I wouldn't have it any other way. Shaking my head, I pull the door closed behind me before heading out to meet him.

Walking past the front of the car, I stick my tongue out at Cooper through the windshield. I yank hard twice on the driver's side door before it finally opens. "It'd be nice if you'd let me know you were going to the car next time, ya noodle," I say, stepping in. Coop looks at me like it's Christmas morning, his knee bouncing up and down as if he chugged an iced coffee while he was busy waiting.

"Sorry, Mom. I'm just so excited. Let's go, let's go!" He hands me my keys, then waves his hand at me like I'm deliberately wasting time instead of fastening my seatbelt.

"Alright, I'm going!" I turn over the ignition once, twice, three times before it starts and then throw the car into reverse. "So, are you excited for the game, or...?" I ask sarcastically, pulling onto the road.

At twelve-years-old, Coop straddles the line between still a young kid and too cool for his mother. How much information I get from him is hit or miss. Sometimes I say something and he won't stop talking. Other times, I say the same thing, and I get a grunt here and an "mhmm" there. I've learned to ask simple questions, keep the mood light whenever possible, and let him take the lead.

"Obviously, Mom," he says, looking out the passenger window and pulling his beanie lower on his ears. "The Flames are going all the way this season, I know it. Anderson is such a stud, and Monte is an absolute legend. They got robbed last year, but not this time."

*I guess today I have the chatty Coop.*

He wiggles his whole upper-half back and forth. "I feel it in my bones." I laugh knowing as much as he sounds like a teenager sometimes, he's still my silly little boy underneath the long shaggy hair and full hockey garb.

When Nick and I went our separate ways, I was terrified of being a single parent. Despite not realizing it until I was older, I had watched my mom struggle my whole life to raise me on her own. She worked too hard and slept too little, and I was so worried that I wouldn't be able to follow in her massive footsteps. That all changed the moment I laid eyes on Cooper. I was devastated that Nick and I had drifted apart and that the person I thought was "the one" ended up being someone completely different. But looking into Coop's round baby blues, I saw the love of my life. And the only boy—besides his father—to ever take my breath away.

"So, whose jersey are you wearing? Sanderson?"

"Anderson!"

"Okay, okay, sorry. Anderson. And the coach is... Montel?"

"Mom! It's Monte." He lets out a sigh and rolls his eyes, while I mentally high-five myself for riling him up. Tipping my chin, I let my mouth form an O shape. "He's only like the best coach in the league. Youngest too. He played for the Wolves for ten seasons before he tore his ACL. Total bummer. I YouTubed the video like a million times. He was cutting across the ice and got wrecked by The Goon." I glance at him straight faced. "Joe Morris, Mom." My expression doesn't change, but he still continues. "Anyway, Monte's knee puffed up like a watermelon." He takes both hands and holds them in front of his face in two, mirroring C shapes. "It was awesome!" he says through the hole in his hands.

My brow furrows while the rest of my face falls in disgust. "Okay first... ew. Second, what's so great about the two of them?"

He turns now so he's facing me, his face riddled with excitement. "Anderson is an absolute sniper, and Monte is a stud behind the bench. Trust me, Mom. They slap."

I turn down my lips and widen my eyes in mock impression. "I mean, if they're snipers and studs, then obviously they slap."

Now it's Cooper's turn to look at me blankly. I nudge him with my elbow, and a chuckle escapes his lips as he rolls his eyes away from me. Preteen or not, we're still as close as can be, despite that half of the time I have no idea what he's talking about.

That's another thing that used to scare me. My mom and I were best friends while I was growing up, minus those few teenage years where everyone hates the person making the rules. But we had so much in common. We liked the same classic chick flicks and watched soap opera reruns whenever they were on. She'd tell me what color shoes to wear with which belt and give me advice when my friends at school were acting bitchy—girl things.

Coop and I don't have that. He's into games that I know nothing about and sports that I can barely keep up with. He watches superhero movies and shows where people prank each other for fun. I can help him learn how to treat a woman and with what girls like when you go on dates, but I don't know anything about what it's like in a locker room. I can't tell him from experience what to do when he wakes up with morning wood or how to navigate when kids hit growth spurts before him and pick on his small size and changing voice. That's all stuff he needs a male perspective on. One Nick could offer him if he were ever consistently around, but that I will never be fully qualified to give.

Clearing my throat of my sudden sadness, I change the subject. "So, what's the plan for tonight?"

He pulls out his phone, Nick's previous "I'm sorry" gift, and the thing I specifically told my ex that our son didn't need. Nick insisted that its sole purpose is to be a means for him to communicate with Cooper, but last time I checked, he hadn't sent more than a "good luck at your game" text in the few months he's had it. When he's with me, the phone is for weekends and nights where he has hockey only. If he has practice and I'm at the restaurant, he is to call me if they end early or if his coach asks him to stay late. Outside of that it's kept at a minimum. He can use it for pictures or games, but he's too young for social media or to be texting with friends. In my opinion, there is absolutely nothing that important for twelve-year-olds to be discussing without parental supervision.

Cooper turns his screen so I catch a flash of the schedule on the Junior Rocket's website. "It says the facilities tour starts at four-thirty in the offices. Then, we get to see the locker room and a few other things before we walk out through the tunnel. Some of the players and Monte are supposed to be there for the tours, and there's time for questions and autographs before the game. Oh my God—"

My gaze snaps to his. "Coop..."

"Gosh. Oh my gosh! What if Anderson signs my new jersey? Dad will freak!"

I roll my eyes, then dart them back in Cooper's direction, thankful that he's looking down at the picture on his phone. Nick's presents always make Coop forget about the fact that his dad has been basically useless since his ninety-second performance that helped to conceive him. I, however, see right through his bullshit, but it's not something that I want to advertise to Coop. Regardless of how good at it he is, Nick is Cooper's father, and he's the only one he gets. Sometimes I wish I had a dad around even if he was a shitty one.

My dad left my mom when she was pregnant with me just like Nick did, but unlike Cooper's father, mine never came back. Nick takes Coop one weekend a month and every other major holiday each year. Of course, he can see him whenever he wants, but most of the time, those random visits get canceled last minute, just like today. Sometimes I wonder which is worse—a degenerate dad who you've never met or a workaholic one that thinks gifts and grand gestures make up for him prioritizing his job over his son.

I'd never let Cooper know that though. As far as he's concerned, Nick and I are peaches and cream. Best buds. Perfect pals. If Mom taught me one thing about being a single parent, it was to never let your storm get your kid wet.

"That'd be pretty cool, buddy," I say, offering Coop my brightest smile. He bobs his head up and down with wide eyes. "Maybe Monte will too."

Cooper laughs and shakes his head. "That'd be awesome, but Dad would freak for a whole different reason if that happened." I must look at him questioningly because he explains. "Dad hates Monte. He says just because he played doesn't mean he can coach. I heard him tell Grandpa that he got lucky last season making it to the Cup, but he bets his ass he can't do it again."

"Cooper Bennett. Language!"

"What? I didn't say it! Dad did."

"Of course he did," I say to myself. Nick never remembers to watch his mouth around Cooper. Probably because something like that takes practice, which he hasn't had.

"I'm just saying, everything Monte does annoys Dad for some reason. It's hilarious to watch." I stifle a laugh as Coop looks out the window.

I think this Monte guy just became my new favorite person.

# 4

# Levi

I throw my black Range Rover into park and grab the now cold coffee from my cup holder. I had time to grab it before Ruthie's game like I hoped and did so with the intention of taking it with me. Like an idiot though, I left it in my car, and now it's freezing. Could I get a hot, freshly brewed cup from the three hundred dollar coffee machine in my office, sure. But this is Drippy's coffee. Nothing is better than Drippy's coffee—fresh or reheated.

I do a quick search of my interior to make sure I'm not forgetting anything in my rush to get inside. I'm never late to the arena. I'm never late anywhere. In fact, I typically wouldn't have even left after this morning's practice, but today was important to my niece, and I'd be damned if I missed it.

Pushing open the door, I slide off of my black leather seat. My watch reads 4:36pm, which means I'm not only late for the facilities tour that started six minutes ago, but I also don't have time to put my suit on before I have to face the Junior Rockets and their parents.

I pride myself in always being put together. People eat with their eyes so to speak. They judge you by your cover. That's why my cover is always perfect. Not because I give a shit about what other people think, but because I don't have the time or energy to convince someone of what I already know—I have a lot to offer. Businesswise that is.

But the big brown eyes on Ruthie make everything worth it. That girl has me wrapped around her finger. My rock hard exterior melts to complete mush when she's around. That's why when she asked me to go for ice cream after her game-winning goal, I did it. I had to. How could I say no? I may not let a lot of people fully in, but when you're in, you're in. Especially if you're as perfect as she is. Should I have made her leave after scoop number three? Probably. But one look into those cartoon eyes and I'm putty in her hands.

Dashing through the arena's back doors that lead to our offices and locker rooms, my body freezes involuntarily before the door clicks shut. There's a woman standing outside of my office looking at the team photos hanging at the end of the hall. Her arms are crossed over her chest, and there's a crease in her brow like she's either pissed off or focusing—maybe a little of both.

As I watch her, she uncrosses her arms and shoves both hands into the pockets of her bright, red vest. She moves to the next picture and her long wavy ponytail sways back and forth. The honey-colored streaks in her hair catch the light that's above her, which makes them stand out against the chestnut brown that surrounds them. It reminds me of how the sun beams hit the buildings downtown when the sun rises and sets between them, creating a golden glow over the city. I can't see much else except that she's majority legs, and damn... I've never been jealous of a pair of jeans until this very moment.

Out of habit, I bring my cup to my mouth, and it's only when the cold coffee touches my lips, that I snap from the trance I've apparently fallen into. Cracking my neck to both sides, I take a deep breath before exhaling as I move toward not only my office but the woman in front of it. Voices float from the opening in the door, which tell me that the players are already inside. This is the only circumstance where someone is allowed in my office without me there, and everyone who works here knows it.

It takes my brain nearly the length of the hallway to process that this mystery girl is here with one of the Rockets. It then takes all but a few seconds for that thought to lead to two more. One, she is probably a mom. Two, she may be a wife. I might not want my own relationship, but I'm definitely not a homewrecker. That shit is too messy to be worth it.

When I'm only a few feet from both her and my office door, I pause, torn. The professional in me says to pass her by. I might have my fun after hours, but when I'm on the clock, my focus is here. I never mix work and play. Employees, team family members, moms of those who tour our arena—all off limits to my after-hour affairs.

The man in me, however, tells me otherwise. At first glance, she's beautiful. Sexy, even. She has those long legs I'd like straddling my waist, my face—pretty much anywhere she'd like to sit. But she also just stands out to me. Maybe it's the ridiculous vest she's wearing so confidently or the fact that she's out here alone. Either way, the last thing I want to be with this girl is professional. When she doesn't even look in my direction, I quietly clear my throat, my body choosing before my mind has a chance.

The woman swings her gaze to mine, and sucks in a quick breath before swallowing hard. Either I scared the shit out of her and this is her attempt at keeping calm and collected, or she is just as taken aback by me as I am by her. *Interesting.* Her face instantly falls from the snarl she wore before to a soft smile, and her caramel eyes give me a casual once over. *Interesting again.*

"He's late," she says like it fell from her mouth. I don't speak, mostly because I'm not sure what to say, but also because her voice is like an angel's. It's the perfect combination of sweet and feminine but with a dash of rasp that takes my head places it shouldn't go this close to my office. When I don't reply, she continues talking, filling my silence. "The coach. He's like ten minutes late. He's probably getting paid, what? Like three million dollars, and he can't afford a watch? Typical."

She scoffs and rolls her eyes, and I try to hide my smile by taking a vested interest in the lid of my cup. This I did not expect. "Maybe he got stuck somewhere important," I say, bringing my eyes back to hers. A spot of gold in her left iris pulls me in. It pushes through the sienna around it and lands on me like a lighthouse shines on danger ahead.

"Yeah," she says. "Or maybe he thinks because he has this job and the power that comes with it, that the rules don't apply to him. God forbid he makes time for us little people." She speaks with a bite, but there's now a distance to her gaze as if she went somewhere else for a second. Fluttering her long lashes, she exhales a deep breath, and her frown slowly shifts back into the smile from before. "Anyway, I'm Alex." She drops her arms and extends one toward me as I slowly switch my coffee to my other palm, letting her name cement itself into my mind.

"Levi," I say, meeting her handshake, and celebrating internally when I see a vacant left ring finger. My hand swallows hers, palpable electricity shooting up my arm and then further south. If it happens for her too, she doesn't flinch, but she also doesn't pull away as she continues to speak.

"Which kid is yours?" she asks.

I let the question linger before answering. "Oh, I don't have any kids," I say like a challenge.

Her head cocks to the side, her eyebrows creasing, and she pushes her lips into a shallow pout that shouldn't catch my attention but definitely does. "Then why are you—"

"Monte!" a scrawny boy calls from the crack in the door. He's wearing a Flames beanie with floppy ears and a toothy smile a mile long. As he pulls the door open wide, an echo of cheers and whispers from the rest of the crowd floods through it.

Alex, whose head was turned toward the kids, snaps her attention back to me. She does one more back and forth between me and the group of players now gathered at my door, all the while still holding my hand.

The corner of my lip creeps upward, and she instantly drops our embrace, bringing her fingers to brush an imaginary hair behind her ear. My hand floats down, now feeling empty of hers, as the situation becomes clear. Her eyes widen as she huffs out a breath, then her arms cross over her chest like they did when I first saw her looking at the photos. Her guard shoots up in front of me, her once welcoming smile disappearing completely.

I give her time to speak, but when it's clear she has nothing to say, I do instead. "I should probably..." I point my thumb toward the group of boys looking at me starry eyed and the parents standing behind them, watching their reactions.

She does nothing but raise her brows, and I lick my lips in an attempt to hide my grin. This girl has an attitude she's not afraid of showing. Walking in the doorway, the boys all part to let me through, and despite their close proximity to me, it's her eyes I feel on the back of my neck. I walk toward my desk, shaking a parent's hand here and bumping a player's fist there. Sadie, the woman who runs Spark the Flame, is standing in the corner doing her best to paint a professional smile while she avoids my grey sweatpants and black Flames hoodie. I'm not sure she's ever seen me off of the ice in anything but a suit. I sit my cold coffee on the glossy surface of my desk and turn to the crowd. Propping myself onto it, I scan the lot, doing my best to make eye contact with each of the parents.

"I'm sorry I'm late, everyone." There is a short clatter of responses, none of which I hear because I'm searching for Alex. She enters from the hall as I begin again. "I'm Levi Montgomery," I say, directly to her before continuing to scan the rest of the crowd. "But most of you know me as Coach Monte."

A few of the boys look at their parents and smile, one of which is looking at Alex. He's got the same caramel hair color she does, but his eyes are a contrasting blue. She mirrors his excitement while his gaze is on her, but the second he turns to me, it hardens back up.

"I promise that I do in fact own a watch..." I pull up the sleeve of my sweatshirt and flash my black-banded Apple watch to the group. They all chuckle, except for Alex, whose eyes narrow on me instead. Despite her best efforts, a faint smirk creeps up from the cheek that she's biting, and I'll be damned if something inside me doesn't feel rewarded. "But my niece's soccer game ended in a shoot-out and well, Uncle Levi had to be there to watch her score the winning goal."

Everyone either smiles approvingly or lets out a chuckle, except for the feisty brunette that seems to have my attention. Her face remains cold, but her arms slowly unfold from her chest as she brings her hands back to her pockets. I can tell from her eyes that she's trying to read me, and I know she can tell that I'm doing the same. She's probably trying to decide if I'm genuine or not—if I'm telling the truth. I'm trying to figure out why since the moment I saw her, my heart's picked up speed and my boxers seem a little too tight. Both things happens on occasion sure, but my heart and my dick have never reacted this way together.

"Regardless," I continue, clasping my hands in my lap. I look around the room at the twelve-year-old faces so full of excitement just to be standing here. "I apologize for being late, and I can assure you..." I stand up straight, squaring my shoulders, and look directly into the gold spot I can see even from here. "You now have my undivided attention."

# 5

# Alex

U nbelievable.

One minute I'm talking to the cute dad in the hallway with sexy, tousled hair, grey freaking sweatpants, and no wedding ring. The next, that same guy is standing in this millionaire's office, going on about making plays and changing lines. *Talk about a buzz kill.*

I won't lie, when Levi approached me, I was pleasantly surprised. Not that I'd really be into dating a dad of one of Cooper's teammates, but it would have been nice to have someone to talk to for the next few hours who didn't come with his wife or wear heels to an ice rink. Most of the parents came here as a family, and the ones who came alone aren't really my speed. The moms of Coop's teammates are... stuffy. My idea of a good time is going to a Krunk Fitness class with Brooke and dancing out my stress. These women look like they might shrivel up and die if they even heard the word twerk.

All that said, my surprise quickly turned to disgust. I was so wrong about him becoming my new favorite person. That guy is Nick with a clipboard. A much taller, broader, more athletic version, but I can only assume, after his first impression, that all of the same general qualities still apply. Rich, formal, dedicated to work—he's clearly selfish if he had time to stop for coffee on the way despite already being late. Oh yeah, he cared about making us wait—so much so that he grabbed his fix first.

He's also clearly arrogant as hell. Just the way he acted when he realized I had no idea who he was. *"Oh, I don't have any kids."* And with that smug little grin of his. Typical. He must think it's absolutely hilarious that I didn't recognize someone of his authority. Stupid me, right?

After Coach Montgomery's little office chat, the group moved onto the next leg of the tour. Following Coop around the film room while Sadie, the woman in charge, talks about camera equipment, I can't shake what Levi said.

*"You now have my undivided attention."*

It wasn't only *what* he said but *how* he said it. Strong, annoyingly sexy, and while staring at me with unrelenting eye contact that made my stomach do this weird flipping thing. He doesn't know me from Adam, but it's like he knew what to say to strike a nerve—and he did.

Cooper slaps his friend's arm, which interrupts my thoughts, and directs his attention to the viewing screen that's broadcasting the last game's footage. The camera follows a forward who gets shoved into the boards, and I catch a glimpse of Levi in the background behind the bench.

Much like he did when he uttered those words, he stands stoically. He watches the two players collide into the glass without so much as blinking. His hair is gelled back this time, unlike earlier, but his beard is still perfectly shaped. He fiddles with a pen in his hand, and of course, he's wearing a goddamn suit that for some reason both pisses me off and awakens something just below my belt.

Thanks to Nick, I am so turned off by the idea of ever dating someone like him again—I refuse to fall second to a job, especially when there's Cooper to think about—but damn if Levi doesn't wear that suit like it was stitched right onto his skin.

Suddenly much warmer than I was before, I slide out of my vest and drape it over my forearm.

"Mom!" Cooper calls, and when I turn to find him, I realize the rest of the group is halfway out the door. I steal one more glance at the screen, but the camera has already moved on to the goalie that's in a split way deeper than I could ever go.

I look back to see Coop's shoulder pass the doorframe and hustle to catch up to the other players and parents. I get one foot into the hall when a shadow falls over me. A crisp smell like apple and mint invades my senses.

"Don't want to be late," a smooth deep voice says, too close to my ear for him to be standing up straight.

I turn my head and meet the same eyes that I just watched follow his players on the game footage—dark green like emeralds jabbing my soul. It takes my brain a second to register that the eyes, the voice, and the delicious smell, have all come from the same person who's leaning beside me. Levi's bent down mere inches from me and only stands tall when I pull back from his space. He's smoothed his hair back pristinely and swapped his loungewear for a tailored black suit, the only pop of color coming from the crisp white button-up that lies underneath. With a skinny black tie layered on top, it's different from the navy blue suit and silver tie from the video. This one's more formal, more striking—it'd be more alluring if I didn't know better.

I swallow the saliva that's built under my tongue and collect myself, standing taller. The appearance of this man may be tempting, but if there's one thing I've practiced over the years it's to never let them see me sweat. My mom and I agree that people underestimate a single woman, especially those who already think they're better than anyone else. So, even if it's all a front, I try my hardest not to forget who I am. *Fake it till you make it, baby.*

"How's the coffee?" My tone is sarcastic and snide, but only to me who can't seem to let go that he had time for a latte despite us here waiting.

"Hot," he says as he arches his brow, and it's like the area between my thighs takes it as a command, heating immediately. *But that doesn't mean anything.*

I do a slow nod as I turn away from him, following the crowd. He leaps forward and walks alongside me as Sadie announces that we are heading to the Flames' locker room.

"Is he yours?" he asks, pointing to Cooper, who like the rest of the group, has yet to realize that the god they call Monte is following behind them.

"Sure is."

Levi takes a sip of his coffee, and I make the most of the vantage point to analyze features like his chiseled jawline. I didn't notice from afar, but beneath his well-trimmed beard, the angles under his cheeks and just above his neck are sculpted like artwork because... of course they are. Judging by the pull in his jacket where his bicep flexes as he brings his cup to his mouth, his whole body is carved the same. And those lips. They're full and smooth—almost too pretty to belong to a man.

Pulling his hand away from his face, he catches my gaze, and I dart my eyes in front of me in an attempt to hide my staring. The group stops to listen to Sadie's spiel about the layout of the locker room and the rules of touring it. Coach Monte uses the idle time to his advantage, his voice almost a whisper. "You're annoyed, aren't you?"

I'm caught off guard. He speaks casually despite me being me and him being the star of this show. I hesitate a beat before responding. "I don't know what you're talking about," I say quietly.

"Yes, you do."

I keep my eyes trained forward. "I really don't."

"You're irritated," he says as if he knows me well. He squares his body toward mine, and I mirror his stance. "With me."

"I am not irritated with you," I lie. My mind is running a mile a minute trying to keep up with this man who I met maybe five minutes ago. Whether he's correct or not, his assumption about how I'm feeling only further triggers my hatred of men like him.

"You are."

"Am not."

"Are too."

"I don't even know you."

"Oh, I know," he says quickly, inhaling a deep breath. He exhales slowly, the corners of his lips tugging up gently. Neither of us speak, but there's a tension between us that's got my heart knocking inside of my chest. He parts his lips, and at the same time, Cooper realizes I'm talking to his hero.

"Mom?" he says excitedly, but I can't seem to look away.

"Hey, buddy," Levi says, slowly breaking our eye contact. He holds his hand out to Cooper who shakes it with gusto. "Let me guess... " he says, grabbing Coop by the shoulder and turning him side to side. "Forward." My son's face lights up, and he nods enthusiastically. "Two goals last game."

"Atta boy." Levi nudges his arm, and Coop smiles proudly. "Anderson fan, huh?"

"Hell yeah!" Cooper says, then his eyes dart to mine. I give him the *I Know You Didn't Just Say That* look, and he hangs his head. "I—I mean... yes, sir." I roll my eyes, and Levi lets out a chuckle.

"Me too," he says with a wink. "I think he's around here somewhere. We'll have to trap him for an autograph before you head out."

Cooper's face pops back up, and I can't help but smile despite my annoyance. *Why does it feel like Coach Monte knows exactly what he's doing?*

Sadie pulls open the doors of the locker room, and our group begins to funnel inside. I go to move with them when a hand lands on my shoulder. Cooper continues on as I tilt my head and look first at the fingers that sit right above my collarbone, then completely turn around.

This guy is either extremely friendly or has some serious boundary issues. *Has he ever heard of personal space?* I glance again at his hand branding my skin and make a mental note to add some sort of boundary related topic to my idea list for the blog.

"I'm sorry," Levi says, his hand still by my neck. He pulls it away and goosebumps fill their place despite the layers that I'm wearing. "For being late."

"It's fine," I laugh off.

"It's clearly not."

Adjusting my stance, I tuck a stray hair behind my ear. "It is."

He holds my gaze. "You have a problem with *me* then."

"I have a problem with your kind." I snip back, almost too harshly. Our banter is light, but my chest feels heavy. It's true—ex-boyfriend-lawyers, celebrity coaches, they're all the same. Too much power and too little heart.

Levi scoffs and runs a hand down his scruff. "You don't even know me," he says mockingly, repeating my statement from earlier.

I clench my jaw and pull back just a little. "You're right. I don't."

Cooper's voice trails a few feet from the locker room entrance, Levi and I the only two left in the hall. He calls to me once as he crosses the threshold, then disappears into the room with the rest of his team. I lift my brows once, biting my bottom lip, then turn on my heels.

"Let's change that," Levi says once my back is to him. I remain facing forward, but heat pools below my belly button. I close my eyes and grind my teeth, fighting every urge to turn back around. *No, Alex. Not this again.* Listening to the voice in my head, I walk away from where he's still standing.

When I reach the locker room, I finally look back. He hasn't moved, his hand now tucked into his pocket, the bottom of his jacket pulled open behind it. I unapologetically look him over, from his polished shoes to his slicked back hair. I'm instantly taken back to that cafe twelve years ago where everything changed for me... in none of the ways that I thought it would.

"Sorry," I say unconvincingly. I give him a slight shrug and say out loud the thing I've had to constantly remind myself of since I set eyes on him. "I don't date suits."

# 6

# Levi

The arena roars as the horn sounds for Anderson's third goal of the night. I don't know what happened between practice earlier and puck drop, but I don't care. This morning he was dragging. He had yet to rid himself of the toxins he had more than likely indulged in, and it showed. Now, not so much. Tonight he came with grease on his skates and fire in his eyes. He came focused and committed and has been making moves since he first touched the ice.

It started with a breakaway goal where he slipped past two defensemen before faking out the goalie. Then, there was a rebound shot after the puck bounced off the post, and just now, he ripped a slapshot from the top of the circle at the start of the last period. The kid is killing it, buzzin' around with a hot hand and back to playing the way I know he can—better even—and right when it really counts.

Fans from every level throw their hats and beanies onto the ice as the players skate to their respective benches. They celebrate as the sound of our goal song floods the speakers with a rhythmic beat. After they huddle around Drew, the boys gather in front of me as the ice crew starts to collect the discarded gear.

We're already up by two, and where the Warriors look gassed, we're just getting started. All of the extra conditioning I insist on is paying off, and with Anderson hot, my job's been easy so far tonight. So, instead of a big speech, I let the boys have their moment while the arena settles down, and I take advantage of my free time.

The icing on the cake for an already great game is my clear view of the Rockets' box where little Miss I-Don't-Date-Suits is sitting front and center. Alex is hard to miss in her brightly colored vest, but I have a feeling my eyes would be drawn to her regardless. I don't know a thing about this girl, but I'm intrigued. I can't remember the last time I thought twice about the depth of a woman besides what was going on underneath her clothes. I also can't remember the last time I was shot down by one either, and rather than it pissing me off... it really fucking turned me on.

The suit is usually an aphrodisiac for women. Of course, that's not why I wear it, but it's an added bonus that comes with the territory. The same was true as a player. The girls eat up the uniform, helmet, sweat, blood—but they were just as attracted to the formal wear before and after the game.

Alex, however, turned her nose up to it so fast she nearly headbutted me with the tilt of her chin. The fact that I flirted with her in the first place didn't surprise me, but the fact that she gave me nothing back did and the challenge only enticed me more. There's nothing like the chase. It's just been so damn long since I've had one. Since anyone's made me work for it.

The boys smack Anderson's helmet and crack jokes while they hydrate before we're back on the ice. I put my hands behind my back, which catches their attention. They simultaneously quiet down and give me their focus, knowing this is how I stand when I mean business. "Not much to say." I start. "Keep doing what you're doing."

They all nod along. Burns knocks on Anderson's chest one more time, then points toward his face. Brushing his nose with his finger, Drew wipes away a trickle of blood that must have started because of his last hit into the boards. I speak to the team but bring my eyes right to him. "Don't take your foot off the gas." With his mouthguard hanging from his lips, he tips his helmet forward slightly in silent understanding. The crew exits the ice, and I pull back from the boys.

Instinctively, the next line gets set for the whistle, and once again, I bring my attention to the box in the sky. I look at the leggy brunette that keeps stealing my focus as she sips her drink, only this time, it's not a passing glance. I use this transition to hold my gaze and anchor it to her. It might be the adrenaline coursing through my veins, high on our lead, but after a second, I swear we make eye contact. She freezes for a beat when her eyes find mine, pulling her soda away from her mouth as she sits up straighter.

Crossing one leg over the other, Alex slowly brings her straw back to her lips. She clearly knows where I've been the whole game, so it's not her surprise at seeing me that causes her stiffened reaction. No, my bet is she's been sneaking glances this whole time too, and she's just shocked that I caught her. *Or she caught me.*

From here, I can't make out the *way* she's looking at me, but there's no denying that we're in the midst of a staring contest I don't plan on losing. The ref blows his whistle, and in my peripheral vision, I see movement on the ice, but I don't turn. There's a loud smack on the boards and another whistle, but still, I don't waver. I bring my hands behind my back and hold my steadfast gaze in her direction.

To my surprise, she does the same with her stare. It's only when her son, who's sitting next to her, taps on her leg and points toward our zone, that she finally looks away. Reluctantly, I follow his arm, tearing my eyes from her profile, and focus back on the game I should've been homed in on in the first place.

According to the sign the ref is making toward the scorekeeper, the Warriors' winger cross-checked Petrov into the boards. Their player heads to the box, and I shift back into gear, analyzing every second of our power play.

Despite a two goal lead, I've learned a win is never a win until that final buzzer. The Warriors could decide at any point to turn it on, and there is no way I'd allow for a comeback. This power play is the perfect opportunity to further broaden the gap. Luckily, just like our last rep this morning, it runs like a well-oiled machine. We capitalize on the one man advantage and increase our lead to three.

The penalty ends, and I get wrapped up in the next twelve minutes until the clock winds down to zero. At the final horn, the boys on the ice throw themselves into a pile, and the fans erupt in cheers. The bench is cranked up, the crowd is rowdy, and I'm satisfied with another promising win.

As I shake hands with my assistant coaches, I almost forget to sneak a look at my newest attraction before I walk off the bench—hockey once again proving to be my number one focus. I casually swing my head to her box, but where she was once seated, there's now an empty chair surrounded by Junior Rockets fist-bumping and high-fiving the win. I'm surprised at the disappointment that jolts through my body. Maybe it was the challenge—or her goddamn attitude—but I was hoping to see more of her... and of her legs.

When I get back to my office, I strip off my jacket and put it meticulously back on the hanger I keep on the back of the door. Rolling up the edge of my sleeves, I fall back into my chair and let out the breath I inevitably hold every game.

I always say that hockey gives me the good kind of anxiety. The kind you feel when you're afraid of losing something you love. The kind a mother no doubt feels when her teenager is out for the first time since getting his driver's license. The kind that causes worry but that you can only feel when you're lucky enough to have something to lose.

This sport, besides my family, is the only thing that has never let me down. Even when I gave it every reason not to, it somehow has always been there to pick me back up. When I tore my ACL for the first time in juniors, I thought I was done, but the love of the game pushed me to rehab myself back into playing condition.

When I tore it again in the NHL, I was even more defeated. The "love" of the game wasn't necessarily as prominent. Playing hockey was my job. It was how I made my living. It was the thing that brought me the life I had always wanted—with the girl that I thought I'd be with forever—and I was numb to the pleasure that the actual sport used to give me. Still, it didn't let me get away.

Two years after my second tear, I was at my lowest. I had spent that time nursing an injury I knew I wouldn't be able to play through again. I was mourning the loss of the person who dumped me at the same time I lost everything else. I was partying recklessly because of the hole of depression I fell into—drinking, taking pills, getting in bar fights that nearly put me in jail or the ground.

Then I got the call.

One random night, I was sitting on a bar stool at a hole-in-the-wall, half-drunk and half-high, and yet, I still felt nothing. I had no job, no passion, no partner—no purpose. I had pushed everyone I knew away. Liam wouldn't even let me see Ruthie, who was only two at the time, because of the mess that I created for myself. But I still couldn't seem to get it together.

Then my life changed forever...

*A meathead with tattoos, bulging veins, and a red broken out face, walked in and sat at the barstool a few down from mine, eyeing me the whole time he did it.*

*"Hey, aren't you that washed up Wolf who blew his knee out a few seasons ago?" he called down to me, clearly looking for a fight. Lucky for him, I was looking for an excuse to feel anything at all.*

*"Good one, tough guy. You just buy your roids in the back alley?" I replied, sipping my beer like I asked him the weather.*

*"What the fuck did you say to me?" He pulled himself from his stool and within seconds, was breathing in my face.*

*"Oh, nothing," I said, pushing my stool away from the bar. I had every intention of standing to meet him and asking if he shoots them or pops them, when my phone started vibrating. Normally I would ignore a call in general, let alone at a time like this, but a gut feeling drove me to take it. With Popeye still towering above me, I brought my phone to my ear.*

*"Levi Montgomery?" the voice on the other end asked as our lines connected.*

*"Yep," I said curtly, staring at the ogre next to me. He looked surprised that I took the call but no less pissed than he was before.*

*"It's Johnny Clark from the Flames. I've been chatting with your former coach about you. I'm looking to fill an assistant coaching position..."*

*Instantly, I saw nothing but the last few years rolling past my eyes. I didn't see the bar or the guy standing over me looking to pound me into the ground. I saw the darkness, depression, the hole I fell into... and a small light at the end of the tunnel.*

*"If you're interested, I'd love to sit down to talk more about the details," Johnny continued.*

*Stunned, I sat in silence as I struggled to find words to respond. To say anything at all.*

*"You there?" Johnny asked on the other end of the phone.*

*"Uh, I—yeah, I'm here. I mean, yes. Yes, I'm here, and yes, I'm interested." I fidgeted in my seat.*

*"Great, I'll be in touch."*

*"I'll talk to you soon," I said eagerly. "And Johnny..."*

*"Yeah?"*

*"Thank you."*

*"You got it, bud. I'll see ya."*

*I looked at my opponent who now looked more bored than angry. "Sorry, man. My bad." I threw money on the bar and stood from my stool. He looked at me even more surprised than before. Putting my hand on his shoulder, I looked him dead in the eye and said, "I'm gonna be a coach." Then I walked out the door.*

That was the last time I had a drink and the last time I felt that low. That coaching offer may have quite literally saved my life. It definitely saved my career. It's what landed me my assistant coaching position on the Flames and what eventually got me to where I am today. It was the reminder I needed to take control of my life again in every possible way.

Taking one more deep breath and reveling in the win, I check my phone and see the front screen riddled with messages.

Influencer Olivia

**Meet up?**

Receptionist Emma

**Wanna celebrate the win tonight?**

Spray Tan Kate

What are you getting into after the game?

Liam

Ruthie says good game, Uncle Levi. Now go the
fuck home.

I laugh out loud at the last text. Shaking my head, I type a reply.

Ruthie has a potty mouth. Way to go, Dad.

My brother replies almost immediately.

Liam

That last part was from me. Keep it in your pants
tonight, little brother.

I scoff and thumbs-up the text, then scroll back through the others.

Seeing thirsty messages like these isn't something I take pride in, but I'd be lying if I said I didn't also instigate them. Just because I appreciate my solitude, doesn't mean I want to be alone *every* night.

I'm not the love them and leave them type. I'm just not the boyfriend type either. With me, you know what you're getting. We don't do dinner, we aren't watching movies, there's definitely no happy hour happening before. If we meet up it's for one thing and one thing only. Do I enjoy these women's company? Sure. Do I want to risk even the possibility of them catching feelings? Hell no.

I don't have the time, energy, or need for anything more. What I want is a mutually beneficial couple of hours. Time that's rough and wild, and where again, I'm in control.

And it's all I'm capable of giving them.

My mind flashes back to olive skin draped in that awful red vest and the woman inside it. I smirk just thinking about her ridiculing my tailored suit while sporting a puffer vest the color of a tomato.

Alex seems like a firecracker. She also seems like she's been through some shit in the past. Any single parent has. In one way or another, they ended up on their own thanks to some turn of events. Technically I don't know there's no dad in the picture, but she was alone with no wedding ring and had that attitude—and that came from somewhere.

I think of Liam and all that he's been through and wonder how Alex got where she is. A lot of women would let their circumstances get them down and maybe she does, but it didn't seem that way. She seems fierce, and judging from the fact that she shot me down without a second thought—despite my career and obvious status—it's clear she's wildly independent.

If I had gotten her number, there's no doubt in my mind she'd be who I am texting right now. She doesn't seem like the easy type who would fall to my feet like some of these other women would, but that's the attraction. And I'd like to give that smart little mouth of hers something to do.

Looking back through the names in my previous messages, I realize anyone but her tonight wouldn't cut it. It's a ridiculous notion considering we said maybe ten words to each other, but there's no denying that it's true. I may have options, but there's only one woman on my mind right now.

Rather than waste my time, or anyone else's, I exit out of my messages and scroll to a number that always hits on nights like these.

"Pick up or delivery?"

I clear my throat. "Pick up, please."

"Your name?"

# 7

# Alex

Driving home, I sit in silence for the first time in the last three hours. Cooper got invited to stay the night at his teammate's house and sprinted to their car the moment I said yes. Apparently a spare toothbrush, which Dante's mother swore they have, is all a twelve-year-old needs for a sleepover. Well, that, an Xbox controller, and copious amounts of snacks.

Selfishly, I was happy to have the rest of the night to myself. Between the plan change with Nick and sitting with twenty Junior Rockets and their parents for the length of the game, I'm both mentally and physically spent. Not to mention the fact that my brain has been occupied by one tall, dark, and manscaped coach. It's both a blessing and a tragedy. Yes, he is the epitome of what I avoid in all men, but that doesn't change the fact that I haven't been able to get Levi Montgomery out of my goddamn head since I saw him in that hallway.

It started with the physical, obviously—I'm jaded, not blind. But what really got me was that he didn't even blink an eye at the sight of Cooper. Most men, particularly those I'm interested in, hear I have a kid and react as if I've told them I have a house full of cats. They seem to think it's completely outrageous for someone single and in their early thirties to also have a child. They're either "too young" or "too old" or *"just not ready for kids yet, ya know?"* One guy even told me that he had a dog once and even that didn't work out, whatever that means...

But this is the first time someone has had no reaction at all.

It was almost as if it didn't matter—like I was telling him I had a goldfish, rather than a preteen. He was great with the Rockets, and the way he treated Cooper tells me he's had practice with kids. My son never got his jersey signed, but that's not necessarily Levi's fault. I'd say maybe Monte has one of his own—outside of the niece that he mentioned—but from what I saw on Google in between periods when I shamelessly stalked him online, there are none that we know of.

In fact, Coach Jawline seems to be infamously single, except for one recent picture that may suggest otherwise. There were dozens of photos of him with other coaches, players, and even a few with a guy in a baseball jersey that he slightly resembled. But until the picture of him and a blonde model popped up—where, even then, he was turned mostly away from the camera—there weren't any seen with a woman or child.

Very specific parts of me were thrilled by the realization that he's not plastered on the internet with a confirmed smoking hot girlfriend or a handful of baby mamas. I think I even felt a weight lift that seemed to have settled in the back of my mind. But, once again, I had to remind myself that I'm not going there with him. It's a shame really. If he lost the suit, found a watch, and changed, well, basically everything he encompasses, he doesn't seem like terrible company. Lord knows I could use a good looking man in my life.

Or any man really.

It's been... awhile. But between working two jobs and momming full time, when am I supposed to find a spot in my day for sex, much less dating? Not to mention, I don't make it a habit to bring strange men around my son who seems to know way too much already about the birds and bees thanks to the older kids at the rink. Yes, I have needs, but Cooper takes priority.

It's actually quite ironic considering my day job is writing *Kiss and Tell*, a relationship column for a lifestyle blog. It's how I know I'm at least a half-decent writer. I spend my days typing about love languages, stages of relationships, and navigating intimacy, yet there is no love, relationship, or intimacy anywhere in my personal life.

For the most part, I use the lack of men in that area to my advantage. Having an ex I can barely stand, I know exactly what women *don't* want. And with no dates or boyfriends, I have all day to think about what they *do*. Of course, there are days when I'm lonely and nights when it's worse, but for now, me and my little pocket rocket do just fine.

I'm halfway home when my stomach growls over the beat of the song blaring from my car radio. It seems that I searched for social media accounts of one NHL hotshot rather than dipping into the buffet between periods like the rest of our group.

I pull open the sliding top of my center console and search for anything of substance. I typically try to keep something on hand, if not for myself then for Coop, but without crashing my car, I find only two things. The first is a half-eaten granola bar that's bound to crack a tooth at this point, and the other is a menthol cough drop. Neither sound appetizing, and both are probably expired, so I reach for my phone to pull over and do my second online search of the night.

I could wait until I get home to eat, which is what I normally do, or even stop by the restaurant to see how Brooke's night is going. But the last place I want to be on my only night alone is The Gilded Tap, and I might as well get something besides the wraps I already eat three days a week.

I can't even remember the last time I had a night where Cooper was away and I wasn't working. Anytime he's at a friend's, or on the rare occasion that he stays at Nick's, I always pick up an extra shift. It's not that I don't love the idea of having 'me time,' but I'm not used to it. Being a single mom means it's all on me, so my body—and my brain—are used to *doing*.

Working from home, I never relax. I use every second in between writing blogs and answering emails to throw laundry in or get dinner started. Then, with waitressing, you never stop moving, and on the off chance that I do get five free minutes throughout the day to sit down, my body may be resting but my mind is always racing. What *could* I be doing? What *should* I be doing? What do I *need* to do so that I can have more time to do even more things tomorrow? It's exhausting.

I decide that, for once, I'm doing something just for me and trying somewhere new. As I do, I look up to see the sign for the next exit showing three dining options. Two are fast food and although I love a good greaseburger as much as the next person, I'd prefer one that's not paper thin and pulled from the freezer. The third choice is some place called Petey's. The name doesn't say much, but the curly fries in their logo catch my eye. I contemplate just going home for another half of a second before I give in. Then, I signal to move onto the off ramp and follow the signs for my dining destination.

I park outside of Petey's and am not at all surprised to see that it's basically a dive bar on the side of the road. I am, however, shocked to see how many other cars are in the lot. I've worked in the food industry for many years now, constantly wanting a second source of income, and if I've learned anything, it's not to judge a place by its curb appeal.

I've been to places that look like shitholes but serve some of the best food in town, and I've been to high-class restaurants that serve runny mashed potatoes and dried out steak. What you can judge however, is how busy it is, and my guess is that there are a dozen vehicles parked outside of Petey's for a reason.

I step out of my car and zip up my vest as I walk toward the front entrance. It might only be October, but the cool evening air tells me autumn is here to stay.

That realization chills me more than the breeze. This time of year used to be really tough. With Cooper's birthday in August, the first few months of fall tend to bring back a lot of painful memories.

Babies are hard. Sure, they can't run around or talk back yet, but they also eat like eight times a day and typically only sleep at the worst possible times. Add in doing the majority of the work on your own and dealing with a relationship that's falling apart, and you have yourself one hell of a postpartum cocktail. Unfortunately, that type of poison doesn't lead to a three day hangover. Instead, it drops you into a depression so dark that your mother ends up caring for you like the newborn you're now responsible for.

It was around this time of year that my stamina ran out, and that's exactly what happened. My mom was feeding me, bathing me, and soothing my tears, on top of also doing all of those things for my two-month-old baby. Thankfully, Mom is a saint, and I was fortunate enough to claw my way out of a place I never want to find myself in again. Not everyone's that lucky.

It took time and help from the people I'm closest to, but with weeks of therapy, I started to finally feel like myself again right around Coop's first Christmas. There are still dark days—I think all moms have those—but I try to see them as reminders that the rest of the days are good ones. That's how I like to remember this time of year too.

A low hum of voices floats under the door of Petey's before I even push it open. When I do, the sound is amplified, and I can see why—the bar sits practically at the front entrance. There is a register off in the corner of the wraparound counter and a handful of high-tops off to the side, but besides that, almost the entire front half of the "restaurant" is stools.

A rattle comes from off in the distance where a man in a tight, white tank top slides a rack full of balls up and down on a pool table. There are old street signs plastered all over the walls that say things like *Dead End* and *Keep Out* and one on the door of what I assume is the kitchen that says *Road Work Ahead*.

Knowing this is probably the type of place where the bartender is also the hostess and server, I scan the bar for a stool to put in an order. An older blonde woman with a Petey's t-shirt and pixie cut comes over as I sit down at one of the few open seats at the back end.

"What can I get ya?" she asks, wiping the spot that's in front of me and clearing away the last person's trash.

"I'll take a whiskey on the rocks and a to-go menu if you have one, please."

She smiles at me and without any words, grabs a glass and a bottle, slides a menu in front of me, and fills the cup in a matter of seconds. *This lady is good.*

I scan the stained, clearly worn menu, and my eyes land on the burger up top. Too hungry to bother reading the rest, I set the paper back down and smile at the bartender. She sets down the beer bottle she cracked for the person sitting a few stools down and comes back to me.

"I'll take a burger, extra pickles, medium well." She nods and turns to leave. "Oh, and curly fries, please!" I call out to her. She gives me a polite smile, then turns to the screen by the back wall and starts tapping on buttons.

I slouch into my seat and pick up my drink, swirling the liquid just inches from my nose. I inhale deeply, allowing the chaos of the day to settle over me. Breathing in the strong notes of smoke and cinnamon from the whiskey in front of me, I take in another scent I can't quite place.

"Can I help you?" the bartender asks in my direction. I part my lips, but before I can speak, someone else does.

"Pick up order," a somehow familiar voice says from behind me. A few people look past me as I set down my drink. That one scent remains, and it lends itself to the nagging feeling I have that there's something I'm missing.

"Name?"

I move to look over my shoulder, and it hits me too late—apple. I finish my turn and am hit with the sight of a skinny black tie and the sound of the now recognizable voice of—

"Levi Montgomery."

# 8

# Levi

"What are you doing here?" Alex tries to snap, but her words come out muted. I chuckle under my breath at not only her reaction but the circumstances. What are the chances that she's at my favorite dive?

Petey's is... unique. The customers are about as eclectic as the decor on the walls, and although it's more bar than restaurant, their burgers are the best around. I order from here because the food is amazing, and the type of people that frequent this place don't give a damn about who I am. Sure, there are always some who recognize me, especially with it being only twenty minutes from the rink, but they aren't the kind that are going to throw themselves in my direction.

I still sometimes give them a fake name for my order, Sam Smith or Jim Jones, but on the occasion that I don't, there has never been an issue. In fact, there was one time when a drunk nearly fell off his stool after I came in, throwing around his opinions on our loss that night. Needless to say, I wasn't in the mood, but before I could respectfully tell him to fuck off, another patron sat his ass down and the rest of the bar simply went about their business.

It is a surprise to see Alex here, though. Hell, it'd be a surprise to see anyone I know at this little hole-in-the-wall, but for this woman in particular, I'm shocked. Usually women who carry themselves like she does don't tend to frequent places like this.

"I guess I could ask you the same thing," I say, clasping my hands behind my lower back. She straightens her posture in the chair, and I do the same, standing in front of her.

"I'm getting dinner."

"Well, would you look at that. Another thing we have in common."

She tries to hide a smirk that forms on her lips as her brow furrows into that grouchy face she made at me earlier. It takes everything in me not to reach up to the crease on her forehead and smooth it out with the pad of my thumb.

"Nice vest."

She looks down at it, now fully zipped, then glares up at me with her big, caramel eyes. "I think red might be my color."

"A Flames girl at heart."

Her cheeks flush a lighter version of the vest itself, and I take that as a win. "Nice suit," she quips back.

"I think black might be *my* color."

With that, the small patch of skin at the top of her neck still exposed from her hoodie, mirrors her cheeks. "Just like your soul then."

"Ouch." I cock my head back and run my tongue along my bottom lip. She follows my movement but says nothing more. A brief period of silence sits between us, but despite her hostility, it's not awkward at all. I notice her attitude isn't *with* me but *at* me. There's more to her rejection than meets the eye.

"Eat with me," I say out of nowhere. *What the hell?* I can't remember the last time I shared a meal with a woman, let alone one who has barely given me the time of day.

She shifts in her seat, crossing one leg over the other and then uncrossing it again until it's settled back on the edge of her stool. Something about me makes her uneasy, and I'm not sure why, but I like that she seems just as thrown by me as I am by her. Like we're equally confused by what's going on here.

"It's been a long day," she says, her tone somewhat depleted. "I think I'm just going to take my food and head home."

I begin to nod slowly. This girl is going to make me work for it, and I like it. "Well, if you won't have dinner with me, will you at least tell me what it is about my 'kind' that irritates you so much?" I put air quotes around the word she used earlier, and she rolls her eyes.

I'm finding that irritating her is becoming increasingly thrilling. "I'm serious! You've had it out for me—the *real* me—since before you realized who you were talking to. So, let's hear it." I pull my arms back in front of me and hold them out wide, gesturing for her to let it out. I push open my jacket that she hates so much and settle my hands into the front pockets of my pants.

Alex watches, her face still grumpy, as I open up her view of my chest. She is still sitting in front of me and although she's taller than a lot of women, I'm well over six feet. Her vantage point hits right below where my ribs begin. She swallows hard and makes no effort to hide the once over she gives the front of my body as I pull away the fabric.

"What about all this drives you so crazy?"

"I don't even know you," she says coyly.

"Exactly," I whisper, leaning close to her space. She doesn't pull back and for that half a second, our faces end up just inches apart.

"But I could guess." She says it not with her usual bite but with confidence. Tipping my chin up at her quickly, I encourage her to continue.

Alex clears her throat, and to my surprise, she stands to meet me. She gives me another very obvious scan, then shoves her hands into her vest pockets, almost mirroring my stance.

"Coach Monte. Levi Montgomery." She raises one brow before continuing. "Ex NHL star turned coach. One of the youngest in the league according to my son. Played for the Wolves for—ten seasons was it? Until you were hit on the ice and given a season-ending injury. Torn ACL." We enter yet another staring contest until I lick my lips. At that moment, her eyes waver just an instant.

"So, you do know me," I say through a smirk.

"I know *of* you."

"And my type?"

"And your type. Businessman. Your work is your life, your first priority. You say you don't care about the money—you just want to help people or do something you love—except of course you care about the money. In fact, you care about it so much that you'll continue to work yourself to the bone because you are making approximately one shit-ton to do it.

You sleep with a multitude of women who think you walk on water, but with whom you have no interest in outside of the bedroom. You make promises you can't keep and cancel plans you can't make because of your great responsibilities, but in reality, you're selfish. And really, the only thing you care more about in this world than your work—is yourself." She takes a deep breath and crosses her arms over her chest. "How'd I do?"

I stare at her blankly, fighting any reaction that I naturally have to tell her how wrong she is about most of that. She holds my gaze for a second, then sits back down and lifts one brow, challenging me. I step forward, closing some of the gap between us, then turn and lay my forearm on the bar.

"Two," I say, leaning toward her.

Her confident grin falls flat. "What?"

Lifting her glass off the counter, I tilt it slightly, watching the amber liquid flow toward the rim. Right as it reaches the edge, I counter the movement and set it back down. I move my eyes from the drink back to hers. "I make approximately *two* shit-tons doing what I do."

She snorts through her nose unamused. "Exactly my point." Picking up the same glass I was just holding, she brings it to her lips without breaking eye contact. "You're all the same."

I shake my head slowly while looking at her. This close, I can see the gold in more detail, and I realize it's more of a sunburst than simply a mark in her iris—a firecracker, just like her.

I decide now is not the time to tell her that although she was right about a lot, she was wrong about me being selfish. I may do what's best for me in most situations, but it's never at the expense of blindsiding someone else.

The people that I put after myself know that's their place. Maybe that doesn't make them feel any better about it, but they're never caught off guard when I come first. I guess, by definition, that's me being selfish. But if there's anything I've learned from all of the things that have happened in my life, it's that sometimes it's okay to put yourself first.

"So, was this your son's father or... ?"

She chokes on her whiskey, setting her glass down quickly and covering a cough in her elbow. When she pulls her arm down, a bead of liquid still sits on her lip. I resist every urge I have to wipe it away with my finger or lick it off her mouth myself.

Alex reaches for a napkin and dabs at the droplet that—in my head—I claimed as mine. She glares at me over her hand, but as she lowers it, her face drops too. *Bingo.*

I may not be an expert on love, but I know a thing or two about being jilted. It leaves you resentful and bitter. I bet she and I have a lot more in common than she'd like to admit. A weariness washes over her as she parts her lips.

"Here's both of your checks. Food will be right out." She's saved by the bartender when she pushes one receipt in front of either of us. Alex picks up her purse, and I grab her bill. She slaps her card down on the bar before realizing I pulled it away.

"No," she says, reaching for my hand.

I move it so she can't tear the slip from my grasp. "Stop. Consider this my apology for being late earlier."

Alex freezes, her face now more pissed than before. She reaches again, but I counter her movement. "No!" she says loudly.

"Enough," I say, smirking. "You're causing a scene." She quickly scans the bar and realizes not one person here cares about what we're doing. I slide the slip to my opposite side, putting even more distance between her and it.

"You are not paying for my burger," she says, stepping off of her stool and leaning over me. She lays her body across the counter—and across mine—and I take advantage of the fleeting seconds I have to scan this side of her.

Her puffy vest rises as she reaches, causing the hoodie she's wearing underneath to raise with it. The movement exposes a slight sliver of skin on the small of her back, right above a perfect ass. I dodge her long ponytail that nearly takes me out, the scent of coconut briefly overwhelming my space as she gives one final thrust toward the bill. She's not tiny, but when your wingspan is as long as an NBA player, there aren't many that can beat your reach.

Alex lets out a frustrated groan as she slides back to standing.

"What's wrong?" I ask, grabbing her wrist as it passes in front of me. Her breath hitches, and I hear it first below my belt. She looks at me with a heated expression, her eyes somewhat hooded. Just to toe the line, I brush her soft skin once with the tip of my thumb. "Afraid I can't afford it?"

She rips her hand away from me, but not before I see her throat move up and down. She's pissed, no doubt, but she's also drawn to me. That thought alone is enough to set me on fire.

"Fine." She huffs out a breath, then slams her body down into her seat.

The bartender comes back, her return perfectly timed with the end of Alex's tantrum. I hand her my card and both bills. She spins on her heel to walk to the register, and I slide Alex's card off the bar. Reading it briefly, I survey it for any new information about her.

Unlike my assumption, Alex is her whole first name. It's written there, just four simple letters. Not Alexandra or Alexis—that's all there is—written next to my new favorite last name.

I hand the card back to her, and she snatches it from my grasp, throwing it carelessly back into her bag. I look at her under raised brows, and she sulks into her stool. "Thank you," she mumbles, her voice barely audible.

"Oh, this has been fun," I say sarcastically, signing the receipts sitting in front of me. "You sure you don't want to keep this going?"

She looks at me side-eyed, but the corners of her lips turn up ever so slightly. She clears her throat unnecessarily before responding. "I'm sure."

"Yeah, you seem it." I snatch my bag from the two on the bar and pretend not to notice that Alex's mouth has dropped open, her wet lips forming the perfect shape. I turn back toward her, and she snaps them shut, back into her stoic demeanor. "Next time." Leaving again, I pretend I'm not at all fazed by her. That messing with her hasn't been the highlight of my day.

As I crack open the door, the chill from outside attempts to cool me off from our encounter. This woman has riled me up more than anyone has in a long time, and I can't resist the urge to take one more look back. When I do, my eyes find hers already on me.

"Take it easy, Bennett," I call with a nod. Her teeth find her bottom lip, and before I can rush back to her and let mine do the same, I push the door open fully, hoping the crisp October breeze will help me walk normally.

# 9

# Alex

I snap the screen on my laptop shut and bury it back in my bag to finish my side work after my shift. "How do you feel about personal space?"

Brooke looks up from the silverware she's wrapping and cocks one eyebrow. "Like having it or giving it?"

"Either. Both. I don't know. The overall idea of it I guess. Specifically with strangers of the opposite sex."

"Hold on." She picks up a fork off of the counter that we're standing at in the back of the kitchen and wiggles it in my direction. "Are you talking about Coach McHottie from the other night?"

I look at the utensil in her hand that she's now pointing at me like a possible weapon and instantly regret telling her anything.

The first thing I did after my run in with Levi at Petey's was text Brooke. She answered via Facetime the second she started her break. I called her back as I was walking in the door.

*"Tell me everything," she said, shoving a forkful of salad into her mouth. I could tell from the background that she was in the dry food storage closet at the restaurant, our favorite place to eat—and hide.*

*"There's not much more to tell than what I already texted you earlier." I sat my to-go bag from Petey's down on the counter and finally unzipped my vest. Instantly, Levi's smug face flashed in my mind.*

*Nice vest. Yeah, thanks. These are really in right now.*

*The fake continuation of that conversation in my head only annoyed me more. I tossed my vest off, ridding myself of any more reminders of him, and pulled out my burger.*

*"Alex, you texted me saying, and I quote, 'Met the coach of the Flames. He's hot but a douche.' How are you going to just breeze by every other detail like that?"*

*"We talked for like ten minutes total," I said, reaching into the bag. "Five before the game and another five afterwards when I ran into him grabbing food on my way home. Coach. Hot. Suit. Douche. That pretty much sums it up." I mentally added on another list of things—tall, arrogant, nice eyes, attitude, great lips, no concern for physical boundaries.*

*I began unwrapping my burger when she asked, "So, what about him exactly screamed douchey to you? Besides the fact that your vagina physically shrivels up at the sight of a man in a sports coat?" Brooke knows better than anyone that this whole anti-suit thing is just my way of simplifying how much Nick hurt me. She just also loves to call me on it.*

*"Oh, you've got to be kidding me!" I groaned, dropping my burger back onto the wrapper it came in.*

*"What? That's a fair question! You meet a guy who makes like a billion dollars a year, who, from my quick stalking sesh, is hotter than hot an—"*

*"No, not that,"* I interrupted with a sigh. *"He took my burger."* She stared at me blankly. *"Like by accident. We must have gotten each other's bags."*

*"Ooh, this is good. What's in the one that you got? You can tell a lot about a man from how he likes his meat."*

I looked up at her briefly before rolling my eyes and spreading the sandwich that was, in fact, not mine. *"Looks medium-rare. No onions, tomatoes, sauce... or pickles"*

*"So, just lettuce and cheese?"*

*"Looks like it."*

*"And on the side?"*

I peeked back into the bag. *"Steak fries."*

*"Interesting."*

I set the burger down and tilted my head. *"Please, Brooke, tell me everything you now know about this man because of what he gets between his buns."* I closed my eyes slowly and shook my head. When I opened them again, Brooke was smiling at me with a strip of lettuce dangling from her lips.

*"Good one,"* she said, slurping the green into her mouth. *"Okay, for starters, the medium-rare says he's traditional but also likes the finer things in life. A manly man. You know, not afraid of E. coli and all that."*

*"Uh huh."*

*"And the lack of toppings tells me he's a clean freak, but busy. He wants to eat in his car but doesn't want to risk the chance of dropping a slice of tomato or a drop of ketchup on his suit."*

I ran my tongue along my teeth, wrinkling my forehead, but also considering how sort of spot on it all sounded. *"And the fries?"*

*"Oh, that just tells me he has poor taste in sides. Steak fries? I mean those are like the worst variety of potato."*

*"Okay, I'll give you that one."*

Pushing back my stool, I walked to the fridge to grab the ketchup and a jar of pickles. I could hear Brooke slurping up the bottom of her diet soda, which according to her usual routine, told me we had approximately ten more minutes until her break was over.

*I headed back to the island where my phone with her face on it was propped up on my water bottle. Adding the condiments to my food I said, "Please go on."*

*"So, he likes juicy meat and thick potatoes, coaches hockey, makes a bajillion dollars, and wears a suit. Does that cover everything?"*

*"No," I said, my mouth full of burger. "He has this thing with personal space."*

"Just tell me. Am I crazy? Or was touching me, talking inches from my face, and paying for my food a little... much?"

"Oh, for Christ's sake. It's called flirting, Alex," Brooke says, wrapping a napkin around a set of utensils. "You make it sound like the man groped you then whispered secrets into your mouth. You know, for someone who writes about relationships for a living, you're really shitty at starting them."

I pick up a butter knife and layer a fork and spoon on top of it. "I know what flirting is, Brooke." I think back to the start of my blog post I typed minutes earlier. "I'm just... out of practice."

"Now there's the understatement of the year."

Wrapping a napkin and a paper tab around the bundle, I toss it into the woven basket on the counter. I reach for another knife. "It's hard! Between writing and waitressing, and Coop of course, there's no time."

Brooke exhales and, without asking, I know why. She is the biggest advocate of putting yourself first. She also has no children, and therefore, can only understand so much.

"But I know, you're right," I continue. "I need to start dating." I move to grab a spoon from the plastic bin, but Brooke turns to me and stops my hand.

"Honey, I am going to say this with all the love in the world." I angle my torso toward her, waiting to hear what she's about to say, my body as anxious as my mind for some sage advice. She leans in to meet me and places her palm on my cheek. "You need to get laid."

I scoff and pull away from her dramatically, turning back to finish the silverware. "I'm doing just fine in that department," I say, once again reaching for a spoon.

She places her hand on the edge of the counter and shifts her weight so she's leaning on it, looking at me stubbornly. "Tell me the last time you got off."

Avoiding eye contact, I grab a fork and sandwich it between the other two utensils in my hand. Puffing up my chest just a little, I try to sound confident. "Yesterday," I say.

"Mhmm."

"I did!"

"That little pocket rocket you call a vibrator doesn't count."

"Counted last night," I say, still avoiding her gaze. *And the night of the game when I was thinking of him.*

My cheeks flush, and I pray that Brooke assumes it's because of our current conversation despite the fact that we talk about everything together.

"You know what I mean, Al. That body of yours is just going to waste. We all have needs."

Not knowing what to say, I toss the last roll of silverware into the basket and move it to the shelf underneath our workstation. When I stand back up, she's looking at me with her head tilted down and eyebrows raised, waiting for a response.

"What do you want me to say? Okay, yes, I know. I'll add getting railed to the top of my to-do list." Brooke rolls her eyes playfully, and I reach for my bag.

"You know... Coach McHottie might seem a lot less douchey if you were underneath him."

My head snaps back up. "No," I say definitively, pointing my finger in her direction. "I am under no circumstances getting involved with a suit again." Playing with the chipped polish on my fingernail I add, "Besides, according to the internet, he potentially has a new model girlfriend with perfect hair, no waist, and tits bigger than both of ours combined."

Brooke swats at my arm. "Oh, stop. That's all rumors. I follow that girl online. She does *not* have a boyfriend. It's all gossip. And him essentially being everything you hate on paper is *why* it's perfect. You need a good lay and he—well, judging off of his swagger alone—definitely has experience. But he's not your type at all. It takes all of the work out of it.

No dates. None of that *'What do I say?' 'What do I wear?'* Just the good stuff." She wiggles her brows in my direction.

"No," I say again, thinking of how doing something like that would look to my son. "First of all, think about what impression that would give Cooper."

"Umm, I'm thinking it would look like you're mom of the freaking year. Hanging out with his hero? He'll be calling him Daddy right along with you." She winks at me as I ignore her.

Slinging my bag over my shoulder, I grab my jacket from the closet next to us and look at her thoughtfully. "No."

Brooke huffs out a laugh, grabbing her own jacket and following behind me as I walk out through the kitchen. "Oh, come on, Alex. Live a little!"

Stopping at the system in the back of the restaurant, I clock out and throw on my coat. Brooke does the same once she catches up to me.

"You're not telling me to live a little. You're telling me to have a one night stand."

"That's not true," she says, lowering her voice as we walk past the people still seated at the bar. "I'm telling you to have *multiple* one night stands."

"Doesn't that defeat the purpose of the *one* part then?" I push the door open.

The air is cool but still, and the chill actually feels good after running around all night. We were busy for a Wednesday, which is nice. I don't typically work many weekday shifts because Cooper has homework and hockey, and it's hard to find a sitter that's allowed to be out on a school night. Occasionally though, I pick up an extra shift here and there, especially if Brooke's working.

"You're right. That doesn't really make sense. No one night stands."

"Thank you," I say, throwing my hands up in relief. I walk toward our cars that are parked next to each other in the lot. When I get to the driver's side, I look at her to say goodbye, and there's a mischievous grin painted on her face.

"What?" I ask, pulling open the door.

"Friends with benefits." She nods her head approvingly.

"Goodnight, Brooke," is all I say as I tug on the handle. After a few more pulls—I should really get that fixed—I step into the car and start the engine.

*Friends with benefits. Ridiculous.*

# 10

# Levi

"I'm coming in! You better have pants on!" I shout into my brother's apartment. As if growing up only a year apart wasn't close enough, we also now live in buildings right next to each other.

Liam signed with the Gators baseball team after he graduated college, two years after I was drafted by the Wolves. Golden City has been his home for almost his entire adult life. It was a huge added bonus to getting my first job with the Flames. Being in the same city as my brother was important to me. But after getting my second chance at having at least a version of the life I always dreamed of, being near my niece was non-negotiable.

The beat of a pop song echoes down the hall moments before Ruthie enters the room with a speaker in her hand and her ponytail swinging. "Uncle Levi, of course I'm wearing pants!" She says with a playful eyeroll before turning down her music and bounding into my arms. I hug her tightly, then pinch her cheek like I always do despite how much it drives her crazy.

Leaning down, I whisper, "I was talking about your dad."

Ruthie makes a disgusted face while simultaneously smothering a giggle. "Ew, yes. He's wearing pants too."

"Well good. You know, when we were little, he used to walk around in his underwear all day long."

The sound of my brother clearing his throat floats around the corner. "That is not true, Ruthie. Don't believe a word your uncle says." Liam tugs on Ruthie's ponytail as she shoots him the evil eye for messing up her hair. "It was just in the mornings." I shake my head slyly, a smirk on both of our faces. He kisses her cheek, then looks at me. "And now Uncle Levi can't seem to keep his on at night."

My head stills, and my grin falls to a flat line. Liam raises his eyebrows at me, then toward Ruthie. "Why don't you go draw your uncle a picture with your new art kit."

"What?" I say, my eyes dramatically wide. "That would be great, kiddo."

She pops a knee and puts her hand on her hip. "Uncle Levi, I'm not really a kiddo anymore," she says, breaking my heart. I remember when she was four and propped on Liam's hip all day.

"You'll always be my kiddo, kiddo." I kiss her on her head before she turns to walk away.

My brother rounds the kitchen island, and I follow behind him. "Really?"

"What?"

"Uncle Levi can't keep it in his pants," I say in a deep mocking tone.

"I didn't say that."

"You might as well have."

He pulls two mugs from the cabinet and the coffee pot from the machine. "Am I wrong?" he asks, pouring two full cups. Looking up at me through the steam, I meet his gaze as he slides a mug my way.

Liam and I have a lot in common. We're tall, lean, and handsome as hell. We like to have a good time, but we both have priorities that come before anything else. We also have both dedicated our lives to sports that started as hobbies but became our careers.

In other ways though, we're on two opposite ends of the spectrum. I keep my hair neat with a freshly trimmed beard. He has shaggy locks and a clean face that makes me look like the older one. He's laid back and goes with the flow, where I'm regimented and like to be in control. But what stands out the most in all of our differences is when life gives us lemons, he makes lemonade. I just turn sour.

It's always been that way. Liam's the light one, the funny one, the one who brightens a room simply by walking into it and somehow finds the good in every situation. He's the man who learns that a one night stand turned into a baby and insists on sticking around. The one who takes a two-month-old infant in by himself, no questions asked, when her mother decides she can't be a mom. The man who then raised that little girl to be the most perfect ten-year-old you'll ever meet. The brother who won't even look at a woman because he's too worried about how it might affect his daughter.

I am the darker one, the temperamental one, the one who always seemed to have a chip on his shoulder—even before there was one. I'm the man who got injured and dumped, then fell into a dark place, only to move past it all and take every precaution to never get there again. The brother who sleeps with women despite having no plan to fall in love again—and no real desire to.

We're the same, but we're not—brothers, but still different.

"You make it sound so much worse than it is," I say, sipping my black coffee. He laughs lightly as he adds a spoonful of sugar and a splash of almond milk to his mug—yet another example of how we're opposites. He continues to chuckle as he stirs his drink.

"Dude, for the last couple of years, you've had a different woman in your bed every few weeks. You're telling me not one of them has left you even remotely interested in more?"

"Not one," I say quickly.

"Not even this Olivia girl?" I glare at Liam, and he holds his hands up in defense. "What? I saw it online, sue me."

Dropping my head into my hands, I exhale deeply. Olivia took one picture recently with me in the background when I wasn't paying attention and posted it on her social media. Of course, at least half of her trillion followers are Golden City gossips or Flames fans with a coach kink. Now, it's a topic of conversation for every sports gossip page on the internet. In her defense, she apologized profusely. Apparently she was just trying to show her OOTP?... OOTB?... I'm not really sure, but regardless, the damage has been done.

"Not interested."

"Not interested or not open to it?"

"Both."

"Then why keep it up?" *Because she's wild in bed and, from what she says, has no interest in marriage or kids because that would mean giving up all night benders and possibly botox.*

"Because it's easy. We're on the same page with what we want—no commitment."

"For now," Liam says, rolling his eyes.

I roll mine back at him, but in reality, he's right. It's the reason the woman in my bed changes every few weeks. Everyone's on board with my parameters at first, but eventually that changes. They either catch feelings or try to push for more, and when that happens, I know the arrangement has run its course.

It's not that I wouldn't love to meet someone worth keeping around, but if I've learned anything from my past, it's to be very selective about who I allow into my life. So far, no one has even come close to fitting the bill.

An image of Alex flashes through my mind. Although it's happened more than once since meeting her, this is the first time I'm not sure it's welcomed. It's no secret to me that the girl has caught my attention—which rarely happens. No surprise either if you have eyes in your head. What shocks me a little is that she chooses now to make another appearance. That her bright eyes, long legs, and smart mouth come to the forefront of my mind at this very moment. During this conversation.

I'm ashamed to admit, but I Googled her yesterday. After seeing her for the first time at the game and then again at the restaurant, I was intoxicated, and after a few days without her, I needed another hit. Like coming off of my first high from a drug I had just gotten a taste of, my mind was craving another dose of her. The closest thing I could find was a shitty internet search that barely gave me anything.

Unlike the women who usually flock to me—who live with their phones in their hands—there were no Alex Bennetts on any social media apps. Not that it would matter being that I myself don't have a profile, but it would have been nice to have a closer look at who she is.

What did surprise me was seeing her name pop up on one of those cookie-cutter blog sites where all they talk about is what's current in fashion and what celebrity couples' "ship names" are, whatever that means. Apparently my little "I don't date suits" must date *someone* because she writes for their column all about relationships. *Great.* Exactly what I need. A newfound interest in someone who makes a living on her investment in love and talking about it online. My only saving grace is she doesn't seem remotely interested in giving me a chance.

I sit forward in my seat. "Hold on a second. How come you can give me shit for *having* sex but if I give you shit for *not,* then I'm the asshole?"

"Because," he says, tasting his coffee. "I have a four-foot excuse. Besides, no one likes a man slut."

"Yeah, well, no one likes an abstinent prick either." I raise one eyebrow, challenging him lightheartedly. I know Liam's reasoning is different from mine. I also know it's a sore subject, so I don't press the issue.

"Don't you want more for yourself someday? A family even?"

My mind immediately goes to Ruthie and how much I love that little girl. Without a doubt I want a family, but that's another reason that I won't settle down with just anyone. Not that it happened on purpose, but I've seen firsthand through Liam what can happen when you pick the wrong mother for your children. I may not be all that young anymore, but to me, that doesn't matter. There's no rushing something that big.

"Plenty of time," I say, brushing him off.

He rolls his eyes again. "I'm telling you, man. One day this is all going to catch up with you. You're going to break someone's heart, or something's going to happen, and you're going to become a PR nightmare for the organization... or worse." He doesn't go into detail, but I know what he's hinting at. He himself has experienced casual sex leading to way more. Not to mention the other issues we have to worry about—diseases, pregnancy scares, stalkers. We've all heard the stories. But what Liam forgets is that I don't do anything recklessly.

"Don't worry about me, big brother."

"Oh, I'm not worried about you. I'm worried about myself. What am I supposed to tell Ruthie when her favorite person in the world gets himself into trouble?"

"Why's Uncle Levi in trouble?" my niece says out of nowhere, standing at the entrance to the kitchen and holding a piece of paper with a colorful picture. She walks over and takes a seat on the stool next to mine.

"I'm not, kiddo. Your dad's just kidding." Ruthie hands me the paper. "So, what do we have here?" The drawing is of three people, two larger ones and one that's clearly Ruthie in the middle. The other two, I assume, are me and Liam. One has shaggy hair and a full smile, and the other has shorter hair and a flat line for a mouth.

"That's me," Ruthie says, pointing to the obvious choice. "And that's Dad," she continues, pointing to the man with longer hair and a happy face. She slides her finger over to the person with no smile and looks at me. "And that's you, Uncle Levi."

I glance at Liam, who's hiding a smirk behind his mug, then back down at the paper. "Wait, why don't I have a smile?"

"Well, it *was* because Dad says you're always grouchy..." I glare at Liam as Ruthie shrugs.

"Oh, does he?"

She laughs. "But maybe now it's because you're in trouble."

I tickle Ruthie with my left hand, flipping Liam off behind her head with my right. "The only one who's going to be in trouble is you if you don't go fix my face."

Squirming off of her stool, Ruthie snags the paper from the counter and runs away from the kitchen. "Okay, okay!" she yells through a giggle with a fake attitude. "I'll be back!"

Once she's rounded the corner, I swing back to Liam. "Nice. Really nice."

He shrugs. "Again... am I wrong?"

I scoff and swirl the coffee at the bottom of my cup. "Imagine if I wasn't getting laid."

"That was so good... as usual," Olivia says, buttoning her jeans. I've already pulled on a pair of sweatpants that were folded in my drawer and am secretly waiting for her to leave.

"It was," I say, walking through my closet to my shelf of t-shirts. I grab a crisp white shirt, then turn past my suit I was wearing earlier and hung before Olivia and I got started. I pick a piece of lint from the jacket before stepping back into the bedroom.

"Hey, you want to grab some food or something? I'm starving."

Side-eying Olivia, I throw my t-shirt over my head. "Come on, Liv. You know we're not going to do that."

"Oh, relax, Levi. It's a burger, not a proposal. I don't want that either, remember?"

"Doesn't matter if it's a gas station hot dog. It's not happening."

She huffs as she pulls her shirt down over her tiny waist. "Remind me why that is again?" I walk to the kitchen and pull two bottles of water from the fridge. Setting one on the counter, I crack the other open. *Here we go.*

I could tell her the truth—that I don't go on dates because I don't see the point. Dating leads people to think that there will be more, and more leads to putting your heart on the line for something or someone that's not within your control. That I've done it before and gotten my heart ripped out of my chest. I could tell her that no one, including her, has even come close to seeming worth that. But I won't.

"Because I'm busy," I say. "Trust me, you don't want to date someone like me."

She slinks over to where I'm standing and slips her hands under the hem of my shirt. "You weren't too busy for what we just did." She rises to her tip toes and kisses the side of my neck. For a second I let her, but then I pull away. "You're right. But that's about all I have time for."

Liv stares at me briefly, then smiles flirtatiously. "Worth it." She reaches around me to grab the bottle of water from the counter. "Let me know the next time your schedule opens up."

I give her a grin. "I'll call you a cab."

"No, it's fine. I'm going out downtown anyway." She walks to the door and pauses, her hand on the knob. "Good seeing you, Levi."

"Always a pleasure, Liv." She closes the door behind her, and I finally relax.

Having these women in my life is always fun in the moment. I'm in a space that I know, with no worries about anything shady going down, and I get to sleep with—no, there's no sleeping—I get to *fuck* a beautiful woman. They know what we do stays here in the bedroom. They also know nothing goes beyond having sex, and we do it on my terms—my place, my times, my rules.

Afterwards though, between the time that we're done and the time it takes for them to get dressed and leave, feels like an eternity. All I want when we're finished is my space back. I don't want to grab food or have a postcoital drink. I'm not looking to talk, and I damn sure won't be doing any cuddling. I'm not looking for a wife or a girlfriend. Hell, I'm not even looking for a friend if I'm honest.

Liam's probably right. It's not a great look, and although I don't give one fuck about what other people think, I do care about what he thinks and what Ruthie may think if she ever got wind of all this. I also can't risk any sort of issues with the Flames. I nearly lost hockey once. I won't do it again.

But what that would mean is either not sleeping with anyone or settling down with only one woman. The first one sounds almost as miserable as a broken heart, and I can't see the second one happening anytime soon—definitely not with Olivia. She's cool, and I'm sure one day she'll make somebody worried about their follower count very happy, but outside of our preferences in the bedroom, we have exactly zero things in common. Add in that she's now trying to push the envelope of our agreement, and I think it may be time to wrap it up.

# 11
# Alex

"Tough game," Dante's mother says as we stand to gather our stuff. Kathryn, *"with a 'Y' "* sat next to me today, and she is a yapper—also with a "y." It is, however, the first time so far this season that I've said more than a couple words to another hockey mom, which was... almost tolerable.

Apparently the boys had a great time at her house watching movies and playing video games. She told me all about the snacks they had and how late they stayed up laughing and having fun. Cooper did tell me he had a blast. At least *somebody* enjoyed their night.

She then proceeded to discuss all the gossip she's heard about the other parents from the team. I now know who is getting divorced, who is hooking up, and who she suspects likes to keep things *interesting* in the bedroom. Basically, I have way too much information about anyone, let alone people I see on a weekly basis, and Kathryn and I are new "game besties." I'll come better prepared next time with extra caffeine. Or maybe something stronger.

I'm not the only one having a bit of a tough time here. The final whistle was just blown, solidifying that the Rockets were shut out by one of the best teams in the league. The boys played hard, but by the end of the third period, they were dragging. These kids are bigger and faster than any of our players, and I think our guys were a little discouraged because of it.

"They're so... huge," I say, watching the line of players from the other team skate past the Rockets as they high five each other after the game. They tower over Cooper so much that I can barely see him on the other side of their team.

"They breed them that way over there," Kathryn whispers. "I guess when there's nothing except an ice rink around you for miles, there's not much else to do except to eat, sleep, and breathe hockey."

She was telling me earlier about the town where they're from and made it seem like watching grass grow was the second most exciting thing to do there.

"Well, maybe next time." Cooper slaps the goalie's glove and heads toward the bench. I take that as my out and wave goodbye to Kathryn. "I'll see ya."

"Later girl!" she says. Despite my internal cringe, I force my face to maintain a bright smile.

Stepping down onto the bottom step of the bleachers, I try to catch Cooper's attention and give him a thumbs up. He takes off his helmet and brings his eyes to mine, but they quickly dart away from me. Tapping his teammate on the arm, he nods toward the corner of the rink and the two of them light up as other boys gather around them. I try to read their expressions but am clueless as to what is going on until I see someone walking onto the ice from where they're pointing.

A very good-looking guy, younger than I am, struts slowly toward me with the swagger only someone in their mid-twenties would have. He has shaggy blonde hair that hangs down on either side of his face and a smirk that's cool but confident. He's wearing jeans and black boots and is carrying a dark duffle. I may otherwise be nervous that a stranger with a bulging bag is walking toward my child, but when he raises his outer arm to the boys, I see the Flames logo on the chest of his jacket.

"Who is this guy?" I whisper to myself, leaning closer to the boards.

"That's Drew Anderson," an unexpected voice whispers back.

I startle, almost falling face first into the glass with no way to catch myself thanks to having my hands in my jacket pockets.

Turning around, I see heavily glossed lips and fake eyelashes directly behind me. "Jesus, Kathryn," I say reactively. She looks at me very taken aback, and I try to recover. "Sorry." I pretend to laugh while pulling my beanie lower on my ears. "You scared me."

Kathryn paints a closed-mouth smile. I do the same and try to change the subject. "Who did you say that was?"

"That's Drew Anderson," she repeats. I think back to the jersey Coop was wearing when we went to the game, and it clicks—the Flames forward. I guess they really do look different out of uniform.

*"Anderson fan, huh?"*

The sound of *him* drifts through my mind, the perfect combination of silky and rich. I roll my eyes at myself, rubbing under the front of my hat and cursing my lady parts for heating at the memory.

Bringing my attention back to the Flames player now encircled by Rockets, I watch as my son and his friends look up at this man like he's God himself. He says something, causing the boys to spring to attention, then turns around. They follow his gaze, and I do the same, my eyes landing on a full pout, dark beard, strong jaw... and tailored suit.

I blink hard, feeling my stomach drop toward my toes. *How is this happening?* Opening my eyes, I focus on the spot between my legs. "I blame you," I whisper to the button of my jeans. My eyes grow wide as I quickly snap my head over my shoulder to make sure Kathryn didn't just witness me damning my crotch.

I glance back at Coach Monte as he tilts his head toward the Rocket's bench. Anderson and the boys move in that direction and pile through the opening in the boards. The other parents file down the ramp toward the lobby area between the bench and the locker room—the same place where Levi's standing. I feel like I'm watching a tennis match the way I'm looking back and forth between Cooper's team and the NHL coach that shouldn't catch my attention.

My adrenaline pumps as my fight or flight response begins to take over, but there's really no way out. Unless for some reason Levi decides to leave right this second, or I become invisible, the only way out of this rink, short of abandoning my son, is by interacting with my new curiosity. The boys walk off the bench toward the locker room with Anderson in the middle, who is twice their size.

A warmth rises up from my chest to my cheeks as I brace myself for our inevitable interaction. I'm not sure what I dislike more—him or how I feel around him. A silence surrounds me that says I'm the only one left in the stands not rushing toward any past or present hockey players, and it's time to make my move.

I descend the ramp, taking advantage of the fact that Levi is shaking hands with parents and high-fiving players as they pass. Stepping onto the carpet at the end of the slope, I fake search for my phone that I know is zipped safely inside the front pocket of my bag. As the commotion settles, I come to a crossroads. I can either commit to hunting through my bag for the foreseeable future, or I can get a grip and talk to him. He chooses for me.

"Bennett," he says, low but steady. I pause with my hand wrapped firmly around a pack of gum, his piercing eyes on me.

Squeezing the life from the cardboard box, I play as unbothered as possible. "Monte."

His mouth forms an easy smile. "Good to see you again."

*I wish I could say the same.* "Likewise."

I glance around, happy to see that most of the parents have already made their way into the locker room to see whatever excitement Anderson is offering. "What are you doing here?"

Levi places his hands behind his back. "I promised Cooper an authentic Anderson autograph."

My breath involuntarily hitches and judging by the tension in his jaw, he noticed. "Oh," I say, sounding as caught off guard as I am. I realize that my hand is still stuffed in my purse, so I move it to my pocket instead. "You, uh—you didn't have to do that."

His brows turn in ever-so-slightly. "But I said it, didn't I?"

"Yes, you did."

"So, here I am."

He looks around our little hometown rink, and the weight of the situation really hits me. Coach Monte, as irritating as he may be, is presumably a very busy man.

It comes with the suit in most cases—definitely this one. I'm sure he has games and practices, meetings and interviews—personal matters that he has to tend to. But instead, he's here. For my son. Because he said that he would. *But mostly because it makes him look good,* the voice in my head reminds me.

"I appreciate that," I say stoically. "It's... unexpected."

"From someone of my kind?" he asks, the corners of his lips creeping upward.

"Exactly," I say, leaning in closer. Sweet notes of apple and spicy mint undertones tease me and force me back to standing.

"Anyway, I looked up the Junior Rocket's schedule. I hope that's okay." I nod my head lightly, and he mirrors the gesture. "I told Anderson, and he was all for it. He brought a pile of jerseys that he's signing for the boys as we speak." He turns around and looks toward the locker room. Judging by the squeals coming from a group of otherwise too-cool twelve-year-olds who just got destroyed in a game, I'd say he's probably right.

"That's very nice of him. And you." I cross my arms over my chest, and he tracks my movement, inhaling deeply. "Thank you."

He pulls back, a smirk on his face. "What was that?"

"Thank you," I repeat.

He cups his hand by his ear and leans down, the scent of him, once again, wrapping me up. "I'm sorry, I just—Could you say that one more time?"

Without thinking, I nudge him in the shoulder which meets my hand like a concrete wall. His eyes fall to the spot, then come back to me, my face no doubt flushed with embarrassment. *Why did I touch him?* Okay, maybe the personal space thing is a little contagious.

"Alex Bennett, are you warming up to me?" He looks at me, a cross between surprised and impressed.

I nibble on my bottom lip and lie through my teeth, willing the most recent lust I feel toward him not to resurface. "Not even a little."

"Oh, I think you are. That was just... playful." The word seems so foreign coming from his mouth.

I part my lips to speak, but Cooper interrupts me first. "Mom!" he yells, running out of the locker room in the same jersey he was wearing the other night. "Mom, look!" He turns around, and unlike the one from before, this one has a signature on the shoulder blade. A large "A" and "#12" frame an otherwise illegible scribble right across the nameplate.

"Wow! That's awesome, Coop." I pull him in close, his back to my front, making him a barrier between Levi and me.

"Hey, Coach," he says excitedly, holding out his fist. Levi meets it with his, and I try not to stare at the veins that shoot up his covered forearm from the top of his hand.

"Told you we'd get you that autograph." Levi winks at me, and my eyes roll to the back of my head. I admit it was borderline sweet until he had to go and act pompous about it. *So close.*

"Sweet!" I pinch his shoulders, and he sinks beneath my grasp. "Thank you," he adds.

"No sweat, buddy."

"Alright, let's get going." Smiling politely at Levi, I grab Cooper's bag. "It was nice to see you again, Coach Montgomery."

His full name sounds almost awkward rolling off my tongue, but my body reacts to it as if it was foreplay. *Why does it keep doing that?* Levi's eyebrows grow tense, his eyes heated beneath them. His throat moves up and down.

"Call me Levi... please." Reaching for Coop's stuff he says, "Here, let me carry that for you."

"Oh, no. That's okay." I hold the large bag out to my son. "It's actually Cooper's job."

"You want to play the sport, you'll carry your equipment," Coop groans, mocking my usual phrase. I scrunch my nose at him and ruffle his hair, then nudge him toward the door.

Taking our first step, I glance back at Coach—Levi—and see him staring at nothing, his brow still furrowed.

"Bye, Coach!" Coop calls over his shoulder. Levi's eyes dart from the ground to where we are a few feet away. All of a sudden, he leaps toward us.

"Actually," he says, holding his pointer finger up. "I was kind of hoping you could do me a favor."

Cooper springs to attention, and I squint at Levi, trying to read him.

"Yeah?" Coop asks.

"We're, uh—having a big event for the Spark the Flame program." He reaches up and rubs the back of his neck. *Where is he going with this?* "Sadie thought maybe showing more content with us working individually with kids would help with our mission. You know, spotlighting a local player and having him be more involved with a few things. Help us get some more insight into what we can do to assist the future hockey stars of our area." Cooper is completely still, hanging on to every word that Levi says, as my mind races. "So, what do you think?"

Coop's head snaps to me, the look on his face like he just won the lottery. Probably because to him—he did. I glare at Levi. He did not just put me in this position. I don't even know what this entails, and yet, he put it into my son's head like it was a done deal. Any previous desire for him flies right out the window. I'd thank him for that if I wasn't so pissed.

Peering at me, and probably reading my reactive expressions, Levi continues. "You'd have to talk to your mom, of course. I don't need an answer today, but... " He brings his eyes to me. "We'd really love to have you." Now I'm the one completely still until my brain catches up with the rest of my body. *Nice try, Coach. But it's a little too late for all that.*

Levi pulls out a business card from his back pocket and holds it up to me. I hesitate before finally taking it because Cooper is looking up at me like it's a golden ticket.

"Talk with your mom and have her email me what you think. If you're interested, we'll get all of the details ironed out."

"Oh, I'm interested," Cooper says, his head nodding like it's falling off his neck. "Can I, Mom?"

I squeeze his shoulder. "We'll see," I say, looking down at him. I then move my gaze, heated with annoyance, to Levi and find his sea green eyes already on me. "We'll talk about it."

He nods once, and I swear the corner of his lips raises slightly. "Sounds good," he says. "We'll talk."

# 12

# Levi

"Thanks for meeting with me." Rounding my desk, I sit on the ledge facing a mousey spitfire I've come to know, tapping her Apple pen against her tablet case. "You can sit down, you know. I promise nothing will fall apart without you for a few minutes."

Sadie, the director of Spark the Flame, smiles politely but remains standing. "I perform best when I'm on my feet," she says before inhaling deeply. She looks like the Energizer Bunny with an iPad instead of a drum.

I hired Sadie to run this program when I started it. She is quick, efficient, and organized. She's also a ball of anxiety with a caffeine addiction. Much like me, she finds it hard to relax—always on her toes. Because Spark the Flame is still a smaller foundation, she's in charge of a few other activities here—meet and greets, signing events, sponsorships—but despite her schedule, she thrives on more work.

"I want to add some new marketing for Spark the Flame before the gala," I say, reaching behind me to grab my hot Drippy's cup.

Immediately Sadie whips open the cover on her device. "Great. I didn't know you were thinking that."

Lifting the lid, I blow on the hot contents inside. "Honestly, I didn't either." *Not until Alex tried to leave.*

I can't say what came over me after the Junior Rockets' game other than I fucking panicked. I went there planning to make good on my promise to Cooper—and to scratch the itch I've had all week to see her. I thought that would be enough, but the moment my eyes locked on hers, I knew I was wrong.

After talking with Liam, the thought of Alex was already nagging at me—my own mind betraying me by leaping to her when he talked about my lack of relationships. I don't even know this girl, yet I can't seem to move past her.

Then, after meeting up with Liv, with the intention of screwing her out of my head, it was worse. Olivia is fine, and we've had a good run, but when I saw her face, I wished it was Alex's. When I kissed her lips, I pictured Bennett's, and when I was fucking her from behind, I fantasized that it was the same perfect ass I saw leaned over the bar at Petey's.

It's as if Alex Bennett has altered my brain chemistry—changed what I've come to know in only a few conversations. I haven't decided yet if that's a good or a bad thing, but I knew I needed to see her more to find out.

The only issue is that I went and walked myself into seeing her in the one situation that I probably shouldn't. I'm not sure it would look great professionally to suggest this whole initiative and then for the board to find out I'm interested in the player's mom. Of course, the consequences of this weren't exactly at the forefront of my mind when she looked at me with her little frown. I'll just have to cross that bridge if and when I get to it.

"What are you thinking? Bigger names? More teams? We had talked about partnering with the community center a while back." The sound of Sadie's voice interrupts my thoughts as she rattles off ideas, her hand flying across the screen. "We could look into sponsorships with companies related to both kids and hockey—Learn to Skate programs, gear, those cool Gatorade bottles with the flavor pods that they all seem to love."

I let Sadie finish spewing, having no idea how long she's been at it, and buy myself time by sipping my coffee. When she finally comes up for air, I stop her before she can begin again. "Actually, I have an idea."

She pulls her face back and turns her lips in. "Oh... okay!" I can't help but chuckle at the change in demeanor. It's like she went from drill sergeant to soccer mom in a matter of seconds.

"I was thinking we put a face to the program—make it more relatable for kids and more endearing to the donors. I know we advertise pictures of all of the teams that come through, but I'm talking about choosing one to spotlight and really get to know. Maybe that kid changes every so often, but we can pick one to have specifically for gala content. It makes things seem more personal than just giving these players a one-time experience.

I want our program to be more than that anyway. The whole point is to connect with young athletes from neighborhoods nearby and get them excited about the game we all love. What better way to show that we're doing that than to have one of them speak on our behalf?" I know I have a slightly ulterior motive, and I came up with this on the fly, but I really do think it's a great idea.

Once again, Sadie starts tapping on her tablet. "I like it," she says. "So, what are your thoughts? Pictures? Interviews? We could let them be the kid-coach for a practice and maybe get them on the bench for a game or two?"

"Yes. All of that. We can let it come naturally. Honestly, I haven't thought much about those details in particular." *Or anything really.* I just knew that I needed to get Bennett in the same room as me—to give her a reason to be where I am.

"We could host a contest or raffle to choose the child. Maybe we can have the young teams nominate players they think deserve to be spotlighted?"

I rake my nails down my beard. "Actually, I already have a kid in mind."

Sadie repeats the same reaction as she did before, tapping away. "Perfect!"

"He's a good kid, local player—his team was here the other night, the Junior Rockets. He loves hockey, raised by a single mom..." I hate to throw that in there, but like it or not, it's a relatable angle. Sadie's eyebrow cocks up as I mention that last part, and she does some more typing on her screen.

"Name?" she asks, looking down at her iPad.

"Cooper." She pauses and then looks up at me, patiently. "Bennett," I add on, feeling the weight of that name in both syllables. The name of the woman who I can't get out of my head. *Why is even that small detail having an effect on me?* "Cooper Bennett." Sadie taps some more.

I got an overwhelming, yet completely ridiculous sense of pride when I searched the Junior Rockets' roster and saw Alex gave Cooper her last name. I don't know what went down with his father, but I already hate the guy. I should have known though. In the few brief interactions we've had, I can already see that she's a no-bullshit kind of woman. She's sharp, quick-witted, and completely independent. She seems like the type of woman who thinks everything through. The type that if she's honest... wishes she didn't have to.

Checking my phone again, I open my email. Still nothing. "I'll handle reaching out to the parent and will keep you updated on any response that I get."

Sadie nods once and slaps the cover of her iPad closed. "I think it's a great idea, Coach."

"Thank you," I say. *Can you pretend it was yours?*

"Yo, we missed you at breakfast this weekend," Erik, one of my two assistant coaches says as I walk out of my office, skates already on. He hands me a coffee, and I nod my head in thanks for the mid-morning buzz.

Every Saturday that we don't have a game, or aren't traveling, the three of us coaches try to grab food at one of the local diners downtown. It only happens occasionally, but it's nice to get together outside of the rink. More importantly, taking the time to talk about things other than hockey, helps to build our chemistry and success on the bench.

"I know," I say over the lip of my cup. "I took Anderson to sign some jerseys at the Junior Rockets' game that day".

Erik glances at me sideways and keeps walking, his blades clunking against the rubber floor just like mine. "The team that was here for Spark the Flame last week?"

"Yeah, I promised one of the kids I'd get him Drew's autograph, but Anderson was with Tammy when they came into the locker room."

He raises his brows and nods his head, completely convinced. "Well, that was nice of you two."

Pulling my lips in, I give him a closed mouth smile.

It's not a lie. Drew was technically in with our trainer when the Rockets had their locker room tour. He came in toward the end, but the boys were already headed to the player's lounge. I, however, don't think I would have even noticed had he been in the room. Considering Bennett had left me in the hallway completely rejected, I'm pretty sure my mind was on nothing but figuring out what the fuck just happened.

"Well, you didn't miss much," Erik says. "Gavin's dog had puppies again. I saw pictures. They're pretty damn cute."

Pushing through the door to get to the tunnel, I look over at him. "I'm sure they're adorable."

"I'm sure Ruthie would think so."

I stop in my tracks. "Don't you dare say a word. Liam would kill me."

"Kind of the point."

"And then he'd kill you. I know you're out for my job, Erik, but I'm telling you, man. That's not the way."

He nudges my shoulder, both of us knowing that's an absolute lie. Erik loves his job, but he consistently reminds me that he has no idea how I do mine.

The boys are already stretching at center ice as we step onto the bench. Gavin stands in the middle of their circle talking to them. "Not a word," I say, looking at Erik when Gavin nods toward us.

Skating onto the ice, I join the group. "Alright, let's go, boys. Give me two lines in and two lines out." The guys take their sticks and head to their designated areas for the drill we run regularly.

A ding sounds from inside my warmups, and I all too quickly slide my phone from the pocket.

Influencer Olivia

> Still thinking about the other night as always.
> Round 2?

"Come on, Bachelor Boy. We have a practice to run," Gavin jokes as he skates over to me. "Enough flirting already."

"Not even close," I say back.

"Oh, so you're telling me that wasn't a girl you've slept with before? Olivia maybe?"

My eyes narrow at him before falling closed. These two guys know me better than everyone, besides my brother. If I deny it, it will only make it seem like I'm trying to hide it for another reason.

"It was." Gavin cocks an eyebrow, a cocky grin growing on his face. "Unfortunately," I add.

"Damn," he says, shaking his head. "Not into it?" *Jesus, will people stop asking me that?*

"Not like that."

Gavin scoffs. "Tell that to the internet. You're in even more sports gossip than normal recently."

I throw my head back as I come to a definite realization that this has to end. As solid as our sex has been, we've reached our expiration. Besides, if I have my way, and am granted a gift from God, I'll have Alex soon enough. If there's one thing I don't do, it's sleep with multiple women at once. *Talk about messy.* I pull out my phone and swipe open her message.

> I don't think that should happen again. Sorry,
> Liv.

Instantly three dots bounce up and down in the bottom corner of our texts. I brace myself for her response.

Influencer Olivia

> That's cool, Levi. You're a good lay, but you're also boring as hell. Take care.

She adds another text with a kiss face emoji, and I breathe a sigh of relief. That's taken care of.

Holding up my phone to Gavin, I say, "It's handled. Happy?"

He laughs. "Man, for someone who gets more tail than a dog with two left paws, you sure don't seem to like many women."

I stare at him, so confused by the majority of what came from his mouth. "I like women just fine," I clarify, as we skate to where the boys are forming the lines that I instructed them to. "It's loving them that I have a problem with." I blow my whistle, starting the drill, and ending our conversation.

The last thing I ever want to discuss again is my past love life—specifically Rachel.

Like most kids freshly drafted, I took advantage of being in the spotlight. I partied for years, and I ate up the fact that so many women were giving me attention. But then I met Rachel.

In a sea of puck bunnies, she was a breath of fresh air. She was fun and sweet, and she genuinely seemed to like my company, unlike the others who draped their half-naked bodies over me every chance they got. At the time, she was different. Now, she's the entire reason that I've sworn off being in a relationship. She's also half of the reason I almost lost any chance I had at keeping hockey in my life.

Don't get me wrong, my light went dull the second I heard that pop in my knee almost eight years ago. But at the time, hockey wasn't all I had. Rachel and I had been together for years at that point. Quite literally, I thought I hit the jackpot. I had accomplished my dream, I was playing well, and I had a girl on my arm with a heart of gold. She loved me and supported my career, and as far as I was concerned, she was it for me.

Of course she didn't hate our lifestyle—the house, the vacations, the cars—but that seemed understandable enough. Who wouldn't like those kinds of lavish things? It never occurred to me that she was the type who was only in it for the money. *Stupid fucking me.*

The second the doctors told me I would never play professional hockey again, not only did my light dim, but so did Rachel's. She encouraged me for a while to bounce back and tackle the rehab head-on, but when it was clear to everyone that this was it for me, *that* was apparently it for her.

She told me she had been feeling us grow distant for a while. That for as long as she had endured it, the stress that my job put on our relationship and the time we spent apart was too much for her to deal with anymore. But that was all a lie.

In the end, I realized the reason she had been pushing so hard for me to recover had nothing to do with me at all. Either she had become so accustomed to the life that we had that it ended up changing her without either of us realizing it, or she had me fooled from the very beginning.

Immediately following our break-up, she was on to the next professional athlete—this time a basketball player. Clearly the traveling, the schedule, and the distance between us weren't the reasons she ended things if she was willing to jump right into bed with the next guy with the same lifestyle. No, the difference between him and me wasn't only the sport we played. It was that he was just getting his start in the professional sports world, signing with a seven-figure deal, and I was on my way out the door.

In a matter of weeks, I had lost the two things that I loved the most in life. Or that at least I thought I did. Luckily, the one that came back to me was the one that really mattered. The one that despite our struggles, has never let me down.

I'm over Rachel now. The last time I checked, she was off living in another state and with an even newer athlete, but the whole thing really fucked with my head. I realized that with me back on track to make professional hockey my career, I'd be surprised if anyone ever seemed special enough to take any of my focus away from the game. I'd also be surprised if I ever thought about love again.

What was even worse though, was it made me feel like I could no longer trust myself. I loved Rachel for years. We lived together, talked about a wedding someday, and were thinking of starting a family eventually. Still, I was blindsided. From that point on, I decided I would never let anything like that happen again. Rachel doesn't haunt me like she used to, but I learned from my mistakes. For now, the only person in this world who can hurt me is myself.

# 13

# Alex

"*H*arder," *I cry, sitting back on the same desk Levi did the first day we met. It was the day he uttered those six salacious words:*

*"You now have my undivided attention."*

*If he didn't mean it then, he damn sure does now as he pounds into me from the standing position. "Harder, Levi," I breathe into his ear as his chiseled body hovers over me. "Please."*

*A groan climbs from his chest as he thrusts into me, obeying my command. His hands straddle my half-naked body as he leans his weight onto the desk. "Good girl," he growls. "So polite."*

*The fabric of my skirt, pushed up around my waist, flutters against my bare stomach with every rhythmic movement. Our breaths tangle as we rock into each other.*

*"This was such a good idea," I say, letting my head roll back so I'm staring at his office ceiling. My elbows nearly buckle under the weight of my upper body as I get closer and closer to coming undone.*

*"I was hoping you understood what I really wanted when I brought Cooper on as our spotlight player."*

*I giggle. "That you wanted to have sex with me on your expensive desk?"*

*"That I wanted to fuck you on my expensive desk. And all over the rest of this office."*

*"Oh, Coach," I moan.*

*A guttural sound escapes Levi's throat. He pulls out, and I whimper from his absence. "Say it again."*

*"Coach."*

*He pushes into me once more, with more force this time. "Again."*

*"Coach." My voice comes out gravelly. He drives in again and my legs start to tremble wrapped around his bare ass. I know he's close, and so am I.*

*"Again," he says through gritted teeth.*

*"Co—"*

"Mom!" *What?*

"Mom!" *There's a pounding sound that doesn't match the cadence of our bodies.*

"Mom!"

My eyes fly open, and I throw myself into the sitting position, the sleep mask I'm wearing already halfway down my face.

"Mom!" Cooper calls from the other side of the door. "Will you shut that thing off!"

It takes me a second to survey my surroundings and process what's happening. I'm not with Levi, and I'm not in his office. But I *am* going absolutely insane. *A sex dream, really?* Who is this guy, and what is he doing to me? And how come even asleep he was the best I ever had.

I swat at my phone alarm that is croaking from my nightstand and remind myself that I have to stop listening to smutty audiobooks before bed. Frazzled, I throw the mess of a blanket, that's all bunched around me, to the side and reluctantly force myself out of bed. The air hits my balmy skin, and it's exactly what I need to cool myself down. I couldn't tell you the last time I slept through an alarm, but I didn't get much sleep this past weekend.

I was up well past midnight both nights after closing at the restaurant, and despite my resistance, my brain won't shut off about Levi since Cooper's game on Saturday. *Clearly.*

You always want what you shouldn't have.

You'd never believe it from my nighttime fantasy, but I'm more pissed at him than anything. I have no idea what his intentions are with making Cooper some sort of Spark the Flame mascot. I guess I should thank him for reminding me of why I was reluctant to let myself think about him in the first place. He didn't even consider the position that he put me in. First of all, it was so unexpected, and he gave me essentially no helpful information. More importantly, he didn't even mention it to me before dropping it on Cooper. Ever since we left the rink, that's all he's been talking about. *Have I thought about it yet? Have I emailed Coach?* The kid is like an addict waiting on his fix.

The truth is, I selfishly want nothing to do with seeing Levi Montgomery more than I have to. If I can't control his presence while I'm sleeping, the least I can do is distance myself from him when I'm awake. My body feels torn when I'm around him because my mind knows exactly who he is, and the only way to ensure that ends is to stop spending time with each other—something he just made almost impossible.

If only for the sake of getting Cooper off my back, I do have to figure it out. Doing this would be an awesome experience for him—there's no doubt about that—but before I agree to anything, I need to know the ins and outs of what exactly we're getting into. The only way to do that is to reach out to Levi, the one person I'd otherwise avoid. If that doesn't say I'd do anything for my kid, I'm not sure what would.

Looking at my clock, I calculate that I have only twenty minutes until we're supposed to walk out the door. One upside to working for an online blog is, nowadays, we all work from home. That means I don't technically have to get ready for the day until I feel like it—or ever if I don't want to. Ten minutes—one semi-cold shower—and a lounge set later, I walk into the kitchen.

"Mom, can you please email Coach Monte today? There is no way you can say no to this. Spark the Flame has never chosen a kid to be the face of their program before. I Googled it last night."

"Oh, yeah?" I ask, walking to the coffee pot and popping a K-cup into the holder. "And how did you do that on the phone that's supposed to be off and away before you go to bed?"

Cooper's spoon of cereal pauses on its trek to his mouth as his eyes search the room for any possible excuse. "Did I say last night?" he asks, his voice breaking mid-sentence. "I meant first thing this morning."

Raising one brow, I cross my hands over my chest and lean back on the counter. "Mhm, sure you did."

"Come on, Mom. Please?" He drops his spoon in his bowl and brings his hands together under his chin. "I'll unload the dishwasher for a week."

"You'll do that anyway for having your phone on after bedtime," I say, grabbing my now full mug, a smile dancing across my lips.

Cooper slouches in his stool. "Fine."

After a moment, I add on. "But I'll also email Coach Montgomery today. I promise." A vision of Levi suspended over top of me flashes before my eyes, the steam coming off of my mug floating past my neck like his breath as he pants out his command. *"Again."*

I'm brought back to reality as Cooper all but falls from his chair to rush around the island. His face springs to life as he throws his arms around my waist. I hold my coffee above my head to stop the impact from sloshing it around. "Thank you, thank you, thank you. You're the best mom I've ever had."

"Yeah, yeah," I say, soaking in his embrace. "Remember that when I'm in the nursing home. Now go get your stuff. We're leaving in five."

Back at home, I swirl my iced latte and stare at my computer screen. Extra caffeine is needed today. I have a blog post on personal space to finish, and I can't stop thinking about the man who inspired it.

I know I have to email Levi. Cooper's begging may be a pain in my ass, but if there's one thing I don't do, it's break my promises—especially to him. Nick does that enough for the both of us.

Minimizing my draft page, I pull up my email. Maybe getting this out of the way will help me focus on the work I actually need to complete. My eyes shift to the shiny business card sitting next to my desk, taunting me to use its listed information.

Clicking the button to compose a new email, I take a deep breath. The screen pops up, and the cursor begins its relentless blinking. *Tick. Tock. Tick. Tock. Tick. Tock,* it seems to say as I start with the subject.

Having worked in an industry where most communication is done through email, I've learned the person's address is the last thing you enter. All I need is to be drafting my message, having not yet gone back to edit out typos—or take out any impression I may actually want to see him—and hit send by mistake. This way, there's nowhere for the information to go until I'm ready for it to be out in the world.

Starting with the greeting, I begin to type.

---

**From: Alex.Bennett@Gmail.com**
**To:**
**Subject: Spark the Flame Campaign**

**Dear Levi,**

---

I erase his first name even though he told me that's what I should call him. It sounds too... casual. Too personal for the tone I'm going for.

---

**From: Alex.Bennett@Gmail.com**
**To:**
**Subject: Spark the Flame Campaign**

**Dear Coach,**

---

Once again, my memory taunts me. *"Say it again."*
I delete the whole line before starting again.

---

**From: Alex.Bennett@Gmail.com**
**To:**
**Subject: Spark the Flame Campaign**

**Dear Coach Montgomery,**

---

Fine. Next, I start the message.

---

**From: Alex.Bennet@Gmail.com**
**To:**
**Subject: Spark The Flame Campaign**

**Dear Coach Montgomery,**
**This is Alex Bennett, Cooper's mom from the Junior Rockets. You asked us to email you our thoughts about Cooper helping with the Spark the Flame campaign. After some consideration, I have come to the conclusion that we need more information before making a decision.**

**Cooper is already quite busy with his schoolwork and hockey schedule, and I myself work two jobs. In addition, as someone who is already very cautious of Cooper's usage of the internet and social media, I'd like to know what is required of him specifically.**

**As exciting as the opportunity may be, I am hesitant to agree without hearing all of the terms and conditions. It would have been helpful to talk about this before getting Cooper involved.**

**I hope you understand. I look forward to discussing the details with you.**

Rereading my message, I know it sounds professional—borderline cold—but that's exactly what this would be. A business opportunity for Cooper, essentially. And despite the thought of Levi satisfying my obvious need in my dreams last night, that is not what this is. It's not about the two of us seeing each other again. In fact, that's the part of this I'm dreading the most.

Sure, Coach Montgomery is sexy and intriguing, but he's also everything that I actively avoid. I mean, Nick was so similar and look how that turned out. There is no way I am even entertaining the idea of that ever happening—at least in reality.

A tingle begins its descent between my legs, and I squeeze my thighs together in response. *Don't even think about it.*

For good measure, I go back to my email and edit the last lines of my message.

**I hope you understand.**
**Thank you,**
**Alex Bennett**

I finally add his email to the recipient line and hover my mouse over the send button.

"This is for Cooper," I say to myself.

Another added bonus of working from home is you can talk to yourself like a crazy person without anyone else hearing you.

I click down on the touch pad, and the *swoosh* sound of the email being sent teases me on its way through my laptop speakers.

Immediately, I slam my screen shut and resist every urge I have to throw it across the room. I almost don't want Levi to answer, but at the same time, I can't stand the idea of waiting for a reply.

I decide burying myself in work is probably a more productive way to distract myself than staring at the mound of laundry now in my view on the other side of my room. Cracking open the screen, I quickly exit out of my email and mute the sound so notifications can't chime through.

I pull up the blog post I started over the weekend. It's almost finished, I just have to add my final edits. I reread the draft, and as my fingers move to the keyboard, my phone tweets from next to my computer.

Glancing at the screen, a notification for a new incoming email sits bolded right below the time. Damnit. I clearly didn't think that one all the way through.

All it shows is the sender and the subject line of the email, but even that is enough to get my palms sweating as they sit hovering over the keys on my laptop.

> **Levi Montgomery**
> *RE: Spark the Flame Campaign*

"Fuck me," I say out loud and as if in response, another email comes through.

> **Levi Montgomery**
> *Calendar Invite - Office of Levi Montgomery*

Almost instantly, my heart rate picks up. Why did I think I could somehow avoid ever having to see that desk again?

Like ripping off a band aid, I swipe across to read the email first.

From: LeviMontgomery@NHLFlames.com
To: Alex.Bennett@Gmail.com
Subject: RE: Spark the Flame Campaign

Hello Alex,
Thank you for getting back to me. I am happy to hear that Cooper is interested in being spotlighted for our program, but I also understand your concerns. I do apologize for not speaking with you first. I was excited to fill Cooper in on the possibility. Maybe it's a little too late, but how about we discuss the specific terms first before getting Cooper even more involved. Does that sound okay to you? I will send you a calendar invitation request following this email. Feel free to block out any time I have available that is convenient for you.
Thank you,
Levi

Slouching back in my seat, I reread the message. Then, I read it a couple more times for good measure, coming to the same conclusion each time—he doesn't sound like an ass at all. *Shit.*

Seeing him own up to his mistakes makes it really hard to hate him at the moment. I remind myself he's just another arrogant, suit-wearing, rich guy with a punctuality problem, but his response—and the image of him shirtless in my dreams—threatens to cancel all of those out.

Picturing this new version of Levi, I drop my head into my hands. It'd be nice to somehow know for sure that I was right about him, that he's a bad apple, exactly like Nick. But right now—after that dream and his email—he's starting to feel more like forbidden fruit.

# 14

# Levi

"Are you guys off tomorrow?" Liam calls through the fence that separates me from the machine shooting baseballs toward him at eighty miles per hour. He swings the bat and, of course, makes contact again.

Sliding my fingers through the loops of metal in front of me, I lean into the fence. "Yeah, but I still have to go into my office. At least for the morning." The pitching machine shoots another baseball from its opening, and Liam winds up to swing again.

Being a player on the Golden City Gators, he has access to their top-of-the-line practice facility with technology way more advanced than what we're using now. But this batting cage holds a lot of memories for us.

Liam and I used to come to Three Strikes as kids. We were always both into baseball, and this was what we did when we saved enough money doing chores or raking leaves. It's also what Liam used to cheer me up when we were younger.

When life handed me those lemons I refused to turn into lemonade, he would bring me here to help make things right. When I came home upset in kindergarten because I was the only kid who hadn't lost a tooth yet, Liam convinced my mom to take us to the cages. When I got detention in middle school for not doing my homework—batting cages. When I got in a fight with someone at school and Mom took my license away, Liam used the car we shared to bring me here.

Now, the tradition continues, only I'm mature enough to return the favor sometimes too.

This is where Liam brought me the week after my injury. I couldn't hit the ball, but he made me sit and watch him swing in silence for hours until eventually I couldn't take it anymore, and I finally broke.

When a girl Liam slept with once showed up with a two-month-old Ruthie saying he had to take her or put her up for adoption, all three of us came here. I hit balls, and they both cried until the owner practically kicked us out. I guess in a lot of ways, Three Strikes is another thing that's never let me down.

Liam was always better than me, obviously, but I held my own. Plus, I made it a point to even the score on the rare occasion that we decided to go skating instead. Despite not playing professionally like Liam, I always loved baseball, and we still try to come every once in a while for the hell of it. It's nice to take some stress out by crushing balls, and it's even better to shoot the shit with my brother somewhere that makes me feel carefree again.

"Do you have meetings?" Liam asks, catching the edge of a ball and sending it into the net strung above him.

"What?" I ask, still thinking about all of the times we've come here before.

"Is that why you have to go in?"

With my hands still resting on the fence, I hang my head between my arms, brushing the dirt around on the ground with the tip of my sneaker. "Oh, uh, yeah. Just one."

Laughing to himself, Liam asks, "Is Jack on your case about the PK again?"

One time the general manager of the Flames made a joke about how our penalty kill could use some work. He was obviously kidding considering our percentages but I, of course, didn't find it funny. I made the mistake of venting to Liam about it, and now he brings it up on occasion just to piss me off.

THE BOARDS BETWEEN US

"No," I say sharply, and he chuckles in response. "It's uh, with a mom of one of the peewee players in the area. We're hoping to spotlight him for the Spark the Flame gala."

I'm surprised by the way I feel awkward telling Liam about this. It's not that I'm uncomfortable talking to him specifically about the Bennett situation, it's just that I'm uncomfortable in general with how I've been feeling about it being a situation at all.

When Alex's first email came in, it was like Christmas fucking morning. To finally hear from the woman I couldn't get out of my goddamn head was truly a relief I didn't know I needed, which was strange enough.

How many times has a woman's name popped up on my phone screen and I don't even blink an eye? Hell, I don't even answer half the time. But seeing her message come through gave me an energy that felt almost foreign.

Then, to read her tone in the message—all formal and polite—was entertaining to say the least. I can count on one hand the number of times I've interacted with her, and during exactly none of them was she ever anything but full of attitude. Talk about lighting me up. For way too long after reading it, I thought about all of the ways to help strip her of those manners—among other things.

What wasn't amusing though was hearing that she not only takes care of her son—presumably by herself considering there's never been sight or mention of his father—but she works two jobs on top of it. The journalism thing I knew about, thanks to my lack of control when it comes to searching for her on the internet, but I had no idea she did anything else. This girl is an absolute anomaly.

The other women that tend to run in my circle are typically, in their minds, still too young to have children or are holding onto their youth for as long as possible. Not to mention, they're entirely too selfish to even think about raising another human being. They also don't tend to have even one thing in their life that qualifies as a respectable job, unless you count posting overly edited photos as a way to earn an honest living. Alex just seems so different, and all of a sudden, I seem... very into her kind of different.

"Wait? Shouldn't Sadie be in charge of that kind of thing?"

My foot pauses mid-sweep over the track I'm making in the dirt, and I internally curse myself for telling my brother way too much about my life.

Yes, Sadie should be handling all of the inner workings of STF because, well, that's her job. But there was no way I wasn't handling this when it's because of me that this is even happening in the first place. Because I needed another excuse to see *her*.

"Technically I guess."

"Then what's the deal? Don't you have enough on your plate?"

"I think I can handle it."

"But you don't have to."

"But I want to," I blurt too quickly. Liam turns to me before snapping his head back toward the machine as another ball flies toward him.

"I know you're a control freak, little brother," he says, still turned away from me. "But that's a little much even for you."

With no argument there, I say nothing at all. I sandwich the cool metal of one link of the fence between the thumb and forefinger of each of my hands, occupying idle time. The thought that even Liam can see that I'm acting outside of myself makes me nervous. Like he said, I'm a control freak. So why can't I control my feelings about some woman I just met?

A ball pounds the metal I'm holding, barely missing my hand. "Holy shit," Liam says as I look toward him.

"Seriously dude. What the fuck? Pay attention. That almost took off my finger."

"That's not what I mean." He rips off his helmet and hangs it by his side. These old cages don't have the type of technology that can tell you how many balls you have left, but Liam's always had a knack for knowing when the pitching machine was empty. "You want to sleep with this woman," he says.

Rolling my eyes despite my stomach doing the same, I enter the cage and pull the helmet from his grasp. I reach for the bat now tucked under his arm, but he pulls it away before I get a chance to grab it.

"Admit it," he says.

"No."

He holds the bat above his head like he used to when we were little. "Do it."

"No," I growl, lunging toward it again. Unlike when we were kids, I'm not four inches shorter than Liam anymore, so his little game shouldn't pan out like it used to, but I still can't manage to get it. "Will you give me the fucking bat?"

"Sure," he says, handing it to me. I glare at him cautiously before slowly reaching for the metal.

"Why?" I ask hesitantly, curious why he gave up so easily.

"Because I don't need you to admit it." He walks out of the cage and takes my place on the other side of the fence. Leaning closely to the links he speaks again, his voice just above a whisper. "The fact that you won't, tells me all I need to know."

On instinct, I smack the bat against the links. Liam snickers to himself before crossing his arms over his chest. "See."

Holding the bat parallel to the ground, I point it at him. "Shut up."

I hit the start button so the pitching machine springs back to life. I'm not sure why I'm suddenly flooded with anger, but I'm ready to hit the shit out of something. The first ball comes toward me, and as I make contact with it, a cracking sound fills the space. That's a start.

As I think about why Liam's comment set me off, he leans on the fence. Just when I think I've survived this conversation, he interrupts my thoughts. "I was right, wasn't I?"

He says it as the next ball comes flying toward me, and I swing hard, missing it completely. "About what?" I ask, now even more pissed from missing such an easy hit.

The hum of the machine signals another opportunity to whack the hell out of something, and as that ball begins its journey toward me, Liam says, "That your meeting is more sex than business."

I snap, hitting the ball so hard my hands tingle from the impact, and my brain aches from the realization of what set me off. I'm not pissed because of what he's saying—no one would blame him for assuming that Alex is my next conquest. But it bothers me that him seeing her that way is pissing me off. *Why? I'm not quite sure.*

"Damn, brother. Keep hitting like that and they'll give you my job."

"It's not like that."

"What?"

Taking off my helmet, I step to the part of the fence that's out of the pitching machine's firing line. "The mom, Alex."

Liam hangs his hands on the fence like he's giving me his full attention. "Oh, she has a name."

I tilt my chin down and give him my *stop talking* face. "It's not like that," I repeat.

"So, you don't want to sleep with her?"

"Of course I do." My mouth blurts what I'm thinking before my mind has a chance to stop my reaction.

Liam shakes his head. "I'm so confused."

Dropping my forehead into the crook of my hand I exhale heavily. "So am I."

"Wait a second," he says as a ball slams into the fence. We both startle, forgetting that the pitching machine is still going. Three Strikes is so old there's no stopping mechanism when it comes to the power. You hit the big green button on the wall to start and when the balls run out, the machine shuts off.

Moving away so he doesn't get hit by a ball, Liam walks to the opening around the side of the fence. "Do you like her?"

"What are we, preteen girls?" I ask, dodging the next ball and meeting him at the gate.

"Oh, God no. That sounds terrifying. Please take Ruthie for me during those years." He shutters at the thought. "I just mean, do you actually *like* this one?"

Mimicking his tone, I say, "I don't even *know* this one." I'm not sure at this point who I'm convincing, my brother or the part of me that is intrigued by a girl for the first time in years.

"You always did lead with your dick," he quips. I push his shoulder, and he stumbles back dramatically.

"My dick doesn't know her either." *Not yet at least.*

"Well, we can work on both of those things. Preferably in that order."

I scoff at him, but the thought of my dick coming anywhere near Bennett is enough to get me going. "We'll see," I say, beyond done with talking about this.

"We will," Liam says, throwing his arm around my shoulder. Another ball smacks the fence, and I move back to the batting position. "But in case you weren't sure, whoever she is—I fully approve of her wifing you up."

# 15

# Alex

P ulling into the Flames' parking lot, my thoughts are perfectly torn between wanting to be there already and wanting to handcuff myself to the steering wheel of my car.

Half of me is fine coming here and seeing Levi. There's so much about him I want to hate that it will be easy to forget that my vagina clenches at the sight of him. The other half of me, however, would literally rather be anywhere else. How does this guy drive me crazy in both the best and worst possible ways?

As I park, I repeat the mantra that I've rattled off in my head over and over on the drive to get here.

*I am strong. I am independent. I do not need a man to take care of me or my son. I will not let said possible man intoxicate me with his ridiculously good looks and intermittent good nature. Suits are stupid, and men who wear them represent everything you have learned to despise.*

I'm still working on its eloquence—and extensive length—but it works for now.

I pull my car into a parking spot around the back entrance like Levi told me to. According to his email responding to my calendar request for today—Wednesday at 10:00am—I am to park here and hit the buzzer at the back entrance. From there, someone will come to let me in and lead me to his office. It took everything in me not to make a comment about him not being able to use the front door like the rest of us little people, but I decided against it considering I was trying to give him polished answers.

Glancing at myself one more time in the rearview mirror, then cursing under my breath for even caring what I look like, I take one extremely large inhale before throwing my shoulder into my car door. The driver's side sticks a little sometimes—among other issues that it has—so you have to be aggressive with it.

I'm not hurting for money by any means. I make a decent living writing the column, and I have plenty of regulars at The Gilded Tap that consistently tip me well. Nick, for whom money is the only way he knows how to show up, pays for hockey and contributes a decent amount in child support every month that covers most of Cooper's other expenses. But I don't need a new car.

So, the door sticks. And okay, on occasion it makes a weird noise or does this grinding thing when I step on the brakes—my grandma has foot bunions and a bum hip, and nobody's trading her in for a newer model. Yes, I say a prayer most days before I start it up, and sometimes I have to crawl out through the passenger side, but I'm flexible!

I live a simple life, and I watch my money because I want to—and because I've always had to. Because I could buy a new car with a few hundred dollar car payment, or I could put a little muscle into getting out of this one and be home with Cooper the extra night a week it would take to earn that back. Slamming my door shut surrounded by cars that could financially eat mine for breakfast is a little disheartening, but it's also the little reminder I need of the two completely different worlds Levi and I live in. The perfect nudge to end this fantasizing once and for all.

Walking over to the door, I see the buzzer that Levi mentioned in his email. My finger sits suspended in front of it for just a second before I force myself to get this over with. A bell chimes out from the other side of the door, and moments later the sound of footsteps adds to the ringing. A click joins the melody before the bell shuts off completely, the opening of the door silencing the sound—and momentarily stopping my heart.

As the door swings toward me, a familiar smell moves with it, and I freeze where I am. When Levi said someone would come let me in, I assumed he meant an assistant, a security guard—God himself—not the one person I needed the extra length of the hallway to prepare for. I'm not ready to see the eyes that I want so badly to make me feel nothing. Not ready to hear the voice that both puts me on edge and makes me melt. And for the love of all things holy, I am not ready to smell the weirdly arousing combination of apple and mint.

"Bennett," he says, holding the door open with one massive hand.

I try to speak, but I'm too busy staring at the broad chest in front of me covered merely by a thin, white shirt. On his lower half he's wearing dark blue jeans and black Nike sneakers—looking so normal. *Damnit.*

This isn't fair. My saving grace in coming here and *not* constantly thinking about my wet dream, was that I could hyper-fixate on him wearing a suit and channel all of my association abilities to compare him to Nick. But, that's out the window because in place of his suit is a casual, non-professional, totally fuckable, t-shirt and jeans. *Now what?*

"Are you going to come in?" He's still leaning against the propped open door, but there's a vein in his bicep that definitely wasn't there the first time I looked.

Pretending I forgot to lock my car, I turn back toward the lot and hold out my key. I close my eyes, push down on the button, and use the fleeting moment I have to summon the version of myself that I need to maintain. Once again, I channel an inner strength that I'm not sure I actually have. *Fake it till you make it, Alex.*

"Now I am."

I walk through the door with all the false confidence I was able to muster in that half of a second I had to recover. He moves aside to make room for both of us in the width of the doorway, and I ignore the fireworks that shoot up my arm as it brushes his chest when I step inside.

Once I'm fully in, I pause, waiting for Levi to walk ahead of me. Technically, I remember exactly where his office is. I have been there before, and it was the setting of my favorite fantasy to date, but it feels presumptuous to take the lead on this one. Instead though, he holds out his hand, gesturing for me to go first—maybe so he can look at my ass.

"I didn't expect you to be the one to meet me at the door," I say before I make a move.

Levi narrows his eyes at me as the corner of his pouty lips turn up. "Who did you expect?"

I shrug. "I don't know? An assistant? A guard?"

His smirk turns to a full smile that makes my stomach turn in a good way. *A bad way?* I'm not sure I know anymore.

"I'm a hockey coach, Bennett. Not a prince."

I nod curtly, caught off guard by his humble response. That would have been the perfect time for something snarky. *Ugh, what an ass.*

Instead of replying, I begin slowly moving forward, and he quickly falls in line right next to me. The silence between us is palpable. I'm not sure what I expected in terms of casual conversation. I know what I planned to address as far as Cooper is concerned, but I guess I thought the lulls in between would include more of his smart aleck comments and irritating remarks.

He's quiet though, glancing back and forth between my profile and the hallway in front of us. I can see his movement from the corner of my eye and from the glances that I'm sneaking myself. If I wasn't mistaken, I would think that Mr. Hotshot-Hockey-Coach is almost... nervous.

Thankfully, the trip to his office is short. I know we're there before we even reach the door because of the pictures mounted on the wall that I remember staring at when he first approached me. Back when I didn't know who he was.

The door is pushed all the way open, and I inhale an obvious breath when I look in and see *the* desk staring back at me. If Levi notices, he once again acts unpredictably gentlemanlike and doesn't call me out on my weird reaction. Instead, he simply leads me through the door.

"Thanks for coming in," he says, sitting on the edge of his desk. His choice of seat helps a little in bringing me back to reality. Choosing the superior position to mine in a chair is definitely a power move, and I focus on that to counteract the rest of it. "I thought this might be easier to answer all of your questions, rather than going back and forth through email."

"That makes sense. Thank you for meeting with me."

Levi crosses one leg over the other, looking down at his shoes while he does it. When he lifts his eyes from the floor, they glide over my body with such speed that I can't tell if he did it on purpose or if I just so happen to be in his line of vision.

"So, Alex..." In our few interactions, I've noticed how often he says my name. Half of the time he only uses my *last* name, but I'm sure that's the athlete in him. There's something about it though that doesn't piss me off. I just can't put my finger on it. "What questions do you have for me?"

Pulling out my phone, I open my Notes app and find the tab labeled Spark the Flame. "I have a few," I say, scrolling the list.

"A woman who does her research."

"It's the journalist in me," I respond without looking up.

"I assumed so."

My finger freezes, and I glance at him without lifting my head. "How did you know I was a journalist?"

His jaw tightens, and his eyes find the floor before flicking back to me as if, for a second, he was contemplating whether or not to lie. "I Googled you too," he says, the last word catching my attention.

My heart rate quickens. "What's that supposed to mean?"

Levi places his hands on either side of his massive thighs. *Hockey legs.* I make a mental note to check out his undoubtedly muscular ass the next time I get a chance—for additional research. "You're telling me you didn't Google me before this meeting?"

I'm impressed with how little my face changes when I know damn well I was searching his name the second we got to our seats that night at the game. "Just doing my research," I quip.

"I assumed. Have you been a writer for a long time?"

His question catches me off guard, and despite knowing the answer, I feel put on the spot. "It's what I went to school for." I leave out the part about dropping out. He doesn't need all the details.

Titling his head down once, he offers a grin, and whether it's directed at me or the fact that he was right about knowing what I do is left undetermined.

Clearing my throat as an attempt to move past this, I ask, "How often would you need us—Cooper—to be available for this?"

"I wouldn't say there's a set schedule, but I'd like to give him a chance to be involved in a couple of things over the next few weeks—a practice, a team dinner, maybe a few games, home and away. That would give us plenty of material for the annual gala that's coming up in about a month or so. Ideally this would all end with him coming to that event and speaking on behalf of the youth we partner with. Does that feel doable?"

"Sure," I say, satisfied with his answer. I'll have to give back some nights at the restaurant, but I assumed that coming into this. "And how about expectations as far as media? Working in the industry, I see way too many young faces plastered on the internet. Especially when it comes to celebrities. Pictures are taken and misconstrued, children's lives ruined by gossip or idiots bullying kids while they sit behind a screen. I don't even let Cooper have any—"

"Alex," he interrupts. *There he goes with my name again.* "Whatever you're comfortable with is what we'll do. This is all for the gala anyways, but if you'd rather we not use the content for anything else, then that's fine."

"Oh," I say, taken aback once again. "Um, okay, yeah. That would be great."

"I'll make sure of it," he says strongly.

I nod in understanding. I think I expected a little more of a fight here between us. "And don't worry about money," he adds. *There it is.*

The change in subject—especially to this one—shifts the mood. "What?"

"All of the expenses—the tickets, meals, whatever he may need as far as wardrobe goes—will be taken care of."

Is he for real? This guy has to be making a game of all of this. Every time he says or does something decent, he goes and spoils it with something so typical. Do people like this even realize how condescending they sound?

Nick is the type who flaunts his wealth like this. He buys expensive gifts and makes extravagant gestures, and neither of those things impress me at all. He thinks that he can shower people with money in place of giving them actual attention. He does it with Cooper, and if he does it with his own son, I'm sure he does it with everyone else. Maybe to some women that's attractive. To me, it's the furthest thing from it.

"I can get Cooper whatever he needs," I say reactively.

Levi shakes his head. "Well, you don't have to."

"But I can."

"I understand that, but—."

"But what? I'm a single mom so you assume that I can't afford to take care of my kid? We do just fine, thank you very much. I'd like you to know that—"

"Actually," he interrupts. "I was going to say that the organization will handle it. It's a part of the deal. It has nothing to do with me."

I swallow, staring at my phone instead of looking at him with cheeks I know are flushed. Okay, so maybe I was a little quick to judge Levi here, but could anyone blame me? If it looks like a duck and quacks like a duck...

"Understood," is all I manage to say.

Setting my phone in my lap, I shift in my seat. I know I'm being hypocritical. It's not fair, and I get that, but it's a defense mechanism I've built up over time. To me, it's being cautious. I let my guard down once and that person turned out to be someone I never saw coming. What kind of woman—or mother—would I be if I blindly trusted someone with the same M.O.? Some may not get it, but until they've walked in my shoes with a baby on your hip, I'm not sure they'd ever understand.

Completely forgetting that my phone is sitting balanced between my thighs, I cross one leg over the other and a bang echoes around the room as it hits the floor. Levi leans down for it at the same time that I do, but because he's a giant—and I'm already sitting—I reach it by the time he's even halfway there.

Lifting my head before the rest of my body, I come almost face to face with Levi who is still bent over but frozen in place, his eyes glued to what I think is the back of my chair. Snapping my head behind me, assuming there's a spider or something crawling on my seat, I find the object of his focus. Oh, how I've never wished for a tarantula to be on my skin more than this moment right here.

Whipping my hand to my sweater now pulled several inches above my waist, I yank the fabric down so it covers the black lace g-string poking out from my jeans. Of all the days for every other pair of underwear to be in the wash but these. *Of all the fucking days.*

I smile awkwardly at Levi, any quick one-liner I may normally have, hidden away with every last ounce of my dignity. It's bad enough that I can't stop thinking about sleeping with this man, but now it looks like I wore my sexy underwear just for him.

Pulling his chest back up and leaning into his position from before, he returns his hands to either side of his body, only this time, they're clenching the desk so tightly that I can see the veins in his forearms bulging beneath his skin.

He clears his throat. "Any other questions?"

# 16

# Levi

As Bennett messes with her phone, trying to once again find her list of questions, I adjust the crotch of my pants as discreetly as I can. As if I didn't already have a mental hard-on for this girl, she had to go and flash me the dental floss she has on beneath her jeans.

It's hard enough having to sit here, mere feet from her, and speak professionally, acting as if I haven't thought about her since we met and pictured bending her over every piece of furniture in this place. But then she had to throw black lace into the mix. *Yes, I've caught myself thinking about her more than sexually, but... I'm still a man.*

For a second, when we got to my door, I thought I heard her breath hitch at the sight of my office. If I knew it didn't sound crazy, I may think she has had the very same thought as I have about taking her right here in the place we first met. But she wouldn't have? Would she?

I can tell Bennett thinks I'm attractive. I've been around enough women who want to sleep with me to know what it looks like on their face. Besides, not to sound more full of myself than everyone already thinks I am, but I know I'm good looking. I keep in shape and have a naturally athletic build, not to mention a head full of hair. Plus, I did win "Best Smile" in high school. But I can also tell she kind of hates my guts.

Most women don't try to play coy around me. They see what they want, and they go for it, no matter their morals or how desperate it sometimes makes them look. But with Alex, it's like she's fighting her own internal battle every time her eyes float over my muscular frame. It's as if she's cursing herself every time she lets her gaze slip from my eyes to the other features of my face.

I know she has it out for guys like me—or rather guys she *thinks* I'm like. It's the reason I went against the outfit I first picked out this morning. Normally for meetings like this, I would dress the same way I would for an event or a game—business only. But if there's one piece of the Bennett puzzle that I have fit perfectly into place, it's that the idea of a man in a suit is enough to make her stomach turn. It begs the question, *who drove her there?* But in the Google search I reluctantly admitted to earlier, there were no hints as to who that could be.

Turns out, at this exact moment, I'm not as bothered by this preference of hers as I may be otherwise. The thickness of the jean fabric is doing a far better job masking the growth beneath it than the linen of my suit pants would have. *Blessing in disguise.*

"I think that's all I have," Alex says, and the statement reminds me that we were in the middle of a conversation about her twelve-year-old son helping to showcase a program meant to foster children's love for hockey. *And there goes the problem in my pants.*

"Alright then," I say, grateful that there are no other factors that may deter her from agreeing to this. "I think our next step would be to talk to Cooper. Just to make sure this is something that he genuinely wants to do."

There's no hiding the way Alex pulls back, a surprised look on her face. I'm borderline confused. "What?" I ask.

"Nothing."

"What's that face?"

"I don't have a face." I tilt my head slightly, and she rolls her eyes. "I mean, I didn't *make* a face."

"You absolutely made a face." *I could detect a change in that crease in her forehead from a mile away.*

"I'm just surprised you're considering Cooper's feelings so much in this, that's all," she says with only half of her typical bite. Now, I'm the one stunned by her statement, mirroring the same look she gave me.

"Wow, Bennett. I know you're harboring some sort of grudge against all of my... kind," I say, hiding my amusement. "But I'm not actually evil despite what you may think."

Her face softens, and she licks her lips. My dick reacts like she stripped naked. *What the hell is going on?* One sweep of her fucking tongue, and suddenly I don't care if she thinks I'm the devil himself.

"I'm sorry. I'm just, uh—not used to people being so understanding and protective of Cooper like I am."

A burning sensation begins a slow crawl up from somewhere deep inside of me. It's a primal feeling that I haven't tapped into in what feels like forever. Something that, outside of Liam and Ruthie, I haven't had the need for until this very second. *Like I said, kids are my soft spot.*

"Why do you say that?" I ask without thinking.

She pauses, blinking several times before answering. "We just have a small village, that's all. And even some people in it aren't cautious with his feelings like they should be." I tighten my jaw in response.

Training as a defenseman my entire life taught me to be several things. The first is controlling. When the opponent has the puck, it's a d-man's job to command the ice and control the game. I'm in charge of stopping them, clearing the crease, and taking back possession.

The second is decisive. When a puck is too close to our net, I don't have time to pussyfoot around making decisions about where I'm going to skate or who I'm going to send it to. Hesitation can lead to loss of control. See description number one.

The final thing is protective. It's the defenseman's job to guard our zone and everything in it. My goalie, my net, the puck the second it crosses that blue line—is mine. And I protect what's mine.

Although the number of people who fall into the category is small, if I care about you being in my life, that last one rings true even off of the ice. I will do everything in my power to make sure you're safe—to keep you protected.

Seeing Alex shocked by me simply wanting to make sure that Cooper is comfortable sets something off in me. No one, especially children, should ever feel unprotected. Now, on top of all of the other unexplainable urges I have around her, I can include wanting to watch over Bennett and her son.

"Cooper's feelings about this are the most important thing to me here, Alex," I say seriously. Her eyes light up but not with a brightness that twinkles—more so with a fire that blazes. I ignore the heat from her stare and the one in my chest. "This is all about growing the program that we use to connect with these players. If he's not happy, then what's the point?"

She gapes at me before she catches herself doing it, then quickly snaps the wall back up that I've noticed she constantly tries to keep from falling. But I see her before she's able to—the real her—for just a second. The one who wants someone else to lean on. The one who wants someone to take care of *her* for a change.

For reasons foreign to me, I think for a second that maybe *I* could be that someone. That I could take care of Alex and Cooper. If both Bennetts were in my zone, it'd be my goddamn mission to care for them accordingly, no matter how insane that sounds coming from me—or how unnatural it may feel.

"I appreciate that," she says, and I swear she sounds almost breathless as she does it.

"Well..." I take a moment to reset from my latest thoughts, then throw a smirk in her direction. She drops her head and lets an angelic giggle escape her lips, her mood lifted. *Mission complete.* "I appreciate you... being here. Are the two of you available tomorrow? We have a home game that I'd love for Cooper to be at. It would give him a chance to see how we operate from the inside. Maybe get him more excited about the process. And you too of course."

With that last addition, her throat bobs up and down as if she forgot for a second that she'd have to be here. Is she upset about seeing me more? Better yet—is she nervous about it? There's only one reason I can think of that Bennett would be worried about being around me, assuming she doesn't have a fear of me physically, and that is that she doesn't think she can trust herself around me either. Do I tilt her off of her axis the same way that she does for me?

The thought of Alex's world falling out of its typical orbit because of me makes my pulse race more than it should. But I felt it the second I laid eyes on her. An uncanny gravitational pull drawing me to her. Is it possible she felt it too?

"It's a school night," she finally says. I catch my shoulders before they fall completely and try to conceal the disappointment on my face while my brain searches for solutions—or other opportunities. "But we could do Friday..." she adds, and once again, I try to hide my reaction. "If you have a game."

"We do," I say quickly—too quickly judging by the bashful grin that appears on Bennett's beautiful face.

Smiles look good on her. Shit, everything I've seen so far looks good on her, but this is definitely my favorite. *Until I'm on her.* Then, there's no doubt in my mind what my favorite will be.

"Okay. So, Friday then." Her words come out slow and calculated, as if she's waiting for me to make the next move.

"Friday," I say, neither of us budging despite the natural break in conversation. *I don't want to be done here.*

"You'll email me the details?"

"Sure."

She nods once, then rises to her feet, and all too eagerly, I do the same, pushing off the desk. Pointing her thumb behind her toward the door she says, "Then I guess I'll—"

"Or we could talk about them now," I interrupt. "The details." *Smooth.* "There's this coffee bar downtown, Drippy's—the name's a little off putting I know—but I swear it's the best—"

"Levi." Now it's her turn to interrupt *me.* "I told you, I don't date suits."

My heart rattles in my chest, either from my desperation or her quick rejection. "Then it's a good thing I'm not one. And look," I gesture to my outfit. "I'm not even *wearing* one."

Her face drops slightly. "You know what I mean."

"Actually, Alex..." I close half of the gap between us which somehow feels both too much and not nearly enough. "I have no idea what you mean. It's also very presumptuous of you to assume I meant as a date. It's

a coffee..." I narrow my eyes at her and shake my head. "Not a proposal."
*Oh, how the tables have turned.*

She doesn't speak, but her lack of response is promising. "One coffee,"
I continue. She peers at me like she's annoyed, but her body still faces
mine. "I'll drive." She turns one shoulder to the door. "You drive?" Her
other shoulder follows suit.

"We'll both drive," I say, reaching for her arm. I gently grab her elbow,
and like I bumped a trigger, her cheeks flush the perfect pink. "That way
if this becomes at all date-like, you can leave."

She squares her body back toward me in defeat and groans. She points
her finger to my chest. "One coffee. And it is *not* a date."

"Obviously. But I'm still paying." She rolls those pretty eyes. "I mean,
it's not like you're the one making two shit-tons a year."

# 17

# Alex

**"W**e could do Friday," I mock. "God, Alex, could you be any more thirsty." *Have we learned nothing in the last twelve years?* Driving in my car, following Levi to Drippy's, I replay the last half-hour in my mind like I've done every other time we've spoken. Like those, I leave feeling like I have whiplash from my reactions to him. Between the learned resentment and obvious attraction, I can't decide if I like that I hate him or hate that I... don't dislike him.

I thought maybe it was just the physical—his strong jaw, tight ass, and what I can only assume are flat abs below those two obvious pecs. I mean, people are attracted to serial killers for Christ's sake. It's not a crime. But hearing him talk about Spark the Flame and how sincere he was in wanting Cooper to enjoy his part in it—how curious he was about my reaction—shocked me in the strangest way.

It's been obvious since day one that my vagina likes him, that traitorous bitch. But there's no denying that there's things he's said and done that I don't necessarily hate either. That's is my bigger problem.

The thing that makes it easier is that Levi still possesses all of the qualities that I avoid in a relationship. There is no way someone in his position doesn't live and breathe his job. Work is important and so is money, but for someone who has been put second too many times by my ex, I'd take a simple life over wealth and status any day.

Not to mention, I have Cooper to think about. My son already has one man in his life that is unavailable and unpredictable. I'm not okay adding another one to the mix.

Levi slows as we near a parking lot, and I read the sign on the front of the building as we get closer. *Drippy's Coffee Bar* is hanging in light wooden letters above the door.

Pulling into the spot next to his, I follow his movements as he shuts off the ignition, then casually runs his hand through his hair before pushing the door open. He threw on a sweatshirt since leaving his office because his once exposed arms are now covered, a hood peeking out from behind his head. He exits his black on black Range Rover, which probably has a monthly payment that's more than my rent, and stretches his arms above his head. His top raises to expose a sliver of skin above his jeans, the V I assumed he had at his waistline momentarily visible. A heat rises in my chest, so I tear my eyes away from watching him any longer. From my side view, I see him leave his car and round the hood of mine, walking toward my driver's side.

"Let's go, Judas," I say to the part of me most affected by Levi and the one that I blame for agreeing to come here in the first place. *This could have been an email.* At the same time, he attempts to open my door.

Once again, it sticks, and Levi looks at me through the window. I realize he thinks I have the door locked, so I wave my hand at him telling him to back away. A puzzled expression spreads across his face, but he listens, taking a step toward the building. I ram my shoulder at just the right spot that will successfully open the door, and right on cue, it does.

Levi looks at me, his eyes wide as I step out of the car. "Don't," I say, trying to get ahead of whatever comment he plans on making.

"I wasn't going to say anything."

"Sure you weren't."

"I wasn't." He throws my door closed, and the two of us walk toward the front entrance of Drippy's. "I was just taking notes for my guys. That was one of the best checks I've seen in a while."

Hitting him with the biggest evil eye I can muster, I pause in my tracks. "Ha ha," I say sarcastically.

"Oh, come on. I'm kidding." He holds the door open for me, and I walk through only because of the rich, nutty smell that floods my senses. The first thing I notice is the red brick that runs from floor to ceiling in the back of the small room. On it hangs a chalkboard menu framed in stained oak wood, with coffees of various flavors and varieties written in boxy lettering. Every square inch of the countertop in front of it is covered in different coffee machines and mugs. There are over ten different types of tea and a handful of flavor syrups off to the sides and a pile of to-go cups at least two feet high.

The bar itself is a dark granite, almost the color of the beans themselves that are visible from inside the machines. A register sits pushed off to one side, a handful of covered pastry stands displaying everything from croissants to cupcakes scattered on the counter. The vibe is so different than a chain shop, and everything smells and looks ten times better.

"What is this place?" I say in awe.

Levi smiles at me sincerely, a slight raise in his brow. "*This* is Drippy's. Best coffee in town."

"Hey, Coach." The younger kid behind the register says as we walk over to the bar. Levi pulls out two stools, then takes a seat on one. "Your regular today?" he asks from underneath his visor as he pulls a to-go cup from the stack.

"I'll take the coffee, but you can put it in a mug for now," Levi answers. He looks at me. "I'm not leaving quite yet."

Taking the stool next to him, I let my eyes linger on his. "And then whatever she wants," he says, still looking my way.

Reluctantly, I tear my gaze from his. "I'll take an iced vanilla latte, please."

"You got it," the barista says as he nips at his lip ring.

Levi shifts so he's facing me on his stool. "So, what's with the car?"

"Oh, that? The door sticks sometimes, that's all. It's no big deal."

He looks at me lazily. "Bennett, you're gonna tear a shoulder one of these days. And don't think I missed that sound that came from your brakes when you parked. Those two things alone are kind of a big deal."

I sigh, resting my cheek on my fist, my elbow propped up on the counter. "Didn't we come here to talk about the game?"

"We did. But that was before I had to watch you cross-check your car door to get it to open."

I turn away from him. "We're not talking about this."

"We *could* talk about it."

"But we won't."

"Bennett."

"Levi." I swing back in his direction.

His jaw tightens at the sound of his name—the first time he's heard it fall from my lips. His eyes immediately drop to them. My mouth dehydrates, and right on time, the barista sets my latte down in front of me. I grab it like a lifeline and take a long sip, all the while feeling his eyes still on me. *Damn that's good.* The latte, I mean.

He inhales loudly, turning sideways. "So, about the game." His subject change isn't lost on me.

I mirror his stance, my legs now set between his, merely inches apart. "About the game," I say to our thighs rather than him.

My voice comes out borderline breathless. I may otherwise feel embarrassed—I'm doing a shitty job at maintaining my cool—but judging by the way he's looking through me tells me hockey is the last thing on his mind right now too.

We stare at each other briefly, both of us daring—or begging—the other to speak. All of his potential red flags fly through my mind like warning signs approaching a cliff.

After several year-long seconds, Levi shifts in his seat so he's slightly closer to me. Anxiety continues to rise in my belly when he says, "Alex, I—"

"You know what?" I pull back, no longer able to stand it, and slide off of the stool. "I have a lot of stuff to get done before I have to pick up Cooper from school. I should probably go."

Levi stands to join me. "Wait, Bennett, I didn't mean to—"

"If you could email me the details for Friday, that would be great." Flashing him the best smile I can muster, I pick up my latte. "Thanks for the coffee." I jiggle my cup and take a dramatic sip. "Seriously, so good."

*Alex, please stop talking.*

I reach for my keys, but Levi stops my arm, pinning my wrist to the counter in front of us. Everything in me wants to be livid—how dare he put his hands on me?—But nothing in me actually is. Instead, I feel the same quickening beat in my chest that I feel beneath his grip.

"Alex," he says, his tone serious. I slowly roll my head toward him, and his eyes are there waiting for me.

In my mind I tell him that I can't do this. I can't grab a latte with him while secretly hoping to fall into his lap. I can't sit here and talk about my son and a damn hockey game and pretend I'm not thinking about what his lips taste like. I definitely can't allow my heart to hammer against my ribs like it is for someone who will only bring me trouble.

In reality I say, "You'll email me?"

My brain tells my legs to move, but he clenches his teeth, and the cut of his jaw makes me weak in my knees. I pull on my hand, but it barely budges from under his grasp. He slowly releases his hold on me, and the second his skin leaves mine, I miss it.

"I'll email you," he says, reaching around to rub the back of his neck. It takes everything in me not to throw my arms around him and do the same. *I have to get out of here.*

"I'll talk to you later then," I say, turning toward the door. I take my first step before he replies.

"Take it easy, Bennett."

*Easy. Yeah. Sure thing.*

"You what?" Brooke shouts into her phone, and because mine is hooked up to my car, I get the pleasure of hearing it in surround sound.

"I bailed. I couldn't do it, Brooke."

"You couldn't do what, Alex? Drink coffee with a guy?"

"No, I couldn't drink coffee with *that* guy."

She sighs, making no attempt to hide the sound. "And why's that?"

"Because I can't stand him! Because he's arrogant and annoying. And because he, um, he—"

"He reminds you of Nick?" There's a silence on the other end of the phone that's really Brooke screaming for me to be honest.

"Yes. That's the one."

She sighs. "Listen, Al. I know it's hard, but you have to stop punishing yourself—and your vagina—for your past mistakes. For *Nick's* past mistakes. Are you sure it's Levi you can't stand? Or is it just everything he represents to you?"

Groaning, I take advantage of the red light I'm at and hang my head on the steering wheel. "I don't know," I whine, my voice muffled by the position.

"Well, why do you have to know right now? Or at all? If you're not interested, you're not interested, but it sounds to me like you're sort of..."

"Interested?"

A chuckle escapes her. "Yeah."

"He's kind of like... beautiful, B."

"Oh, I know. I've seen the guy. I'd let him bend me over that bench he stands on and do some pretty wild—"

"Yep. I get it," I say, driving again. "So, what would you do if you were me?"

"Ha," she scoffs. "Do you really want me to answer that?"

*No.* "Yes."

She pauses. "Honestly?"

"Brooke."

An exhale floats through the speakers before she says, "I'd bang the fucking Coach, Al."

"Ugh, that feels like a terrible idea."

"Does it?" she asks. "Or does it just feel like it's out of your comfort zone? Hear me out. When was the last time you did something because you wanted to? Not because you thought you *should* or because you thought you *had* to. Not even something you did because it's what was best for Cooper."

I actively search for an answer, but come up short, exactly like she knew I would. "I don't know."

"Exactly."

She waits for my reaction, but there's too much going on in my mind to form words. I know Brooke doesn't mean go wild and crazy. She doesn't mean for me to be reckless or proceed with no caution at all. But telling a mom to do what's best for *her* is like asking a vulture to kindly eat only half of its roadkill, then politely save the rest for later. It's unnatural! And it's a lot harder than it sounds.

"Now, I'm not saying go get a neck tattoo or fly across the country with some guy you just met—without me, I mean—but go have fun! Let yourself *do* for a change. Stop thinking—about what he wears, or how much he makes or that he reminds you of your ex—just stop thinking in general. *Do*, baby, *do*. And do him."

"Even if I hate him?" I ask dramatically, knowing I don't know Levi enough to actually feel that strongly.

"Shit, especially if you hate him. Hate sex is great sex. Just make sure he wears a—"

"Yes, I got it, Brooke. Thank you so much."

"But in all seriousness, Al—live in the moment. Carpe diem and shit! This guy is hot, and so are you. If you don't want to date him, then don't, but please for the love of God—let him between those fine ass legs."

"You're insane," I say, clutching the steering wheel, attempting to shake it like it's Brooke's shoulders in front of me. When I finally stop, I take a deep breath. "But I'll think about it."

"Yes! I knew it." She lets out a slow laugh, and I can hear her smiling on the other end of the phone.

"I said I'll think about it."

"Mhmm."

"No promises."

I hear her suck her teeth. "Sure."

"I'm serious, Brooke."

"Roger that," she sings.

I groan, only I'm not sure if it's toward her or myself. Is even entertaining the idea of just sleeping with a guy I potentially can't stand a slippery slope? Probably.

But will I think about it?

Also likely.

# 18

# Levi

S itting at my desk, reviewing game film and filling out paperwork, my mind drifts back to Bennett. Those few moments in Drippy's where our eyes met and her perfect legs hovered between mine were fucking torture. If there was one good thing to come from the blue balls I got, it's that I now know that she wants me. But I also know she's scared.

Her attitude and cardboard walls might fool someone else into thinking she's uninterested—or doesn't care—but not me. I know all too well the feeling of being too afraid to let someone in.

What happened with Rachel was a long time ago, but I've learned to live a new normal where I'm cautious of anyone who may have access to my life. And my heart. It's the reason I've put my own walls into place. People who are careless with others' hearts have consequences like loose pucks to a crowd. They're dangerous and hurtful, and half of the time, you don't see them coming. The boards I've built around myself are meant to keep those contained, and it seems like Alex is the same.

I'm guarded, and so is she, and thanks to Liam, I know that being a single parent only compounds that. As a mom, Alex likely feels like she has to worry for her *and* for Cooper. As a *single* mom, she thinks she has to do that twice as much. What she doesn't know yet, and what I can't explain, is I already know I wouldn't hurt them. Her son is safe with me.

I would never intentionally harm a child—physically or emotionally. I may even take it a step further and say I would cause damage to anyone that ever did. And as far as she goes. This is why I'm always honest. Of course, her body would be safe with me if she ever decided it's mine. I wouldn't take that goddamn gift for granted. And her heart? Fuck, if that isn't starting to intrigue me too. But after suffering a pain like mine, there's no way I won't proceed with caution. For both our sakes.

Glancing at the clock yet again, I let my forehead fall into the palm of my hands. Like a goddamn teenager, I told myself I had to wait until 3pm to email Alex.

After our little coffee incident, I went to the gym to blow off steam, then decided that I'd get some stuff done around here to keep me busy—and keep my mind off of her. That worked like shit, and instead, I've been checking the clock every half hour, counting down until it seemed like a less eager time to message her. Basically I've been playing the game. And I hate the fucking game.

"Screw it," I say out loud, pulling up my email. There's one new notification at the top of the page, and I freeze in place when I see who it's from.

> **Alex Bennett**
> *Friday's Game*

My fingers can't move fast enough as I move my cursor toward the name.

*Her name.*

---

**From: Alex.Bennett@Gmail.com**
**To: LeviMontgomery@NHLFlames.com**
**Subject: Friday's Game**

**Hi Coach Montgomery,**
**I wanted to let you know that I talked to Cooper, and he is really looking forward to Friday's game. So am I.**
**Please let me know what you need from us.**
**Alex**
**P.S. Thank you for the coffee.**

---

After reading the email three times, and over-analyzing it like the juvenile I apparently am, I have come to the conclusion that I am so royally fucked.

I'm thrilled Cooper is excited. He seems like a great kid, and I think this initiative is going to really boost the donations for the Spark the Flame program. But I'm ecstatic that Alex says she is too.

Those three little words weren't at all necessary— *"So am I"*—but the fact that she included them tells me two things. One, she's happy to be coming. *Could that have anything to do with seeing me again?* Two, she's not afraid to let me know. I'm not sure what changed between Drippy's and now, but I'm not questioning it.

*"Please let me know what you need from us."* From "us?" Nothing. From *"you?"* That's a loaded fucking statement.

Smiling again at her little add on at the end, I hit reply.

---

**From: LeviMontgomery@NHLFlames.com**
**To: Alex.Bennett@Gmail.com**
**Subject: RE: Friday's Game**

**Hi Alex,**
**Levi please. I am glad to hear the two of you are excited. I will send a car to pick you and Cooper up on Friday at 4pm. This will give Cooper a chance to interact with the team a little before warmups and you and I a chance to go over the details for the next event. He can join me on the bench for a period**
**if he'd like. I will take care of securing a suite for you and for him when he's not down with me.**
**Does all of that sound okay to you?**
**Levi**
**P.S. You're welcome**

Twiddling my thumbs, I stare at the screen expecting an instant reply. When it doesn't come, I push my laptop away and look back down at the notes in front of me. I make the mistake—or not—of leaving my email screen up and spend the next several minutes making myself motion sick from looking up at the page, then down at my desk, over and over and over again. It's worth it when a new message finally loads at the top.

---

**From: Alex.Bennett@Gmail.com**
**To: LeviMontgomery@NHLFlames.com**
**Subject: Nice Try**

**Levi,**
**Your plans for the game sound fine. Cooper would love to be on the bench with you for a period. The suite is not necessary but sounds great. Please don't worry about the car. Mine works just fine.**
**Alex**
**P.S. Drippy's really was amazing. I'll definitely be back.**

---

Grinning like an idiot, I pull my keyboard closer to me.

---

**From: LeviMontgomery@NHLFlames.com**
**To: Alex.Bennett@Gmail.com**
**Subject: I Insist**

**Alex,**
**The suite is something I always have open. My brother sometimes makes an appearance at the games with my niece. It's not a problem. Please let me send you a car. It would be terrible press for the program if our spotlight player got trapped inside yours.**
**Levi**

**P.S. You didn't even get to try their pastries.**

---

For some reason, the word pastries shoots straight to my dick. Maybe it's me already thinking about Alex's muffins or buttering her biscuits, but there's something about her name and dessert being in the same thought that does it for me. The sweetness, the warmth, the trail of whipped crea—

My screen lights up again with a new email.

---

**From: Alex.Bennett@Gmail.com**
**To: LeviMontgomery@NHLFlames.com**
**Subject: So Do I**

**Forget the car, but send the pastries. I try not to make a habit of driving around with strangers, but I'll take a donut any day.**
**Alex**

---

"Are you flirting with me, Bennett?" I ask my empty office.

A sensation that can only be described as tingling spreads throughout my body. Is this what it feels like to actually care when someone's talking to you?

My brain races with all of the things I want to say to her—*I'll send you whatever you want. How about you take me for a spin. Let me send the fucking car.* Then, another thing hits me.

I can't say any of this through my work email. In reality, even this back-and-forth banter is borderline inappropriate for my professional account. Despite now having competition, hockey and work once again prove to be at the forefront of my mind, causing me to second guess even responding to Alex at all.

Instead, I take a leap of faith and do something I would unwillingly do under any other circumstance.

**From: LeviMontgomery@NHLFlames.com**
**To: Alex.Bennett@Gmail.com**
**Subject: Number**

**I'd be happy to have a driver bring you anything you'd like**
**if you'd let me send one.**

**P.S. Please text me if you have any more... concerns. My**
**number's on my card.**

I couldn't help one more flirtatious response, but that's it. No more. I exit the screen, then a thought hits me that I can honestly say I haven't had in as long as I can remember.

*I hope she uses my fucking number.*

"Uncle Levi, why are you smiling like that?" Ruthie draws a line through her three Os and adds a tally to her side of the score sheet. "You just lost."

"Oh, nothing kiddo." Shoving my phone back into my pocket, which is way harder than it sounds when you're lying on your stomach, I boop her on the nose. "Just having fun playing tick-tack-toe with my favorite niece."

Ruthie rolls her eyes. "First of all, I'm your only niece."

"Still my favorite."

"And second, you just lost for like the one, two, three, fourth time in a row. How could you possibly be having any fun?"

I actively search my mind for the right "uncle-ish" thing to say to not only keep her happy but also get her off my case. "Because it's not about if I win or lose. It's about spending time with you!" She looks at me knowingly, her chin low and eyebrows high. "Okay, yeah. I can't even pretend to agree with that. It's way more fun to win." Ruthie nods in agreement, adjusting her weight on her forearms. "But I do love spending time with you."

"But that's not why you're smiling," she says, being the stubborn girl she is.

"Zip it and draw the next game," I say, being the guarded uncle that *I* am.

The truth is, as much as I love losing to Ruthie in childish games—which is only happening because I'm distracted—that's not why I can't get this dumbass grin off of my face.

The reason behind my cheesy smile is that Alex listened. *What a good girl.* She texted me a couple of minutes ago, and I'm not sure I've ever been this content while losing before—tick-tack-toe or otherwise.

The text was no confession of her lust. She simply asked if Cooper also needed to wear a suit—and I quote—"so he fits in with your kind." But it's not necessarily about the contents of the text. It's about the fact that she sent it at all.

Alex Bennett, who acted like she hated my guts up until recently, just willingly texted me of her own accord. If that's not proof she's warming up to me, I don't know what is. And if the fact that I saved her number as simply "Bennett" isn't proof that I'm more than warmed up to her, then I don't know what is there either.

Adding an X to the top left of the board Ruthie drew, I try to forget about Alex enough to stop embarrassing myself with a fifth loss.

"Daddy thinks you need a girlfriend," Ruthie says, drawing a circle in the bottom right corner. I look at her completely confused, and she looks at me like it's my turn to go.

I make my move, putting an X in the middle square of the left column, right below my other one. "Your daddy should probably mind his business."

She puts an O below my pair, cutting me off from getting three in a row. "Well, I think you need a girlfriend too."

With my hand halfway to the paper, I pause. "Your dad doesn't have a girlfriend."

She looks up at me and says matter-of-factly, "No, but he has me."

"Well, don't I have you too?" I ask, putting my next letter between hers in the bottom row, stopping her from yet another easy win.

"Yeah, but it's not the same." She considers her options on the board then places her third circle in the top right corner.

"How is it not the same?"

"Because me and Dad are a pair—like the pitcher and the catcher. He can't be without me, and I can't be without him. We're on the same team, but it's more than that. It's like we have our own mini team inside of the regular one." She looks up at me genuinely, then reaches across the board and puts her hand on my wrist. "You're on our team too, Uncle Levi."

My heart stutters in a way it only ever does for her. Swallowing the lump that now sits in my throat, I place my hand on top of hers. "Thanks, kiddo."

Ruthie is ten and is only repeating something I'm sure Liam has explained to her before about the two of them, but in a lot of ways, she's also right. The only people I truly have are Liam and her, and at the end of the day, they have each other first and foremost.

I was never one who needed to be surrounded by a lot of people outside of my hockey team. In fact, I've gone out of my way to keep my circle small. But I can't help but think maybe it wouldn't be so terrible to have another person in my corner.

"But it's not the same. You need your own catcher," she says, pulling away from me. She picks up her pen and points to the board. "It's your turn."

Looking down, I see Ruthie has me trapped. I glance up at her without lifting my head. She gives me a wicked fishhook smile. *Did she plan this whole thing?*

This girl is diabolical. She brings up a topic she knows throws me off, then weasels her way into making me reconsider my entire stance on relationships—all with the intention of kicking my ass once again.

"You did this on purpose." I choose a square at random and add the last nail to my coffin.

"You're easily distracted," she says brightly, securing her win with a very bold O.

Liam walks in right as Ruthie draws a dramatic line through her three in a row. "Yes! Another win. You're right, Uncle Levi, this is fun!"

I look at Liam who is already doing a shitty job at hiding his amusement.

"Tick-tack-toe?" he asks. I nod with an exasperated look on my face.

"Did she trap you?"

I nod again. "In the game and our conversation."

He shakes his head, winking at Ruthie. "Gets 'em every time."

# 19

# Alex

I caved and texted Levi first yesterday. Okay, I emailed him first too, but part of the reason for that was because both things were very important to Cooper's involvement in the program. *At least that's what I'm telling myself.* Another part of it may also have had to do with my little talk with Brooke.

She's not crazy. Well, she might be a little crazy but not about the Levi thing. Women sleep with men they have no intention of dating all the time. I don't personally make it a habit, but it's a thing. Doing so would definitely be out of my comfort zone, which we talked about, but I said I would try, so I will.

I have no idea how to initiate that. Do people just go up to someone and ask them to sleep with them? Do they say things like, *"The whole idea of you is kind of nauseating, but your body is great, and I'd like to be underneath it?"* Is there flashing involved? I don't know. Maybe for some, but not for me. So, I started by texting him first.

I did genuinely need to know what Cooper was supposed to wear to the game, so channeling my inner Brooke, I sent him one message. Of course he was a smartass about it—no shocker there—his response the usual combination of flippant, and yet, somehow charming.

Coach Montgomery

> He can wear whatever he's comfortable in. Unless he also has a fire-engine red vest. Then he should wear that.

After reading his reply, I rolled my eyes, then immediately thought about seeing him naked. Levi likes to lead with his tough exterior, but I'm learning that underneath his three-piece suit is someone I didn't see coming. It's that unexpectedness that's making this worse. It's hard to know which side is real, which is what I failed to see with Nick.

There's also the fact that our—whatever this is—is technically more professional than anything. Sure, Cooper's doing the Flames a favor in a sense, but in return he gets to make incredible memories. It's a transactional relationship—one I'm not sure anyone would be a fan of going any further. My guess is neither my son nor the organization would necessarily approve of the coach and the spotlight player's mom getting it on. *Or whatever was to happen.*

It was because of all this that I decided not to send a second message. It's one thing to dip my toe in. It's another to completely drown myself. I told Brooke I'd think about it. What I meant is I'd overanalyze it all and go back and forth at least a few times before actually deciding. But isn't that better than shooting it down completely?

"You ready, Coop?"

The question is rhetorical considering Cooper has been dressed for the game since he got home from school. He's in the suit and clip-on tie that I bought him last year to wear to my Uncle Ben's funeral and his only pair of dress shoes. With his hair brushed back but falling loosely in his face, he's the spitting image of his father.

"I am so ready," he says, shoving his hands in his pockets. He looks handsome, and I'm so proud of him for doing this. As much as I was put off at first, it takes a lot for a twelve-year-old to put himself out there like this. *Take notes, Alex. If your son can do it, so can you.*

"Then, we're out of here."

Slinging my belt bag over my shoulder, I grab my keys from the island. Cooper and I walk side by side down the hallway, and I pause at the mirror, giving myself a once-over.

Despite my temptation, I decided against the vest today. Instead, I went with tight black jeans, low-heeled booties, and a red sweater that hugs me in all the right places. I honestly didn't gravitate toward it because it shows off my toned figure and makes my boobs look like a college student's, but that's what pretty much sealed the deal.

"You look great, Mom," Cooper says, with no humor in his tone. He smiles at me and for the first time all night I feel nothing but excitement for him—and gratitude toward Levi for allowing him to have this.

"Thanks, hunny." I go to ruffle his hair, but he slaps my hand away before I even come close.

"Mom," he whines.

"Sorry."

"Alright, let's go!" He opens the door, and as he does, a familiar black SUV pulls into our driveway.

"No."

"What?" Coop asks.

"He didn't."

"Who didn't?"

"Unbelievable," I mutter under my breath.

"Mom!"

I part my lips to explain what's happening, but I don't need to. One long, muscular leg steps out onto the blacktop, followed by the rest of Levi Montgomery.

"Coach!"

"What's up, buddy?"

Cooper runs over to him as I pull the door shut. Somehow closing it behind me with Levi out front feels representative of something. I'm just not sure what.

"What are you doing here?" Coop asks, holding his fist out to him. Levi returns it, then steps out from behind the car door. He's wearing a light gray suit and a deep maroon tie that almost looks purple until the sun catches it.

"I thought I'd pick you guys up. Hey, nice suit." He looks at him impressed, and Cooper pulls on the fabric at the front of his jacket, a humble smile across his face.

Levi chuckles, then finally lets his gaze wander over to me. He drags one hand down the scruff of his beard, then shoves it in his pocket, the other still settled on the top of the door.

"Hey, Cooper," he says while still looking at me. His eyes trail down the length of my legs, then over to my son. "Why don't you hop in the car? There's a TV in the back with everything you could want on it."

Like a typical twelve-year-old, Coop doesn't ask questions. "Sweet," he says, rounding the hood.

Levi shuts his door as Cooper slides into the back seat and meets me halfway up the walk. "Bennett."

"Montgomery."

He licks his lips, then rubs them together. He does a terrible job trying to conceal his smile but a perfect job showing off the dimples hiding beneath his cheeks.

"Why are you at my house?" I ask bluntly.

"You needed a ride."

"I have a ride."

He tilts his chin down. "You have a lemon with a faulty door."

I part my lips and step up to him, one finger pointing to his chest without actually touching it.

"Mom! You've got to see this! There's like a million movies on this thing!"

I peer around Levi to see Cooper hanging halfway out of the back window of the car. I flash a thumbs up, then return my finger to Levi's lapel, this time, brushing it slightly. He peers down at the contact, then back at me. I purse my lips, too irritated by his audacity to react like I otherwise might.

"One time," I say. "I will let you drive us this *one* time."

He smiles slyly. "I'll take what I can get."

Levi turns and gestures for me to move toward his car. I oblige, but I stomp more than walk.

Stepping inside, his typical smell hits me first, but as I look around, I realize I'm surrounded by all of him. The black interior is spotless. There's no snack wrappers in the backseat or empty water bottles rolling around on the passenger side floor. No dust rests on the dashboard, and despite the smell, there's no dried out air freshener hanging from the rearview. In fact, there's nothing in this car that I can see besides the three of us and two coffee cups in the front console.

"Iced vanilla latte, right?" Levi asks, catching me staring at the drinks.

"Right," I say, my voice somewhat thick.

He picks up the coffee and holds it out to me. "A peace offering then."

The shock that I'm in from this whole situation, mixed with the annoyance I still have with him over it, makes me hesitate for half a beat. Levi exhales dramatically, and after approximately three seconds of making him wait, I pull it from his hand and take a long sip.

"It's so good," I say, my lips still halfway around the straw. Levi makes no attempt at hiding his eyes on my mouth. My cheeks flood with heat despite the cold coffee sliding down my throat. It's only when I say, "Thank you," softer than intended, that he moves his gaze from me to the windshield.

Clearing his throat he says, "You're welcome," and now it's my turn to stare at him. *God, that jaw.*

My eyes travel up past his full lips that I can't stop thinking about tasting—or them tasting me. His beard line is even more cut than it was the last time I saw him. He must have cleaned it up before the game. I land on one of the forests of green I've gotten lost in so many times since we've met. Have they always been framed by lashes I'd kill for? *God, Alex, get it together. You're pissed at him, remember?*

Cooper cuts through our silence. "This is so cool," he says. I turn to see him wearing headphones and holding a remote that looks nicer than ours at home.

Abandoning my view of Levi, I find Coop in the rearview mirror. "What are you watching?" He doesn't respond. "Hello?" I say louder. Still no answer. I turn to Levi who is already looking at me, smiling.

"Noise canceling headphones," he says.

I huff out a laugh. "Oh. Didn't even know that was a thing for a car."

"It is if you want it."

I raise my brows and nod. "So, do you often watch movies from the back seat of your car?"

"Why, yes I do actually," Levi answers quickly. "I find the closed space comforting." Leaning into me, the mint from his intoxicating scent hits me harder. "Especially if they're really scary."

For some reason, the contrast of what he's saying and how he looks right now—strong, powerful, larger than life—makes me explode with laughter. Levi rewards me with the brightest smile and for a moment, all of the differences and barriers between us don't exist.

As nervous as he makes me, and as much as this whole thing pissed me off, I'm also more comfortable around him than I expected to be. The feeling is nice. It's also terrifying. *This is how it starts.* They're charming and make you feel good, then you fall in love. And then they break your heart.

"It's all for my niece," Levi says, pulling me from my spiral. "That girl gets whatever she wants from me."

A different kind of heat fills me than what normally does when I'm around him. "What's her name?"

"Ruthie. She's ten—adorable, wild, downright devious." He chuckles to himself. "She's the best."

I think back to that first day when he said he was late because he had to be at his niece's game. *So, he was telling the truth.* "Anyway, we should probably get going."

He puts the car into drive and pulls onto the street. We spend the next fifteen minutes talking about what will happen when we get to the arena. Cooper will get a chance to interact with the players while they go through their pre-game routine. He'll be on the bench for warmups, then back on during the second period. Sadie will be in and out of the suite to check on things and get some information from both me and Cooper—me for logistics and him for write ups about the spotlight. There's a photographer that will pop in and out taking pictures of Cooper on the bench, and depending on how it goes, Coop can hit the locker room afterwards before it's time to head out.

"Wait a second," I say. "How are we supposed to get home now since you decided to kidnap us?"

Levi looks at me sideways without turning his head from the road. "Kidnap? Really?"

I cross my arms over my chest. "Well, what else would you call it?"

"I don't know, Bennett. How many crime shows have you watched?"

The answer is simple—too many for someone who lives with only a twelve-year-old boy. I may or may not have seen every episode of the few dozen seasons of Law and Order SVU, but there is a lot to be learned from a show like that. Desperate Housewives isn't teaching me to claw an attacker to ensure his DNA is under my nails or to knock a taillight out to wave through if I'm ever thrown into a trunk.

"There are some lessons only Elliot and Olivia can teach," I respond.

Levi shakes his head, which proves two things—one, he thinks I'm ridiculous, and two, he knows exactly what I'm talking about. "Well, in how many episodes did the kidnapper show up to the person's house, park in their driveway, hand every possible streaming service off to their kid, then hand them a latte?"

"Hmmm," I drag out. "None that I can recall, but there are a lot of episodes. I definitely could have missed it."

"I'll bring you home after the game," he says, ignoring my banter. "Or I can call you a car like I asked you to let me do in the first place." He tilts his head toward me and lifts his brow in my direction.

"We'll play it by ear," I say back sharply.

Levi scoffs. He shakes his head slowly, a shy smile on his face that's barely visible at this angle.

"What?" I ask, turning my body toward his.

"Nothing," he says easily.

"Tell me."

He looks at me so long I think he might crash the car or miss a red light. "You surprise me, Alex."

There's my name again.

It finally hits me why I like how often he uses it. Nick always calls me "Lex," and I hate it. My name is four letters—it's not even short for anything else—and yet, for some reason, he insists on using only the last three. Brooke calls me Al, but there's a story there, and for some reason, Lex just makes me cringe. Maybe the first time I felt it, it was my body's way of warning me about Nick, but every time it comes from his mouth, it makes my skin crawl.

When we first started dating, it seemed so petty. It was such a little thing to complain about. Then, as time went on, it became almost insignificant in comparison to all of our bigger issues. I would hint to him that I didn't like it and wince when it was yelled across the room, but he never noticed—or never cared.

Now, hearing Levi relentlessly say my full name feels polarizing. Like one letter separates him from who I think he is. I shake the thought and bring my attention back to him.

His gaze feels almost suffocating, as if somehow losing oxygen could be a positive, and I have to look out the windshield to find any reprieve. "I'm not sure if that's a good thing or a bad thing."

In my periphery, I watch him finally look away. He takes a deep breath in and tightens his grip on the wheel before he responds. "Neither am I."

# 20

# Levi

I promised myself I would be a gentleman tonight. I'm on the clock for Christ's sake, and the last thing I need Alex to think is that I only asked Cooper to do this so that I could get her into bed. *Even if that's how this started.* But then she had to go and wear... that.

When I stepped out of my car earlier, I was grateful to be standing behind my door. There was no way I would have been able to hide my body's natural reaction to her otherwise. She's stunning, truly, and sexy as hell. The small heel on the bottom of her boots only further accentuates her perfect legs, and that sweater painted onto her shows off every curve I want to bury myself in. Her loose waves cascade perfectly down her shoulders, and her golden eyes twinkle under the light shimmer spread across her eyelids. *She's fucking beautiful.*

Pulling into my designated parking spot behind my office, I exhale completely for the first time since leaving her house. I wasn't sure how it would feel to be trapped a foot from Alex for the length of the drive, but I think I underestimated the chokehold that her presence alone seems to have on me. Everything I've come to know flew out the window the second I put this car into gear. I flip flopped the whole time between wanting to unbuckle her seat belt and drag her into my lap or continue to talk about stupid shit like what kind of TV shows she likes.

The first choice, though my usual preference, would have been highly inappropriate with her son in the back seat. And the second just felt unimaginable—not because of her, but because of me. When have I ever cared to have any sort of conversation with a woman outside of whether or not she needed me to call her a cab?

Alex is different, though. I would talk to her all day if it meant learning more about what makes her tick. I'd attempt to make her laugh—all day. Watch her try to maintain her feisty side despite the mask crumbling right in front of me—All. Damn. Day.

My body seems to agree. I'm not sure if it's because all I've had of her is what I've fantasized about in the shower, or the fact that I haven't been with anyone since I cut things off with Olivia, but I am so desperate for contact it's almost painful. And I already know that no one but her will help ease the torment. Maybe that's because for the first time in forever, I'm attracted to more than just her body. Still, I want to touch her, tease her, taste her—and it needs to be soon.

"You ready, Coop?" Alex asks her son.

At the same time, Erik parks into his spot next to mine. I look out the window, never happier to see his goofy face. Cooper clicks his seatbelt in the backseat, then pops in between the two of us as Erik slams his car door shut. The sounds echo around me as if they're magnified—as if I'm hearing them from outside of my body. *I can't coach a game like this.*

Suddenly, I know what has to happen.

Rolling down my window, I call out to my assistant. "Hey, Coach Erik." I nod, gesturing for him to come over. Erik walks to the space between our cars and leans his forearms on the now open window.

"Hey, this must be the newest Flame."

The blood rushes from my head into a pit in my stomach until I realize he's talking about Cooper joining the team and not his mother becoming my newest addiction. "Sure is," I say, collecting myself. "Coach Erik, this is Cooper Bennett. Cooper, this is Coach Erik, one of my somewhat dorky but very talented assistant coaches."

Cooper smiles through a nod. "Oh, I know who you are. You won the World Junior gold medal as the captain of Team USA."

"Hey," Erik sings. "The kid does his research."

The blood that once left my head now rushes to my cock, thinking about Alex in my office with her phone in her hand and her thong peeking—

"Just like his mother," Alex says. My head jerks to her and judging by the color in cheeks, she's remembering too.

"Erik, this is Alex, Cooper's mom."

Alex reaches across me, coconut flooding my senses and her chest now just a few agonizing inches from my face. "It's nice to meet you, Erik," she says.

She moves back to her seat, and I have to catch myself before accessorizing her outfit with a hand necklace, yanking her back to me.

"Coach Erik," I say, through gritted teeth. Thankfully, no one seems to notice my clenched jaw in an otherwise friendly interaction.

"Yeah, boss?"

"Do you think you could take Cooper in with you? Show him where the guys are?"

"Yeah, of course."

"Perfect. Cooper, is that okay with you? I just want to talk to your mom for a second before we go in."

Cooper reacts how any kid would given a choice between staying in the car with his mother or going into an NHL arena. He flies into the back seat and out the door before Alex has any time to object. That doesn't stop her from staring a hole through me, but in a matter of minutes this will all make sense.

"Uh—Okay, Coop, I'll see you in there. Stay with Coach Erik!" she calls out the window as Cooper walks over and stands besides my assistant coach.

"I'll be there in a minute," I say, looking at him.

Erik gives me a knowing, yet somehow encouraging smile. "Take your time."

Alex and I watch as both of them make their way through the back door. It's only when it shuts behind him that she finally turns back toward me.

"What are you doing?" she asks. Her voice isn't quite as pissed as I thought it might be, but her mask is back on, that's for sure.

"I'm sorry about the ride," I say, leading with caution.

Her face melts slightly into one less vicious, then goes cold again. "It's fine."

"It's not. I shouldn't have overstepped like that."

She looks at me side-eyed like she's considering her reaction. "You really shouldn't have." Turning my lips in, I nod understandingly. "But it is kind of a pain," she adds.

My face lights up as I shift toward her. "I can take a look at it if you want. Cars aren't really my thing, but I can give it a shot. Or have someone else do it."

"Oh, no you don't have to do that."

"I know that, Alex."

She pauses, the familiar blush creeping up her neck that seems to happen when I use her name. I noticed it the first couple of times but thought it might be a coincidence. It wasn't. Every time I use either of her names, she seems to react. I'm not sure if it's the name itself or the person saying it, but I'm not willing to find out. Honestly, I just like the way it rolls off my tongue. The way it tastes so sweet on its way out.

"But I will if you want me to."

She tucks a hair behind her ear, then clears her throat. "That's okay," she says strongly, but the way she chips what's left of the polish on her nail tells me that she feels off her game. "Is that all you wanted to talk to me about?"

"No."

My voice comes from the deepest part of my throat. Adrenaline courses through my veins like I've only ever felt near the ice. When I was a player and my line was up, I used to hop the boards like my skates were on fire, and I needed to touch the ice before they burnt through my feet. I have that same feeling now.

The loose wave she tucked away before, slips out again and onto her face. Before I can object to my own natural instinct, I reach over and put it back into place. Alex stills except for her chest that heaves up and down in short breaths, my fingers still lingering by the soft spot on her neck.

"Levi?" she questions.

I inhale deeply, feeling any constraint I have left slowly fade. "Alex."

"I—"

Wrapping my hand around the front of her throat, I pull her to me, our lips crashing together. *Fucking finally.*

She's cautious at first, her body stiff, her mouth closed, but as I let the kiss linger, she dissolves into me. I push my free hand into her hair, the other still at the base of her throat. Testing her first, I sweep my tongue gently across her now parted lips, and when she opens for me, I don't hold back. I plunge deeper into her mouth, and she moans into me, my palm vibrating on her neck from the delicious sound. She reaches for the flap in my shirt where there's space between the buttons, but before she can grab a hold, I stop her.

One kiss is not enough, but the things I want to do to her—the things that will satisfy my need for her—can't be done in a parking lot with her kid inside. In the middle of my internal battle, Alex must lose hers. Pushing me away from her, she rubs her forehead with the tips of her fingers.

"What are we doing?" Alex asks, looking at me, her brow furrowed, her eyes heated. She's somehow even more beautiful than she was before with her now swollen lips.

Dropping her wrist, I reach up to the crease in the middle of her forehead and smooth it with the pad of my thumb. "I've been wanting to do that since the first time I saw that grouchy look on your face." The groove somehow deepens, but I continue anyway. "And this," I say, kissing her hard one more time. When I open my eyes, hers are still closed until her lids lift slowly.

The moment is short lived because almost as quickly as she lets her guard down, it flies back up. "Oh my God, what are we doing? Cooper's in there."

"Alex."

Shaking her head, she says, "No, I don't date—"

"Guys like me," I say, finishing for her.

"I told you this."

I nod in understanding. "And I don't date anyone, but—"

"I knew this was a bad idea."

"Alex!" I place my palm on her leg, which is apparently the wrong move because her eyes dart to it like I'm holding a loaded gun. Raising my hands in surrender, I turn so I'm fully facing her. "Stop panicking."

She freezes momentarily, then says, "I'm not panicking."

"Did you want that to happen?"

"The panic or the kiss?" she asks.

I almost laugh. "Well, I thought we weren't panicking, so I guess the second one."

"Yes," she says quickly, which I notice and so does she. She instantly goes wide-eyed, waiting for my reaction.

"Okay, then," I say, my shoulders relaxing for the first time since she started this rant.

"Okay?"

"Okay."

She looks at me like she's waiting for more. "Well, then what happens now?"

"Now? Now we go inside, give your son the time of his life, and win a fucking hockey game."

My tone is nonchalant despite the fact that my heart is still racing from what may be the best kiss of my life and the semi in my pants I'm still trying to deflate. But Alex is scared, and the quickest way to lose the possibility of having her is to come on too strong all at once. She needs to be eased in. She needs me to be in control of this, so that's what I'll do—control the game. For her.

"Sound good to you?"

She takes a deep breath in, her eyes dancing around the car like she's considering what I said. "Yeah," she says on the exhale. "Okay."

"Okay," I repeat calmly. "Now, please get out of the car so I can stop looking at you, and so this," I say motioning to my crotch, "can figure itself out." Her cheeks turn pink as she reaches for the door.

"Backwards..." I add. "If that's possible. If I see another slip of lace, I'm a total fucking goner."

# 21

# Alex

"Wait, he just reached across the seat and kissed you?" Brooke munches on popcorn on the other end of the phone, and I cross one arm over my chest feeling more exposed than I should in a room by myself.

"More like grabbed but yes."

"Like grabbed in a good way or grabbed in a you-had-to-make-Cisco proud way?"

"Do you have the game on?"

"Yes."

"Does it look like I used my kickboxing instructor's moves on Levi's face?"

"Uhh, hold on." Her crunching stops as she concentrates. "I have to look for him. I've been following number twelve around like a cat in heat."

"Brooke."

"What? He's good isn't he? Plus, he's smoking hot. At least from what I can see in his uniform. Did you know that hockey players stretched like that?"

I roll my eyes despite the fact that she can't see me. "He's also like twenty-five."

"Even better," she laughs. "Oh! I found him. Nope, I don't see any bruises or marks. So, either you severely let Cisco down or you, my dirty girl, liked it when Coach McHottie snatched you up in his car."

My cheeks flush and a lump forms in my throat.

Thankfully, with Cooper on the bench for warmups, the suite is empty except for me. Levi told me in his very few words between the car and now, that his brother wasn't coming to tonight's game, so Coop and I should have the room to ourselves.

Not that it would matter if anyone else was in here. This place is big enough to hold everyone I know. A long table sits to the left of the door when you first walk in, filled with finger foods and all kinds of drinks. In the center sits a large rectangular coffee table, framed on either side by two giant, brown leather couches facing each other. There is a massive TV on the wall for watching the game from the comfort of the sofas and a row of stools at a high-top counter, closer to the opening.

In the very front, near the rail that overlooks the arena, is a handful of high, black chairs with the Flames blazing 'F' on the back. This is where I'm sitting, with a perfect view of the team's bench, my son, and the deadly head coach that stands beside him.

Finding Levi myself, and feeling instantly hot, I groan into the speaker.

"Ha! I knew it!" Brooke yells. "You liked it didn't you?"

"I definitely liked it," I whine. There's silence on the other end of the phone. "Brooke?"

"Sorry, I'm here."

Glancing down at the ice, I spot Drew Anderson with his helmet off, standing by the boards. His overgrown hair is slicked back, water trickling down his neck, and a camera in his face. This man is sweating profusely and it's only warmups. He squirts a bottle once into his open mouth, then tilts his chin up and squirts it one more time so it cascades down his head. I can see Brooke's infatuation, but he's a little young for me.

"Will you focus?" I say into the phone, now knowing what stole her attention. "This is ridiculous, isn't it? I mean the man came to my house unannounced and all but forced me and my son into his car. What is wrong with him?"

"He forced you into his car?"

I bite on the skin at the edge of my thumb. "Forced is a strong word," I admit.

"Did he threaten you?"

"No."

"Drag?"

"Uh-uh."

"Push?"

"It was more like asked politely."

"Oh my God, Alex. The only thing ridiculous about this is you."

"I'm too old for this, Brooke!" I cover my mouth as if anyone could read my lips from here. "I'm somebody's mother," I whisper.

There's a thud on the other end of the phone that I can only assume is Brooke's current snack bowl being set down on her end table. "Yeah, you are," she says with gusto. "But you're also a fucking woman, Al. A whole person with needs and desires. And you're not old because if you're old then I'm old, and I know damn well that I'm not old."

I blow out a slow, shaky breath, letting her words wash over me like I need them to. Sometimes I forget that I'm allowed to be someone outside of Cooper's mom. I'm allowed to have my own dreams, my own passions—my own needs and desires. No, wanting to be in Levi's bed is not a life changing goal, but even that is something I'm allowed to want for myself.

One thing I don't do enough is give myself credit. Good moms are their own worst critics. It doesn't matter how kind or respectful, loving or generous, smart or talented their child is—moms go to sleep at night thinking about all of the things we could have done better or differently. We think about how to make our kids happier or healthier, not even considering ourselves the same way. Are *we* happy? Are *we* taken care of?

I always think about Nick and how selfish he is, but maybe he just possesses too much of a good thing. Not that I know from experience, but maybe sometimes thinking about yourself first is okay. Maybe I'd be happier, healthier—an even better mom—if I was a little selfish from time to time. *I guess there's only one way to find out.*

"Anything else?" I ask Brooke, almost afraid of her answer.

"Yeah, one more thing. We talked about this already but remember—you don't have to sell him your soul. It's okay for you to have a little fun every once in a while. You only have a few weeks left to be around him anyway. Just give it time and see what happens."

A calm passes through me that only a best friend giving you permission to sleep with an NHL coach could cause. Brooke may be crazy, but she offers good advice sometimes.

"Oh, and Al," she says, chewing on something. "Can you ask Coach McHottie if Drew's seeing anyone? That guy could totally—"

"I'm hanging up now," I say, already dropping my phone from my ear.

"Oh come—"

"Goodbye, Brooke!"

Ending the call, I walk back to the leather stools at the front of the suite. Looking back down at the ice, I find Cooper and Levi standing side-by-side. Coop brings his attention to me, then taps Levi on the arm. The two of them look up toward the suite. My son waves, and Levi narrows his eyes at me, bringing his hands behind his back. I wave at Cooper, and he switches his attention over to the team. I make the mistake of looking back at Levi who seemingly never looked away.

Our kiss in the car was completely unexpected—definitely not unwanted—but absolutely out of the blue. Part of me thought I should be irritated that he felt like he could just put his mouth onto mine as if he's done it a million times before. But then I remembered that's what I wanted. I know where my head was before that kiss, but knowing that he feels it too makes me that much more comfortable possibly pursuing it.

I'm starting to think that maybe using Nick as my standard for men is only allowing him to cause more damage in my life. Lord knows he'd be thrilled to find out that because of him, I haven't gotten laid in... a very long time, and any sort of real relationship has been completely nonexistent.

I don't plan to fall in love with Levi, but according to him, he's not looking for that either. We're clearly attracted to each other, and if that kiss was a glimpse at our chemistry, it's safe to say that's there as well. Maybe this solution is sort of a best case scenario for both of us.

Levi slides his phone from his pants pocket, types on it quickly, then looks back at me. As if on cue, my phone pings, still sitting in my hand. Scanning the screen, I see an incoming message from the number I saved as Coach Montgomery. *So we're doing this now?*

Coach Montgomery

> Stop overthinking. I can see your wheels spinning from here.

My eyes dart back to the bench, and Levi smirks. Regardless of what we make of it, this man fires me up in the most irritating, yet awakening way. It's as if everything he does puts me on edge—pleasant or not. But usually the best combination of both.

Standing up straighter, I type my reply.

> I have no idea what you're talking about.

I sneak a glance at Levi reading his phone, a lazy smile on his sculpted face. Before I know it, my phone chimes again.

Coach Montgomery

> Always with the attitude, Bennett. It's okay to admit you can stand the suit after all.

> No.

Coach Montgomery

> Okay... then take it off.

My whole body ignites as I stare at the screen. I can feel his eyes on me as I reread his message. If I wasn't sure before how he feels about me—and how my body feels about his—I sure as shit am now.

Contemplating my response, I realize this is it. This is the moment that will decide the trajectory of our course.

As far as I'm concerned, I have two options. One is to shut this down now and forget all about it. It won't be easy to not still want him, but I can lean into the downfalls enough to move on. The second is I can fully commit. I can answer in a way that tells him without a doubt that I'm on board with whatever he's thinking. Levi already knows that I don't want to date him; so playing back now tells him I'm still interested in just that one thing.

Considering my choices, my mind flashes back to his hand on my throat, my body braced against his palm. Shutting this down is probably safer. It would be better for Cooper and less of a risk to my heart. Lord knows it's the comfortable choice, but for once, I'm stepping—leaping—out of my comfort zone.

> Maybe I'll do just that.

From here I can see the sharp edge of his jaw as he tightens behind his idle grin.

Coach Montgomery

> **Good girl.**

There's an instant pulse between my legs that wasn't there before. I take my time moving my gaze from my phone back to Levi. When it reaches him, he wears a satisfied look, but his eyes seem darker, even from this far away.

He slides his phone back into his pocket as he looks at the clock. The horn blows a beat later, signaling the end of warmups. Sadie steps onto the bench and taps Cooper on the shoulder. He turns and shakes Levi's hand, then heads back through the tunnel to come join me. Levi doesn't look back after that, but his words stay with me.

I thought the idea of hearing praise like that was only able to stir me up when I listened to grade-A spice in my audiobooks—or in my dreams with Levi apparently—but I was wrong. The second I read those two simple words in that message, my panties were soaked. Add in the intensity on Levi's face and now *I'm* the cat in heat.

It makes sense that the mom, no—the woman—in me, who spends her days doing everything for everyone else, feeling overworked and under-appreciated, feels overwhelmed by a compliment. It's just unexpected. It shouldn't be, especially when it comes from someone like him—hot, professional, seemingly untouchable in almost every sense of the word.

"Hey, Mom!" Cooper calls as he walks into the room with Sadie at his side.

*Perfect timing.* My twelve-year-old son might not notice my pulse is racing, my pupils are dilated, and my nipples are hard against my too-tight sweater—should have gone with the vest after all—but another woman definitely might.

"Hey! How was it?" I ask, crossing my arms over my chest.

"So cool! Did you see me down there right next to Monte? Sadie says I was on TV. My friends are going to be so jealous."

"Well, there's plenty more where that came from, Coop. You're a star now!" Sadie shines her smile, but mine deflates.

"How big of a star are we talking?" I ask cautiously.

"Mom," Coop groans.

"Nothing crazy, Ms. Bennett. Coach Montgomery informed me to keep all of that to a minimum."

A wave of calm rushes past my anxiety, washing it away. In its place is a reminder to thank Levi later for sticking to his word. Maybe it's the text conversation we just had riling me up, but my mind filters through all of the ways I'd like to show him my gratitude.

Thankfully, Coop brings me back down to earth right before I begin to pant.

"Look! The game's starting!"

# 22

# Levi

We won our game three-nothing. Once again, Drew played like an animal, and our defense dominated on the ice. We were up two-nothing in the first period and were able to maintain our lead until the final buzzer. Our goalie had twenty-five shots against him and didn't let in one—a shutout.

If I'm being honest, I was the least focused one out there. Having Bennett in the stands again was bittersweet. The view was everything I could ever ask for, but that girl and her flawless curves are distracting as hell.

I got no response to my last text to her. It could be that there was nothing else to say. It could also be that she thought it through and changed her mind—she's not exactly warming up to me after all. Or, maybe I showed my cards a little early.

Learning to take control has transferred into all areas of my life. How I dress, how I work, how I live... and how I fuck. It's not for everyone, but from my experience, it's for plenty. Whether Alex knows it or not, she's looking for someone to take the reins, I can tell. I might crave control, but she's hungry to relinquish it. I'll gladly take that on, but I won't ever do something she is uncomfortable with. Judging by the way her eyes crept back to mine though, hooded from what I could see from afar, she has no objection. Now I just have to convince her to let go.

Walking back to my office, I'm a little on edge, but it's not only from the post-game comedown that I normally have. My energy is heightened because I know Bennett is somewhere close by. I saw her leave the suite with Sadie before I walked off the bench. We all decided beforehand that if we won tonight, Cooper could hit the locker room afterwards for a quick farewell with the boys. Erik planned to take him around, let him talk to the guys, and maybe watch one of their post-game interviews. *But where is Alex?*

Swiping up on my home screen to find our messages, I push open the door to my office. When I look up, my eyes lock on the mouth that has haunted me for the last several hours.

"Bennett."

"Montgomery."

Walking past her, I breathe in her scent, the smell soothing me like a drug. I purposely sit in my chair, rather than on top of my desk like I usually do. The thick wood is the barrier I need to ensure I don't live out my fantasy right now. "You're here."

She steps forward but remains standing. "Sadie said I could wait for Cooper here. I hope that's okay."

*It's more than okay.* "Not a problem. Did you enjoy the game?"

"I did."

"The suite was good?"

"Great."

"And the view?"

She takes a slow breath in and licks her lips. "That wasn't bad either."

My jaw grows tight. I swallow the saliva that's built under my tongue, my body's reaction to looking at the very thing I'd like to devour. I stand slowly. "Alex..."

"So, what happens now?" She repeats her question from earlier, only this time, I'm not blowing it off.

"That depends," I say, rounding the corner of the desk.

She doesn't move, but she takes the stance she always does when she's trying not to let me affect her. She stands taller—wider. She tilts her head up, pushes her shoulders back, and short of throwing her hands on her hips, she stands like a superhero—bold and confident. I recognize it because I do the same.

I first learned it on the ice—be big until you are big. Of course size matters but never underestimate the power of body position. Not only can you take up more space, but you demonstrate something of equal importance—confidence. By manipulating your position, you can not only control the space, but you can offer just the right amount of intimidation.

"On what?" she asks.

I've never worried before about what I say, so I don't plan to start now that I'm standing in front of her. "Are we doing this?"

She lets her posture drop for only a second. "I told you, I'm not falling for you."

"That's not what I asked," I say, moving closer. Of course that's my end goal, but I won't scare her with that.

"Then what do you mean?" Her voice comes out shaky, her tone hushed.

Closing what's left of the gap between us, I run my thumb across her lips. "I think you know what I mean."

She parts them, and her warm breath floats past my hand. "Maybe," she says, but the way she leans into my touch tells me she's already decided. It takes everything in me not to bend her over my desk right now, but starting this off by getting caught by the two people who can't know would not get us off to a very good start.

"Travel with us tomorrow."

The thought comes out of nowhere, but in reality, it makes total sense. It's the perfect time for Cooper to be at an away game being that it falls on a weekend, and it will give Alex and I an opportunity to... figure all of this out.

"What?" she asks, understandably thrown by my statement.

"Come to our game tomorrow in Grand Oaks. You can fly with us, or I can send a car for you. It's not a long trip. Whatever you're comfortable with. It's one night. We leave at ten, we play Sunday at one, then we'll be home by dinnertime."

She shakes her head. "I can't. I have work."

"It's the weekend."

"At the restaurant," she clarifies.

Placing my hand on her hip, I say, "I'll pay you what you would make in tips." Her eyes go wide, that stubborn crease in her brow back once again. "I don't mean like that. I just..." Her chin rears backward. "I'm trying to... " Her head tilts sideways. "Okay, let me start over."

Crossing her arms over her chest, fierce Alex begins to reemerge. Grabbing her elbow, I rephrase my whole thought. "You want this. I want this. But we can't figure it out now. Come with us. It will be awesome for Cooper, and it will give us a chance to talk about things." She sucks her teeth, and I find myself wishing she was rolling her tongue over something else. *Grouchy Bennett is hot—scary, but hot.*

"I'll think about it."

A smug smile spreads on my face as I trail my fingers up the side of her arm. "I'll take what I can get," I say, leaning into her.

She doesn't meet me, but she doesn't back away either. My hand is by her neck again, my mouth so close to hers that our breaths intertwine, when footsteps approach the door.

I swing my arm back, spinning on the ball of my foot, my hand landing on the back of my head. I walk toward my desk, desperately trying to hide the bulge in my pants from whoever is about to walk in.

"Hey, Coach," a familiar prepubescent voice says. I fall into my chair just in time to see Cooper and Sadie walk through the frame.

"Hey, buddy," I draw out, leaning my forearms on the wooden surface in front of me. Alex is turned toward her son, using one arm to hug the other against her chest. "How was the locker room?"

"It was awesome. Mom, I got to see an interview with Drew Anderson. How sick is that?"

"Pretty sick," Alex says, looking at Sadie. There's a lack of enthusiasm in her voice that I can only assume means she's anxious.

"Don't worry, Cooper was only watching."

Alex visibly relaxes, her energy shifting completely. She pulls Cooper to her and hugs him tightly, planting a kiss on the top of his head. "I'm so proud of you."

She lights up when she talks to Cooper—that kind of glow I think you can only get from being a parent. I've seen it with Liam and Ruthie too. They're a pair like Ruthie said about her and my brother. It's them against the world. Part of me hopes to see more of it. Part of me wonders why I even noticed in the first place.

"You guys ready to head out?" I ask Alex and Cooper. Between the constant ache I have for Bennett physically and the feelings that I don't need her pulling to the surface, I think it's time to call it a night.

"Aw, man. Do we have to go home?" Cooper whines.

Alex runs her hand through his hair, and I find myself jealous of her damn kid. "Game's over, hunny. Everyone's leaving."

"That's right," I say, looking at Coop. Turning to Alex I add, "But there's always next time."

She rolls her eyes, and I instantly brainstorm all of the ways I'm going to punish her in my mind for that later. Grabbing my things off of my desk, I thank Sadie for her time. The four of us walk out of my office. Sadie goes back down the hall, and Alex, Cooper, and I head to the lot.

"Are you sure you're okay driving us home?" Alex asks, Cooper already paces ahead.

"I said it, didn't I?" Alex looks toward the ground, a smile that shines like the goddamn stars above us, spreading across her face. *She remembers.*

She peers up at me from the ground. "Yes, you did."

We spend the car ride reliving the game thanks to Cooper who is on cloud nine. Alex and I sneak glances at each other every once in a while, but in all honesty, I avoid her more than I'd like to admit.

Cooper's enthusiasm is the reason I started this program. You would think he walked on the moon the way he's talking about being on the bench. His passion for the sport I love—the sport that means everything to me—is why Spark the Flame exists, and I don't want that emotion dulled by a different kind of excitement I feel when I look at her.

Pulling onto their street, a push and pull of angst and relief rises in my chest. As much as I want a replay of the kiss Alex and I had before the game, I also have to get away from her. I have spent all night thinking about her in those clothes, her *out* of those clothes—those clothes draped over every inch of my apartment. At this point, I think a strong breeze might finish me off right here.

Parking in her driveway, I glance over just as she's reaching her right arm across her body to unfasten her seatbelt. The cross-over results in a perfect view of her chest piled at the top of her sweater. "Come on, Coop," she says over her shoulder.

The three of us exit the car simultaneously, and Alex pauses with her door still open. "What are you doing?" she asks defensively. I chuckle at the walls that have already shot back up.

"It's late and pitch dark out," I say moving toward her. "I'm walking you to your door." I stretch across her and watch as she follows my arm. Whether or not I tense my muscles a little tighter as I throw the door shut, I will never admit to.

Alex hands Cooper the keys, and he runs ahead to the door. "Bye, Coach!" he calls over his shoulder. "Thanks for everything!"

"You got it, buddy. I'll see you soon." Bennett stops on her front step, and I follow suit. "He's a good kid," I say.

Looking toward the door, she grins. "Yeah, he is."

I watch as her wheels once again start spinning. If there's one thing I've noticed about her, it's that her mind is never settled. "That's because of you I assume?"

She pulls the sleeve of her sweater lower on her hands. "Nick works a lot. He's pretty much never around. Coop is supposed to see him more than he does, but something always comes up." The pieces start to fall into place as she speaks. "He's a lawyer. He makes a lot of money, which he doesn't mind throwing Coop's way, but he's always too busy to be an actual father."

I think of Liam who uprooted his whole life for Ruthie no questions asked. He makes money, and he's busy, same as me, but we both know that she's his first priority. "Shame on him. He's missing out on one pretty great kid." *And he let one hell of a girl get away.*

"We'll be there," Alex says suddenly, and if I'm not mistaken, she takes a tiny step closer to me.

It takes me a minute to register what she's talking about before I realize she's agreeing to come to Grand Oaks. My body reacts like I expect it to, my dick on high alert once again. But it's the way the rest of me responds that throws me. Almost like parts I've kept frozen and hidden away begin to thaw.

"But I'm driving. And God help you if you show up to my house."

*There she is.*

Peeking in the window, I spot Cooper sitting on the couch in the room right inside the house. As much as I want to respond to her by putting my mouth on hers, I settle for grabbing her hand furthest from the door.

"But you'll come?" I ask, letting just my first finger trail down her pinky.

"I'll come," she says, with weight to each word.

I smother a growl and lean in close to her ear. Alex sucks in a breath, and I can't help myself. I drop my finger to the loop in her jeans and quickly pull her to me so she can feel just how happy I am that she's decided to join us.

Leaning in subtly, I look past her, hard as a rock on the base of her thigh. "Good girl."

# 23

# Alex

S tepping into the shower, I let the hot water hit my cool skin and cascade down my back. Breathing in deeply, I attempt to settle the butterflies that have been swarming my stomach since the moment I woke up this morning. *I can't believe I'm doing this.*

I blame Brooke and Levi for my unexpected behavior. Between her encouragement and his leg-shaking sexiness, I'm not sure saying no to this trip would have been possible. It's so unlike me, but maybe that's the point. Look at where being *like me* has gotten me so far.

I keep telling myself that this is for Cooper. We are going to Grand Oaks today for Spark the Flame, not for me to see Levi, but I know I'm lying to myself. In that moment on the porch where I committed to tagging along, I also committed to letting this happen.

It's clear there is something forming between us, and by agreeing to this trip, I think I also consented to exploring it. What do I have to lose? Levi told me that he doesn't date, and I think it's pretty obvious where I stand on all of that. If anyone would know that I'm worried about the logistics, it'd be him, wouldn't it? Maybe the boundaries this program places on whatever is happening here is for the best. There's a time constraint and a need for privacy, two things that will keep this from getting too complicated. Other than that, we're two consenting adults looking to satisfy a completely natural desire. *Or at least that's what I keep telling myself.*

I'm not saying anything will happen tonight—I'll be sleeping in a hotel room right next to my son—but I'm also not naive. Cooper isn't a baby. I'm sure there will be plenty of opportunities for us to be alone, even if it's just briefly enough to lay down some ground rules. I need to be prepared for what may come.

To start, I came home last night and right away had to do a load of laundry. Finding out just twelve hours before we leave didn't give my overthinking ass much time to waste. Although I'm avoiding that pair of black lace underwear like the plague, there was no way in hell I was packing grannie panties—the only underwear that I had clean. I'm not sure where all of this will lead, but with the way we left things last night, I wasn't willing to risk another underwear mishap.

Lathering soap onto my body, I let my hands work the bubbles into my skin. Looking down at myself on full display, I'm grateful that I don't have to add that worry to my list. Having already had a baby, some women may be insecure about how they look, but that is one of the benefits of giving birth at the ripe age of twenty. My body bounced back almost instantly after Cooper was born, and I take care of myself pretty well now. Never having time to sit down helps keep me active, but I also try to eat decently, and Brooke and I take different workout classes whenever we can fit them into our schedules. Sure, I'm no social media model, but this is a body that screams "MILF" if I ever saw one.

Running my hands up my arms, I brush my soapy palms across my chest. My nipples instantly peak beneath my touch, and I let out an unexpected breath. Ever since that kiss in the car, my body's felt like it was sitting on the edge of a cliff. I was so worked up by the time I walked in from the porch that even the running dryer was calling my name. Lying in bed, I pushed myself over the edge on my own and still wasn't satisfied. I've never missed the physical hands of another person on my skin like I do now. My body got just a small taste of Levi's touch, and now it's as if nothing else is enough.

Cupping my breasts with my slick hands, I squeeze gently, unable to ignore how much fuller they feel than normal. My head falls back into the water, the warm stream hitting my hairline.

I let my fingertips glide down my slick stomach, toward the part I feel most needy. My breath grows shallow, and I realize that this is crazy. Levi and I kissed exactly one time, and now I'm touching myself—again—to just the thought of him. But crazy or not, I'm aching for him. This is the side of me that is completely on board with testing these waters. The side that says I need to get him out of my system.

The challenge is, if I'm going to do this, I need to be all in. No more wishy-washy thinking. No more back and forth. It's not fair to him, and I'm torturing myself. His suggestion to cover my tips for the weekend did the job well. It was the perfect reminder that we live in two totally different worlds. I'm not sure why I worried in the first place. This could never work. It's the same as how it didn't work with Nick, and Levi bringing up how shitty he is, was the push I needed to fully commit. And to create my newest mantra:

Screw Nick. *Screw Levi.* Remember this is only physical.

Just the anticipation makes me more aware of my own touch, and I allow myself to graze my most sensitive part. My newfound confidence in this situation guides my fingers in tiny strokes. Thinking of Levi and finally having him, I brace one palm on the wall of the shower.

Just when my hips begin to move in rhythm to my fingers, there's a call from downstairs.

"Mom?" Cooper yells. *Holy shit, this kid's timing is impeccable.*

"I'm in the shower!" I shout back.

He calls me again, and my hands drop to my sides in defeat. I push open the curtain and glance at the clock I can see in my bedroom. It's only 8:30am, so there's plenty of time. He probably can't find his controller or something.

"Mom!" he calls again, and just when I'm about to go off about needing just five minutes to myself, he adds, "There's a random car in our driveway!"

Levi got me a car. Okay, he *rented* me a car. But regardless, the thing showed up with keys in the ignition, a TV in the back just like in his, and an iced vanilla latte in the front cup holder.

The white SUV with black leather interior is pretty much a dream, and it has that new car smell that I don't think my current vehicle has ever had. The seats are heated, and the whole front dash is like one giant Siri. I'm pretty sure I could tell the thing my destination, and it would drive me there on its own.

But like I told him through text, it was completely unnecessary—borderline condescending—and if he keeps this up, I'll be able to sleep with him forever. *I just left that last part out to him.*

> I told you that you didn't have to do this. My car works just fine.

Coach Montgomery

> You told me I didn't have to look at your car, and you said I couldn't pick you up. I didn't do either of those things. You're carrying precious cargo, Alex. Now I won't have to worry about my spotlight player getting stuck on the side of the road.

His response made me laugh and him ignoring my wishes made me borderline giddy about walking into the weekend, but deep down, I also felt sad.

Nick has seen me drive this car countless times. Not once has he ever mentioned its condition, and he has plenty of money to make good on the situation. Not that I need him to, but any sort of acknowledgement would be nice. How can someone who is essentially a stranger to us seem to care more about my son's wellbeing than his father? I know Levi went against what I asked, but at least his intentions were good. Cooper deserves the world, and I give him the parts of it that I can, but as hard as I try, I can never be the dad that he's lacking.

After thinking about that, I typed out the only response that I could muster in the moment.

> Thank you.

Coach Montgomery

> I'll see you there.

Now, as I unpack our things in the hotel room, I try to talk to Cooper.

"So, have you talked to your dad lately?" I ask in passing, placing my shoes on the floor of the closet.

"Eh, not really," he says, looking at his phone. "He texted me the other day to see how the first Flames game went."

"What did he have to say about the Spark the Flame program?" Setting my toiletry bag on the bathroom sink, I wait for a reply that doesn't come. "Coop?" I ask, walking back toward the bed where my bag sits open, still half-full.

"I didn't tell him." His face is casual as he scrolls, but his voice comes out laced with sadness.

"Why not?" I ask, pretending to still be going through my things. This is one of those times where you just ask the questions and see where he takes it. I know from experience that if I push too far, he'll just shut down. His walls will shoot up, and he'll pretend that everything's fine even when I know it's not. *I wonder where he gets that from.*

Continuing to fiddle with his phone, he says, "I don't know. What's the point?"

Again, I keep things easy and let him steer the ship. "What do you mean?"

Finally, he looks up from his phone, his eyes finding the ceiling and telling me to give him a break. "Come on, Mom. You know how Dad is."

*I sure do.*

I want to say it out loud, but instead, I walk over to where Coop is sitting on the bed. I gently pull his phone from his hand. He looks up at me, and his face and shoulders both relax in defeat as he loosens his grip around his precious device. "Tell me."

With his phone now gone, Cooper plays with a loose thread in the comforter that we're sitting on. It kills me to see how much even talking about this affects him. I can't help but feel guilty. I should have done more. I should have hidden this better. I should have *been* better and maybe just having his mom would be enough.

"It's always about him or work. I would have told him about this, he would have acted all happy, and then what? Nothing. He wouldn't show up. He wouldn't ask about it until weeks later. There's just no point like I said. He doesn't care."

"He cares about *you*," I say, instantly attempting to plug the holes I see drowning Cooper's boat.

He sighs. "Dad only cares about himself."

Tears bubble up inside me, partially out of sadness for my son—I didn't realize just how much he noticed these things—and partially out of anger toward my ex. How can Nick be so goddamn selfish? How do you look at your child, someone who is half your DNA, and not treat them like they walk on water? I know Nick loves Cooper, but Cooper doesn't know that.

It sounds harsh, but it's true. It's hard enough for adults to understand unconditional love, let alone a child. Wrapping your mind around someone caring for you no matter what, despite your flaws, and despite everything else that other person may have going on in their life, is hard. It takes confidence in who you are and the relationship you have with that person. It takes trust and fulfilled promises and that person showing up. Cooper doesn't have those things with Nick. I don't blame him for feeling this way.

"Your dad does love you, honey, but I understand why it's hard to believe that. I'm sorry that he makes you feel like his job is more important. Sometimes even adults have a lot of growing up to do."

This is killing me because I know how Cooper is feeling. I've been here with my own father not showing up, and I've been exactly where he is with Nick. It's hard to understand how a parent doesn't put a child first, second, and third on their list of priorities. Looking at Coop, I know I'm not the perfect mom, but I also know now that's one thing I got right.

Cooper throws his arms around my waist, and I revel in his embrace, the tears that were once bubbling up, lodging themselves in my throat. "I know, Mom," he says. "But at least I have you."

That breaks the dam and my eyes fill, tears slowly escaping.

When he eventually lets go, he looks up at me. I give him a smile and wipe my cheeks dry. Cooper makes the awkward face of a typical preteen who knows I've been crying and would rather do literally anything else than acknowledge it.

"I don't know about you, but I'm starving," I say, cutting him a break. His head perks back up instantly. *There's my boy.* "We have a couple of hours until dinner with the coaches. Should we grab some lunch? I hear there's a good pizza place nearby."

Cooper smiles at me, hops up, and grabs his sweatshirt from the bed as if this conversation never happened. *If only we were all so resilient.*

"I'll never say no to some freaking pizza, Mom," he says excitedly.

I look at him with all the sincerity in the world. "Cooper, I love you."

He smiles at me. "But language."

# 24

# Levi

"**A**lright boss, where are we headed to eat?" Erik asks, leaving our team meeting as he rubs his palms together. The captains are leading a players' dinner with the rest of the guys, but us coaches usually do our own thing for meals. Team bonding and all that.

"Actually, I think I'm gonna take Alex downstairs to the hotel restaurant. We have some things to go over."

Erik looks at me side-eyed, his mouth twisted in that knowing pout that he often does. "Mhmm. I'm sure you guys have a lot to... discuss."

Staring at him blankly, I consider arguing but decide against it. Erik isn't stupid. He knows me, and I can only assume he knows what I'm getting at. The good news is, he doesn't care. He is the most laid-back guy I know. As long as you're not a defenseman who turns the puck over in our zone, he doesn't seem to have a problem with much of anything that goes on around here.

Besides, there's nothing in the program that says I can't try to get to know the spotlight player's mother—have a conversation. I would know—I invented it—and I just made up this spotlight player thing a week ago. Would it be frowned upon if they found out that we're making arrangements to sleep together? Probably. But it's not like I'm going to fuck her on the restaurant table. *Unfortunately.*

"Just drop it."

Erik drags his thumb and index finger across his lips as if he's zipping them shut. *This guy's a total dweeb.* "Consider it dropped."

*He's also a great fucking friend.*

"Thanks, man," I say. I tap his arm lightly as we continue walking. "Oh, I need one more thing."

He glances over. "Now you're pushing it."

"I need you to take Coop to the players' dinner. Let him hang with the guys for a while."

"You mean babysit the kid again so you can talk to Ms. Fine-With-The-Nice-Legs?"

My fists clench at my sides, then slowly relax. There are not many people I'd let talk about Bennett that way thanks to my newfound need to protect her—even if they're kidding—but lucky for Erik, he's one of them. And he's doing me a solid.

"I would say it'll be the last time, but I don't like to lie."

"Hey, if it means maybe you'll actually settle down for once, I'll do whatever you need. If I have to go on another double date with Tasha's book club friend and her husband with his weird soccer obsession, I'll lose my mind."

Shaking my head and laughing to myself, I correct him. "Let's not get ahead of ourselves, but I'll do what I can." Stopping in front of my door, I extend my hand, and he takes it in his. "Thanks, I owe you one."

"Oh, I know," he says. "I'm keeping count."

Waiting for Alex in the lobby, I go over everything I have planned for her. I know she wants to keep this strictly physical, so I'll start strong there. Once we lay down ground rules, I'll take full advantage of catering to her in every way that I already have in my mind. I have no objection to sleeping with Alex, but I also think, as crazy as it sounds, I just might want more.

I'll have to approach that part with caution. I know she's afraid that I'm the same as she pictures everyone in a position like mine to be. I don't know her history, but there's clearly a reason that she feels this way. Who am I to question her walls when I've had my own built up around me for as long as I can remember? We each seem to have a reason behind them. The difference is, mine have been cracking since the first time I saw her. But she doesn't need to know that yet.

I'll use this time to chip away the idea of me she has in her mind. For once I'm actually hoping that the girl I plan to sleep with catches feelings. Dare I say, my endgame is to be with her, but I can have plenty of fun in the meantime. My short-term goal—give this girl the best sex she's ever had to keep her coming back for more. My long-term goal—use that time to find out her history, hear what she's thinking, and prove to her that I'm not the person she thinks I am. It might take some time to get there with her, but I'm patient when it counts.

The sound of a child's laughter from outside the hotel doors reminds me that there's just one thing I have to accomplish before any of this can be put into action. With perfect timing, Cooper walks through the revolving door and jogs over as soon as he sees me.

"Hey, buddy," I say, giving him a pound. "How was the drive?"

"Uh, sweet! All my mom's car has is a radio and a seat full of crumbs. I could live in that thing that we rode in today."

I huff out a laugh. "Glad you approve. How about your mom... ?"

"Eh, she acted annoyed, but I caught her cranking up the seat warmer the whole way here."

A satisfied feeling fills my chest. The thought of spoiling both Bennetts even a little bit makes a smile grow on my face. The thought of warming Alex's perfect ass makes something else grow entirely.

As if on cue, I see the outline of her figure round the door. As the wall spins in front of her, it slowly exposes the body I've dreamt about and the face that makes my heart skip a beat. It's also apparently the face that now makes me say things like "heart skip a beat." *God help me.*

The unhurried reveal is almost torturous, but it also makes it last, and I savor every millisecond. When Bennett finally walks through the opening, the first thing that catches my eye is the black hoodie she's wearing. The Flames logo is stitched large on the front, and the sight of her in my team's gear might be the sexiest thing I've ever seen. The other thing I notice is her posture.

Too often I've seen Alex looking defeated when she thinks nobody's watching. Like she's worn down or stressed out from just life itself. Of course, when she realizes other people are paying attention, she perks up like she was never down in the first place. But not now.

Now, she's standing strong before she even sees me. She looks bold and confident, her arms swinging freely by her side instead of across her chest or in her pockets where I normally find them. It's selfish, but I can't help but hope this means she's thought about us. *Fucking please tell me she's at least thought about me.*

"Nice hoodie," I say, hoping the droll comment will keep the mood light. I want this version of her for as long as I can have it.

"Funny story," she says, tugging down on the sweatshirt. "I found this in the back seat of the car that you sent me."

"I got one too!" Cooper chimes in.

"Hmm. That's weird," I say coyly. "I wonder how those could have gotten in there." Cooper gives his mom a knowing smile, and she looks up at me under raised brows.

"Thank you," she says.

"I have no idea what you're talking about."

Alex shakes her head, her lips tugging upward before she changes the subject. "So, you two off to dinner then?" Both her and Cooper look at me for an answer.

"Actually, Coop. Do me a favor. See that lady over there at the desk? Can you go ask her if she can bring some extra water bottles to the guys' rooms? We don't want them to be dehydrated for the big game tomorrow."

"Sure!" he says enthusiastically, running toward reception.

I take a deep breath in, turning back to Alex. I learned my lesson last time by bringing things up in front of her son before talking to her first.

"I was actually wondering if you would be okay letting Cooper go with Erik to the players' dinner. I thought he'd like that." With the risk of overdoing it, I take a step closer. "And I thought we could get dinner and talk."

"Oh." Her lips part and her eyes widen in surprise, but it's not half as bad of a reaction as it could have been.

"We'll eat here at the hotel restaurant. That way you're nearby just in case Cooper needs you."

"Okay, sure," she says softly.

"Yeah?" I ask too eagerly.

She smiles shyly. "Yeah."

We hold our stare as Cooper runs back to us. "That was weird."

"What was weird?" Bennett asks, her gaze still on me.

"She said they just stocked their rooms with water like an hour ago."

"Strange," I say, only now tearing my eyes from her. "Well, thanks anyway, buddy. Hey, what do you say to eating dinner with the boys tonight instead of us old coaches?"

"Really?" Coop says, his eyes growing wide.

"Yep. Coach Erik should be here any minute to walk you over to the event room."

"Yes! Mom, can I?"

Alex leans down to her son. "Sure, honey, but let Coach Erik know if you need anything, okay? I'll be right down here."

"Yeah, yeah, sounds good. Where is he?"

"Where's who?" Erik asks, coming up from behind us. "Oh, the coolest coach on the bench? Right here." Cooper laughs but rolls his eyes in his direction. *I'm really starting to like this kid.*

"You ready?" Erik continues. "If we don't hurry up, there will be nothing left for us after those animals get their hands on the menu."

"Oh, I'm ready," Coop says, turning to leave. "See ya, Coach. Love you, Mom!" he calls over his shoulder.

"Have fun you two," Erik adds casually.

The second they're out of sight, the mood seems to shift. There's a potential in the air that wasn't there when Cooper was around. Now it's not the team's coach and the player's mom. It's just me and Alex.

"You ready?" I ask.

She answers with only a nod, but she's the first to take off toward the restaurant.

The hostess seats us at a two-top table in the back corner. There are other people here, but most of them occupy the bar up front. For the most part, we have privacy. Enough at least to have this conversation.

The waitress takes our drink orders, club soda for me and a red wine for her.

"You don't drink?" she asks when the server walks away.

"Not anymore."

She narrows her eyes. "It feels like there's a story there."

I nod, leaning back in my chair. "There is."

"Care to share?" she asks casually.

"Long story short, when I got injured a while back, life got... pretty dark. My ex and I broke up around the same time, and basically my whole future was up in the air. I turned to any vice I could find that would numb it all just a little. But it almost cost me everything."

She sits forward in her seat, picking the cloth napkin off of the table and playing with the corner. "I'm sorry. That must have been really hard."

"It was. But I'm stronger for it now."

Her eyes jump to me, but she pauses before she speaks. "I thought you said you didn't date." She says it with a tone that's a cross between curious and accusatory—almost as if she's calling my bluff.

"I don't anymore. Not really at least."

She visibly relaxes, sitting back in her chair. "I get that. As you can probably guess, my relationship with Cooper's father was kind of a trainwreck. Still is in a lot of ways. I haven't dated anyone seriously since."

Now it's my turn to lean forward, knowing this is where I find the answers I've been looking for. The reason why she is so up in arms around me. "He's the suit, right?" I sit up straighter.

Alex bites her lip, and I lick mine in response. "He is," she says. "He pretty much found out I was pregnant and decided that Cooper and I didn't fit into his life plan. His career is the only thing he's ever cared about enough to put everything else aside for. You'd think it'd be his son, but..." Her voice trails off in thought. I set my forearms on the table, move in closer, and finish for her.

"But he's a piece of shit who has no idea what he's fucking missing?" I stare into her gold spot like it's the light to latch onto at the end of a tunnel, and for me, I think it just might be.

Alex meets my intensity, her chest rising and falling quickly, the Flames 'F' dancing from the rhythm. "Yeah."

She holds my gaze for what feels like both a flash and an eternity. The tension lingers like the calm before a storm, and I've never been surer that I want—*need*—more of her.

I watch Bennett's pupils dilate in front of me, her eyes hooded as they drop to my mouth. Standing suddenly, she grabs the hem of her sweatshirt, slowly lifting it high above her head. She has a plain white v-neck t-shirt underneath that hangs loosely around her curves, and I've never found something so basic to be so captivating.

"I'm going to go to the bathroom," she says sheepishly, but her eyes are set on mine. She lingers before finally turning and walking toward the doors not far behind us. *Is she challenging me?*

My mind reels with all my next possible moves. Do I follow her? What if that's not what she meant? Imagine me walking to that bathroom door, and it's locked. Or worse. It's not, and she's in there not expecting me at all. *Talk about ruining any chance I may have had.* But what if I don't follow her, and that *is* what she meant? Then it looks like I don't want her.

*And I really fucking want her.*

Eventually, in the midst of my back and forth, the waitress comes with our drinks and sets them on the table in front of me. "Do you guys need another minute?"

Still following Alex, I watch her reach the bathroom, then peer over her shoulder before stepping inside.

I swallow dryly before answering, my eyes still on the dark, wooden door. "A couple minutes would be great," I finally say.

*Challenge accepted.*

# 25

# Alex

S tanding at the sink right in front of the bathroom door, I stare at my reflection in the mirror. *Did I actually just do that?* I don't know, maybe Levi won't take the hint. Maybe he won't follow me here like I insinuated. For a second, I can't even remember why I did that in the first place. Then I remember.

*"But he's a piece of shit who has no idea what he's fucking missing?"*

Okay, so, that was pretty sweet... also very true, which is what I'm choosing to focus on. I've been around Nick too often to know when someone is a pretentious prick and when they aren't—I don't think that's Levi.

He's been fairly open since we sat down. Nick would have lied through his teeth about any personal issues he had going on—it's hard to admit to a flaw when you're perfect in your mind. He also remembered how I felt about talking about things in front of Cooper without speaking to me first. I'm not sure Nick would have even been listening to me when I complained about that, let alone cared enough to remember for next time. But that doesn't change all of the other things.

What led me to this freaking bathroom was the reminder that Nick is no reason to keep myself from having what I want. As if my conversation with Cooper today wasn't enough, hearing how much he sucks from someone who I've compared him to, was the icing on the *screw my ex* cake. So here I am.

Maybe the public bathroom of a five-star hotel in the early evening isn't the best time to initiate this little... arrangement. But I had to capitalize on the guts I had all of a sudden. *Thank God it's a single stall.*

Just when I'm starting to think that Levi didn't understand my innuendo—or worse—did, but doesn't want to join me, the indistinct sound of footsteps brushes the carpet on the other side of the threshold.

I still, my palms leaning on either side of the sink, my body frozen except for my chest that heaves up and down with built-up anxiety... and anticipation. White-knuckling the porcelain, I attempt to catch even the faintest of sounds that suggest it's Levi—and that he's coming in.

And then I do.

The delicate grind of the knob slowly turning, rips through my ears like it's been amplified a hundred times over. All my blood rushes to my feet, and my palms grow warm and slick against the cool sink. I watch as the door pushes open an inch at a time, pausing halfway.

The person on the other side now has a view of the whole room, minus where I'm standing, and I have a view of an open door, minus the person behind it. As if the emptiness of the rest of the space was an invitation, Levi slips in quickly, quietly shutting the door behind him.

I turn away from him, suddenly shy, but our eyes meet in the mirror, both sets of them heated. His jaw is somehow tighter than I've seen it before, and his build seems bigger in such a small space. His hand remains on the knob when he speaks. "Hi."

Pushing any second thoughts out of my mind, I home in on the reflection of this beautiful man. This man with dark hair, striking eyes, and lips I need to taste again. This man who just might be nothing like I thought he was. "Hi."

With that, the click of the lock echoes off the walls as he glides to me in one full stride. He stands completely behind me, our bodies closer than we've been before. He seems taller like this, probably because I can barely see his whole face in the mirror. I'd be intimidated if I wasn't so damn turned-on.

Steadily, he lifts his hands and places them on the lower halves of my shoulders. Never taking his eyes off mine, he runs them down the length of my arms. Goosebumps trail their path, lighting up my skin. Levi's being cautious, I know he is, but as much as I appreciate the thought, being careful is the last thing that I want right now. *I need to let myself have this before I change my mind.*

With his hands wrapped around my wrists, Levi lets his eyes fall just briefly to scan the rest of my reflection in the mirror. When he brings them back to mine, they're full of need, and so am I. To show him that, and grant him the access he's so patiently waiting for, I push my hips back into him slowly. My body lands on him already hard between us, and I watch his lids fall shut with the contact.

As soon as they open, his hand cups my chin and turns my mouth so it's tilted toward his. "Bennett," he says, his tone low and husky.

"Montgomery," I answer breathlessly.

"I've waited way too long to taste you again." His voice is hushed, a reminder that we're in a hotel restaurant. The thought only makes me crave him more—the excitement something I haven't had in so long. "Tell me I can kiss you."

I hold back a smile from the irony that *now* he chooses to ask for permission. His full lips hover just above mine, and when I nod my head in agreement, they almost touch. A lazy grin forms on his mouth. He runs the tip of his nose from the base of my cheek to the shell of my ear. "Say it," he whispers.

There's a pulse between my thighs as if I answer there first. Then, my words follow suit. "Yes."

He collides with me, both of us hungry. His kiss is deep and smooth, his tongue meeting mine like rain to a drought. Still, I want more.

Reaching my hand up behind his head, I rake my fingers through his hair. Levi groans into my mouth when I take it in my fingers, tugging it gently. He releases my chin without interrupting our kiss and runs his fingertips across the bare skin above the neckline of my shirt.

My nipples strain against my bra as he grazes one on his movement south. When he reaches the bottom hem, he slides his hand under my shirt and across the sensitive skin below my belly button. Dipping his fingers only slightly into the waist of my jeans, he runs them back to where they started.

A whimper is the only sound that escapes between us, and it takes Levi pausing his touch for me to realize I was the one who made it. He inches toward the button of my pants, and adrenaline courses through me. My hand begins its slow fall from the back of his head as I realize what we're doing. "Wait," I say, pulling back slightly.

He pushes his hand into my hair. "Okay."

What am I thinking? Can I do just the physical? I've never been that way. If I had, there wouldn't be a bulk pack of batteries in my nightstand drawer. *But we're trying new things,* I remind myself. *You want this. You want him,* and you're about to get a taste.

"If you don't want this, I'll turn around and walk out of here like this never happened," Levi says. He rests his forehead on my temple. "But please, Alex—don't ask me to stop."

It's then that I realize, I don't *want* to go back.

"Levi," I all but beg. He answers with his silence. "Touch me."

With a growl, his lips find mine again, and he rips open the button of my pants with two fingers. He pulls my zipper down slowly, a contrast to his first movement, like he's realized he wants to savor this. Just his hands this close to the place I've thought about him being so many times makes my hips buck into him. He twitches below his belt with a fullness that should scare me but only increases my need.

Levi sinks the tips of his fingers into my satin thong. *God, I'm so glad I did laundry.* My breath increases, and I realize this will be the first time I've been touched here by someone other than myself in a long time. I think the anticipation alone might unravel me.

Sliding his hand further down, he runs two fingers past my middle and freezes. "You're so fucking wet for me, baby."

The last word alone, coming from his mouth, makes my legs waver beneath me. Levi reaches around me and takes my outside wrist, bringing it back behind him. He slides both of our hands, his guiding mine, into his back pocket. Leaving mine there, he slips his out and brings it to my waist.

"As much as I'd kill to see it, I don't want you on your knees just yet, Bennett. Hold onto me."

On command, I pull him flush against me. My hand feels so small on his ass, his massive muscles tight as they help to brace my weight. "Good girl," he whispers, and as if it's my reward, he slides his middle finger into me.

I suck in a breath as my heart hammers against my rib cage and my pussy pulses around his knuckle. It's not surprising that I'm this close already being that the entire last week has felt like foreplay.

"Patience, baby," Levi says, sliding out of me. I miss him instantly, my body begging to be filled again. "I've waited too long for this to be over so fast."

He uses my arousal to brush circles around my most sensitive spot. Unable to just stand here and take it without touching him, I slide my hand from his pocket to where he sits between us. I palm him over the outside of his jeans, feeling how big he really is.

Levi makes a guttural sound and plunges back into me, adding a second finger this time.

I put pressure on his length. He works me from inside, his thumb rolling gently over my clit. The pressure builds like I've never felt before. I know how to get myself off, but *this* with *him*—it's almost too much to take.

There's a knock at the door and both of us freeze. "Just a minute," Levi says, clearing his throat. I look at him with worried eyes, and he somehow manages to smile. "This won't take long," he says with a wink.

I might be annoyed with him if I didn't know he was right. I've been on edge for him for so long, just one more word, stroke, graze, will cause me to free fall.

"Look at me," Levi says, nudging my chin upward.

Finding the mirror again, I see myself first, but I'm almost unrecognizable. There's something different about the person staring back at me. It could have something to do with the large NHL coach standing behind me or his slick fingers still inside me, but I don't think so. Not in that way at least.

I think the difference is that I see a new version of myself. A version that only comes to the surface when you do something just for you—when you allow yourself to have something you really want. Levi is that for me, and I'm letting myself have him.

"Alex," Levi says. "Eyes on me." Coming back to the moment, I find a familiar dark green gaze in the reflection. "That's it."

He slips his fingers from me, runs them the length of my slit and then pushes them back in. Twirling them inside, pleasure I've never experienced before shoots through me. I let my head fall back onto his shoulder, and he stops instantly. My walls quiver around him, and he exhales at the feeling. "I said look at me, Bennett."

My head snaps up, and his fingers start again. *Was that punishment for looking away?* The thought takes me higher, and I have to move my hand from his body to brace myself on either side of the sink, hanging my head between my arms.

There's another knock that Levi ignores and that I'm incapable of answering. Instead, he drops his head to my ear, nibbles it roughly, then tilts my chin until our eyes meet again. "Come for me, baby," he whispers. And I do.

Staring into his eyes, my body trembles, his name escaping my lips barely audible. "Levi."

At the almost silent sound, he withdraws, leaving his palm cupped around me, and bringing his other hand to the base of my throat. It's so big that his fingers still reach the side of my cheek, and he turns it so I'm facing him.

"You're perfect," he says, crashing our mouths together again.

A door slams shut, and I realize the person waiting must have gone into the other bathroom next door. Levi breaks our kiss and slides his hand from my pants. I turn and watch as he buttons them and pulls the zipper back up, my knees still weak beneath me.

"You go," he says, kissing me once more. "I need a minute."

We both look between us at where he strains beneath the threads of his jeans. A heat creeps up my cheeks as if *that* is what would make me blush amongst having Levi get me off in a bathroom.

"Okay," I say, fixing my shirt.

I'm not sure what else to do so I reach for the door, my back turned from Levi when he says, "But I'm not done with you yet."

# 26

# Levi

The second the door clicks shut behind Alex, I let out the heaving sigh I'd been holding. I have never been more afraid I'd come in my pants than I was just now, and that includes the time Daphne Summers gave me a lap dance in a hot tub after the sophomore formal wearing only her bikini. Apparently Bennett makes me hotter than a half-naked girl makes a fifteen-year-old Levi, and that's really fucking saying something.

It's not even her body that did it to me, although finally being able to put my hands on her perfect form was a definite bonus. But it was more the way she finally let go. When she uttered my name for the first time, I would have sworn she was going to tell me to stop. As hard as that would have been, I meant what I said. I would have respected her wishes and made every attempt to put this behind me and just move forward with the Spark the Flame campaign.

When she didn't—I almost fucking lost it.

The idea that I may be getting through to her fulfilled me more than it should. I've never cared before about a woman being into me. Maybe that's because, if anything, I've had the opposite problem. But for once in the last eight years, I do care.

I know this is just physical to Alex, at least for now, but if I can read people like I think I can, this is not the usual for her. The only reason she let this happen is because she realized who I am doesn't completely disgust her after all. Or at least that her attraction to me outweighs her dislike of my so-called "kind." That realization for some reason, is fucking erotic to me. It's also one less roadblock that we'll have.

My new problem is, I'm not even close to finished with her yet—physically or otherwise.

Glancing down at my gold watch, I do the fastest math I've ever done and calculate just how much time we realistically have. The players' dinner usually lasts about an hour and a half depending on how fast the kitchen can fill their orders. That gives Bennett and me about another hour. It's not nearly long enough, but it'll have to do.

Psyching myself up, I take one last look in the mirror and run through another list of hockey players' ugly faces to get this situation under control. *Gretsky, McDavid, Crosby, Anderson, Petrov.* My mind lands on Burnsey and with it comes his nauseating laugh. *Yep, that'll do it.*

Pushing open the bathroom door, I nearly run over our server heading back toward our table. *Perfect timing.*

"Excuse me," I say, still somewhat out of breath.

She turns to me and paints a professional smile. "Can I help you sir? I was just heading back to take your order."

"That won't be necessary. We actually need to leave. Can you please send a burger, medium-well, with extra pickles and curly fries to room 308 and one medium-rare with just lettuce and cheese to room 316?"

"Sure thing," she says cheerfully. "Any sides with the second?"

"Steak fries," I add, saying a silent prayer to thank God that Bennett and I switched bags at Petey's.

Alex's caramel hair flows down the back of her chair as she sits at our table. I step beside her and nonchalantly slide my hand underneath it, cupping the back of her neck. "We're leaving," I say calmly.

The wine glass in her hand pauses at her lips, her breath catching before the cup makes contact. I slide my hand off of her, sweeping her hair to one shoulder as I do it. *Fuck, she's beautiful.*

"Are we not eating?" She looks at me eagerly, lowering her glass to the table.

"Which are you hungrier for?" I ask, still standing above her. I lean in closer and rest my palm on the empty spot in front of her. "Because I sure as hell know *my* answer."

She looks at me torn, surely working the same numbers that I just did moments ago. "We have at least an hour, and I'll shoot Erik a text on the way to tell him to let Cooper hang with the guys for as long as he wants." She looks at me, her expression unreadable, but when I extend my hand, she answers without hesitation. She places her palm in mine, and I pull her to stand. Then, reluctantly, I drop our embrace as soon as she's up.

She may be coming around to this, but I don't want Bennett to get the wrong idea. This isn't a date, and I know that. It couldn't be even if she changed her mind. Whether it's holding hands or locking lips, Alex and I can't be seen by Sadie or anyone else from the team doing anything more than having a chat. Not to mention there's always a risk Cooper is out walking around for some reason. As willing as she seems to be right now, from what I know so far about Alex, Cooper finding out about this would blow any real shot I have with her.

Instead of holding her grasp, I place my hand on her lower back and guide her toward the exit. I am a gentleman despite what people probably think, and it gives me a reason to touch her again. She shivers in reaction to the contact as she grabs her sweatshirt off the table. She takes only one step before I take hold of the material in her grasp.

Alex goes to move forward but freezes when there's a tug on her hoodie. Looking side-eyed over her shoulder, she watches as I look down at it in her hands.

"Next time..." I growl into her ear. "You leave that on."

Her throat moves up and down as I flatten my palm once again, nudging her on before dropping it completely.

As we cross through the lobby from the restaurant toward the elevator doors, Alex scans her surroundings. "He's fine," I say in a tone I hope is reassuring.

I press the up arrow, and she crosses her arms over her chest. Reaching over, I tug on her elbow until both arms fall back to her sides. *Be big, Alex.* "And so are you."

Her lips turn in as the doors separate, inviting us inside. I don't move. I won't. Not until she does. *I'm challenging you, Bennett.*

Alex takes her sweatshirt by the sleeves and ties it around her waist, then slowly steps through the doors.

*Challenge accepted.*

I step in behind her, the two of us standing side-by-side but staring straight ahead. The doors ding as they slide closed. The second we're alone, we both turn to each other. Wrapping my arm around her waist, I lift her and carry her to the elevator wall before setting her back down on her feet.

Resting one palm high above her head, I bring the other to her chin, holding her flawless face in the curve of my hand. "I told you I wasn't done with you yet," I say, dipping down to place kisses up the length of her neck.

Turning her head in my hand, I open up her throat for me and feel her pulse quicken beneath my lips. I wedge my foot between hers, her two perfect legs now framing mine. Alex leans in to grind against me, and I meet her with my thigh, giving her the friction she so desperately wants. Seeing her need me like this again so quickly, only works me up more.

I push harder into her, and she moans as she moves her hips faster. I dive down to her, sweeping my tongue into her mouth, when all of a sudden, she lifts my shirt and plunges her hand into the front of my jeans in one fell swoop.

She hums into my mouth, and I groan into hers as she takes me in her hand through my boxers. Shifting upward, she attempts to dip her fingers beneath the final layer that sits between her palm and me, rock hard just for her.

"Not yet, baby," I manage to plead. When I have her on me, I don't want to feel like I have to hold back. I want more than the mere seconds we have left.

In perfect timing, the elevator jolts to a stop. Alex rips her hand from my pants, but I stay put, sliding the hotel key out of the front pocket of my jeans. I hold it up, wedged between my first two fingers, in the few inches that separate us. "Are we still doing this?" I ask playfully.

Her eyes drop to the card, then back to me. She runs her teeth over her bottom lip, then snatches it from my grasp.

Stepping off the elevator, she turns back to me. "316," I say with an obvious grin.

Alex follows the signs on the wall until she reaches my door. She scans my card on the pad above the knob but turns back when it clicks open. She's once again asking me, *"What happens now?"* This time, with no words at all.

Reaching around her, I push the door open without breaking eye contact. She walks in, and before the door latches, I'm flush to her back. "Bed. Now."

Bennett's breath hitches, but in spite of that, she strides quickly to it. *My eager girl.* Before her shins reach the mattress, I spin her around. She tucks her hair behind her ear, and I brush her lips with the pad of my thumb.

Pulling her by her belt loop like I did last night, I rest my forehead on hers. Breathing her in, the scent of coconut is like foreplay to my senses. "Off," is all I say as I tug once again on her jeans.

Alex brings her hands to her waistband, slowly fidgeting with the button. When it releases, it takes everything in me not to reach right for my prize once again. But I can't. Not yet.

I have no problem taking control here. In fact, I encourage it. But I need to know that Alex understands how fucking perfect she is. I don't want her to hesitate. I don't want her to second-guess that this is exactly where she should be. I want her confident in herself—and in us. Always. Not just when she decides she can do it. I want the Alex that walked through that revolving door earlier tonight.

She glides the zipper down and begins peeling her jeans from her hips. When they hit the floor, I drop there too. Pulling up on the sides of her thong, the material between her legs comes into view. The navy fabric is shades darker here, drenched from our moment before. I peer up at Alex whose lips are parted at just the pressure that the lifted fabric creates. I slide the sides past their place, then down to her feet, exhaling heavily on my new view. *Fucking perfect.*

Her knees buck at the warm air on her clit as I pull the thong from under her. Standing, I scan Bennett's body, now naked from the waist down. I hold the satin up to her, the darkened material clearly visible.

"Do you see this?" I ask her, my voice gravelly. She nods shallowly. "*I did this.*" Her head, once again, moves up and down. "Say it."

"You did that," she says breathlessly.

"That's right, baby." Sliding all four fingers between her legs, I cup her in my hand. "And I'm gonna do it again." I kiss her neck. "And again," I whisper into her ear. "And again."

My mouth crashes to hers as I plunge two fingers into her. Alex whimpers as I reach around to grab her ass that I finally have access to.

With my hands still where they are, I drop to my knees for the second time already. *This girl.* Adding my mouth to her bundle of nerves, I twirl my tongue in rhythmic circles. Bennett finds my hair and pulls me to her.

"Good girl," I say, still making contact. The vibrations from my words only cause her to put more pressure on the back of my head, but I don't care. Suffocating here, like this, would be the perfect way to go.

When her legs grow weak around me, I lick my thumb, then stand, bracing her back with my forearm and using the pad of my finger to finish her off. Alex tightens around me and grabs the outside of both of my arms, hanging on for dear life.

"Let go, baby," I say, and we both know I don't mean her grip. Obeying, she releases her hold and melts into me, her tight pussy clenching around me once again.

My cock strains painfully against my jeans watching her come undone. I would pleasure Alex for hours, but between cutting things off with Liv, this past week with Bennett, and now tonight, I need contact like I need air in my lungs.

Alex comes down from her high, her eyes not just hungry, but starving. She reaches for my waist almost immediately, undoing my button and zipper with twice the speed she did her own. This is exactly what I want—for Alex to gain that confidence from watching me take care of her.

"Off," she says, mimicking my command, and I immediately slide my jeans and underwear down in one strong motion.

Springing to life in front of her, Alex's eyes grow wide, and she reaches for me right away. I groan under her touch finally on my bare skin. She explores me as I bring my hand to her cheek, using the opportunity to glance quickly at the watch on my wrist.

We still have time, but I'm not willing to risk this not happening again because we have too close of a call with Cooper. I'm also not willing to waste a single second on just me. Knowing how just her *hands* feel on me, I can't wait for her pussy tighten around my cock. And that is something that won't be hurried.

Sliding my shirt up and over my head, Alex pauses, her grip on me growing tighter. She scans my broad chest and the body I've worked for since I was a kid, her mouth open like she's shocked to see it.

"You're beautiful," she says in a daze. I can't smother the laugh that escapes my throat or hide the smirk that spreads on my lips. Instead, I reach down and pull her shirt off the same way.

Unlatching her bra, I reach out and cup her in both hands. "No... You are."

The contact with her chest brings Alex back to the moment. For good measure, I brush the pads of both thumbs across her peaked nipples, and she moans, mirroring the stroke against me. Precum coats her finger, and she uses it to slick the tip.

Unwilling to waste any more time, I pull her hand from me. "On the bed, Alex."

Sitting back on the mattress, she wraps one arm across her chest, hiding some of the most beautiful tits I've ever seen. Her wheels start spinning, and I know I'm losing her from this moment. Her head is anywhere but here. "Drop your arm, baby."

The tips of her fingers slide down the length of her forearm as she slowly obeys.

"You think too much," I say, leaning down to straddle my arms around her. I take one peak in my mouth and put pressure on it with my lips as I flick my tongue against it. Alex drops her head and arches her back, pushing it harder into me. "I'm gonna take that all away."

Releasing it with a pop, I hover over the next. "When you're with me, I want you here." I repeat the motion on this side, my cock growing more and more impatient for her as I take my time. Sucking it once again for good measure, I move my mouth away. "Got it?" Alex hums in response. "Words, baby."

Lulling her head back up, she lets the natural effect of gravity pull her knees open underneath me. "Yes," she says, and I know that's her way of answering twice.

"Good." I push her one knee toward the other, her whole body rocking to the side. "Now, crawl toward the headboard."

Alex swallows before rolling her hips so her ass is on full display. I take advantage of the time to reach back into my jeans and pull a condom from my wallet. When she reaches the top of the bed, she goes to turn back around, but I stop her in her place, steadying her hips with my hands. "Not so fast."

Starting at her neck, I run my hand down her spine until I reach the dimple at the bottom. Goosebumps trail my hand as I lean over and place a gentle kiss in the middle of the divot, then slap her full cheek. "Look at me," I say sternly.

Alex glances back, her eyes full of want and need. I stretch across her and wrap her hair into one fist. Tugging it gently, she pulls up onto her knees, her back to my chest and my cock sitting perfectly between the cheeks of her ass.

Releasing my grip, I reach around with one hand and graze her soaked pussy, using the other to cup her full breast. "So fucking wet," is all I say before my need for her overpowers my want to explore. "Turn around."

Flipping over, Alex lets her weight fall back on her elbows, her body on full display once again. This woman is stunning. Not in the plastic way that most of the other women I've been with are. She's naturally breath-taking—real, effortless. On top of that, this body has accomplished more than I would ever be able to. It's strong, resilient—*mine.*

Leaning down, I kiss her with a passion and intensity that I can't describe. It's like a normal kiss doesn't have enough pressure or entan-glement for the need that I have.

But now I have to be inside her.

Reluctantly pulling away, I rip open the packet in my hand and begin rolling its contents over my length. Sitting up, she stops my hand. "Let me." Using her own fingers to finish it off, she watches me as she brings it down to the base. Seeing her come back to me—take charge in this way—is almost too much.

She leans back again when she's finished, and without hesitation, I take one leg in each crook of my arm. Centering myself against her, she grinds her hips, rubbing her sweet middle against my tip. As if it was permission, I ease myself into her. We both groan on contact, and Alex fists the sheets beneath her.

"You okay, Bennett?"

She nods while licking her lips. "More," she says.

"That's my girl."

I push further into her, watching for her reaction. I know this isn't Alex's first time, but her walls are so strained against me that it might as well be. As much as I want it hard and rough, I don't want to hurt her. She bites her bottom lip as a sweet whimper escapes her throat.

"You're so fucking tight, baby," I say, halfway in.

Her cheeks flush with embarrassment. "It's been a while," she admits.

"Perfect," I say, and just like that, the newfound confidence is back in her eyes.

"More, Levi," she repeats.

Those sweet words are all I need to bury the rest of myself inside her. She quivers from the fullness alone, and it takes everything in me not to finish right now. Instead, I begin shifting slowly, picking up speed as Alex's hips meet my rhythm.

Dropping her legs, I lean down to her, kissing up the side of her neck as we move together. "So fucking good," I say into her ear as I hold her wrists against the bed above her.

"Levi," she moans, wrapping her legs around my waist.

Straightening my arms, I leave both of hers pinned beside her head. I kiss her lips, sucking on the bottom one as I pull away. She arches up into me, driving her heels into my lower back, and I fill beneath her.

My breaths come out in short pants, and as hers matches mine, I push my thumb into her parted lips. "Suck."

She does as she's told, wetting my finger with her mouth as I sit back on my knees.

Using it to brush quick strokes across her clit, I quicken my rhythm and finally let myself go. Alex cries out as her walls tighten around me, and that's all that it takes for me to empty inside her.

"Fuck, baby," I groan as I drop to my forearms. Our thrusts slow, and our chests meet at each breath as we come down from the high.

After we both start to settle, I pull back from her. "You okay?" I ask, holding my breath.

She looks at me with a twinkle in her eye and a grin on her lips. "Yeah," she responds, short of breath. "I'm great."

# 27

# Alex

W hat the hell just happened? No, scratch that—What the *fuck* just happened?

I don't know who that girl was who just possessed me for the past ninety minutes, but I like her. Shit, I *am* her. And I have Levi to thank for that.

If I wasn't sold on giving this physical relationship a chance before—I am now. I think my vagina might somehow torture me from the inside out if I don't. Those three—*three*—orgasms were undeniably the best I've ever had in my life. I don't think I knew what sex was until I experienced what just unfolded.

Doing that with him was so unfamiliar, but somehow, he made it feel perfectly natural. It's almost like him taking control made *me* feel more empowered. It's hard to explain, but there's one thing I know for sure. I want it to happen again.

Levi pulls his shirt down over his chiseled abs, and I gawk as he does it. This man's body is like a Greek god's, and I didn't get to worship it nearly enough. Seeing me stare, his face morphs into one of playful amusement.

"You like what you see?" he asks, buttoning his jeans.

I shrug nonchalantly. "Maybe."

Gliding over to me, he grabs hold of my wrist and lifts his shirt. He runs my hand down the length of his torso, allowing my fingers to explore every peak and valley of his frame. "How about now?"

"Hmm," I hum playfully. "I'm not sure." I reach for the hem of his shirt. "Let me look again."

Levi stops my arm in its track and pulls me to him, thigh to thigh, chest to chest—nearly mouth to mouth. "You're making me feel like a piece of meat, Bennett." He kisses me hard, then pulls back quickly. "I kind of like it."

A slow heat travels both north and south. "So do I."

Levi breathes in deeply, then drops my wrist and takes a step backward. Exhaling, he says, "As much as I would love to take you again—and again—we need to go get Cooper."

I nearly pout despite the fact that I'm not sure my body could take much more today anyway. Plus, he's right. It's not that I forgot about Coop—I could never—Levi just did a very good job at taking my mind off of my everyday life.

For once, I got lost in the moment. I wasn't worried about housework that had to be done or lunches that had to be packed. I wasn't dealing with Nick drama or the aftermath. For once, it was about me—me and Levi. We just still haven't talked about how to ensure that this continues.

"We didn't get the chance to um—talk," I say, sliding my sweatshirt back on. Levi steps into his shoes and straightens his hair in the mirror.

"You mean go over ground rules?" he asks coyly to my reflection.

"Basically."

"I know," he says, turning around. "Tomorrow. Let me drive you to the rink? Cooper can go with the boys on the bus. I just have to be there around the same time as the team to game plan. We can talk in the car?"

"Okay." I smile naturally, and I realize it's because I'm genuinely excited for this conversation. *Amazing what an orgasm can do.*

Levi closes the gap between us and slides his hand down the back of my unfastened jeans. Cupping my ass, he says, "We'll figure it all out. I can promise you that." He dives in and nips the skin above my collarbone. "For now, I just need to know you're still in." He trails the tip of his nose up the length of my neck, and the contact sends shivers up my spine.

"Oh, I'm in," I say heatedly.

His lips move against the side of my ear, the teeth from his smile hitting my cheek. "You better be." After a quick peck, he pulls away. "You ready to go?" he asks.

"Yeah," I answer. "Let's go save Erik from Cooper."

Levi laughs. "More like let's save Cooper from Erik."

It seems Levi and I were both wrong. When we went back downstairs and walked to the event room, there was no one in need of saving.

According to Erik, one of the players had the hotel staff hook up a TV and gaming system in one of the corners. He and the boys were standing around Cooper and Drew Anderson, who were sitting in chairs in front of the television.

I learned later that Cooper made a comment about being a better "Anderson" than Anderson is. Apparently, his "Chel game is top notch," and Drew set out to prove him wrong.

I got the full story later, about how we walked in on game three of Coop being proven right. I also got the inside scoop from their dinner and how much fun my son had hanging with the guys. I spared him the details of *my* night, but did share some pictures and write-ups that I got from Sadie in my email.

She's done a great job at capturing the spark in Coop's eyes whenever he's around the team. And the stories and captions really showcase the point of the program. There's talk about how happy Cooper says hockey makes him, and his goal to play professionally in the future. All in all, I'd say the first day was a success... for both of us.

Now, sitting in the passenger seat of the rental in the hotel parking lot, I'm hoping that today goes just as well. Our arrangement shouldn't be that complicated as long as nobody finds out about us and we're both able to keep our feelings in check. I think I have a good grip on the first part. It's the second one that I'm more worried about.

I glance out the tinted windows as Levi walks to me in a navy blue suit. His tie hangs undone around his neck, his face stoic until he gets to me. "Hey, nice car," he says, opening the driver's side door.

"Eh, it's okay. The door opens a little too easily for my taste."

He smiles lazily, then reaches over the center console. Grabbing me by the collar of my hoodie, he pulls me to him. "You're wearing the sweatshirt again," he says.

He kisses me deeply, his fragrance filling my nose as he explores my mouth. As much as I like it, I'm caught a little off guard by the gesture. I make a note in my mind to bring it up when we get to the rules.

"Well, I only had it on for a little while yesterday," I say, ignoring it for now.

"Don't remind me." He narrows his eyes, our faces still close.

His apple smell floods my senses even more and my question falls from my mouth before I can stop it. "Okay, what is that smell?" Levi sits back quickly, his face covered in panic. "No, it's good. It's just so... different."

I've nailed down the mint as the gum he always seems to be chewing when he's on the bench, but it's the sweetness I can't seem to place. Leaning forward, I grab him on either side of his face and bring it to mine. I may otherwise feel embarrassed at the fact that I start sniffing him like a dog, but if this has a chance in hell at working, I need to not be distracted by that freaking aroma.

"There!" I yell, inhaling the scent from his chin. "What is that?"

Levi's eyes almost glisten, and this close to his cheek, I catch a glimpse of the dimple that's hidden beneath his shaped-up scruff. "That's my beard balm."

Trying hard to read his expression, I search for any indication that he's kidding. I knew he kept up with his appearance with his fresh fade and trimmed brows but... beard balm?

After a long pause, I respond. "Isn't that for..."

"Longer beards?"

"I was going to say lumberjacks."

Levi purses his lips and cocks his brow. "Ruthie gave it to me for Christmas last year. It's not really necessary, but it's from her, so I've worn it every day since. It's supposed to smell like—"

"Apple," we both say together.

"Yeah," he says sheepishly. "They're her favorite."

I laugh out loud as I picture a formal Levi with gold watches and tailored jackets smearing green apple beard balm over his cheeks. It would be sweet too if I was letting myself think that way.

Grabbing his face, I turn it back to me and graze my thumb over the balm-coated hairs. "I like it."

Levi turns and nips the palm of my hand. "Good because that's rule number one. No hating the beard balm. I'm pretty sure Ruthie smells my face every time I see her just to make sure I have it on."

We both laugh together as he puts the car into drive. "I'm just kidding." He pulls out of the parking spot before continuing. "So, go ahead, Bennett. What's the *real* rule number one?"

Looking straight ahead, my hands grow slick from a sudden wave of nerves. A million things run through my mind, I just don't know where to start.

"You're overthinking again," Levi says, glancing over.

"How do you do that?" I ask quickly, another question escaping my lips.

"Do what?"

Fidgeting with the strings of my hoodie, I say, "Read me."

He shrugs. "It's the player in me—and the coach, really. I like to think that I can read people well—pick up on little things, judge their next move, plan my reaction. It's actually what got me where I am now with all this. My ex was apparently the only person I've ever read wrong. After that, I figured it was easier to stay away from women entirely."

"Entirely?" I ask under a raised eyebrow.

"Well, maybe not entirely."

I smile back. "My ex was the same way," I admit unexpectedly. "I thought we would be together forever—our own little family once Cooper came along. But I was wrong too. Now he makes a living out of deceiving people, so I guess it worked out for him. Me, not so much."

He grins. "We've got a little baggage between us, huh?"

"I guess so," I laugh.

Levi's face grows serious. "For what it's worth, I think you've done a pretty great job all on your own."

My cheeks heat. "Okay, rule number one."

"What?" he asks, his brow creased.

"That's the real rule number one. If we're going to do this, you can't be saying things like that."

He squints at me, then asks, "Like what? The truth?"

I swallow the emotions those last two words cause. "Compliments like that. And no greeting-kisses... I'm not your girlfriend. And I don't want your charm."

He huffs out a laugh. "Okay, Bennett, I'll try my best."

I roll my eyes. "This needs to be strictly... physical."

Levi sucks his teeth but eventually smiles back at me. "I can do physical."

"Yeah, I figured that."

He tilts his head and winks. *This guy knows exactly what he's doing.*

"Yes, keep doing things like that instead. Much better."

Narrowing his eyes, he pauses momentarily before saying, "You know, don't take this the wrong way, but I didn't take you for a 'sex-only' kind of girl."

A low hum of anxiety creeps up from my belly, but I swallow the familiar feeling back down. "I'm trying something new."

"Happy to be your guinea pig," he says, lightening the mood again. He reaches over and squeezes my thigh. His pinky grazes the sensitive skin at the top, and I inhale quickly.

"No one can know," I say suddenly. "That's rule number two."

He nods slowly. "I agree.".

"I don't want Cooper to feel weird about the whole thing with being around you all the time."

Levi replies as he pulls into the arena. "You don't have to explain. Honestly, it'll save me from having to have a difficult conversation with Sadie and the board. At least until these few weeks are over."

*At least?* Does Levi think this may go past the time he's working with Cooper? I guess I never really considered it. The Flames organization not finding out about us is kind of Levi's thing. The reasons that I want to keep this hidden away don't really have an expiration date. We could technically keep this up even after Spark the Flame, but Levi will still be Levi, and I will still be that single mom who was hurt by someone like him.

Levi's not Nick, I know that. But the fact that I think about my ex when he does something I don't like and compare him to Nick when he does something I do... is exhausting. I just don't think I could ever move past it.

Besides, Cooper will still be his biggest fan. I would hate for him to think he got this gig because me and the coach had something going on. Cooper already has one parent he can't trust. I don't even want him thinking I could possibly be the same.

"So, what else?" Levi asks as he pulls into a parking spot toward the back of the building. I contemplate skipping over this one, but now it's gnawing at me. This has to end somewhere.

"Rule number three—this stops at the end of all this. When Cooper's done here, so are we."

Levi looks almost shocked as he puts the car into park. Holding his chin in the crook of his hand, he rubs his beard with his first few fingers. He takes his time inhaling a long, slow breath, then exhaling it the same way.

Out of nowhere, he slides the driver's side seat back and reaches over to me. Unbuckling my seat belt, he hoists his hands under my arms and yanks me out of my seat so I'm half on top of his legs. Crawling the rest of the way over, I find myself straddling his lap. Levi braces me on either thigh and says, "You scared you're gonna fall for me, Bennett?"

Hearing my name while seated on top of him growing bigger between us, makes it hard to think, let alone respond. He slides his hands up the sides of my jeans, and I feel every inch of his movement on the material like he's branding the skin beneath it. Tucking his thumbs into the waistband, he somehow pulls me even further down onto him.

My mind and body fight for control. I lean half an inch closer to him, but I think about how, on paper, I know this is going nowhere—how am I supposed to trust someone like my ex again?

*Another half inch.*

But when I'm with Levi, there's these glimmers of a guy that's nothing like Nick.

*Another.*

It's easy to focus on the rest of it for now, but will it be like that forever?

*Closer.*

Not to mention the mind-blowing sex that will keep pulling me in.

*Closer.*

Will I fall for him eventually? I don't know.

*Closer.*

Will I grow addicted at some point? That feels more realistic.

Before I have a chance to verbalize my thoughts, my mouth lands on his. I guess my body wins this war.

But that *was* the whole point of this in the first place.

# 28

# Levi

Alex and I are really doing this. We're basically fuck buddies, but after this past weekend, I'll take whatever parts of her she's willing to give me. At least until I can convince her to give me more.

There are two major ground rules—keep it physical and keep it secret. There is also a third rule that may or may not be in play. Alex's suggestion to end this when Cooper's time with Spark the Flame is finished wasn't necessarily settled. She mentioned it, sure, but at the first tease of her falling for me, she had nothing to say. It didn't bother me much—she used her mouth in other ways—but I am curious to know what her real reaction to that would have been.

The other two requirements are easier to work with. I may have to check myself sometimes, but keeping things physical with Alex is no fucking chore. Rule number two is even easier. I've never been one to over share parts of my life anyway, and who I'm sleeping with has definitely been under lock and key. Not that I'm afraid of people finding out about her for the reasons I may have been with the others, but I would like to keep from stirring up trouble at work.

My biggest problem now is breaking down Alex's walls. I'm no stranger to those either, but it's going to make changing that potential third rule a little harder.

Some of the reasons that she's guarded, I can't control. I can ease her mind and try my best to work around them, but I'm a hockey coach. It's who I am, and it's who I plan to be for as long as they'll have me. There are some, though, that I do have control over. I can make sure she never doubts that she can trust me, and I can keep our little secret. I can also show her that I'm nothing like her selfish piece of shit ex. I care about my job, of course, but I've never been one to put that above someone else's feelings.

Alex has told me a little about Nick the Dick. I know their back story and how he all but abandoned her and their son when he was born. I also know he's flighty, unreliable, and a shitty example for Cooper of how a man should behave. Which is why I plan to work in as many things as I can, in the time that I have, to right someone else's wrong. Hockey is a sport, and there's plenty to learn about the game, but it also lends itself to learning so many lessons found in life.

"Alright, buddy," I say to Cooper on the bench. It's one of our mid-week practices, and Coop happened to have the day off from school for a teacher in-service. Alex is sitting behind us in the stands, her headphones in and her laptop perched on her thighs, working from here.

"The next thing we're going to do is practice backchecking. Mistakes happen all the time during games, but it's more about how you respond to those mistakes. It's everyone's job to help the team recover. You're going to set the boys up in the corners, and Drew's line will start them off. Every time you blow the whistle, a new group will go and try to recover the puck from the group before."

Coop nods in understanding, his whistle in hand. "Got it," he says, skating to the center.

While Cooper leads the team in a drill the captains could run in their sleep, I take advantage of my free time to skate back to the bench. It'll give me a second to catch up with Bennett, and it will give Sadie and her photographer, who are lurking around the ice, a chance to take some pictures with just Coop and the guys.

When I reach the bench, I part my lips to call to Alex but stop when I realize that she probably won't hear me with her headphones in. It may also look a little suspicious to the team and her son if I'm screaming to the spotlight player's mom through the boards.

Instead, I tap on the glass discreetly. When she doesn't even flinch, I grab an extra stick from the pile and use it to do the same.

Finally, she looks up from her screen and smiles that hidden smile she's perfected over our past few interactions. It's one that says, "I'm happy to see you, but I'm pretending that you're just another face in the crowd."

Sliding my phone from my pocket, I hold it in front of my stomach with my back to the ice and wiggle it back and forth. Taking the hint, she reaches for hers in the bag next to her.

> You look busy.

Without looking up, she replies.

Bennett
> I am busy.

I snicker to myself. *The mouth on this one.*

> You also look like a snack.

Dragging her eyes to me, she arches her brow. Without looking down, she texts back.

Bennett
> Are you hungry?

My head snaps sideways. Little Miss Blogger is always so cocky behind her screen.

The image of Alex on her knees for me flashes through my mind. Unfortunately, it's the last image I've had of her in that capacity since our trip. After the game, the boys and I flew right back home, and since we're not exactly testing these waters in public yet, I couldn't meet up with her afterwards on a whim.

It's the main reason they're here today. I've been struggling without at least seeing her face but also dying without her touch. It's hard enough that I still don't know everything about her—what she tastes like or feels like from behind—but being completely deprived from everything is fucking fatal. Of course, it's great having Cooper here—for the program and the team—but I'm not mad about the chaperone he brought with him.

Considering all of this, I answer with heat in my body and truth in my words.

> Starved.

Bennett licks her lips. The movement is possibly unrelated, but it drives me wild either way. She shifts in her seat, and her expression tells me she's eager for me too. I almost chicken out. This is not at all setting a good example for Cooper, which is supposed to be my new priority. It could also be obvious as hell to everyone around us, but I want her more than I seem to care about that.

> Go to my office.

I'm surprised at how easily I hit the send button. For someone who loves to be in control, there are a lot of other factors at play here that could make this all go terribly wrong. But this is what Alex does to me. I went from only allowing women to come to my apartment to fuck in my space, to hooking up in public bathrooms and sneaking off the ice.

Bennett

Like after practice?

Like now.

*Come on, Alex.* You know what you're doing.
I go through all of the reasons she's going to object. She's busy. They'll notice. What if Cooper gets suspicious? I prepare for them all.

Bennett

Okay.

*But not for that.*
I haven't been this excited in a long time, and it doesn't even have to do with the quickie I'm hoping we can have in my office—It's her.

Tapping my phone against the palm of my hand, I bring my gaze back to Bennett's without dulling my smile. Glancing behind me, I see the boys, Cooper, and my two assistants engaged in the drill. Turning back to her, I nod toward the exit telling her to move.

Thankfully, Sadie showed Alex how to get to my office from the stands and vice versa through the concourse. Of course, the precaution was more for if Cooper needed something, but in this exact moment, I'm more grateful than ever for her attention to detail.

Knowing it will take her twice as long as me to get back to my office, I head back onto the ice to check on the guys.

I skate around, watching them run through the drill almost a full time before looking at my watch. After the longest five minutes of my life, I tap Erik on the arm. "Yo, I'll be back." I wiggle my phone in front of me. "I've got to make a phone call."

Erik tips his head up once in understanding, preoccupied with watching the guys, and I take that as my cue to fucking run.

I skate back to the bench and nearly trip as I step off of it and into the tunnel. I practically sprint toward my office, still in my skates. Reaching the door, I take one deep breath because of the running I just did and a second one to ease my adrenaline. Pushing it open, I find Alex sitting on the edge of my desk looking like the goddamn goddess she is.

"Bennett," I say, my dick responding to her name like she owns it already.

"Montgomery."

I move to her and kiss her sloppily. "We don't have much time." I plant kisses down her neck, rubbing the tops of her thighs over her jeans.

"I know." She looks at me wickedly, then reaches for my waistband. Pulling me by the fabric of my warmup pants, she watches them stretch open and sticks her hand inside.

"Oh, shit," I say, not expecting her to dive right in. She grips me tightly, and if I wasn't ready before from just the idea of having her again, I am now.

I slide my fingers to the button on her pants and flick them open. Halfway through pulling on her zipper, she stops me.

"What?" I ask, already short of breath. I look at her as she nibbles her bottom lip.

"I want to repay you."

"No, that's not—"

"Levi," she interrupts as she twists my hips so now I'm at the desk. "I want to."

My jaw clenches, and I twitch in between us. "And I thought I was the hungry one."

"Tell me what to do," she says.

So, I was right. She likes it when I take control. The realization makes me want her more. Right fucking now.

"On your knees, Alex."

I go to speak again before she does it—to tell her that just because I take the lead doesn't mean she has to oblige—but she falls like an angel right in front of me, dragging my pants down with her.

Taking me in her hand first, she rolls her tongue around just the tip, teasing me. I let my head fall back, closing my eyes and running my fingers through her hair. Unexpectedly, Alex takes all of me to the back of her throat. I groan, bringing my gaze back to her, her gold spot glistening from the way her eyes water. If I thought watching her be fulfilled was intoxicating, seeing her pleasure me is completely addictive.

She runs her mouth up and down my shaft before I decide I need more. "Touch yourself," I say as she pulls back, sucking hard. She looks at me, unsure, her wet lips parted. "Show me, Alex. Show me what you did to yourself when you were alone this week and thinking of me." It's a gamble to be so bold in this moment—to assume that she got herself off with just me in mind. But if she has felt even half of what I have since I've met her, I like my odds.

Proving me right, Alex drops her free hand down and pushes it into the opening in her jeans, making it a double win for me. "That's it," I growl as I guide myself back into her mouth.

Taking all of me again, she starts to play with herself at the same time. Watching her do both is almost more than I can take. If I thought I had good sex before, I was wrong—and she and I are just getting started.

As if it was even possible, I grow harder in her mouth, filling beneath her touch. Alex's hand moves as she twirls her tongue back up the length of me. Pausing toward the top, she separates her lips with me still half inside and pants. *She's close.*

The warmth of her breath inches me closer and closer with each exhale. "Goddamn, Alex."

Suddenly unbalanced on my skates, I brace one palm on the desk behind me. Reaching down with my other, and thanking God for my wingspan, I slip my hand under the V of her sweater and stroke her swollen nipple. She hums around me as she takes me again and the tremor from the sound is almost more than I can take. I squeeze her peak between my knuckles, and the next noise that escapes from her mouth around me, finishes me off.

"Fuck," I grunt through gritted teeth. The way her lower half twitches beneath her as I buck my hips into her quickly, tells me she's coming with me. *And that thought alone is everything.*

When we've both fully unraveled, and Alex stands, I wipe her mouth with the pad of my thumb.

"You okay?" I ask, realizing she's seemingly quiet.

She grins devilishly. "Great," she says as she rolls her eyes.

"What?" I ask, completely confused.

"Now even when I touch myself *not* thinking of you... I'll think of you."

The laugh that falls from my lips, despite what just happened here, is almost as unexpected as what she said. *Another surprise.*

"Good," I say, grabbing her ass and pulling her body back to mine. "Maybe that was my plan all along."

"Defense, Roo! Get back!" Liam yells, standing in front of his tailgate chair. He shoves another nervous energy orange slice into his mouth from the snack bowl by his feet.

"Those are for the kids, you know," I say, watching him gnaw at the rind.

He throws the peel into the garbage can behind him and pulls another from the collection. "There's like a hundred of 'em. They're fine."

I chuckle, shaking my head. "You nervous there, soccer dad?"

"It's a tied youth community game, little brother," he says, looking over at me side-eyed. "Of course I'm nervous."

Resting my wrists on the arms of my chair, I full belly laugh. "I can tell."

"You'll see one day, man. Just wait until you have a mini-you in the rink."

I follow Ruthie as she darts across the field. "Whatever you say."

"Speaking of minis on the ice, how's that going with the Junior Rocket?"

Sitting up straighter, I play it cool. "Yeah, it's good. We have another few weeks, and then he'll come to the Spark the Flame gala to finish everything off."

"Mhmm and his mom?" he asks, taming a smirk.

"Fine," I answer, clearing my throat. "She's fine."

Liam pauses the chewing of his latest orange slice and turns toward me. "You totally slept with her, didn't you?"

"What? No," I argue defensively.

He sucks his teeth. "Sure."

"I didn't."

"Liar."

"I'm not!"

The moms sitting on either side of us snap their heads in our direction. Liam and I both flash them a charming smile and pretend to go back to watching the game. It seems like Liam may have finally let it go when I see him out of the corner of my eye.

Leaning into me sideways without taking his gaze off the field, he whispers, "Know how I know you're lying?" I meet his question with silence. "You're causing a scene at a youth community soccer game."

I push to stand, ready to argue, when I see the moms turn toward us again with judgment in their expressions. "Fine," I grunt through gritted teeth, mostly because these ladies scare me. "We slept together."

"Bingo," Liam says. I wave at the women who are still staring at us and turn back just in time for my brother's next question. "So, was this just a one time thing?"

Shoving my hands into my pockets, I stare straight ahead and say nothing.

"No," he says with a judgmental tone.

I look at him sideways.

"No," he repeats.

"Holy shit, just say what you want to say, Liam."

"You didn't sleep with her. You're *sleeping* with her." My silence answers for me. "Are you at least getting to know her too, like we talked about?"

"I'm working on it," I say casually. Liam scoffs. "I am! But it's been a long fucking time, and she's putting up a fight. Apparently I'm not her... type," I explain.

"Wow," Liam drags out, his eyes back on Ruthie. "Never thought I'd see the day where *the* Levi Montgomery wasn't someone's type."

"Well, it's here."

"Huh." Liam puts his hands on his hips. "So, what's the plan then?"

"I just told you."

"*Get* it in until she *lets* you in? That's your big plan?"

I turn to him, irritated by the situation and the fact that he's only making it worse. "She just wants to keep things physical. I'll stick with that while I work on changing her mind."

Before he can respond, Ruthie comes over to grab her water bottle at a time-out. Looking over her, I mouth *"not a word"* to Liam.

"What are you guys talking about?" she asks through gulps.

I peer at my brother with my eyebrows high, then turn to Ruthie. "Nothing, kiddo. Just keep your head in the game."

Liam bends down to her level. "That's right. Listen to your uncle and go try your best."

Ruthie grabs her water and an orange slice and kisses us both on the cheeks. "You guys are weird," she says before running back to her team.

"Oh, so we're keeping it a secret too?"

*That's right.* Just me and Alex... and my obnoxious big brother. "Yes we are."

"Whatever," he says, dropping his hand on my shoulder. "I won't pretend that I get it. I'm just happy you're finally feeling something." He tightens his grip, then pats my back. "I'm proud of you, little bro."

I smile awkwardly, but if I'm honest, I'm sort of proud of *myself*. I feel a little like an idiot pining after a girl that pretends she can't stand me, but at least I'm putting myself out there. I'm constantly telling my guys to play fearlessly and to leave it all on the ice—you miss one hundred percent of the shots you don't take—but I wasn't applying those things to my own life outside of the rink. Now I am.

"Thanks. I guess we'll see how it goes."

Liam grabs two orange slices and hands one to me. "Levi Montgomery—falling for a girl instead of just falling into her." He shakes his head and sinks his teeth in. Ripping the wedge from the peel, he laughs through his chewing. "Who would have thought?"

# 29

# Alex

"No. No. No." Brooke huffs out a breath and pulls out yet another piece of clothing from my closet. "Hmm... no." She tosses the floral print top onto the bed, adding it to the pile of rejects.

"Why should what I wear even matter?" I ask, sitting on the mattress as my clothes stack up next to me. "It's just breakfast with the coaching staff. The guy has already seen me naked," I mumble.

"Exactly. We have to make sure he keeps that shit up—pun intended." I snort out a laugh while rolling my eyes. "Speaking of, catch me up."

"Well, I told you about the first situation," I say, trying to remember where I left off with Brooke.

"You mean how he finger-banged you in the hotel bathroom? Uh, yeah. I've already pitched it to all of my favorite porn sites."

Slapping her playfully, I continue. "Then there was his hotel room."

"I still can't believe you let him pop your cherry. I am..." She wipes away an invisible tear. "So proud."

"I have a child, Brooke."

"Yeah, but he's practically a teenager. I'm pretty sure that thing seals back up eventually."

Staring at her, a puzzled look on my face, I process that sentence. "That is absolutely not how that works."

"You know what I mean. This is so exciting! Okay, what else?"

Playing with the sleeve of one of the discarded tops, I say, "We sort of hooked up in his office the other day when I took Cooper to their practice."

"You what?" she yells.

Leaning over, I lay my palm across her mouth. "Shh! Coop is right downstairs."

"Oh, please. That kid has his video game up so loud he couldn't hear me if I was standing behind him. Watch this. Cooper!" she yells. After waiting briefly, she does it again. "Coop!" Crickets. "See. Please continue."

"That was it."

"What was it? Details, lady. Was it like on the desk, over the desk... *under* the desk? I just need this dream to become a reality."

Regretting having ever told Brooke about that, I say, "We, uh—we didn't have sex."

"But you just said..." Her face lights up, and she squeals while clapping her hands in front of her face. "Oh my God... did you have Coach McHottie's thing in your *mouth?*"

"That's it. You can go," I say, standing and walking over to my closet.

Brooke shifts so she's facing me. "Okay, I'll stop obsessing over the fact that you blew him in his office, but Alex... You blew him in his office! Who is this naughty girl, and where has she been hiding?"

She rifles through sweater after sweater as I consider her question. "I don't know," I finally say. "I just feel comfortable with him I guess."

"Aw, I love that, Al. When's the last time that happened?"

"What?"

"You letting someone in."

"I let you in," I say.

She laughs. "Bitch, I clawed my way through, and even then you resisted."

She's right. We met seven years ago, and nothing about our meet-cute was easy. Cooper had a half-day from school for some holiday or another, but I still had to put in a full day online. To occupy him, I thought it was a good idea to let him get lunch out at a restaurant, which was a treat for us back then. We sat at a booth closest to the servers' station, but apparently we weren't the only ones with this idea because the floor was flooded with kids and their parents.

Brooke and one other waitress were the only two working, and we were seated in her section. When she came over to us to take our drink orders, I was ten minutes out from my column deadline, and Coop was having a meltdown because he was bored.

*"Hey, little man,"* Brooke *said to him, crouching down so she was at his level.* *"Tough day?"*

*"I'm sorry,"* I said. *"I know you guys are busy. I'll try to keep him controlled over here."*

Brooke *stood back up and smiled at me.* *"It's fine, seriously. Like seventy-five percent of the customers waiting are kids who got chicken fingers. They take about five minutes to fry, and everyone's orders are already in."*

*"Oh, okay,"* I said shyly. *"I just have to have this done in the next couple of minutes, but once it's sent to my boss, and I can give him the attention he's looking for, he'll be okay."*

Brooke *paused a moment then looked at Cooper.* *"I'm Brooke. What's your name?"*

*"Coopah,"* he said, the way kids his age always mess up the "R" sound.

*"Hi, Cooper. I'm Brooke. How about we give Mommy a minute to finish her work, and we go find some crayons at the hostess stand? Does that sound okay?"* She asked that last question looking at me.

*"Oh, you really don't have to do that."*

*"I know,"* is all she said. I nodded gently and watched as Cooper so willingly placed his hand in hers.

*They came back five minutes later. My writing had been sent, and I had a glorious minute to spare just to sit by myself.*

*"Mommy, look! Bwooke gave me candy!"*

*"I hope that's okay. I swear he does have crayons and paper there too."*

*"That's fine. Thank you for that, seriously."*

*"No problem. It was a good break for me honestly."* She leaned down to my son. *"From all of these stinky grown-ups, right?"* Cooper put his hand to his mouth and giggled. *"Oh, and apparently I also met my new best friend... Owex."*

*Now it was my turn to giggle. "Oh, is that right?"*

*"Yep. Cooper told me himself." She looked at him, but he was too busy unwrapping the lollipop he had in his hand. "He did, I swear."*

*Despite knowing that at five-years-old, Cooper was just making small talk, I was embarrassed at the idea that my kid felt the need to find a friend for me. When I didn't respond to what Brooke was saying, she filled the silence between us. "Alright, well, I'll come back to check on you guys. I'll see you soon, Cooper. You too, bestie."*

*She came back over several times that day, always with something for Cooper and always calling me "Ow" like the way Cooper said the first half of my name.*

*A couple of days later, I returned to the restaurant while he was in school and thanked her for being so sweet to us. That day, she talked, and eventually, I started talking back. We've just been yapping ever since.*

"Thanks for being so annoying," I say, squeezing Brooke's wrist.

"Then or now?"

"Both but let's not get ahead of ourselves. That's not what's happening here with him. I'm comfortable sexually. That's it."

Brooke turns away, but not before I catch a slight roll to her eyes. "I know, I know. Strictly physical."

"Exactly."

"Well, I'm on board if you weren't sure. You always are, but just be careful, okay?"

I turn my eyes up. "Yes, Mom. Don't worry, we used protection."

"Good," she says, a slight drop in her expression. She reaches over and squeezes my arm, grabbing my full attention. "But that's not what I meant."

I part my lips to respond, but she continues before I have a chance to speak. "Okay, now I'm going to go say bye to your kid and get out of here."

Before I can stop her, she's halfway out the door. I follow her out of my room and down the stairs to where Cooper is still sitting playing his game. I pull one headphone away from his ear. "Hey, say bye to Aunt Brooke."

"Bye," he says, still hitting buttons on his controller. I pull it from his hands, and he snaps to attention.

"Mom!"

"Cooper. Say goodbye."

He huffs out a breath but does as he's told. Sliding his arms around Brooke's waist, he says, "Bye, Aunt Brooke."

"See ya later, little man, and hey—sleepover soon. The newest Batman movie was just added to On Demand." She leans into him and whispers. "PG-13."

"Sweet!" he says. "I'm in."

Brooke turns to me and winks, then walks toward the door. "Love you guys! See you later!"

"Love you!" we respond simultaneously.

Once she's out the door, I look back to Cooper. "We're leaving in fifteen minutes for breakfast."

"Oh, yeah!" He throws his headset on the couch and runs to his room. *Now he's done playing the damn game.*

Once I'm back upstairs, I finally pick out an outfit. Slipping it on, my mind wanders to what Brooke said before.

*"You always are, but just be careful, okay?"*

She's right. I am always careful, and where has that gotten me?

Running my fingers through my hair, I give myself one more once over in the mirror. I study my mock turtleneck sweater hanging over black leggings and my hair cascading down one shoulder, but for a second, it's not my reflection staring back at me. It's the girl I was twelve years ago with a messy life and a broken heart.

Much like the current me, she's nervous about the changes that are happening. She's a little anxious and a little insecure, and the fear of the unknown sort of scares the shit out of her. We're still the same in a lot of ways, her and I. Looking at her though, I realize something. I don't want to be that way anymore.

Of course, things will always cause me concern, especially when it comes to Cooper. That's just what being a mom is all about. But picturing myself before he was born, I see the same person I am today. Nick did a number on me, that's for sure, but I am so done with feeling stuck in that place. His actions have caused me to worry about all relationships, but especially the one with myself.

Staring at the younger Alex, I hate that we're still so alike. We're both afraid to take risks—in jobs, in love. It's the reason I'm still single and working for a lifestyle blog instead of writing about things that actually matter. So much of the way we see ourselves is through Nick-colored glasses, and we deserve better. *She* deserved better.

*I* deserve better.

Taking a deep breath, I look myself in the eye. "We're done being careful," I say aloud.

# 30

# Levi

Waiting for Alex at the restaurant is like waiting for the referee to drop the puck at game time. All kinds of emotions rush through me—nerves, anxiety, excitement, anticipation—and I even put my lucky socks on that I got from Ruthie for my birthday.

I just want today to go well. Of course, I can't wait to see her and maybe touch her again if I'm lucky. But mostly I want to use this time to get her more on board. Talking to Liam about this made me realize how good it feels to be changing. It's fucking wild—and terrifying and completely unnatural—but it's happening. And that's because of her.

I understand that this meal is just the usual coaches' breakfast we have occasionally when we're off, but it's the first time that Alex and I will be out together with other people. I'm not sure eating with Erik, Gavin, and Cooper counts as mingling socially, but I'm hoping that it's a good way to ease into actually being seen together.

The bell on the diner door chimes, and I look up way too quickly, not even pretending to be interested in Gavin's new puppies' eating schedule. Coop walks in first, the hood of his new Flames sweatshirt up over his hat. An arm reaches through the door behind him, yanking the material from his head, exposing his Junior Rockets cap underneath.

Alex steps through the doorway, her nose pink from the cool air outside, and I have a strong urge to back her into a corner and ask her why she's not wearing a jacket. I don't know why it feels so normal to want to take care of her—or to make sure that she's taking care of herself—but I've never been so compelled to scold someone for not checking the weather.

Cooper searches the room as Alex speaks with the hostess and at the same time, the employee and Coop point in our direction. As they weave through the tables, Bennett's full body comes into view, and I audibly groan—quietly, thank God. *Fucking leggings.*

As if it wasn't already going to be hard enough to keep my hands to myself sitting next to her, she had to go and wear one of the most tempting articles of clothing.

The two of them get to our table and the three of us stand.

"Hey," I say, looking first at Alex, my gaze eventually landing on Cooper.

"Good to see you guys," Erik says.

Gavin holds his hand out to Coop. "What's up, bud?" He shakes it before Gavin moves on to Alex. "Nice to see you again."

"Likewise," she says, taking his hand in hers. "Hi, everyone." Her eyes meet Erik's, then land on me as she takes the seat beside my chair, Cooper sitting on my other side.

I may be new at this, but I'm not dumb. There was no way I was risking not sitting next to her. I made sure to save both seats on either side of mine at the diner's round table, thankful they're all so close together. *Possible crisis averted.*

"Thanks for coming," I say, trying my best not to openly stare at her mouth. "We do this every once in a while, so I thought it would be nice for Cooper to see this side of things."

"Thanks for having us."

She glances down at the paper menu in front of her and nonchalantly runs her tongue across her bottom lip. No one else, including her, seems to notice, but my dick definitely does. *Al-fucking-ready.*

Erik starts talking about how we're not all business all the time and how the three of us actually do hangout outside of the team quite a bit. Gavin joins in, and Coop starts asking questions about how long we've known each other and what we typically order, when Alex throws her hair over her shoulder, her coconut scent makes me hungry for more than just breakfast.

Without even thinking, I reach under the table and put my hand on her knee. Her eyes freeze on the menu.

"Stuck on what type of juice to order?" I ask casually as I follow her gaze to the beverage section.

Her throat moves up and down before a polite smile spreads across her face. "I think I'll just get a coffee."

I nod, amused at how calm she's being, but then she raises her head, her warm palm settling on the inside of my thigh. "Extra cream."

My hand freezes, and I shift my body so she's recklessly close to where I'd actually like her. At the same time, Erik speaks, reminding me that's not a good idea.

"Isn't that right, Monte?" he asks, his eyebrows raised expectantly.

Alex tiptoes her fingers into dangerous territory. She looks at me the same way Erik does despite more than likely having no fucking clue what he's talking about either. "What's that?"

"The puppies," Gavin chimes in. "You won't let us talk Liam into getting one for Ruthie."

Before I can answer, Cooper speaks up. "Wait a second. Liam Montgomery is your brother?"

Erik and Gavin both laugh. I throw a smile his way but am borderline uncomfortable making direct eye contact considering the things I'm picturing doing to his mom right now.

"Crazy right?" Erik says. "A Flames' coach and Gators' all-star. Talk about good genes."

Alex quits her shenanigans long enough to tilt her head in my direction. "Your brother plays baseball?"

Having some breathing room now that her touch has fallen further down my leg, I'm able to string more than two words together. "Yeah, he plays shortstop for Golden City. He's Ruthie's dad."

Her expression changes to something I could only explain as surprised. Is she impressed by my brother or by my ability not to name drop the star of our city's baseball team as my closest relative?

"He's a legend, Mom."

Her face relaxes, but she narrows her eyes. "I had no idea."

"So, anyway," Erik says. "I thought Ruthie would love it, but Monte seems to think..."

His voice trails off as I get lost in Bennett's gaze. Her stare grows more heated as she looks through me. Suddenly, her hand is back on my leg, her thumb swirling slow circles near my growing hard-on.

I reach higher on her lap, and she mimics my movement. At this point, we're playing a game of chicken where one of us winning may actually mean losing. Not wanting to bring any attention toward the two of us, I initiate my next play. If there is one thing I learned about controlling a situation, it's to always have a game plan.

"Do you know what you want?" I ask Alex, fully aware of the double entendre.

She almost doesn't respond, but when the other two coaches and her son look at her curiously, she searches for an answer.

"Um, I think I'll have a veggie omelet."

"Perfect," I say, pulling my hand out from under the table. "You guys know my order. We'll be right back. Alex?" I nod toward the door, and she looks right to Cooper who is busy scanning the pancake toppings.

Erik winks in my direction, and Gavin takes a sip of his coffee. I stand from my seat, quickly turning from the table and grateful that I went with my black joggers instead of grey. I glance back at Alex who finally stands and follows behind me.

Bobbing between tables, I reach the exit and head straight through it, only slowing down to listen to the door close behind her. I walk around to the back of the building and stop at my car.

My senses heighten as the sound of gravel crunching underneath Bennett's shoes amplifies as she approaches. When she must be just a foot or two behind me, it stops altogether.

I turn, taking in the cars around us. There are a few sprinkled back here, but most of them sit in the lot up front, something I knew when I decided to park around back. I'm not saying I assumed this would happen, but I sure as hell prepared for the possibility.

That's why I brought the Spark the Flame t-shirts for Cooper's team today and purposely left them in my SVU. That's also why I made a point of telling Erik and Gavin that, sometime during breakfast, I was going to get Alex to leave the table so I could put them in her car without Cooper seeing—as a surprise to him and his team of course.

I knew it wouldn't take me long to initiate contact, seeing how I have been restless without her these past few days, but I didn't expect to be out here before the waitress even took our orders. The second her hand grazed my leg though, that was it. There was no way I was making it through breakfast like this.

"I have shirts for Cooper's team I wanted to give you," I say, shoving my hands into my sweatpants' pockets. Dare I say there's a flash of disappointment in Alex's expression.

"Oh," she says, crossing her arms over her chest. "Great. My car's up front, but we can put them in on our way back inside."

"Sounds good." I nonchalantly walk to the door behind the driver's side of my SUV and pull it open so it stands between me and the inside of the back seat. Alex walks in front of me, and looks into the car.

"So, where are the shirts?" she asks, her brow slightly furrowed in that adorable crease. She leans further inside, searching for the box, putting her lycra-covered ass in perfect sight.

"They're in the trunk." She stands back up, looking at me questioningly. "Get in the car, Bennett."

As if a switch was flipped, Alex's face relaxes, her caramel eyes darkening to more of a chocolate. I round the door and stand in front of her, waiting for her to make her move. When it clicks that I'm serious, she drops one foot into the car. Holding onto the headrest in front of her, she sits down and brings the other leg inside.

"Keep going," I say, stepping in too. She scootches across the black leather seat until there's room for me to join her. I sit behind the driver's side and close the door behind me, thanking God that I sprang for the tinted windows and expanded backseat.

I reach over and grab her legs, swinging her so they're now flat against the bench. "Leggings? Really?" I ask, sliding my palm up her calf. Leaning closer to her mouth, I add, "You knew exactly what you were doing."

"I wanted to be comfortable," she says flippantly.

I drag my teeth over my bottom lip as I flood my senses with coconut. "Oh, you will be—with them wrapped around your ankles. Pull them down."

An almost excited grin frosts her mouth as she moves her hands to the elastic around her hips. She shimmies them down, and it takes all but two seconds for me to see there's nothing underneath. Sitting back, taking in the view completely, I run my hand down my face and smile.

"What?" she asks conscientiously.

I snicker as I lean down to her. "Good. Fucking. Girl."

Immediately, I lunge for her, not even bothering to start slow. We don't have time, and I don't have patience—not with this piece of art on display. I use my tongue to lap up the length of her, then focus on the bundle of nerves at the top. Alex's hands fall into my hair as she arches her back beneath me.

Making room to dive in deeper, I slide one shoe off and rip the legging from around her ankle. Bending that leg, I lift it so her knee rests closer to her hip. Adjusting my long body, I straddle the leg that still lies flat against the seat.

"Holy shit, Levi," she cries out.

In this position, I have more space to continue devouring her while slipping a finger inside. Alex points her toes, the shift of her leg underneath me causing some much needed friction to my throbbing cock that's pinned against it. I groan at the contact and curl my finger inside her, all the while still sucking her clit. The shudder from my mouth only adds stimulation, and Alex's hips buck underneath me. She whimpers when I pull out of her and is rewarded with two fingers slipped back inside.

"Oh my God," she moans. Using my other hand, I reach under her sweater and bra and rub her nipple between my fingers. "Yes, right there."

I slow my movement and steady my fingers, not enough to torture her, but enough to delay the inevitable. "Are you on the pill?" I ask, pausing briefly.

"What?" she responds quickly.

In her defense, now is not the ideal time to bring this up, but I want to feel her with nothing between us, and I won't just do that on a whim.

I also don't want to always have to worry when things like this come up spur of the moment.

"The pill," I say again, kissing the insides of her thighs. She shifts her ass underneath me, begging for me to come back to her.

"Yes," she says breathlessly. "Yes. I have been since Cooper was born."

"And clean?"

She sits up on her elbows. "Seriously?"

"I am." I deadpan. "Got tested last week."

"I haven't been tested since my last annual," she says. My hope deflates until she continues. "But I haven't been with anyone since then. I'm clean."

My body rejoices from her response. Surprisingly, my mind does too. Something about knowing Alex has been only mine for much longer than I expected makes this even better. I do nothing to hide the growl that crawls out of my throat as I lean back down. Resuming my movements, she rocks back into me, the pause seemingly making this better. When her legs begin tensing around me, I slide my hand from her shirt—and her dripping, wet pussy—and sit back on my knees.

Alex sits forward again and snaps her head up. She's ready to object, but before she can, I'm halfway inside her. *Thank God for drawstrings.*

"We're coming together, baby," I say, inching in further. "I need you to relax." She leans back on her forearms and lets her head lull back as I bury myself deep inside her. "Fuck, Bennett."

At the sound of her name, she tightens around me. "You feel so good, baby," I say, my voice growing husky. "But we have to be quick." I add this on so she knows why I'm rushing, but I know damn well I wouldn't last long regardless.

She nods her head in understanding. "Please," she exhales.

With that, I pound into her, her body sliding closer and closer to the door, thanks to the slippery leather beneath us. She braces herself against the headrest of the passenger seat and the back of the bench. We rock together in one fluid movement, both of our pleasures building simultaneously.

"Levi," she cries. "I'm, I'm..."

Her walls clench around me, her pressure the final pull that I need. I slam into her one last time as I explode inside her, the high continuing until the moment I reluctantly pull out.

Bennett sits up, her face flushed and body beautiful. She reaches for my lip and brushes herself from the hairs of my chin. When she goes to pull back, I grab her wrist in my hand and put her thumb in my mouth, sucking it clean. Her eyes grow hooded, and if I had time, we'd go again—right here, right now.

"We should probably get back," I say instead.

She slides on her leggings as I tuck myself back into my pants. While she finishes up, I slip out of the car and head to the truck. I pop it open and take out the shirts I really did bring for Cooper and his team. Closing it again, my eyes fall to my reflection on the rear window. My hair is tousled, and my cheeks are red, but that's not what I notice most.

What I see instead is that for once, after sex, I don't appear almost miserable. Like what we did was just something that happened on autopilot. I look... happy. Like I have that postcoital glow that you're supposed to have after you sleep with someone. Alex comes out from the car and when I look at her, she has it too.

Maybe that doesn't mean anything, or at least not to her, but it leads to a realization for me. Regardless of how this ends with us, I finally fucking feel something again.

And that, to me, means everything.

Thankfully, no one had anything to say after we came back from the parking lot. Checking the time, we definitely took longer than necessary to move a box from one car to another, but the boys were too invested in talking about Anderson and how crazy he's been performing on the ice to even notice we were gone.

Our meals came out shortly after we got back. Eating occupied the rest of our time, but Cooper seemed to enjoy himself, which was the main reason for even having them here. Alex didn't look too disappointed either, wearing a cute little grin that only an orgasm can cause. I never thought she'd lean so far into this, but she's proving to have a little bit of a wild side. *Or maybe I just do that to her.*

As we put on our jackets to leave, I drop the final piece of my little surprise for our player.

"Hey, Cooper. What do you say we have all the Junior Rockets back for the game next weekend? Maybe you guys could hop on the ice in between periods?"

With eyes as wide as the pancakes he ordered, he answers. "That'd be awesome, Coach!"

"If that's okay with you," I say, turning to Alex. I know she doesn't like when I drop things like this, but I meant to ask her while we were outside. I just got a little preoccupied.

"Actually, it's your dad's weekend," she says. "But I'm sure he'd be happy to take you."

My body tenses, and I try not to show it, but Alex's gaze goes straight to the clench in my jaw.

"Cool," Coop says, sliding his phone from his pocket. "I'll text him right now."

"Sounds good, buddy." I say it as if I'm calm and collected, but inside I'm reeling. I don't like the idea of not only missing out on seeing Alex but having to see her ass of an ex in her place.

We all walk out of the building, but I pause when I remember I'm not parked up front with everyone else. "I'm in the back," I say, reaching my hand out toward Erik. I clap him on the shoulder, then do the same to Gavin. "I'll see you guys at the rink."

They both nod, then say bye to Alex and Cooper before heading to their cars.

"Coop, I'll have Sadie reach out to your coach and set you all up for next weekend, okay?"

"Thanks, Monte."

Leaning down, I tousle his hair. "You got it, buddy."

As I stand back up, I resist the urge I have to say goodbye to Alex in the way that I want to. To pull her close and kiss her hard before watching her walk away. Instead, I say, "I'll see you soon?"

"You will," is all she answers back before throwing her arm around Cooper and turning away.

They make it just a few feet before I call back to her. "Hey, Bennett!" I shout.

Alex and Cooper both turn around. Without specifying who I meant in the first place, I plaster a smile on my face and simply yell in their general direction. "Thanks for breakfast."

# 31

# Alex

I haven't seen Levi these last couple of days. His team has two away games coming up, so they'll be traveling for most of the week. Between working at the restaurant this weekend and him leaving first thing on Monday, this has been the longest we've gone without seeing each other since this whole thing began.

We've had essentially no contact since the breakfast incident, and as weird as it sounds, it's strange for me. I think, in a way, I've gotten used to him being around. I know my body definitely has. It's funny how that works. You go way too long without any sex-life at all, then finally get a taste and—BAM! You're addicted. I guess the saying "you don't know what you don't have" applies here. So does the one about distance making the vagina grow fonder.

It's now Thursday night, and I'm sitting down in the snack bar to watch Cooper's practice. The little eatery at our local rink may not have suite seats like the Flames do, but they have tables by a window that overlooks the ice and cheese fries for only three dollars.

There may also be an added bonus of a TV hung in the corner of the room that just so happens to be airing the NHL game of one sort of maddening—very sexy—head coach.

I stare at the screen while Coop does his stretching and try to picture Levi without the suit on. Sweatpants, jeans—no clothes at all—anything really besides the bane of my existence. As always, he looks freshly groomed, his beard perfectly shaped, his hair properly faded. My mind flashes to running my hands through it while he went down on me in the backseat of his car, and I have to quickly look around to make sure there's no one near me who can hear my thoughts.

The fact that the parking lot situation happened at all, shows I'm starting to get the hang of this whole benefits thing. Would I say that we're friends? I guess not. I think to be friends you have to hangout with the person outside of obligations, and I don't plan to start that up. Most importantly, I would never admit that Brooke was right. The benefits, however—those have been exactly what I've needed.

The clock on the jumbotron winds down to zero as the Flames late-afternoon game comes to a close. The good news is, that means Levi will be on his way home tomorrow. The bad news is that I still won't have an excuse to catch up with him being that Cooper is with his dad all weekend. Supposedly, Nick will finally get to meet the coach that he just happens to hate. He answered Cooper's text about going to the game with a resounding "sure" and called me later to confirm the details.

The day after tomorrow, Nick will take Cooper to meet the rest of the Junior Rockets at the game just like they did the night this all started. The boys have a suite once again and will get a chance to play on the ice between periods. All I asked Nick to do was take pictures. I'll make sure to catch the game during my shift at the restaurant, but I'm sad that I have to miss this.

Technically, I could have tagged along, but I'm trying to force him into the parenting role. If I went with it would just be me chaperoning two preteen boys. Not to mention the idea of being with Nick and Levi in the same place freaks me out for two reasons. One, seeing them act the same—or, even worse, get along—would probably be more than I can take to continue doing what we're doing. Two, seeing them act nothing alike—or, even worse, hate each other—would make continuing to do what we're doing even harder.

The idea of solidifying that Levi is not the less Nickish version of my ex is the worst thing that could happen. That would make keeping this relationship strictly physical nearly impossible. With sex like this and a reality like that, I'm not sure I could resist giving into him more than I want to. And none of that would change that his job, like Nick's, must still be his priority.

"Whatchya watchin'?"

A high-pitched voice comes out of nowhere and makes me jump out of my seat. Turning around, I see Kathryn With a "Y" hovered behind me. I fake a smile, my hand on my chest, and turn back toward the TV.

"Oh, I was just watching the—" I stop mid-sentence when I realize my latest overthinking session has caused me to miss seeing the guys leave the ice, and now it appears like I was staring at a tampon commercial, completely mesmerized. "Never mind."

Kathryn scrunches her nose, an energetic smile on her face. "Can I sit down?" she asks eagerly.

I swallow my real response and point to the seat across from me, also facing the ice. "Sure thing."

"So, are you excited for the Flames game this weekend? That was awfully nice of them, wasn't it?"

"It was," I say dryly. "But Cooper's dad is actually taking him so..."

"Oh, I didn't know his dad was around. I don't think I've ever seen him before."

Kathryn waits expectantly for me to fill her in on the details. I hesitate knowing that I'll just be the next story in her gossip line to the mom that she runs into after me. Parting my lips, I try to figure out how to word this the right way—or avoid it altogether—when my phone pings from my bag. *Saved by the bell.*

"Just one second," I say, reaching into my purse. I slide just the top part of the screen from the pocket and read "Coach Montgomery" written across the top of a message. My body floods with excitement, partly because I've somehow escaped Kathryn's questioning and partly because... why would he be texting me?

Unwilling to even peek at the words that he's sent in Kathryn's presence, I look up at her. "So sorry, I'm actually going to take this." I mentally point across the rink. *Way, way, way out there.*

"No problem," she says brightly. I offer a genuine smile for her incessant positivity and slide my still warm cheese fries in front of her.

"Enjoy," I say, throwing my bag over my shoulder and booking it for the ramp toward the lobby.

I walk to the furthest bathroom from where I am, somehow feeling like this must be read completely secluded or not at all. Luckily, most of the people at the rink right now are male and there's another bathroom closest to where Coop's team is skating for the moms that may need to use one.

I lock myself in the largest stall and lean back against the door. Bringing my phone back out of hiding, I swipe open the message.

Coach Montgomery

**Did you catch the game?**

I'm caught off guard by the simplicity of the text. I guess in my mind I thought there either had to be an important or sexual reason for him sending it in the first place. I consider not answering at all. Casual conversation is definitely not just physical, but I'm already here, and leaving would mean going back to making small talk about my disastrous past love-life.

I did.

I tap the back of my phone case with my fingers, watching the three dots blink in the corner of my screen.

Coach Montgomery

**Wish you were here.**

"What?" I say aloud.

My eyes grow wide with a feeling like somehow someone just heard me talk to myself in the bathroom stall. I hold my breath and pause my movement, verifying that there's no other sound to be heard. *I'm alone.*

In my head, I question why he'd say that. Messages like those are definitely against the rules. *We are not doing this, Levi. I am not your—*

Coach Montgomery

> To celebrate...

*Oh.*

Well, in that case... *this* I can do. I take a deep breath, channel the bold attitude I seem to have stumbled upon during our time together and use it to respond.

> And what would we do to... celebrate?

He answers instantly as if he was sitting on his next text, just waiting for me to reply.

Coach Montgomery

> I'd take you back to my hotel.

> And...?

Coach Montgomery

> Your turn.

Despite being alone, I blush just reading those two words. It's true, I've found this whole new energy since being with Levi, but that doesn't mean I'm not still a little timid at first.

> First, I'd undress, and then I'd strip you of that god-awful suit.

Coach Montgomery

And then?

Your turn.

*Two can play this game, Coach.*

Coach Montgomery

I'd send you to your knees.

A tingle shoots south of my belly, and my chest begins to move in bigger waves. The memory of taking Levi in my mouth causes a faint heat to creep up my neck. I wouldn't say I've ever been a particular fan of that act in the past, but there's something about making such a stoic and serious man buckle at the knees that really does something to me.

I would suck you until you were close, but not enough to finish you off.

Just typing that out sends a pulse between my thighs, the material of my bra suddenly like electricity against my sensitive skin. I let my fingers explore my breast from the outside of my shirt, only flirting with the idea of actual contact.

Coach Montgomery

Good, because before that happens, I'd want to wrap your legs around my waist and carry you to the bed, your begging pussy pressed against my skin.

I can almost feel him on me as I read over his message, the fictional friction creating a very real reaction. How does this man turn me on using only words? I'm desperate for more.

> Then what?

Coach Montgomery

> Nuh-uh. Nice try, baby. Your turn.

Swallowing the saliva that's built in my mouth from drooling over the image of Levi holding my naked body to his, I unconsciously run my fingertips down the middle of my chest to the waist of my jeans. Holding the phone in one hand, I play with the button, not quite undoing it but tempting myself.

> Drop me on the bed. I'll crawl on all fours.

Coach Montgomery

> Good girl, Bennett.

The praise quickens my breath even more as my head lulls back against the door of the stall. *What is it with us and bathrooms?*

Coach Montgomery

> I'd slide into you slowly. Savoring every fucking inch of your grip around me.

> Grabbing the headboard with one hand and touching myself with the other, I'd look back at you, watching as you sink yourself deep inside me.

I watch in anticipation as the three dots show again at the bottom of the screen. Waiting for Levi's reply like I need it to breathe, I run my fingers past the material between my thighs.

As quickly as the dots appear, they disappear again. I go to text a second message reminding Levi that it's his turn to make a move when a drop-down notification with his name flashes across my screen.

On instinct, my finger flies to the red reject button, my heart starting to race even more than it already was. *Is he crazy?* As if it's the universe's way of reminding me of how different my world is from Levi's, he's Face-timing me from his five-star hotel. Not that he knows I'm standing in a hockey rink bathroom, but—I'm standing in a hockey rink bathroom!

Before I have a chance to type out a message telling him that I will under no circumstances be answering a video call, he texts me first.

Coach Montgomery

> **Answer me, Bennett.**

And now, apparently, I'll be taking his call. *Damn him for unlocking this kink.*

I panic comb my fingers through my hair and throw it over my shoulder. Digging through my purse, I pull my headphones from their case at the bottom of my bag and place them in my ears. Within moments, my phone rings again, and although I'm tempted to reject it, I'm also surprisingly tempted to answer.

Sucking in a huge breath and hitting the green button, Levi's face pops up on the screen. He's shirtless, lying flat on the bed, one arm up with his hand tucked under his head and the other straight above him, holding the phone in place. His hair is still set perfectly, his eyes somehow greener through the view from his camera.

Unsure of where this conversation is headed, I remain silent. He does too until he says, "Where are you?" His voice comes out husky and that tells me everything I need to know about what we're doing—picking up right where we left off.

"I'm at Cooper's practice. In the bath—*Standing* in the bathroom."

*Good correction, Alex. That definitely makes this way less weird.*

"Are you alone?" he asks, his eyes narrowing.

I nod slowly. "I wish I wasn't."

"You have no idea," he says, moving his hand from behind his head and clenching his jaw. Tilting the phone down, I get the full view of his naked body on display, his massive hand holding himself. The veins shoot up into his forearm as he strains against his size. I suck in an audible breath, and he brings the phone back so that we're looking at each other. "Even when you aren't here, I'm fucking rock hard for you."

My lips part at the confession, and his eyes shoot to my now open mouth. I never imagined such a statement could be considered flattery, but my body responds to it as if it's the biggest compliment I've ever received.

"Where were we, Bennett?"

# 32

# Levi

I t has been exactly one week since I've touched Alex—not that I'm counting. I haven't had phone sex since college, and that was fun—and so goddamn necessary after so many days without her—but I'm dying for the real thing.

I also just... miss her? I know I'm not supposed to. I also know I probably sound like the biggest pussy saying that about someone who has been nothing but open about not wanting to date me, but I don't care. She can resist me all she wants, but I'm leaning into the one thing outside of hockey that has made me feel—anything—and that's her.

As if all of that wasn't enough, she isn't even the one bringing Cooper tonight. If he shows up, Coop's dad is supposed to be joining him and the rest of the Rockets for the game. This isn't a spotlight player-specific event, so I don't have to be too one-on-one with Alex's ex. I did, however, ask Sadie to bring them to my office before warmups so I could meet the guy whose past actions are keeping me from taking Bennett as mine.

Glancing at my watch, I see warmups start in exactly ten minutes. I asked Sadie to bring them up here at least a half-hour before so I didn't have to rush—and so I had time between our meeting and when I had to go out on the ice. I can't imagine meeting Nick will leave me in the kind of headspace I have to be in before a game. I'll need time to reset myself before it's time for action.

Picking up my cell phone, I scroll to Sadie's name to call for an update. Just as the line connects, there's a ringing from the hall. Before she has a chance to pull her phone out, Sadie walks into my office, followed closely by Cooper and a very average looking guy in a jersey.

"Hi Coach, sorry we're late," Sadie says, an obvious uneasiness about her. She is detail oriented, almost to a fault. I already know that *she* wasn't the reason that they weren't here on time. "Mr. Mercer got stuck at work." She smiles politely in Nick's direction, clearly uncomfortable.

I stand from behind my desk as Nick steps forward. He reaches his hand out to me. "You know how it is," he says casually.

My eyes slip to Cooper who looks almost as awkward as Sadie. I guess to some extent I technically do know "how it is." My schedule is sporadic. Games run late and travel times change, but I can't imagine I'd let it affect the one night I've had with my son in the last two weeks—probably more. Since I met Cooper, I haven't heard of Nick being around even once.

Meeting his hand, I respond evenly. "To some extent, sure." A flash of understanding taints his expression as he slows our handshake. *That's right, asshole. I know.*

We drop our hands, and Nick shoves his into his pockets. Cooper steps up and holds out a fist. "What's up, Coach?"

I touch my knuckles to his. "Hey, buddy. Thanks for coming."

"Of course! The team is stoked to be here. Mom wishes she could have come." I perk up a little too quickly at the mention of Alex. Nick definitely notices, but I pass it off as it being my reaction to the first half of his answer.

"I'm, uh, so glad the team's excited."

"No way your mom wanted to be here," Nick says, the statement hitting me like ash from a fire—an unexpected sting.

"Yes she did."

"Since when does she like professional hockey?"

Cooper's face flushes as he looks at me with anger in his expression. I try to respond with reassuring eyes, but he flicks his gaze toward the ground. "It's not about the game," he says to the carpet. His head is cocked toward Nick, but he doesn't bring his eyes to him. "She likes spending time with me." It's clear Coop's pissed about Nick being late. It's also clear Nick doesn't even seem to notice.

"Well, you have me tonight, buddy. Come on, it's gonna be great!" Nick ruffles his hair, and Cooper winces beneath his touch.

"Yeah, okay," he says despondently.

"Has Coop told you everything he's gotten to do as our spotlight player?" I chime in.

Furrowing his brow, Nick turns to Cooper. "Wait, what? You didn't mention anything about that."

"It's not a big deal," Coop says.

"Actually," I interject. "It's a pretty huge deal. Cooper is going to be the face of our community outreach program called Spark the Flame at our annual gala. There will be a slideshow of photos and videos of him with the team, a scholarship given to a local player in his name, and he even gets to give a little speech in front of all his heroes."

Cooper shines as Nick steps behind him squeezing his shoulders. "Hey, that's my boy," he raves.

Coop looks up at him, a slow smile now hiding his previous disappointment. "It is pretty cool, isn't it?"

"Totally. My boy, the star." Nick turns to me. "If you guys need any donations for anything I can—"

"We have it all covered, but I appreciate the offer."

The balls on this guy. He does realize the Flames are a billion dollar organization, right? And that bringing up money at a time like this, where his son finally has his attention, really plays into his whole douche reputation. It's the first glimpse I have of this guy and even I hate him. I can also see now why throwing money around makes Bennett cringe.

There's nothing wrong with being wealthy. In fact, some of the best people I know have more money than they realistically need, but it's how you use it that matters. I haven't offered to pay for Alex's meal, rent her a car, or gift her merch because I'm trying to impress her. I damn sure didn't bring up covering Cooper's expenses because I thought it'd make her fall for me. I did these things because I can and because I wanted to. Because the money isn't a big deal but making her feel special and at ease definitely is.

It hits me now that this is one of the many reasons I finally feel like I want more with someone. Rachel left me because I no longer was able to offer her what she really wanted from me—my wallet. Alex, on the other hand, would probably prefer it if I didn't have it at all. It's as if my wealth is a trigger for her to stay away, and that quality in her is one that I needed to find to finally feel like I could let someone in.

Nick purses his lips and raises his brows just once. "Alrighty then."

Scared of what I'll say if I let my growing annoyance for this guy stew any longer, I cut our time off. "Okay, I'm headed to warmups, but Cooper, have fun tonight. You tell Sadie if you need anything." He nods, and Sadie smiles from the corner of my office. "And Nick..." Mr. Rich Guy's head snaps back. He's either caught off guard that I used his first name or just surprised I know it in the first place. "It was nice to finally meet you."

I let the weight of each word sink in before I nod to Sadie. She steps up and gestures to the door. After letting his gaze linger on me for an extra second, Nick finally twists Cooper's shoulders without responding to my comment. *I hate this fucking guy.*

It takes everything in me not to call Nick out and tell him how big of an idiot he is for spending any free second of his time doing anything but worshiping that kid and the mother that's raising him. I know what it's like to have a demanding job that requires a lot of your day and almost all of your brain power. But Nick can't even be a decent enough guy to appreciate the time he does have with them.

When they reach the threshold, and I'm almost out of chances, I give in just a little to my temptation. If I'm right about Nick, he's an entitled prick who, despite not wanting this family of his, doesn't want anyone else to have them either.

"Hey, Cooper," I call before he turns down the hallway. He pops back in, and I make it a point to wait for Nick to appear behind him. "Do me a favor."

"Yeah, Coach?" he asks.

I look directly at Nick. "Tell your mom I wish she could have come too."

The Junior Rockets take the ice in between the second and third period. As much as I want to stand and watch, I have about three minutes before and after I have to be in the locker room to do that. We're fucking losing, and there's no way I'm missing my chance to have a little chat with the boys.

I watch as Cooper skates onto the ice. He glides over to his position and looks up to the suite that the parents are watching from. Nick stands in plain sight, but he's leaning into his palm that's curved around his mouth, his other hand held up to his ear. Coop waves to him, but Nick doesn't wave back. The asshole may be facing the ice, but his attention is with whoever is on the other end of his call rather than his son.

Cooper's body posture deflates as he falls into position, two hands on his stick. I think back to watching Ruthie play soccer and how often she glances over at Liam or me. This is like the Cup for this kid, and his dad is too preoccupied to even pretend to be watching. As if I wasn't already fucking heated enough about being a goal down going into the third, my insides spark an actual flame. That spark starts to blaze as it hits me that if I realize how Cooper must feel right now, Alex, who is no doubt watching from home, definitely does.

There's a deeper anger that courses through me. One that is so beyond the fact that we're losing or that Nick the Dick isn't paying attention to his kid. It's one that can only be described as protective in nature. It's a passion that burns in you when anyone hurts someone you care about—and I do care about Cooper. He's a great kid, and I've enjoyed the time I've had to get to know him.

I mess with my tie, it's familiar hug on my neck suddenly too tight, as I realize why my feeling is amplified. It's not only Cooper that Nick is hurting here. You hurt him and you hurt Alex, plain and simple, and the combination of the two is almost too hard to let go.

Realizing I really need to get back to the locker room, and therefore don't have time to dangle the loser lawyer from the balcony, I fix what I can from where I am.

"Hey, Cooper!" I yell from the bench. His head snaps up to where I'm standing. "Go get 'em, buddy!"

Even through his mask I can see a smile spread across his face, his black mouth guard on full display. He taps on his helmet and sits back in position, and there's no hiding the way his shoulders no longer hunch forward over his stick.

Blowing out a smooth breath, I'm finally at ease enough to turn around and walk through the tunnel. Glancing at my watch, the numbers tell me I'm over the time I allotted myself to watch in the first place. It's only by two minutes, but it's still surprising that the pull I had to make tonight better for Cooper and Alex overrode the pull I had to get back to the boys. What's even more surprising is how much I don't seem to care—and how now all I can think about is making all of this up to the both of them.

# 33

# Alex

The Flames won in the final seconds of their game. They were down by one most of the time but tied it with two minutes to spare. Drew had a breakaway with thirty seconds left and deked the Renegades goalie to secure the win.

Shockingly, I seem to care about the score. Partially because of Levi—just because I don't think we'd work doesn't mean I hate the guy—but mostly because of Cooper.

Nick picking him up late at the restaurant was bad enough, but then they showed the Rockets on the ice and the parents in the suite. Nick was on his phone every time he was on camera as the kids played between periods, and I'm sure Cooper noticed every second. I'm hoping the win brought at least some joy.

From the corner table in the restaurant, I had a clear view of the TV hung on the wall and an obviously disappointed Coop. Just the way he stood told me everything I needed to know, and it took all of my restraint not to fling my pad of order slips at Nick's stupid head through the screen.

I actually tried calling his cell. The bastard denied me but was still on the phone the next time the camera flashed to the suite. All of the other parents around him were swooning for their players but not Nick. He was undoubtedly on a work call about someone's record or trial evidence. It can never seem to wait.

The whole thing put me in such a funk that our manager cut me first. Normally, I wouldn't want to leave early, especially when I've given away too many shifts lately, but I wanted to be at the house in case Cooper decided he was done with Nick too and asked to come home early.

I texted him after the game but haven't heard back. That could either mean he has forgotten all about it for now—probably thanks to some elaborate gift or grand gesture—or that he doesn't want to talk about it and is already on his way here.

Pouring myself a second glass of wine, I snuggle into the couch. There are highlights from the game playing when I turn on the TV, thanks to Cooper constantly watching our local sports network. Of course they're at the part where the Junior Rockets take the ice.

The camera shows Coop waving to the stands, and I contemplate torturing myself by rewatching the scene all over again. I opt not to, instead pointing the remote at the screen to change the channel, when his face lights up again. They didn't show this view during the live filming, and it floods me with relief. My heart warms and my anxiety dulls, no doubt a result of both the wine and seeing that my son did in fact have fun despite his father's underwhelming attention.

I continue watching, looking for the source of his cheer, maybe a fellow player or the silly mascot he loves that dances around like he's quite literally on fire. But when the camera scans across the ice, Levi pops into the corner of the screen, a thumbs up raised in Coop's direction. The bench behind him is empty, the other players and coaches must have already headed into the locker room, but he's still there watching my son.

I tell myself that it's his job. He needed to put on the outreach hat and at least act interested in the Rockets being there. But I'm grateful for him still. Whether or not he realized that Cooper was down, I don't know, but he seemed to have an effect on his mood either way.

My mind immediately runs through all of the ways I could thank him for that... also no doubt a result of the wine. The physical flush in my cheeks from the alcohol now mirrors the heat that heads south, and I find the time since I last saw Levi feeling longer than it has been.

Twelve years of history leaves me still unconvinced this could work in the real world, but here in our short window of time, he's making it really easy for me to keep coming back.

I was on board with this physical thing even before I started warming up to him. But seeing his different sides that are nothing like the other suit I know, erases any hesitation I may have had before about giving him my body.

As if the universe wants to slow my thoughts, the doorbell rings. Looking at the time in the corner of the screen, I can only assume it's Cooper, and he forgot his key. Nick wouldn't bother texting me if he insisted on coming home. He'd be too annoyed and too busy convincing himself that somehow this was all my fault.

I stand, turning off the TV and letting the buzz that rushes to my head give me the kick in the ass that I need to finally tell Nick off. With my heart pumping and my blood boiling, I stomp to the door. Taking one deep breath to gain my composure, at least until Cooper gets to his room, I pull the door open.

The beating in my chest halts completely, then immediately begins pounding again, my body temperature increasing with its rhythm,

"Bennett."

My lips part, but no words come out. My brain is playing catch up to my body that seems to be one step ahead. Levi stands in front of me on my doorstep, his black tie hanging loosely around his neck, his suit jacket sitting open.

His eyes drop right to my lips as I will myself to speak. His gaze travels the length of my cream quarter zip and soft matching lounge pants before rising again. "Wha—What are you doing here?" I finally force myself to stammer out. It's not him that throws me, it's that he's here. In this moment. Just as I was thinking of him.

He clears his throat. "Can I come in?"

Nodding, I step aside, and he brushes past me, the thick material of his sleeve like lead against my arm. I give myself the few seconds it takes for him to walk inside to shake the shock before I ask again.

"So, what are you—"

He slams into me, our mouths, chests, hips—all flush against one another. Sliding his hand into my hair greedily, he deepens our kiss. "I needed to see you," he says between pecks, and I can't help the validation it gives me to know that after such a win, I was how he wanted to celebrate.

"Good," I manage to say, my voice already breathless.

With that, he walks me backward toward the living room. When the back of my thighs reaches the arm of the couch, Levi stops pushing me forward and reaches for the hem of my sweatshirt. He's already hard, his movements quick yet unhurried. They aren't frantic or rushed, just swift and productive—deliberate regardless of speed.

He lifts my top over my head in one smooth motion, tossing it to the ground by the table. His eyes fall on my naked chest underneath and for the first time since he walked in the door, he remains motionless.

"Fuck, Bennett," he groans, eventually breaking his pause to reach out and hold me. His hands fit perfectly around the cup of my breasts that now sit heavily in his palms.

His eyes laser focus on each peak as he rolls them between his first two fingers. I whimper, a pulse growing between my thighs matching each squeeze that he gives.

Feeling an extreme need to touch him too, I slide my hands under the fabric that sits across his shoulders. He lets out a growling exhale as I slide his jacket down his arms, letting gravity pull it down behind him.

I reach for his buttons as he leans into me, bringing them closer and planting nips and pecks up the side of my neck.

"I need you to know something," he all but whispers as he runs the tip of his nose across my jawline.

"Mhmm," I hum, undoing his last button. He reaches around me, freeing his wrists from the cuffs as he talks.

"I know we're not supposed to say things like this..." I drag my fingertips down the length of his now exposed chest, and an escaped groan interrupts his thought. "But you deserved so much better."

I freeze, my fingers hovered over the space above his belt. Levi undoes his second sleeve and allows his shirt to join his jacket on the floor. "So did Cooper." He kisses me, but I don't let myself sink into him like I did before.

"You're right. We aren't supposed to say things like that."

It comes out unconvincingly, but I'm proud of my mouth for speaking what my brain knows it should say. The rest of my body, on the other hand, is now even hungrier for Levi, as if his confession somehow doesn't break our first rule.

"I know. Strictly physical." Ripping me from my thoughts, Levi lowers his hands to my hips and twists my body so the arm of the couch now faces me. Bringing his palm to the space between my shoulders, he bends me in half, forcing me to brace my hands on the cushion of the couch. "But let's pause all of that and pretend for a minute."

My ears perk up at his words, and at the clanging of his belt, as he pulls it from the loops of his pants. I glance back in time to see him lick his lips and watch as he reaches for my waist. Stripping me of both my sweats and underwear, he reaches beneath me. "Pause?" he asks, the heat from his hand sending chills up my spine.

I squirm from his touch. "Pause," I answer, needing more of it.

He smiles, slowly dragging one finger from my front to back. "Nick is an asshole, Alex," he says. A sigh escapes from deep in my throat. "You know that, right?" He slips just his fingertip into me, palm to the floor.

"Yes," I exhale, confused at his statement and still unable to argue again that we shouldn't be talking about things like this.

"Good." He begins moving only the top of his finger in slow circles as if to reward me for my answer.

"And hypothetically, you know that despite our jobs having similarities, I am *not* an asshole?" He slows his movement when I don't respond. "Right, Bennett?"

His finger barely inside me was already a tease, but his lack of motion leaves my body begging for more. "Right," I pant.

I'd like to say his touch is what gets me to confess, but after everything I've seen, and having watched him pick Cooper up on TV tonight, regardless of his intentions, I know he's right.

He squeezes my ass, his finger still teasing. "Are you sure?" he asks roughly. "You know I'm not like him?"

I nod desperately. "I know."

He pushes his finger in until his second knuckle sits inside. "Do you?"

I clench around him, needing him deeper. "Yes."

Levi sinks in further. "I need you to say it."

I moan, my chest heaving in short gasping breaths. "You're not like him."

He twists his finger without pulling out until it's fully inside me, his palm now face up. The tilt provides some relief, but it's still not enough. He doesn't respond, but I know what he wants—and I know what I need.

"You're not like him, Levi. You're not like Nick. I know that now."

"Good girl." Without warning, he pulls out, leaving me hollow and deprived, but just as quickly, he thrusts into me... hard.

I cry out. The pressure is the most I've felt in days. Not yet moving, Levi leans forward and wraps his hand around my throat, guiding me back to him.

"And if we *were* talking about this..." he growls into my ear, my back now flush with his chest. There's a deep pressure from this angle as he fills me completely. "I'd tell you that if you were mine, you'd never question whether or not you were a priority."

My thoughts run wild, this twisted game he's playing messing with my mind, body, and heart all at once. I don't know what to say. Now doesn't feel like the time to start an argument, but how do I respond without feeding into this? We had an agreement, and although he's doing a damn good job distracting me from that, I have too much to protect to let those rules fly out the window.

He wraps his free arm around my ribs and holds me tightly. "Do you understand?" he asks, raising his hand to brush across the center of my breast.

"Levi."

He drops his grip from the base of my neck to rub small circles between my legs. "Tell me."

My head lulls back onto his shoulder as he starts moving slowly inside of me, continuing to brush and stroke simultaneously.

"Tell me," he repeats, quickening his pace.

My legs start to tremble as he switches to my other swollen nipple. "Levi." At this point I don't know if I'm saying his name to stop his words or to continue his actions.

He pounds harder, his fingers still moving at a relentless pace. When my walls start tightening around him, I reach up behind my head and wrap my arm around his neck. He slams in once more and right when I'm about to come undone, he stills all his movement completely.

"Say it, baby."

In my most vulnerable state, I have no more fight left. Everything in me, inside and out, begs for release. "I understand," I plead. He pulses inside me, and I clench around him. "I understand."

# 34

# Levi

W aking up after a win is nice. Waking up with the memory of Alex thrown over her couch is even better. Not to mention that, in a roundabout way, she finally admitted that I'm not the complete asshole she convinced herself I am.

So, I may have pulled it out of her—teased, edged, tortured—but after realizing how truly invested I am, there was no way I was leaving without her admitting she can at least stand to be around me.

My only problem is, now that she has, I'm even more screwed. Knowing she was completely against this made changing her mind like a scrimmage for me. Despite actually liking her, there were no real stakes. If she changed her mind, then I'd get to have her. If she didn't, I at least could say I finally put myself out there again.

Now, seeing that the door isn't completely slammed closed, it's like the fucking playoffs. Knowing that at least some of her concerns have been eliminated, it's almost as if there's a chance that if I play my best game, we could take this all the way. That right there is scary as hell. There's so much more to lose.

Putting myself in this position means doing what I've said for almost the last decade that I would never do again—opening myself up to get hurt. I'm allowing something other than hockey to make me happy, and although I may regret it, I'm shocked at how naturally it's come.

Surprisingly, the most unnatural thing about this is how I have to try to pretend that I'm not falling for Alex. Something tells me if talking to her like she's my girlfriend breaks a rule, telling her I'm starting to have real feelings for her might end this altogether. It's the reason I dropped the whole thing after we finished—the first time—and why I didn't bring it up again before I left.

Finally forcing myself out of bed, I throw on a set of workout clothes. It's not late by any means, but mine and Bennett's mini marathon last night took more out of me than I thought it would. That being said, I probably don't *need* to get a workout in, but it's my norm, and I'm sticking to it.

After my morning routine, I head to my car just in time for my phone to start ringing the second I unlock the driver's side door. Sliding it from my joggers, I sit down before I look at the screen. I'm embarrassed at the smile that darts across my face thanks to the name that flashes on the device. Starting my car, I lean back in my seat, letting the engine warm up as I connect to the call.

"Bennett," I say hesitantly. There's a heavy exhale on the other end of the phone that causes me to sit up straighter. "Alex..."

"Hey," she finally answers, her voice despondent.

My heart rate picks up. "What's wrong?"

Another massive exhale. "I need a favor."

I let out a silent chuckle. Resting my elbow on the window, I sit back and relax once again. "Last night wasn't enough for you? I mean I know this is a physical relationship, but I didn't expect you'd be calling for—"

"Not that kind of favor."

A strange feeling invades my chest. One that can only be described as pride. Alex needs something—I have no idea what, but that doesn't matter—*I'm* the one she called. "What do you need, Bennett?"

"Iz mah car," she mumbles.

"Huh?"

She groans and repeats her statement more clearly. "It's my car."

A scoff escapes me. "Of course it is."

"It was making a noise, so I pulled over, and now it won't start."

"What kind of noise?" I question.

She takes a deep breath before responding. "Like a shh skrr clunk."

"Like a what?" I deadpan.

"Shh skrr clunk."

I swallow a laugh. "I'm sorry, say that one more time."

"Shh skrr—ya know what? Never mind."

"Okay, okay, I'm kidding." *That was too easy.* "Where are you?"

"Halfway between my house and the restaurant. On that side street by the Kwik Mart on Cherry."

"With the slushies?"

"Yeah, how do you—"

"Ruthie," I say.

She snickers a sound that's heaven-sent. "Right."

I throw my car into drive. "Are you okay?"

She groans quietly then says, "Yeah, I'm fine."

"Okay, I'll be right there."

"I'm sorry. I'd call Brooke, but she's already clocked in, and Cooper has a game, or I'd call—"

"I said I'd be there."

"Thanks, Levi," she says softly.

I smile to myself. "No problem, Alex." *Anything for you.*

I pull up behind Bennett's car and get out of my SUV. Luckily this street doesn't get a lot of action. Walking around her car, I find her sitting on the hood with her sleeves pulled down over her hands and a Kwik Mart cup to her lips.

"Ridiculous," I say, crossing my arms over my chest.

"Can we save the 'I told you so' please?" She slurps her drink, and a shiver runs through her.

"I just meant that your lips are bright blue, and I'm not sure if it's because of the slushie you're drinking or the fact that it's freezing out here and you're, once again, not wearing a jacket."

She sticks her tongue out at me, and it's even bluer than her lips. "My coat's in the car, but I didn't feel like getting it once I was already outside. And this," she says, holding her drink in the air, "is delicious."

Her attitude makes me laugh, but her hardened nipples showing through her shirt make me feel something else entirely. "Want to try?" she asks, sipping the straw. My eyes drop to her mouth that's perfectly formed around the plastic.

I step to her, shoving my leg between hers. "Yeah, actually."

Lowering her drink, she arches her brow and bites her colored lower lip. She holds her cup out to me, but I push it aside. Brushing my palm past her cheek, I pull her mouth to mine and take my time exploring hers with my tongue. After I've thoroughly swept her, I break our kiss, but not before sucking that same bottom lip. "Mmm, that *is* delicious."

Alex's face is one of surprise, but her thighs squeeze mine without reluctance. She grabs me by my drawstring and pulls me to her. I let my weight fall forward causing her to fall backwards onto the hood, her hand outstretched to her side still holding her drink.

With my arms straddling her face—amber eyes, pink nose, blue lips—it takes everything in me not to have my way with her right here. But, as I lean in to show her how much I want her, she trembles once beneath me.

"You're lucky it's cold," I growl into her ear, pushing myself back to standing.

"I don't feel very lucky." She braces herself on her forearms while I try to decide if she means because of the car or me withdrawing my body from hers. *Possibly both.*

"Maybe next time you'll wear your coat," I say, slinking away from where she is.

"Wait, it's in the car. I'll just grab it!" she whines.

I shake my head without turning around. "Nope, too late. I'm teaching you another lesson, Bennett." I get to the headlight of my car when her feet hit the ground.

"Ya know, teaching me these lessons—even the fun way—feels a lot like breaking our rules, Coach Montgomery."

I stop in my tracks, the formality of my name leaving her lips hitting me differently than it did a few weeks ago. Then, it felt too proper for all of the things I wanted from her. Now, it feels like a fucking cock tease.

The dirt on the road crunches beneath her shoes as she stomps toward me. As her steps grow louder, I spin around, our bodies now mere inches from each other. "Yeah, well, so does me rescuing you."

Her brow creases into her usual grouchy face and once again, I reach up and smooth the lines between her eyes. On my contact, goosebumps crawl up her exposed chest and something tells me it has nothing to do with the temperature outside. *Does this battle between us turn her on?* "Get in the car, Alex."

Walking to my passenger side door, I realize I'm hard for her, my body's response to her open denial that there's more to what we're doing here. *Clearly it turns me on too.*

"But what about mine?" she protests, stepping back toward her car to grab her coat from inside and her cup from on top.

"Leave the keys in the ignition. A tow truck's on its way."

She opens her mouth to speak but decides not to. Brushing past me to step in the car, it's my turn for goosebumps despite my thick hoodie.

I shut her door, walking back around to my side. When I sink into the leather, she looks over at me, her cheeks flushed and her brow finally relaxed. "Thank you," she mumbles.

"What happened?"

"I was on my way to the restaurant when the noise started."

I can't help but grin. "What noise was that again?" She reaches over to slap me but smiles, and I'm embarrassed by just how good her response makes me feel.

"So, the noise that shall not be repeated started, and then there was some chugging and puttering, and it pretty much died on the side of the road." Turning my lips in, I stare straight ahead. "I know, okay. I'll get it taken care of."

"No," I object, snapping my head back to her. "*I* will get it taken care of."

"Levi, you're not—"

"You can pay every cent of the bill, but that car is not touching your driveway until my guy at the shop gives it the all clear, understand?"

Surprisingly, without any protest, she nods her head and looks out the window. Reaching for her chin, I turn her back toward me. "What's wrong?"

Her eyes glisten. "Nothing," she says.

"Pause, Bennett." Her throat moves up and down, no doubt a reminder of our time last night. She doesn't speak, but she doesn't stop me either. "Tell me," I insist.

"I just hate this," she says, avoiding my gaze.

I tilt her head up. "It's fine, Bennett. This shit happens."

She stares through me, discouraged. "I'm not talking about the car."

"Neither am I." Her eyes grow wide as she searches mine for understanding. "Sometimes even an independent woman like you needs a favor."

She sinks her weight into the crook of my hand, leaving me with a feeling that somehow tops every other one I've had with her. The idea that Alex feels seen, heard, and understood means so much more than any of the rest of it.

*This.* This is how I make it up to her. This is how I show her that I'm not like her ex—not like who she thought I was. Not with showering her in praise and compliments, though she deserves that too and more. But by supporting her. By showing her she doesn't have to be alone in this—that she's already not.

In a strange way, it's kind of like how hockey was there for me. I felt lost and abandoned and had the weight of the world on my shoulders. It seemed like no one understood. Like no one could possibly know what it felt like every day for me to push through the pain and resentment that I still harbored for the things that broke me.

For me, it was my injury and Rachel, and I'm lucky to have gotten that phone call that gave me hope. The one that finally gave me something to believe in again—that made me feel whole all by myself.

For Alex, it was Nick and his actions. Not unlike my situation, he left her feeling like she had no one else to turn to—like she couldn't trust anyone but herself. Having Cooper, I'm sure she threw herself into him, and for a while, that probably helped her forget. Her role as a mother superseded her needs as a woman. But now, with Cooper older and, hopefully, with me in the picture, she's realizing that all that's left is that same feeling that I had at the bar eight years ago. Now she just needs to pick up the ringing phone.

With tears in her eyes, she looks at me, neither of us really sure what to say next. Instead, I press my lips to her forehead and suck in a deep breath. For the first time, she doesn't argue with me about saying something outside of our rules. She doesn't say anything at all, but that's okay. I don't need her to validate what I know to be true. Her actions say that all by themselves. Now, I just need to give her space and security to lean into that. To let me be that call for her. And until she answers, I'll keep trying—over and over and over.

"Unpause."

# 35

# Alex

My boss emailed earlier with a "brilliant idea" for my next blog post. According to her, "situationships" are the new relationships, and it's time we talk about it. Only I don't want to talk about it, Cynthia, because that right there hits a little too close to home.

Upon further investigation, a situationship is a type of romantic relationship where there is no clear definition, no consistent communication, and no future planning. Basically, there may be physical intimacy, but there is no obvious label as to what the connection means emotionally to one or both parties. I personally feel attacked by Cindy's suggestion, but without explaining why, I can't shoot it down.

Which leads to me sitting at my desk right now, brainstorming ways to talk about how the hottest new trend in the dating world seems to be not necessarily dating at all. In reality, I should be happy to know my current condition is the popular one, but I'm anything but glad.

The truth is, I have no idea what's going on anymore. I thought I had a handle on this thing with Levi, but the last few times I've seen him have left me more than confused. When we started this arrangement, I knew it was outside of my comfort zone. What I didn't realize was that the sex-only thing would be the easiest part. It's keeping it that way that's proving to be more of a challenge.

Never in my life did I think that I could even consider falling for another suit like Nick. Right or wrong, I thought the whole idea of someone whose life is dedicated to their work and who lives in such a different world than me—a single mom with no padded bank account—was revolting. Until now.

It's only been a few weeks, but in that time, Levi has shown me he is ten times the man that Nick ever was. Between him looking out for Cooper and taking care of me in more ways than one, he's making it harder and harder to continue telling myself that this side of him is all a facade.

His mid-sex pausing may have been a little heat of the moment, but Levi doesn't have to sweet talk me to get into my pants. And that doesn't explain his words in the car on the side of the road after rescuing me like my knight in shining joggers. There have been no real reasons for saying all of these things unless he's genuinely a really good guy. The problem is, where does that leave me?

Levi's been proving himself to be unlike Nick as a person, and he told me that we'd be a priority if I was ever his. But that doesn't mean things won't happen that are outside of his control. His job is important and sometimes spontaneous, and people are counting on him to be available. Not that we need to be the center of someone's universe, but I'd like it if we didn't get left behind every time something comes up for work once again. I'm sick of feeling second best, and even more sick of seeing my son let down. Also... is it too much to ask to finally be the center of someone's goddamn universe?

My mind starts running numbers and dates—his game schedule, practice schedule, travel time—until I realize that none of this matters if I don't admit to myself how I'm feeling and accept what that might really mean. But every time I think I have an idea, the voice in my head echoes the same thing it's been saying since this all began. *"We're not going there, Alex."*

It's getting harder and harder to swallow these potential feelings down until whatever this is runs its course. I used to think it would all go away when our arrangement was over. Having him inside me a few times a week doesn't help to make him any less attractive. That guy knows what he's doing in the bedroom—or bathroom or car—that's for sure. So, I figured that ending this would bring me back to reality. But then you add in that he's really starting to become someone that Cooper and I can both count on, and now, I'm not so sure. Part of me thinks I may be starting to lose my grip on any control I might have once had on this situation... ship.

---

Kiss and Tell Blog Post Draft #1:

**Situationship or Situationship-wreck**

*Apparently chivalry isn't the only thing that's dead. According to the latest dating trend, so is just about everything "typical" about a relationship. Labels? Dead. Communication? Dead. Feelings? Dead... DEAD DEAD DEAD DEAD.*

---

Feeling the beat of my heart in my finger still hovering over the "D" key after smashing it down, I stop. Okay, maybe now is not the right time to start drafting ideas for this specific topic. Instead, I turn to my newest addiction since realizing that maybe I don't hate Levi after all.

Opening a Google page, I type in his name. The bar at the top of my screen lights up blue as my computer remembers the previous searches. Clicking enter, I watch as the most recent information populates on the screen for Levi Montgomery.

Most of it is what I've seen before—coaching interviews, team pictures, game schedules, previous athletic career statistics—but there's a new image at the top of the screen that I don't recognize from the last time I looked. Clicking on the article, I'm taken to a local Golden City newspaper page dated from Monday.

The picture is of him and a beautiful woman with dark skin and tightly woven braids that fall effortlessly down her back. He's in a black suit with a sage green tie, and she is in a silk, emerald dress that flows to the floor. They're standing side by side, her arm wrapped around his back and his hand sitting loosely on her hip. The camera caught them laughing, smiling at each other. Her deep brown eyes sparkle while his squint with his genuine reaction to whatever is *so* hilarious.

I realize there's a feeling brewing in me that I haven't had a need for in quite some time. As soon as I recognize it, I quickly exit the screen, reading no more than the heading of the article: *No Crocodile Tears for this Gator Brother.*

Staring straight ahead, I tell myself I have no right to be jealous. In fact, I should be happy for the reminder that Levi and I aren't together—a reminder that I so clearly need. But repeating that to myself doesn't help to calm the storm that's growing inside of me. Winds in my mind swirling my thoughts, puddles of anxiety flooding my belly—my heartbeat like thunder clapping inside my chest. Emotions pour out that I haven't felt in so long, and I'm not sure what's worse, the envy that rises from seeing Levi with someone else or the anxiety of knowing I care so much—and I shouldn't.

What's even worse is that I haven't seen him in days, so, I'm already needy for him there. The way I constantly crave him isn't helping, and the thought leads me to a new feeling—concern. Levi and I never got a chance to talk about whether or not we were still having sex with other people. I know I haven't, and I know he was overly cautious with me, but I can't assume that because we're being intimate, he gave up sleeping with everyone else.

After stewing for far too long, I come to the conclusion that there's only one way to find out. *Yes, this is good, Alex.* That's the perfect thing to focus on here—not my ever-growing feelings, but my deep concern for our sexual safety. Is it an added bonus that I now have an excuse to see him? I guess if that's what I was worried about...

Picking up my phone, I try to wipe the last ten minutes from my brain and text Levi like I would any other time we talk. I may be acting like a lunatic, but I don't need him to know that.

Busy?

Biting my nail, I wait for a reply. Luckily, it's a game day, so their practices are usually done by now.

Coach Montgomery

> Just leaving the rink... Meet me at my apartment?

Immediately some of my anxiety lessens. I'm not sure if it's his response or just him, but I already feel better about this whole situation. Going to his place for the first time might not grant me immediate peace of mind, but I definitely won't deny some peace of body first.

> Sounds good. I just have to get Cooper in a couple of hours from school.

Coach Montgomery

> Works for me. We have a game tonight anyway.

Ignoring the swell in my heart from his last reply, I stand from my desk. "I'll come back for you," I say to my laptop. *Have I mentioned there are benefits to working from home?* My phone pings once more with Levi's address. I grab the keys to my rental—Levi somehow managed to get the same one as before—and stare down at my hand.

"I bet he didn't rent her a car to replace her broken down piece of shit," I say to myself. I glance back at my closed laptop that I know is only hiding the picture of Levi with that perfect woman and her white teeth and banging body. *Okay, I'm really losing it.* Shaking my head, I snatch my phone from my desk and punch Levi's number into Maps. *Perfect.*

> I'll be there in twenty.

I was greeted by a doorman... a *doorman*. Levi lives in the type of building where someone is paid to say hello to him when he gets home. I'm sure Walter, as his name tag said, does more than wave and nod and tip his hat, which in my mind is what a doorman does, but the fact still remains. Levi has a goddamn doorman.

This is crazy. No, this is good. What another perfect reminder. It's a great time for a reality check—right before I walk into his penthouse apartment, sleep with him on his million thread count sheets, then confront him about a picture I had no business seeing. Or in whatever order things happen to land.

Walking straight toward the elevators, that look bigger than my bedroom may I add, it hits me that I stick out like a sore thumb in this place. The floors are golden marble, there are chandeliers hanging every ten feet that probably cost more than my salary, and a fireplace roars in every section of the lobby. *How warm does it need to be in here?*

I glance down at my slip-on sneakers, faded jeans, and beige vest layered over a black knit sweater. I don't belong in this place. Hell, I don't belong in this world—one of money and status and three-piece suits. But I know who belongs in this world—women who wear emerald dresses and have braids for days. *Damnit.*

As I'm considering turning around, the elevator doors open just a few feet from me, drawing my attention. A woman walks out in a pencil skirt and white blazer, but it's the man who stands from the shiny, black leather couch facing her that steals my attention. His back is to me, but I know that hoodie—I have the same one—and I'd recognize that ass in jeans anywhere at this point.

Levi turns around, his hair damp, his cheeks flushed like he rushed to get here, and a smile that's so genuine I would drop to the floor right here if I didn't think I'd get yelled at by Walter for inappropriate lobby behavior. *Has he always looked this... normal?* Hot and sexy but not formal and completely out of my league? The suit typically throws me, but seeing him wear pretty much the same thing as me in this fancy building, means we either both stand out or we both fit in. Either way, I instantly feel less like an outsider.

"Hey," he says, his face lighting up, or maybe that's the crystal that hangs right above him. "I was just gonna come wait for you outside."

"Hey," I mimic, my nerves once again calmed by just his presence alone. "Did you know you have a doorman?"

Levi's face drops, and his brow creases as he looks past me toward the entrance. "Huh. Is that who that man is that's always standing there? I just thought Walter was a nice guy with a waving problem."

"Who wears a name tag?"

"Well, you keep wearing vests, and I haven't called you on *that*," he deadpans.

My face warms as I try to hide the smile that throws itself across my lips. Levi glides toward me and pushes his hands into his pockets. "A little bit of a tease leaving the red one at home though," he says leaning down to whisper in my ear.

There's no masking the way I naturally lean into his breath on my neck, my body's way of saying it's been way too damn long. He notices too, his jaw tight when he pulls away, his pupils dilated so it's hard to see where the dark green ends and the black begins.

Turning to stand next to me, Levi places his hand on my lower back and guides me toward the elevators. "Upstairs, Bennett."

Even through my vest and sweater, I can feel his touch like embers on my skin. Levi presses the up arrow on the elevator wall and looks down at me hungrily.

Anticipation blows through me, the weakness in my knees and race of my heart reminding me of why I felt this way less than an hour ago. The doors ding open and stepping inside, the combination of wanting him but needing to have answers, makes it feel like I might bubble over before we even get to his place. Not to mention, I won't be able to focus on what I hope will happen if I can't get out of my damn head.

"Are you sleeping with anyone else?" I blurt, the words spewing from my mouth uncontrollably. *Smooth.*

Levi glances down at me as he presses the button for the top floor, then waves a card from his pocket in front of the sensor beside it. "Do you want me to be sleeping with anyone else?"

"Well, no, but we never really established if that was one of the rules or not."

Levi snorts out a breath, shaking his head slowly. "You and your rules, Bennett."

Trying to decide how to approach the subject of the girl from the picture, I flip back and forth between asking about his weekend and pulling the article up on my phone. Deciding both would be equally weird and passive, I go with our most recent play. "Pause?"

Levi's head snaps to mine, realizing what I am too, which is that this is the first time *I'm* initiating a time-out in our arrangement. After seconds that feel like hours, he finally responds. "Pause."

"I saw a picture of you with a woman at some Gators baseball event over the weekend." I turn from him and stare at the elevator doors to see they mirror our images back at us. *Of course they freaking do.* "I know it's not my place to care that you went, but it got me thinking about how we never really decided if we were sleeping with other people and just for the sake of knowing—plus there's the cleanliness part of—"

"I'm not sleeping with other women, Alex." Levi speaks to the side of my head, but I watch as he responds in our reflection.

"Oh, okay," I say awkwardly. "Good. I'm not either... with men... or women if that matters..." I finally brave looking at him and despite his strong eyes, his lips curl up ever so slightly. "I'm not sleeping with anyone else."

"Good," he says, moving his gaze straight ahead. Another few floors pass by in an audible silence before he speaks again. "It wasn't a date FYI. You know, not that it matters."

I unexpectedly release a heavy breath and look at him sideways, both of our bodies still positioned straight ahead. "Okay." The last few floors crawl by and just before the doors open, I ask the question I've been holding onto this entire time. "So, who is she then?"

# 36

# Levi

T he elevator dings and the doors open leading right into my apartment. Alex takes in the place while I consider how to go about answering her question.

So, she saw the picture from Sunday night—the one Liam sent me saying that for once I look genuinely happy in a photo. Of course he thought it had to do with the time I was having at the Gators' event. Thanks to Liam's suggestion, the Golden City baseball team is trying to start up their own program similar to Spark the Flame. But although the dinner was very nice, I don't think the smile had anything to do with the food or the fundraiser.

I was in a state of bliss the rest of the day after picking up Alex from the side of the road. It didn't amount to much for us, I just dropped her off at work, but the moments before couldn't have gone any better.

I could be wrong, nothing may have changed at all, but it felt like some sort of elemental shift happened between us when my lips touched her forehead. Like maybe just a little piece of what I'm feeling was reciprocated, or at the very least, she finally saw that there's potential here. That night was one of the best I've had in a long time, and it had nothing to do with the event itself. I was just happy and hopeful, and the camera happened to catch me and Tasha laughing.

Walking to the kitchen that sits off to the side of the living space, I watch as Alex runs her hand across the back of my couch. The leather does feel like butter beneath your touch, but the reason I picked it was because it matches the rest of my place—clean, bold, dominant—all high-quality pieces in neutral colors.

"That was Erik's wife," I say, reaching into the fridge. I pull out two waters just in time to catch Alex's hand pause. "We were talking when a photographer came over to us. Tasha was mid-sentence, telling me that Erik was over asking the waiter for more pigs in a blanket." Alex chuckles, but she still looks unconvinced.

"He meant bacon-wrapped scallops, but he kept calling them—never mind you had to be there. When she said that, I started cracking up. For some reason I thought it was really funny at the time." *Probably because I was already floating on cloud nine that night, thanks to you.*

Alex walks over to the island, and I slide one bottle to her from across the counter. "Anyway, that's why we were laughing so hard. Tasha's a trip," I say, unscrewing the top. "And Erik's an idiot." I take a long sip but don't miss that she exhales slowly.

I don't even notice I'm smiling at her relief until Alex narrows her eyes at me. "What?" she asks, resting her hand on her bottle.

"Nothing," I answer. I walk around the island and lean against the space in front of her.

"What?" she repeats again, this time more sternly.

I set my water on the island and pull hers from under her palm, setting it next to mine. Brushing her cheek with the back of my knuckles, I ask, "Were you..." I tuck a loose hair behind her ear before continuing. "Jealous?"

Alex tries to play coy, but not before arching just a little bit toward me. "I was curious..."

I look at her in the same way that I feel—like I've been deprived of her for way too long. "Mhmm."

"And concerned."

I drag my thumb slowly down her jaw. "About being safe..."

Leaning into my touch, she whispers. "Exactly."

"Right," I whisper back, brushing her lips. "And not at all jealous?" I let my hand fall from her chin to her throat. She sucks in a breath and her neck moves up and down beneath my grip.

She doesn't respond, so I tighten my hold. "Answer me, Bennett."
Alex's chest heaves so hard, it touches my forearm in front of it on the inhale. I lean into her mouth, just grazing her lips. "Answer. Me."

"Unpause," she breathes out.

"That's what I thought."

I pull her to me and kiss her with all of the relief that fills my chest. An excitement spreads through me that I haven't felt in too long. A fire for something that's not hockey-related, sparking deep inside for the first time in years.

So, she didn't actually say it, but there was no denying it either. I might be out of the game, but I'm not completely clueless. I just have to get her to see that her world won't completely fall out of orbit if she were to admit it. But not right now. Now, I have other plans.

Alex Bennett is in my fucking apartment. She has no idea how many times I've thought of her here, but I know all of the fantasies I want to fulfill. "Bedroom," I say between kisses.

I tilt my head toward the door behind us, and Alex nods in agreement. She twists her shoulders, but I stop her before she's fully turned around.

"Wait." She looks at me blankly, waiting for me to go on. "Pants off first."

"Here? Before I even get into the—"

"Now."

She grins teasingly, reaching for the top of her jeans. Slipping out of her shoes, she slides her denim down to the floor. Her vest drops with it, and she stands in front of me in a tight black sweater and a thong to match. Not just any thong—*the* thong.

I run a hand down my face. *She did this on purpose.* "Jesus, Bennett," I groan, my eyes still pinned to the lace. "And I thought the vest was sexy."

She slaps my arm playfully, the contact reminding us of where we left off. "Now walk," I command.

She tilts toward the door once again, but this time I let her turn around fully. Her perfect ass—and that goddamn dimple—are on full display as she reaches the threshold. I almost forget to follow her, my attention captivated by watching her leave, until she spins back and nibbles her lip.

As if her teeth pull a trigger, I spring toward her, scooping her up in my arms. Alex gasps, her legs wrapping around me as I walk through the frame. On the other side of the wall, I stop. Pulling my head back, I look at her in my hands, then glance around the room, taking this in.

"What are you doing?" she giggles, leaning in for a kiss. I dodge her mouth, continuing my wandering gaze.

"Just noticing..." She looks at me curiously. "How this room somehow looks different with you in it."

Bennett's jaw grows tight but not from annoyance or anger. Her eyes tell me she knows exactly what I'm trying to say, and I could be wrong, but she might even like it.

As bad as this sounds, a lot of other women have been where she is. Maybe not in my arms, but they've been in this room. But nothing about this is the same. It looks different, feels different, and I've never prayed for the time to pass so fucking slowly. I want to savor every second of this.

Sitting her on the edge of the bed, I take advantage of the fact that I'm already halfway to the ground and drop to my knees. Bennett's legs slide from around me and land on either side of my thighs, opening her up to me. She reaches down for my sweatshirt, and I let her slide it off my body, my crisp, white undershirt gliding off with it.

We both stare, taking each other in, the skin that's revealed, a contrast to one another. Without being told, Alex reaches for her sweater and pulls it up and over her head. Her body now sits in front of me with only her most precious parts covered.

"Beautiful," slips from my mouth.

She parts her lips with her eyes narrowed at me, and I jump in to stop her from speaking. "I don't care what you call us, I'm not pausing to tell you how fucking perfect you are."

Rather than closing her lips, her mouth drops open wider, and just the sight of it sitting in that shape makes me hungry.

I stand before her, and she follows my move, her eyes trailing up to my face, then back down my body. We both reach for my jeans at the same time, my hands immediately retreating to let her do the job. She unzips and unbuttons, then drags the material to meet our other clothes on the floor. Now, all that's between us are three black, flimsy materials that feel more like walls than the fabric they are.

Alex frames my bulge with her fingers, trailing them down my length. I groan at the tease of her touch, and she runs her tongue across her top lip. Leaning down to her, I kiss her wet mouth, her grip squeezing tighter around me. Setting my hands on either side of her body, I nudge her backward until she starts moving toward the top of the bed. I pause her long enough to unclasp her bra, removing one of the remaining barriers.

When she reaches the headboard, we collide with each other, needy and wanting. I palm one perfect peak, and she whimpers the most inviting sound. Sliding from her mouth down her neck, I trail wet kisses in the perfect valley of her chest. Alex's legs squirm beneath me in anticipation.

I pause to look up at her eager face. She smiles flirtatiously, and I smile back. Not because she's ready but because she's not afraid to show it. This girl deserves to be worshipped, and she may finally be starting to realize that.

Pulling up on the material on both of her hips, I nip and suck my way up and down each inner thigh. Bennett arches her back from the pressure of the fabric on her bud of nerves, but I take my time getting to my prize. Reversing my hold, I slide her thong to her feet, sitting back on my knees to take her all in. *This* is mine. *She* is mine. *And one day she'll be able to see that.*

Falling down toward her, I roll her thighs so her knees point outward. She glistens between them, and I force myself not to dive right in.

"Touch yourself, Bennett," I say, looking up at her. She hesitates briefly, then slowly walks her hands toward her middle.

She lands on her clit, but I grab her wrist. "Not there." I guide her hand lower until her one fingertip sits at her entrance. "There."

She dips it in shallowly, feeling exactly what I wanted her to. She looks at me in a way that can only be described as surprised, her eyes hooded from this angle. "That's how I know how you feel about me here," I say softly, pulling her hand toward my mouth and sucking her sweetness off of her finger.

I wait momentarily, her hips shifting between us, then plunge two fingers deep inside of her. Alex moves her hands to grip the sheets on either side of her ass. I remain still despite her clenching around me and bring my face up to meet hers.

Bending down, I once again kiss the spot between her ribs, only this time it's gentle and sweet. "Here," I say, looking her dead in the eye. "Here, I'm not so sure."

Alex gasps, either from my words or my quick movement back between her legs.

Before she has the chance to respond—or object—I rotate my fingers and add my mouth right above them.

Bennett moves her hands from the sheets to my hair as I suck and stroke simultaneously. We fall into a rhythm—her hips and my tongue—and she starts to tighten beneath me.

"Levi," she breathes. She pushes down on the back of my head, putting more pressure on where she needs it most. I slip out of her, continuing with my mouth and reach up to brush her nipple, my fingers still slick from before. Alex's legs start to quiver, when suddenly my phone vibrates from my jeans.

She freezes, now engrossed with the noise, her attention on that rather than my touch.

"Ignore it," I growl, but she ignores me instead, the relentless buzzing still going strong. It finally ends, and Alex relaxes back into the bed, only for it to start up once again.

"Can you get that?" she pants, sitting up on her elbows.

"Seriously?"

"I'm distracted!"

Like I'm having a temper tantrum, I groan, sitting back on my knees. "Fine," I huff.

I reach down and grab my jeans from the floor, slipping my phone from the pocket. I look down at my screen, which is now lit up with two missed calls from Liam.

"It's my brother," I say blankly.

"Ruthie's dad?"

I nod.

"You should call him back."

My eyes grow wide as they float down her body. "Now?"

Alex's cheeks turn the perfect pink before she says, "What if he needs you?"

Although his timing sucks, Alex is right. Liam should still be at Ruthie's game. He knows I'm meeting them before they get to their suite tonight. If something came up or the timing changed, he would just text me. I'm all he has, but we're not really phone call siblings. Something must be up.

Inhaling deeply, I take her in one more time before standing from the mattress. Adjusting myself, my body still very much invested in what was happening in my bed, I return Liam's call.

Alex's gaze bores into me as the phone rings. "Hey," Liam says, answering immediately. "I called you twice. What are you doing?"

With a grin on my face, I lock eyes with Alex. "Eating."

She looks at me, her expression confused as Liam responds. "So, you couldn't answer your—never mind. Listen, we're in the emergency room."

"What?" I yell. Alex sits up, her face now full of concern. "What happened?"

"It's fine. Ruthie took an elbow to the head. She was a little disoriented, so I brought her here to get her looked at."

"I'll be right there," I say, already reaching for my jeans.

"You don't have to—"

"I said I'll be right there." I hang up the phone, shoving one leg in my pants, before I look back at Alex and freeze.

I'm instantly conflicted. Ruthie's my girl, and I need to be there to make sure she's okay. If anyone knows anything about concussions, it's the hockey coach. But Alex is here, and she's already concerned about not being put first. Liam did say my niece was fine, but my instinct is to go.

"What's wrong?" Alex asks, pulling the side of the duvet up over her body.

I slip my other leg in, sitting on the foot of the bed before I continue redressing. "Ruthie got hit in her game. Liam says she's okay, but they want to make sure she doesn't have a concussion."

Alex's hand flies to her mouth. "Oh, no! That's terrible." She pauses, glancing around the room like she's conflicted too. "Well, go!" she says, nudging my leg. She reaches for her bra and slides the straps up her arms, covering herself.

"Are you sure? We were... kind of in the middle of something..." I say, leaning into her.

"Levi, stop." She moves to the edge of the mattress and stands, sliding her thong up her legs. My dick twitches despite the situation, proving just how much I fucking want this girl. "That's not important. Ruthie is."

I stand, joining her as she throws her sweater back on. "You can stay if you want." *Please,* I beg her mentally. *Be here when I get back.*

"Oh, I'm not staying." My whole body deflates as every hope that I've had over this whole interaction flies out the window. "I'm coming with you."

# 37

# Alex

I t's a little bit of a cop out, me going with Levi to check on Ruthie. I just figured what better way to show him that I'm coming around without actually having to say it aloud. I assume a hospital is a pretty safe place to be seen with each other, not to mention Liam apparently already knows about us. *So much for secrecy.* Not that I have any leg to stand on, I texted Brooke the second Levi went into the bathroom before we walked out the door.

I mostly wanted to make sure that she was okay picking Cooper up from school just in case we ran late. I may be alright being seen in the ER with Levi, but I don't think showing up to middle school pick up with Coach Montgomery in the car would be the best way to run the idea of this happening past my son. I also wanted to give her a quick rundown. She wasn't thrilled with my bulleted list of new details—at his apartment, niece is hurt, possible emotional epiphany—but I promised her an update as soon as I could.

Stepping onto the elevator, Levi looks nervous. His brother said that Ruthie seems to be fine. I don't know anything about Liam other than that he plays baseball, and he's a single parent like me, but his reassurance didn't seem to mean much to Levi. According to him, Liam is a "ray of sunshine" that can see the good in almost all situations. Apparently, that makes his opinion about traumatic events a little hard to believe for his darker younger brother.

"I'm sure she's okay," I say, turning to him. The doors close in front of us as he stares straight ahead.

"Yeah, no, I know," he says, painting a smile. "I just want to be there for her. And for Liam."

The part of me that knows what it feels like to go through everything alone—the highs, the lows, the good, the scary—swells at his words. Nick comes around when big things happen, but it's usually Brooke or my mom who swoop in during situations like these, and I know how nice it is to have someone to lean on when you're the only parent around.

Leaving my eyes on Levi, I think back to that first night we met. Seeing him now, there's no doubt in my mind that he was late to the rink because he was with Ruthie. The care that he has for that little girl is evident from his reaction. I was so wrong about him, thinking that he just didn't care about making us wait. In reality, he was doing exactly what I wish Nick would have done even once for Cooper—putting work second to be there for him. Maybe all of us in that office were his second priority, but that's because the person he cared about most was his first.

Consumed by the thought that I judged him so incorrectly, my mind wanders to every other conclusion I jumped to. So, he paid for my dinner, surprised us with sweatshirts, and rented me a car. He didn't do that to throw his money in my face. That's just what I'm used to. He did those things because he can, and because he's a nice guy.

If anything, Levi resists playing the rich guy card like Nick tries to do so frequently. The whole reason we're here is because he doesn't want to only invest money into the Spark the Flame program. He wants to invest his time as well. He wants the program's mission to hit closer to home for this community and give more players opportunities that they wouldn't have otherwise.

Levi could write a check right now for enough money to cover the hockey tuition and equipment expenses for an entire team or ten. But he doesn't. Instead, he brings them to games, lets them meet their heroes, and gives kids like Cooper a chance to live out a dream.

The elevator doors ding open, breaking me from my thoughts. As we walk through the lobby, Levi still looks a bit out of sorts. "I'll drive," I say as we step through the door. I wave to Walter, who raises a brow toward Levi but winks at me.

"I'm fine, Alex, seriously."

"I know," I say as I walk toward the rental. Levi follows alongside me. "But I have this really nice car that somebody rented for me, and if I'm honest... I'm kind of obsessed with the thing."

Opening the driver's side door, I glance over at Levi who is shaking his head and finally flashing a genuine grin. He gets in the passenger seat without any more protest.

"I knew you would like it," he says, pulling his seatbelt over his shoulder.

"I'm just impressed you happened to get the exact same car two times in a row."

Levi hovers the buckle briefly over the clasp it clicks into, but long enough for me to notice his hesitation.

"What?" I ask, starting the car. I punch the hospital into my Maps while I wait for his reply.

"Confession?" he asks as I pull out of the lot.

"Is this like a pause?" I look over at him, my mind reverting back to my thoughts on the elevator.

"Eh... similar, but not really."

"Okay?" I answer skeptically.

Levi looks forward and scratches his head. "This isn't a rental." A silence rings through the SUV, but he doesn't seem bothered. "You needed a car, and I had an extra. I knew you wouldn't use it if you knew it was mine. You can be pissed all you want but—"

"I'm not pissed," I jump in, surprising us both.

He shifts in his seat so he's turned toward me. "You're not?"

My gaze wanders as I swallow. "Actually, no. That was really sweet."

Levi pulls back, his brows raised. "Don't think for one second that I'm keeping it," I add quickly. He rolls his eyes, the corners of his lips turning up. "But that was really sweet." I avoid making eye contact, knowing I'm giving him more than I normally would, but I can see in my periphery that he now wears a full-fledged smile.

His hand lands on my knee. I look down at the contact, then over at him as he gives it a squeeze. I'm not sure if he's talking about the car or my confession, but when he pulls it back to his lap, he says, "I'll take what I can get."

Walking through the Golden City Emergency Room, you can tell that Levi is no stranger to injury. He pushed through these doors like he'd been here before and switched into complete coach mode as he searched for Liam and Ruthie.

If there's one thing that I'm sure of, it's that Levi knows how to command a room. I used to think it was the formal attire and arrogant attitude, but here in jeans and a hoodie, his hair still tousled from when I dug into it, it's the same.

Unlike Nick who needs to puff out his chest, title drop, and belittle everyone else around him to feel important, Levi demands attention all on his own. His size sure helps, and he definitely has a recognizable face in this city, but it's his confidence and natural swagger that draw you in.

I watch as the nurses, medical staff, and even other patients gawk at him as he walks by. Levi doesn't even notice as he looks for his brother. In his mind, Ruthie is the only thing that matters right now.

"Hey, over here," a deep voice yells from down the hall. Our heads both snap to the source. I recognize the man in front of me from one of the pictures I saw when Googling his brother.

He looks just like Levi in some senses but not at all in others. His shape is the same, and he's undeniably handsome, but he has shaggier hair closer to Cooper's and a fresh, innocent face. You can tell the two are brothers, but Liam seems much more relaxed than Levi does—both visually and personality-wise.

On instinct, Levi grabs my hand and pulls me toward him. A tingle shoots up to my shoulder, a reminder that this isn't our norm despite how natural it feels to have my hand entangled with his.

"How is she?" Levi spits out as soon as we're within earshot of his brother.

"Well, hello to you too, little bro."

Levi looks at Liam unamused as Liam lets his gaze fall to our inter-locking fingers. With an easy grin, he lifts a brow toward his brother, then gives me a knowing look. "She's good, man, she's in—" Levi drops my hand and pushes past Liam. "There."

Liam laughs, turning to me. "You must be Alex."

I nod shyly. "And you must be Liam."

"That depends on how he described me."

"Older brother, great athlete, even better dad."

Liam's lips turn in as he nods just once. "Yep, that's me."

The charm of these brothers makes me smile, but the lull in conver-sation makes me feel awkward. I came along to be here for Levi, but even I don't really know what that means yet.

"So, Alex, what are your intentions with my brother?" Liam quips as if reading my mind. My head snaps to him, and he meets me with a wide smile. "I'm just kidding," he adds.

"What has he told you?" I ask, almost too curious for my own good.

"Not much honestly. Just that the physical arrangement was your idea, which was shocking to say the least." My face must scream *What's that supposed to mean,* because he's quick to continue. "I just mean normally that's Levi's thing. Doesn't get too close, doesn't let anyone in."

"I guess we have that in common then," I say softly.

He snickers. "Not anymore."

I tilt my head, asking for an explanation. "Until he met you," Liam offers. "Levi let what happened with his ex build walls around him. Talk about hockey—it was like his heart turned to ice and everyone besides Ruthie and I were just spectators on the other side of the boards."

Letting his words wash over me, I hear them as if he's talking about my own life. "It sounds like maybe we're not so different after all," I mumble to myself.

"But now..." Levi's laugh echoes through the door in perfect timing. "Now, I think he's finally stopped letting his past control his future."

I swallow hard, and he must notice.

"He's all in, Alex. I know my brother better than anyone. I don't know how you did it, but you did."

My palms get sweaty, and my heart starts to race—my body's reaction to the combination of excitement and anxiety that's starting to swirl. This whole time I've been so worried about keeping my own walls up, that I didn't even see his crumbling before me. Guilt rushes through me. How did I not realize that as I was forcing myself to keep Levi out, he was pushing himself to let me in?

As if he can hear my thoughts, Liam says, "I'm glad you two are finally starting to get out of your own way here. If there's one thing I've learned from my experience, it's that you can't wait for things to stop being hard to start being happy."

Gazing up at him wide-eyed, he chuckles. "We're all still working on that in some ways. I'm just glad Levi finally found his catcher." I look at him sideways, my cheeks growing warm. "Yeah, as soon as I said that out loud, I realized how weird it sounds out of context."

I'm not exactly sure what Liam means by his catcher, but butterflies flutter from the idea of being Levi's *anything*. Liam talks so casually, but what he's saying hits me like a punch to the gut.

Waiting for things to stop being hard to start being happy is exactly what I'm doing. For almost twelve years, I've convinced myself that love is too much—too scary, too risky... too hard. I'm waiting for it to feel easy to feel ready. To feel easy to me and to feel easy for Cooper. But Liam's words remind me that love isn't easy. Even if Levi lived in the same world, shared the same schedule, had the same exact priorities, it still wouldn't be simple.

Love by definition is intense. It's deep and fierce and so powerful that it can literally rewire your brain. It's hard, but it's also kind and exciting and with the right person, it can be so worth all of the struggle. You just have to take that first step like Levi has and face the fears that are holding you back.

The step that I know I need to take.

"Dad," a little girl's voice calls out, bringing me back to the moment.

Liam inhales deeply and says, "Guess that's my cue. You coming in?"

"I think I'll give you guys some time. I just wanted to be here to make sure everything was okay. Can you get Levi home?" Liam nods and I smile, so glad that I came.

"You coming to the game later?"

I glance over my shoulder, having already started walking toward the door. "We're not supposed to," I say. "For Spark the Flame I mean."

Liam cocks one brow as he takes a step toward Ruthie's room. "Something tells me if you want to, Levi will figure it out."

# 38

# Levi

R uthie's fine.

The girl took an elbow to the temple and still royally kicked my ass in three games of tick-tack-toe. The doctors suggested she take it easy, which much to her dismay means missing the Flames game tonight, but other than that, she should be good as new soon enough. *Thank God.*

This situation freaked me out way more than you'd think it would considering concussions are far from rare in hockey, and that doesn't include those that go undiagnosed. But Ruthie is my ten-year-old niece, not a two-hundred-pound professional athlete, and I love her just a little more than the guys on my team.

There was one silver lining to all of this happening though, and that was how things ended with Alex. I'm sure the mom in her was worried for Ruthie, but it was the way she handled my reaction that spoke the most to me. She didn't have to be so understanding, and she definitely didn't have to come along. She may be too nervous to admit that this means more to her now than it did before, but her actions speak louder than her silence.

I understand her hesitation. Falling for her doesn't mean that I don't still think about how much pain this could bring. But if having her there today was a look into what it's like to not feel so fucking alone, I'll take the risk of losing this over not having it at all.

Walking into the arena, I'm more ready for this game than ever. We're coming off of a winning streak, which fires me up, Ruthie is fine, and Alex is coming. She texted me earlier asking if it was okay if she came with Cooper and her friend Brooke who I've never met.

Of course, Liam had already told me what she said at the hospital. I called the manager of ticket sales almost immediately to make sure there were tickets available at Will Call. But it was nice hearing from her about wanting to come. It was also nice to mess with her.

Bennett

> Hey, is it okay if Cooper and I come tonight? My friend Brooke is with us too if she can tag along.

>> Hmm, is this for official Spark the Flame business or something?

I was abnormally anxious waiting for her response, but the peace I felt at her two simple words made these last few weeks worth it.

Bennett

> Or something.

At this point, nothing can ruin this night. Losing would come pretty close, but everything that's happened with Alex may just be capable of curing that too.

"Hey, boss," Erik calls from his office. His door is open, and he's at the edge of his desk like he's been waiting for me to walk by. "League rep is here. No-notice drug test."

Dropping my forehead into the crook of my hand, I brush my finger back and forth across my brow. Twice a year the league is permitted to do a piss test on every player. They're random and not even us coaches get notice, but it's mandatory for every team.

Their timing is shit considering the headspace my guys are in and the downer this puts on things. Not that I'm worried about the actual tests, but it completely throws off their routine that's obviously been working. However, it's great for me considering what would normally be a huge annoyance is now only minorly inconvenient thanks to my high on Bennett.

"Alright," I say, blowing out a heavy breath. "I was going to go, uh, talk to Alex, but I can—"

"I got it. You go. Not much you can do here except wait around anyway."

"Are you sure?"

Erik looks at me seriously. "How many times do I have to say it? Double dates, book club, soccer—not workin' for me."

I laugh probably too hard for such a stupid statement, but him giving me time to go see Alex seems to release some sort of endorphins in me. "Hey, I'll take it. Thanks, man."

He tips his chin up to me and grins. "You got it."

Knocking on the door of our suite, Alex, Cooper, and the brunette I can only assume is Brooke, all turn around. Of course I first lock eyes with Bennett, but there's no missing the way her friend looks me up and down. Then, I see Coop.

"Hey, bud," I say, greeting him first.

He bounds over to me, and I hold out my fist. He taps it quickly but then jumps into asking, "Wait, is it true that your niece took a bow to the chicklets?"

"Cooper!" Alex calls from afar.

"Sorry." He clears his throat. "Is, uh, is your niece okay, Coach?"

I laugh, rustling my hand in his hair. "She's okay, buddy. It wasn't to the teeth, but she's got a pretty nice shiner."

Cooper's eyes grow wide, and his mouth falls open. "Woah, on a girl? That's so—"

"Coop."

"Terrible. That's so terrible."

"And pretty sick," I whisper, leaning into his ear.

He smiles and nods, then walks to the snacks. The brunette with hair to her collarbone, wearing heeled combat boots and a jean jacket, comes forward next.

"You must be Brooke," I say, extending my hand.

"You must be Coach Mc—"

"Brooke," Alex interrupts sternly.

"Coach Montgomery," she says with a mischievous smile. I make a mental note to ask Bennett about that later and shake my head yes.

"Nice to meet you."

"Likewise," she says. "Hey, little man," she calls to Cooper. "How about we go get one of those pretzels the size of our faces before warmups start?"

"Yes!" he yells, dropping the fruit on a spoon back into the bowl.

Brooke winks at me, and I can't help but chuckle. She totally planned this to give Alex and I time to talk, which is greatly appreciated but also greatly suspicious. *So much for secrecy, Bennett.*

As they walk away, I turn my attention to her. She's standing in front of me, as beautiful as ever, in dark jeans, her Flames hoodie, and that damn red puffer.

"Nice vest," I say, taking a step toward her.

"Nice suit," she echoes, matching my move. Her eyes don't wander like they would have before. I know we're alone, but it's as if for once she's not worried about who might be around us.

Being that technically other people could walk into this suite, I keep my hands to myself. After Saturday, we have free reign for whatever we decide to do, but until then, I'm technically still the coach who is working with her son.

Alex looks at me with hopeful eyes, then glances at my lips. "How's Ruthie?" she asks, her voice somewhat softer.

"She's good. That girl is tough as hell," I say with a grin.

Her smile grows. "I'm sure she is."

Closing what's left of the gap between us, I add, "Kind of like someone else I know."

Alex's cheeks flush, and she drops her head forward. When she picks it up, a loose wave falls in front of my favorite gold spot.

"Just so you know," I say strongly. "If we weren't here right now, I'd be tucking that hair away from your eye. Maybe brushing your cheek once it's pushed back."

Her lips part as she moves the stray hair from her face. "Just like that," I whisper.

She goes to speak when my phone rings in my hand. Glancing down I see it's Erik. "Sorry, one second." Rolling my eyes, I bring the phone to my ear. "What's up?" I answer.

"Boss, you're gonna wanna come down here."

"What's wrong?"

Erik sighs on the other end of the line. "We have a problem."

"Shit."

My mind starts racing. There is no way there's trouble with these tests. I make it my mission to know every detail about what's going on with this team. With the boys right downstairs, I decide not to get into it over the phone. I want to be here with Alex, but the last thing she needs is for me to worry her about anything else. "Okay. I'll be right there."

Ending the call, I look back at her. "I'm sorry, I have to go."

"Oh, okay," she says timidly.

"Can I see you tomorrow? You can come over, or I can meet you somewhere. Whatever you want."

"Why don't you come over to my house. Brooke already asked Cooper to sleepover after school and watch some movie that he shouldn't be watching."

I can't help my flirtatious expression. "I think Brooke might be my new favorite person."

"Hey," she says playfully.

"Besides Ruthie." Alex rolls her eyes but smiles. "And you."

Glancing around to make sure we're alone, I prove my confession by quickly crashing my lips to hers. Before her body can even catch up to mine, I quickly pull away.

"Tomorrow." I step backwards two strides. "Six?"

She bites her lower lip. "Six," she repeats.

"He fucking what?" I pace back and forth behind my desk, Cal, the league representative and Erik sitting in the seats in front of me.

"He failed. His test came up hot for cocaine." The rep turns his clipboard toward me where he has a big, red X drawn next to Anderson's name.

"Holy shit," I say, mostly to myself. We've been on a ridiculous streak, and now, our star player fails a goddamn drug test.

"He's out for the next twenty games," Cal says, clearing his throat. Legally, he's obligated to tell us the consequences for a failure, but right now it feels like salt in the wound.

Rubbing the back of my head with my hand, I watch the next twenty games flash before my eyes. "Fuck."

He sits forward in his seat. "Look, these kids are young, you remember how it was. They're here for what? A few hours a day. That's a lot of time to be influenced by the world they live in."

I know that—better than anyone else. I did my fair share of partying as a player, and I definitely remember the pressure to fit in—or stand out. But I have higher expectations, and they know that. I just didn't see this coming from my guys right now, and I didn't prepare for it at all as a coach.

Cal stands. "We'll refer him to the league's substance abuse program so he knows he has resources, but other than that, I'll go talk to Jack and let you take it from here."

Sucking my teeth, I shake my head. "Yeah, thanks."

Cal leaves, and I look at Erik. "Where is he?"

"In the locker room," he says. "How did this happen?"

"I don't know," I say, a panic still low in my gut. "I don't fucking know."

Erik clasps his hands under his chin, his elbows resting on his knees. "I mean, I guess there have been signs."

My head whips to his, this shitty situation making me quick to react. "What?"

"Signs," he repeats.

"What are you talking about?" I snap with a bite.

"I'm just saying, you've seen him. He's so hot and cold lately, but when he's hot, he's really fucking hot. I mean that kid has been unstoppable, even more so than normal."

The last few weeks race through my mind. Erik's right. Drew has been on fire. He has ridiculous natural talent, but his performance has been something very different lately. I guess I didn't notice. Or wasn't paying attention.

My natural reaction is to throw myself in that locker room and ask Drew what the hell he was thinking. How could he put his team in such a vulnerable position? And for what? So he looks like the cool guy? Like the hero?

But then the coach in me steps forward, and now I'm questioning myself. How did I miss this? Was I so distracted by pursuing Alex that I didn't see what was happening right in front of my face?

Yes, it is my job to win games, but it's also my job to shape these guys into men and to know everything that goes on in this arena. I'm supposed to lead by example, but my attention has been completely divided since Bennett walked into my life.

Erik's statement echoes in my mind. *"I guess there have been signs."*

Images of Drew skating harder and faster than I've ever seen him before pop into my head. I see him scoring multiple goals every game, picture the time blood was trickling from his nose in our huddle. His solitude between periods, his sweat, his aggression—all of it obvious. Just not until now.

I have never been any less than one thousand percent dedicated to my work. Unless it was Ruthie or Liam, hockey came first. But then Alex appeared in that little hallway outside of my office, with her puffy red vest and her grouchy little attitude, and everything changed.

Anxiety washes over me. I'm torn up about Drew, but what hits me worse is the realization that I don't know how to be both of these people. I clearly can't be the coach that my guys need and the man that Alex deserves at the same time. In this scenario, I missed seeing the signs that one of my players was spiraling into very dangerous territory. What happens when it's something more? When it's worse? When it's something that can hurt Alex or Cooper?

This time, it was hockey that got the short end of the stick. How long until Alex feels like they're the ones who aren't getting enough? That's her biggest fear. It's the one thing that she has been very up front about since the moment we met. She doesn't want her and her son to be second best. To be let down. What if I finally get to have her, and I throw it all away?

I don't know how to be exceptional in both of these roles, and I'm not used to how that disappointment feels. How do I give one hundred percent to the sport and the girl? Better yet, how do I not fail the two things that I want to be great at more than anything in the world? How do I choose between hockey and her? Between my first love and the potential love of my life?

# 39

# Alex

The biggest story in the hockey world today isn't about the Flames' win yesterday, despite missing their best forward, or even their extravagant gala tomorrow. It's about how Drew Anderson—number twelve, star forward—failed his no-notice drug test.

I'm not sure who's more upset, Drew or my twelve-year-old son who now has to go twenty games without watching his favorite player skate the ice. There wasn't much being said about it before Coop left for school this morning, but seeing him off the ice yesterday devastated him. Even Brooke acted weird when I told her about it. I think realizing her crush is an actual human threw her off her game more than she'd like to admit.

Drew was clearly torn up about the whole situation. I saw one interview this afternoon, and he looked like he hadn't slept all night. I'm sure this is embarrassing. I'm also sure this isn't the turn he thought his career was going to take after doing so well these last few weeks.

I can imagine that Levi was also shocked, although I can't be sure since I haven't spoken to him since we talked before the game. I texted him last night to let him know I'm here for him, but I haven't heard back. There's plenty being said online about his involvement and reaction to everything, but I know better than anyone not to believe whatever you see in the media.

It would be nice to hear that he's doing okay. I know that he takes a lot of pride in his team and their performance, but I keep reminding myself that he probably has a million things he needs to deal with today.

Between handling the drug test situation and the big Spark the Flame event tomorrow, I'm sure he's super busy. He said he'd come over today at six, so I won't worry about anything until then. And when that time comes, I plan to finally tell him how I feel. That just means I have to occupy the next couple of hours so I don't go crazy from the lack of contact.

It's a good thing I myself have a gala to prepare for—something I never thought I'd say. According to Sadie, I have to find a dress for myself and a tux for Cooper all within a specific budget determined by the program. Not that money should be any issue considering the number she sent me could pay my rent. I considered arguing that it was way too much, but I thought against it. That chick is scary when she wants to be.

That assignment is how I find myself on the luxurious side of downtown Golden City on a Friday afternoon. Instead of catching up on emails and getting ahead of next week's blog post, I'm drinking a nine dollar latte and browsing stores I've never even heard of before. *So, this is how the other side lives.*

After countless failed places, I finally spot a store I somewhat recognize. The writing on the front window sparkles in the sun, the swirl of the letters dancing across the glass. I can't place how, but I know this brand. Stepping inside, I hope that the familiarity will bring me good luck and finally lead me to the perfect dress.

After walking into the store, I'm greeted by an employee who doesn't even attempt to not judge my sneakers. I struggle to find my bearings, surrounded by crisp colors, clean lines, and crystal fixtures. Everything looks much different than the places where I normally shop that are lit up by fluorescent lights, and it's a little intimidating. I head right for the back, spying floor length gowns hanging in all colors by the checkout.

Running my fingers down the expensive materials, my eyes are drawn to a satin dress the same color of my infamous vest. Pulling it from the rack, I spin it around on the hanger. It has straps that are meant to fall down on your shoulders and a tight bodice to hold everything in. The back laces up, and I blush thinking of Levi untying the knot that sits right above the waistline. Holding my breath, I check the price tag. It's well within the budget the Flames allowed, but it's still more than my utility bills.

"Wow," I whisper to myself. I contemplate trying it on when a voice calls out to me from behind.

"Lex?"

I whip my head around like I've been caught stealing, which is how it feels to even hold something this expensive, and a shiver creeps up my spine. "You've got to be kidding me."

"Nice to see you too," Nick says with a smug grin. He has a suit bag thrown over his shoulder, and it's only when I see the logo on the wall behind his arrogant face that I finally place where I know this store.

With disappointment in my tone, I admit, "I forgot that you shop here."

"Best suits in GC," he replies. "Didn't know you did though." He points to the dress in my hands, and I hang it back up like someone lit it on fire. I hate my reaction. *How does he always make me feel so small?*

"I don't," I respond. "But I have to find something for the gala tomorrow."

"Oh, that's right. I forgot about that. Am I supposed to go too?"

I make a poor attempt at hiding my eye roll. I never even thought about whether or not Nick was invited. Technically, as Cooper's father, I'm sure he'd be allowed to attend, but it probably says something that no one even thought to ask if he'd be coming with us.

"I guess you can, but you don't have to," I answer honestly.

He nods, turning his lips in. "So, is your new boyfriend footing the bill for that one?" Changing the subject, he tips his head toward the gowns and raises his brow.

A slow heat creeps up from my chest either from his condescending assumption or the fact that it's borderline true. "I don't know what you're talking about," I say.

"Oh, come on, Lex." The nickname only adds to my annoyance. "I'm not an idiot."

An uncontrollable laugh escapes me, but I manage not to say what I'm thinking. "And what's that supposed to mean?"

"I've heard him talk about you. It doesn't take a rocket scientist to see it. You're sleeping with him." He says it as a statement instead of a question as if there's no doubt he could ever be wrong.

"That's none of your business."

Shaking his head in the most condescending way, he snickers. "Exactly. Just one of many in his bed I'm sure."

"You don't even know him," I shoot out defensively.

He scoffs. "And you do? You learned his name, what? Like a month ago?"

My heart threatens to beat out of my chest. "Why does it even matter to you?"

"It matters if my son is involved."

This time I don't hold back my laugh *or* my thoughts. "Oh, so *now* you care what happens with Cooper?" I say through a chuckle.

Nick adjusts his stance while watching his feet, which is ironic considering he has not one leg to stand on. "Forget it," he says. "Just don't let this fuck Cooper up when the Flames thing is over and Monte's on to the next..."

I step toward him, my finger in his face. "Finish that sentence."

He clears his throat but doesn't back down. "Woman," he says, choosing his words wisely for maybe the first time in his life.

"How about you let me worry about Cooper like I always do, and you stay worrying about only yourself like *you* always do."

Nick shakes his head slowly, running his tongue along his top teeth. "Whatever. You know what, tell Cooper I'll be there tomorrow," he says, turning around. A hum of nerves stirs in my belly before I remember that there's a better chance of seeing God than Nick following through on his promise.

"Oh, and Lex," he calls as he stomps toward the door. "Red's not really your color."

I fume with the same shade he's describing. "It's Alex!" I yell back.

He waves over his shoulder, and I, once again, grab the dress from the rack. It's now even more perfect than before.

After my run-in with Nick, and a solid half hour of dissociating in my—*Levi's*—car, I grabbed gold, strappy heels and a new tux for Cooper.

Seeing him was horrible. It doesn't help that when all I want is to talk to Levi, the man I wanted to see least showed up. I never imagined a life where my ex was such a dick, but if there's one thing I've been forced to learn, it's that Nick's behavior says a lot more about him than it does about me.

Shame on me for ever thinking Levi was like him. Nick's right, I haven't known Levi all that long, but he still talks to me with more respect than the father of my child ever has. The revelation fills me with gratitude. I pull my phone out to no notifications from Levi but decide to send him another text anyway.

> Can't wait to see you tonight.

Exiting out of our messages, I see one I missed from Brooke.

Brooke

> I'll be by to get Coop around five.

Perfect. That gives me enough time now to catch up with Cooper and enough time later to get ready once he leaves. Liking the text, I pull up to school pick-up. Cooper walks out of the building moments later with his phone in his hand only inches from his face.

"How was your day?" I ask as he buckles his seatbelt.

"It was fine," he says, looking back at his phone.

"Excited for your sleepover?"

He doesn't answer with words, just a distracted, "Mhmm."

I wait for him to say literally anything else, but he is so engrossed in whatever he's watching. A few minutes pass before I try to get his attention. "Cooper." He doesn't respond so I wait a beat longer before trying again. "Coop."

"Yeah?" he finally says without looking at me.

I pull his wrist away from holding his phone. When his head snaps to me, I see he has a headphone in his outside ear. Rolling my eyes at what should have been obvious from my twelve-year-old son, I ask, "What are you watching?"

Turning the screen toward me, I finally lay eyes on the man I've been waiting to hear from all day. He looks worn down, his pewter green eyes sunken in, rather than bold and piercing like they usually are.

"The Flames' press conference," he says. "Monte's talking about Anderson's test."

I sneak one more peak at Levi before the screen goes black. It's crazy how much my heart aches to hear from him, but it only makes me more excited to see him tonight and finally tell him how I really feel.

"There. Sorry, it's over." He pulls his headphone from his ear and tucks both that and his phone into his pocket.

"How was it?" I ask, more curious for answers than conversation. Seeing Levi busy does help me feel better about not hearing from him, but now I want all of the details I can get.

"I mean, Anderson's out for weeks, but Monte did a great job going through it. There's like nothing that guy isn't good at."

My cheeks flush as I think about all of the things I know he excels in that are completely inappropriate in this exact moment. Right as I go to ask for more information, and distract myself from my current thoughts, Cooper speaks again.

"I don't think I want to play professional hockey anymore."

I look at him side-eyed, completely confused. I try to sound casual as I reply, careful not to look like I'm prying. There's no better way to cut this conversation short than Cooper feeling like I'm interrogating him. "Really?" I ask simply.

"Yeah," he says. I start to form my response in my head, organizing my thoughts about how it's okay for him to change his mind, that he has plenty of time to think about it, when he continues. "I think I want to coach like Monte instead."

A wave of validation surges through me. They say kids are the best judges of character, and knowing now how I feel about Levi, I am more comforted than I could have imagined to hear that Cooper wants to be like him. I've been noticing recently that he seems to have a knack for reading people. Sort of like a certain coach I know.

"I think you'd be great at that, Coop."

He nods confidently. "So does Monte." *He's confided in him?*

"You like him, huh?" The question comes out as if my need to know for sure has bubbled over.

"Duh." He looks out the passenger window, and just when I think the conversation is over, he turns back to me. "You do too, don't you, Mom?"

My stomach instantly churns, my hands white-knuckling the wheel. I thought I was cautious. Did he see my phone? Did he hear me talking with Brooke? Does he know why we walked out of the diner?

Keeping my cool, I swallow my nerves and ask, "What makes you say that?"

"I can just tell," he says.

My behavior over the last few weeks runs through my mind. I go over everything I've said *to* and *about* Levi. I analyze everything I've done at the games, the practices, and any other time I've interacted with him. I'm scrutinizing every tiny detail that could have given Cooper any sign when he continues. "You seem different when he's around. I don't know, like happier."

Tears build behind my eyes as I realize even he has seen a change in me. There he goes, reading *me*. "And would that be okay?" I ask. "If I did like Monte?"

Cooper nods, then grins as he says, "Sure. As long as he keeps the tickets coming." Nudging him playfully, I wipe a quiet tear that falls from relief. "You deserve to be happy, Mom."

"I love you," is all I can manage to say.

"Yeah, yeah, love you too." Cooper looks back out the window.

I let the highs and lows of this conversation wash over me—the panic of thinking Cooper was upset and the solace in knowing he isn't. It's a whirlwind. But what really breaks me is pride. I did that. I raised my son to be sweet and compassionate and a great judge of character. And I did it all on my own.

"You really are good at reading people, you know that?" I force out, swallowing down my emotions.

"I know," he says matter-of-factly. "You can call me Coach Coop."

# 40

# Alex

It's seven thirty, and there's still no sign of Levi. Not only is he late, but there have been no calls or texts from him all day. Part of me feels like I have no reason to be upset. I know he's in the middle of something important, and technically, we are still playing by the guidelines of our arrangement. But most of me is totally pissed.

For weeks I attempted to keep this casual. I told him over and over that this was supposed to be strictly physical between us. I swallowed down whatever feelings seemed to grow and tried to stick to our original plan. But he's the one who pushed me. He's the one that started this.

If I check my receipts, Levi was the one who first paused our situation in order to break certain criteria—and then did it again. He was also the one who ignored my attempt to put an expiration date on what we're doing and initiate a rule number three. Basically, he was the half of our strictly physical relationship who weaseled his way into my heart and made me feel things for him that I told myself from the very start I was going to avoid. And now, where is he?

My mind jumps right to the idea that he decided that he's done with me. The drug test happened with hockey, and he realized that he doesn't have the time or want or need for anyone else—or at least for me. But of course, there are other possibilities. He could be hurt or sick or stuck on the side of the road with no phone or access to civilization. Those things just seem harder to believe.

The old me would assume it's the first one—a me problem—that something or someone else better or more important came up, and he didn't care enough to tell me. Thanks to Nick, I was programmed to assume that I'd always be second best, especially when it came to someone with a job like Levi's. It's the reason that I judged him so hard when we first met and why, until recently, I convinced myself that despite his actions, there was no way that this could ever work. But things are different now. *I'm* different now.

These last few weeks have taught me a lot about myself, but there are two things that stick out in particular. The first is that I was letting Nick control my actions and keep me in the stagnant place that he left me in twelve years ago. The other is—I'm done with that.

Levi came into my life and changed everything. Not only did he give my son a one-in-a-million opportunity, but he gave me the best sex I've ever had in my life—or my dreams. He showed me that you can have a full wallet *and* a full heart, and that I was quick to judge based on my past.

Most importantly though, he helped to open my eyes to the idea that, even as a mom with baggage, I deserve to be happy and put myself first. It's the reason that I finally started looking for a new job today where I can find fulfillment by writing about something meaningful. And why when he came over tonight, I was finally going to tell him that I was wrong. I do want more, and I want it with him.

With that in mind, I decide that I'm not letting Levi do this. Whether he's second guessing us or something else happened that's completely unrelated to the connection we have, he's not getting off this easily. Countless times, he's begged me to talk to him. He's asked, commanded, and teased his way to getting answers from me. It's time for me to use the confidence I've gained through him to do the same.

With the plan to call him one more time, I pick up my phone. Clicking his name, the call connects, but it doesn't even ring—straight to voicemail.

"That's it," I say aloud. I grab the keys off of the island, which are just another reminder of how Levi overstepped our situationship before I decided to do the same. Clenching them in my hand, I let the fear, anxiety, and irritation I have work their way out of my body through the teeth of the keys digging into my palm. There's such a cluster of emotions going through me that I'm not sure which will win out first. All I know is that the only way to figure it out is to find Levi.

Pulling up to Levi's place, I still haven't decided how I'm going to get to him. From the one time I was here, I know you need a special card that tells the elevator that it's allowed to go up to his penthouse apartment. I never thought I'd be saying that about the guy that I am pining over, but I started this journey to step out of my comfort zone, and here I am.

Walking toward the door, I see a familiar face. "Hi, Walter," I say cheerfully.

He waves and smiles politely like he did that first time I was here. In his defense, he probably doesn't recognize me considering the amount of people that walk in and out of this building, but I certainly recognize him considering the number of doormen that I know.

Stepping closer to where he is, I inhale deeply and shoot my shot. "Walter, have you seen Levi around?" He stares at me blankly. "You know—big guy, bigger butt. He's got green eyes and lips that should be illegal on a man?" More staring. "Yay high," I add, stretching my arm dramatically above my head.

He holds his gaze, his genuine smile now straightening out, and just when I think maybe doormen are like those guards that stand outside of Buckingham Palace who are trained not to speak, he parts his lips.

"Alex?" a voice says.

So engrossed in Walter, I scan his face for any sign that it was him who said my name. His eyes flit off to his side, and I realize the sound didn't come from Walter's mouth.

Looking toward the exit, I find Liam standing next to me on the sidewalk. He must have walked out when I was describing Levi like a missing person and analyzing the doorman code of conduct.

"What are you doing here?" he asks.

Smiling at Walter, then turning my body toward Liam, I say, "I was looking for Levi. He was, uh, well—he was supposed to come over a few hours ago, but he didn't."

My skin feels like it's crawling as I say it, embarrassment and doubt creeping in. Maybe Liam knows something I don't. Maybe Levi has talked to him about us since I saw him last at the hospital, and now, me being here just looks pathetic—and a little stalkery.

"I was worried," I add. *And pissed.*

Liam's face falls. He creases his brow, then tenses his jaw, and with this expression, I can really see the resemblance between him and his brother.

"When's the last time you heard from him?" he asks, his voice serious.

"Not since before the game yesterday. I was with him when he got the call about the drug test. That's when we made plans to meet today at six, but he never showed."

"Shit," he says, running his hand through his shaggy hair. "I knew he was gonna take this hard, but I didn't think it'd be this bad. I haven't heard from him either."

A slight panic starts to take over the annoyance that I was feeling before. Liam is Levi's person. If he hasn't confided in him—or at least taken his calls—this has to be worse than I thought.

"I assume you already checked his apartment," I ask, glancing at the doors that lead into the lobby.

Liam slides a card out of his pocket that looks exactly like the one that Levi used the other day. "Yep. He's not there, and his phone was turned off and sitting on the counter."

In case I wasn't sure before, a lump builds in my throat that proves just how much I care about Levi. I should be angry about this. I should be pissed off that something happened with work, and he completely abandoned me without so much as a text. That's what I was afraid would happen. It's exactly what Nick would do.

But I'm not mad—not in the slightest. If anything, I'm more upset that I didn't make him believe that he could come to me. I'm worried that I pushed him away so much... that it worked.

"I never thought Levi would run from his problems," I say, picturing the strong man who has been a rock for me in so many ways these past few weeks.

Liam laughs, then reads my change in expression. "I'm sorry, it's just, this is exactly what I'd expect him to do. Maybe not literally run away, but Levi takes things like this really hard. He might put on a tough act, but deep down, he holds himself to impossibly high standards, and anything short of meeting those feels like a failure to him."

I nod in understanding, although until right now, I didn't see it that way. That's why he's so dedicated to his job. Not because of the money that it makes him or the status that it brings, but because he loves it. And because of that, he gives it everything he has.

"If you ask me," Liam continues. "That's why he took the break-up with Rachel so hard. At the end of the day, I don't think he ever really saw himself spending the rest of his life with her, but he saw her leaving as his failure. Not because she screwed him over, but because he missed the signs that it was coming. To him, he should have been able to predict what she was going to do."

"Kind of like with Drew and his drug test."

"Exactly. That guy sees the best in everyone but himself." Liam shakes his head with a grin. "My little fucking storm cloud."

I smile despite the conversation, thinking back to the day that Liam called about Ruthie. "And his ray of sunshine," I whisper. I glance up at Liam who is already grinning.

"Yeah," he laughs. "Something like that." He looks around, a smirk still on his face, when all of a sudden, he nods knowingly. "Come on," he says, pulling my arm.

"Where are we going?" I ask as I follow him to the lot.

"I think I know where he is."

Liam stops his car in a gravel parking lot in front of a rickety building beside an old rusted fence.

"Batting cages?" I ask, sitting forward in my seat to look out the window.

Before he can answer, I see movement coming from behind the cage where a tall figure stands holding a baseball bat. All I can see from here, thanks to the one hanging light, is his large frame, tousled hair, and grey freaking sweatpants.

"You go," Liam says, tipping his chin toward the passenger door. "I'll wait here."

I offer him a grateful smile and push the door open. Walking toward the cage, Levi doesn't even turn around. He's swinging at balls one after another like he's in battle, and they are the enemy.

"You should really be wearing a helmet," I say boldly as I slip my fingers into the links of the fence.

When he turns around, Levi's eyes grow wide as they land on mine but then settle into an expression I can only describe as relief. He pauses his movement, taking me in, then swallows hard, hanging the bat by his side. "You always did have a thing for safety, Bennett."

I shouldn't be surprised that even now, he can still make me blush, but I try to hide it anyway.

"You never came over," I say, bringing my eyes back to his. I get a glimpse of the color, so dark that it almost matches the sky, before he puts his one free hand on his hip and drops his head toward the ground.

A ball whirls past his shoulder and lands on the fence, causing me to jump back and him to look up. The machine shuts down right after, the whirring sound that's been in the air now silenced. I take the opportunity to round the fence, and when I get to the entrance, Levi turns toward me. I walk to meet him, grabbing the bat from his hand and leaning it against the metal behind him.

"I'm sorry," he says, his voice low.

"What happened?"

He rubs his brow with his first two fingers, twisting so his back is to me. He exhales heavily then turns back around. "I don't know how to do this, Alex."

"Do what?"

Lifting his head, he lets his arm drift slowly back to his side. "Be two people at once. I can't be the coach I need to be for my team and the man that I want to be for you."

Taking one step closer I say, "But you *are* being both of those things."

"Am I?" he yells, throwing his hands in the air. "Because it feels like I'm failing as a coach, not even realizing that my star player is using fucking drugs." He lowers his hands and his volume, then continues. "And here I am trying to convince you that you can trust me with your heart and with Cooper, and what do I do? The one thing I know that you won't stand for."

Closing the gap between us, I move toward him and take his hand in mine. His grip is weak, but he doesn't let go. "But I do trust you, Levi. That's what I was going to tell you tonight. And I'm sorry that it took me so long to see that. That's a me problem," I say, my voice drifting off. "I know that now."

He lets his eyes slowly fall shut before bringing them back to me. "I still don't know how to give you the attention that you deserve without sacrificing my commitment to my job." He inhales deeply. "And I know that sounds like everything that you don't want to hear, but hockey is like my baby, Alex."

"I know," I say, bringing my hand to his cheek. "I have one of those too." He huffs out a laugh that I feel in my soul and leans into my touch. "I'm serious, Levi. I'm not expecting you to be perfect. I know things will come up and your work will come first, but I also know now that it's the way that we handle that—together—which will make things different from my past. Nick chose his job over us because he felt that we had less to offer—"

"He's a fucking idiot," he interrupts, and now it's my turn to laugh.

"I know, but *you're* not. When this all went down with Drew, I didn't want you to push it to the side to come be with me. I wanted you to come to me so I could be there for you while you face it head-on. Nick made me feel insecure in his love. That's why I thought afterward that I always had to be first. But with you, I'm more confident in myself than I've ever been before. And that's because of how you handle things." I tip his chin up. "How you communicate with me."

His eyes fill with understanding. "So, if you still want to do this," I continue, my voice growing stern. "I'm gonna need you to keep that shit up." He flashes me a full-tooth smile, and I do the same.

"You didn't even say pause," he eventually says coyly.

Finally feeling like I can relax a little, I let my shoulders settle. "Would you look at that."

Levi bites his lower lip, then slips his finger through my belt loop and tugs me toward him like he has so many times before. "Alex Bennett, are you warming up to me?"

Looking back and forth between his eyes, I think of the first time he spoke those exact words to me at Cooper's game. Back then, I was so stuck in the past that I couldn't see beyond who I judged him to be. I thought I hated him, but really, I hated who I assumed he was. I thought he was the type who would think less of someone like me because I'm not rich or lavish. I thought he would think his job was so much more important than a single mom.

Now, I know how wrong I was. Levi is nothing like what I imagined. He is kind and genuine and one of the least selfish people I know. He's sweet and compassionate and someone who, despite everything he has to offer, worries that he may not be enough for a mom and her son.

Levi raises his brow like he's looking for an answer, and I give him one by wrapping my lips up in his. Cradling my face in his palms, he deepens our kiss, sweeping his tongue past mine before he pulls back.

"So," he says with a grin. "What happens now?"

Pushing my chest into his, I sweep my arm past his hip. He sucks in a breath as I grab the bat behind him and hold it between us. "Now, we get out of here."

Levi licks his lips and pulls me to him. "Not a baseball girl, Bennett?" he growls.

"Well, I did hear you were looking for a catcher." He cocks a brow and tilts his head sideways. "Yeah, no, it still sounds wrong."

"Agreed," he laughs.

Throwing my arms around his neck I bring my forehead to his. "How about we stick with hockey then?"

He closes his eyes and takes a deep breath. On the exhale he says, "Now *that* I can do."

# 41

# Levi

"Looking good, little brother." Liam comes up behind me and claps me on the shoulder of my black, three-piece suit before standing next to me in the back of the ballroom.

Giving him an obvious once-over in his dark green tux, I turn down my lips. "Not too bad yourself, big bro."

"You know I had to rep the Gators," he says, running his hands down the front of his jacket. My eyes flutter closed as I nod my head. "So, where is she?"

The nerves that disappeared in the thirty seconds since we started talking come back with a vengeance. "She should be here in..." Pulling out my phone, I check the time. "Six minutes."

"Not that you're counting." I throw my elbow into him as my response, and he stumbles back dramatically. "I was kidding, geez. Little nervous?"

"No," I snap back. One of the waiters who is prepping in the corner looks our way.

Liam snickers and leans into my ear. "Know how I know you're lying." I avoid his gaze, but he continues anyway. "You're causing a scene at a youth community fundraiser."

I roll my eyes, pulling down the cuffs of my sleeves. "Whatever, I'm totally telling Gavin to give you a dog." Liam looks at me confused, but I shake it off. "Never mind. This is just... kinda big."

He smiles, but his eyes grow serious. "You really like her, huh?"

"Yeah, man. I really do." I focus straight ahead on the stage. "And after tonight, she never has to see me again if she doesn't want to."

"Oh, I think she'll want to."

My eyes drift to him. "And why's that?"

He taps my arm and nods his head toward the entrance behind us. "Because if she likes you even half as much as she likes your ass..." Turning around, my eyes land on Bennett who, like Liam hinted, was already staring at my back. "Then you're golden."

My entire body floods with happiness, and without saying another word to my brother, I move right for Alex and Cooper.

I take advantage of the space between us to study her the way I know I won't be able to once I'm standing next to her son. She is beautiful. Fucking stunning in a red I've become so accustomed to seeing her in. The same color as my favorite article of clothing. A perfect match to my tie—and my team.

Her hair falls in loose waves down either side of her flawless face. Her lips are glossed over, her cheeks a soft pink, and her lids are covered in shimmer that reflect the gold in her eye. Every curve of her body is shown off the right amount to make me want more but not nearly enough to satisfy my need.

Cooper stands next to her in a suit nearly identical to mine except for that it's five sizes smaller. His hair is brushed back and tucked neatly behind his ears, his hands shoved into his pockets.

They both wear smiles that light up the room, and I'm lucky that both of them are directed at me. "You're here," I say, my eyes first on Alex.

She nibbles her lip which draws my attention right to her mouth. Thankfully Cooper extends his arm out toward me which pulls my gaze away from her. "What's up, buddy?" I ask, bending down to bump my fist to his. "Loving the outfit."

Coop does a slow three-sixty spin, his hands still tucked into his pockets. "Figured I should probably get used to it if I'm going to coach like you someday."

I glance up at Alex without pulling away. She raises her brow with a grin on her face. "So, we officially decided, huh?"

"Yeah, I mean, I'll still play for a while to stay involved in the game, but give me twenty years, and I'll be right where you are."

Standing back up, I pull my neck back and snort out a laugh. "You've got it all planned out then."

"That's right. Gonna break your record as youngest coach too."

I fake devastation, then rough up his hair. "Bring it on," I say right as Erik walks in.

"Hey, there's our spotlight," he calls, stepping up next to Cooper. "Good to see you, Alex. Coop..." He holds out his palm, and the two of them move their hands in a series of slaps and bumps that form some kind of handshake.

Alex and I look at each other and laugh, but instantly the air grows heavy. Either Erik senses it too or, once again, he's out to find "pigs in a blanket" because he throws his arm around Cooper's shoulders and says, "Let's go find the food." Without so much as looking back at his mom or me, Cooper lets Erik guide him away leaving Bennett and me alone at last.

Unable to keep my hands off of her any longer, I lean in to give her a professional kiss on the cheek. She places her hand on the outside of my arm and squeezes it tightly. "God, red is so your color," I whisper in her ear before pulling away.

She smothers a laugh, then trails down the length of me. "And black is most definitely yours."

I turn my head to the Flames logo plastered on the wall closest to us painted in the same two colors. "I guess we make the perfect pair." Alex parts her lips, then seals them again as a small hand drops on my shoulder.

"We're ready for you, Coach," Sadie says. She smiles at Alex, then tips her head toward the stage.

"I'll be right there," I say to her. She nods, then goes to take her seat next to Cooper, who has already found the table with Erik, a plate of hors d'oeuvres piled high in front of each of them.

Turning back to Alex, a dark heat spreads through me. "Should we be waiting for anyone?" I ask intensely.

"Brooke will sneak in after her shift toward the end. Thank you for letting her come by the way."

"Of course. She's important to you two." There's a lingering silence in the air. "Anyone else?"

Alex swallows hard but smiles shallowly. "That's it."

My jaw grows tight, but my body relaxes. "Then that's all we need." I hold my arm out to her, and she hooks hers on top of it.

"Agreed."

Leading Alex across the room, I realize how natural this feels. For a second, I almost forget that I'm just doing the gentlemanly thing and taking our guest to her table, rather than walking my girl to her seat. I pull out the chair next to Cooper, and Alex goes to sit down, but I tighten my grip on her arm keeping her with me. "I'm so glad you're here," I say, hoping she understands the depth of my words.

She explores my face, taking me in and showing me she does. "Me too."

Alex sits next to her son, and I move toward the stage for my introduction speech. Walking up the few steps, I can't help but pause to look back at her once more. In a sea of people, she stands out like a lighthouse. Moving to the podium, I realize that's exactly what she is—a beacon in the roughest waters. Just like hockey was.

Standing in front of the crowd, I pull the speech from my pocket that Sadie and I wrote for this weeks ago. "Good evening, everyone," I start. "Thank you so much for being here. As most of you know, the Spark the Flame program is something that I hold very dear to my heart, and I am happy to be sharing it with all of you tonight." Glancing down at the rest of my script, I stop reading, deciding I don't need it. I know exactly what to say.

"Looking around, there are so many different types of people here from our city. Some of you are professional athletes, coaches, businessmen, and donors. Others are friends, fans, sons, and mothers." I pause my scanning eye an extra beat longer on Alex.

Trailing over to Cooper, I wink. "Some of us are here because we hope to be like our heroes one day." I take a deep breath in, searching for a familiar face before I continue. "And some of us *are* those heroes." Anderson stares at me intensely as his throat moves up and down.

"My point is, we're all from different worlds. We come from different walks with different life experiences, and yet, we have so much in common. We are all here because we see how important it is to connect the sport that we love so much to the community around us. Of course, we all love to win, and well, I don't know about you, but I wouldn't mind bringing the Cup to Golden City." The group whoops and cheers before quieting back down. I take the time to bring my eyes back to Drew.

"But hockey is so much more than a scoreboard. There's a lot of pressure on all athletes to perform their best every game—all the time—but we wouldn't expect that from these players that we work with in the program. We would tell them to enjoy the game. To try their best. To have fun with their teammates while they do what they love.

That's why I started Spark the Flame. Not just because it's nice for our team to give back to our community, but because that community has just as much to give to us. They serve as a reminder that hockey might be our thing, but it's not *everything*. And we might love winning..." Looking at Alex, I finish my sentence. "but it's not winning if it means sacrificing what you love."

Alex's mouth falls open as I wrap up my speech.

"So, at this time, it is my honor to turn the mic over to Sadie Wells, the woman who put all of this together. Sadie has worked very hard these last few weeks to organize a presentation spotlighting one of Golden City's best peewee players and one of the Flames' biggest fans, who you will hear from soon. Thank you. Sadie..."

The crowd cheers, and Sadie rises from her seat as I walk toward the exit. Both Alex and I have seen the presentation before today, so I know I have a solid fifteen minutes until I need to be back to see Cooper's speech. And as much as I want to go sit next to Bennett, there is no way I'd be able to keep my hands to myself with my veins pumping with this much adrenaline. Not to mention, my nerves are even more shot after a confession like that.

Just outside of the ballroom doors I spot a bathroom. Thinking a splash of cool water to my face and a mini pep-talk in the mirror might be exactly what I need, I push the door open. Bracing my hands on the sink, I take a much needed deep breath, then reach for the faucet. Right as I'm about to run the water, the door clicks behind me. Spinning around, my eyes find Alex just in time to see her turn the lock.

My heart rate increases as I clear my throat. "Bennett."

"Montgomery."

"God, we definitely have a thing for bathrooms," I joke, anxiously.

Alex strides over to me, her gold heels clicking with each slow step. "Did you mean it?"

"The bathroom thing? I guess I—"

"Not the bathroom thing." She stands so close to me that each of her heavy exhales echo through me.

"Oh, you mean the part about me loving you?" I ask, looking directly into her gold spot.

She nods her head sheepishly as she holds her once heaving breath, her lips still parted, and her brow creased in the best possible way. Reaching to her, I run the pad of my thumb down the wrinkle in the middle of her forehead. "I said it, didn't I?"

Tears build behind her eyes as she drapes her arms around my neck. "Yes, you did."

She kisses me, not rushed or hastily, but like we have all the time in the world. Because after tonight, we do. Because the expiration date on our little arrangement is only the beginning for us.

Pulling back, she drops her forehead to mine, and with her eyes still closed, she whispers the four words that feel better than any win on the ice ever could. "I love you, too."

The statement sweeps over me, bringing with them a peace in my heart that I haven't felt in so long. "Was it the suit?" I ask, bringing my head back so I can see her reaction.

She chuckles and smacks me playfully in the chest before snuggling in close. "No, actually," she says. She lays her head on my shoulder, and I wrap her in my arms. "Turns out that didn't matter at all."

# Epilogue - Alex

The ref blows his whistle after Levi calls a time-out, and the Flames skate over to him right in front of us.

Brooke, Cooper, and I traded in our suite for seats behind the bench today. There was no way we were watching the Flames go for the Cup from our usual box in the sky. Sure, those seats are nice, and they come with privacy and half-decent snacks, but down here, we have the perfect view. A clear picture of the ice, the players, and my personal favorite—Levi's tight ass.

This game has been intense. Obviously, NHL games have higher stakes than Cooper's, but now with my investment in the team, it's even worse. I thought I had gotten used to the stress. Turns out I didn't know the pressure of a win until we got to overtime in the championship game.

The Flames were down one-nothing at the end of the first period. The boys played great, but the Kings came to win. After the second, we were up two-one. We scored off of a power play and Petrov shot one in right before the buzzer. Things were looking up going into the third period, but the Kings tied it in the first few minutes, and both teams held steady until the end.

Now there's one minute left in O.T., which means if the minute runs out, we go into double. If someone scores, we will either be NHL Champions or the Flames will have to swallow their second Cup loss in a row. For all of our sakes, I'm obviously hoping for option number one.

For the two most important guys in my life, this would be huge. Both Levi and Cooper would be over the moon if we won. I also wouldn't mind seeing the reaction of the unfortunate third man that I have to deal with either.

Nick has been surprisingly better lately. That doesn't mean I wouldn't love to see him sulk over the fact that Levi came through and brought Golden City a Cup, but he's making progress. It seems in addition to Cooper putting his foot down, having a much more stable and dependable male figure in his son's life was the kick in the ass that he needed to at least start showing up on occasion. I don't necessarily love seeing his smug face around more, but Cooper is happier than he's ever been. He has himself to thank for that.

A few days after the Spark the Flame gala, Coop asked me to drive him to Nick's house. He told me that if he was going to coach a team one day that he needed to start being a leader now—speaking his mind and holding people accountable. I stayed in the car and let him talk to his dad alone, but from the way things have changed, I'd say Coop might be a playmaker after all. Nick isn't winning Father-of-the-Year anytime soon, but he's doing better than he was before, and I think that's all that Cooper wanted.

"So, you're really going to be working with Coach McHottie next season?" Brooke calls over the song playing in the arena, grabbing my attention.

"I'll be working for Sadie, but technically the Flames will sign my checks I guess."

She nods as her body sways to the beat blasting from the speakers. "Well, I'm going to miss you at the restaurant, but hopefully I'll be out of there soon too," she yells, her lip curled up.

"You'll find something."

"I know," she responds, but her voice has gone soft. I assume it's from the idea of finding a new job she's more secure in, which is her biggest goal, but then I follow her gaze to Drew. She's watching him like she always does, her eyes narrowed and face serious, but her body forward like she's ready to pounce.

"He's clean," I mention over the pop song. She glances at me, her eyes bright for just a second. "They just got tested this week before the game." She shrugs her shoulders as if she's saying *why would I care*, then makes every effort to look at anything but him.

"Anyway," I say, changing the subject, noting that her mood seems slightly off. "I'm just excited to be writing about something that matters." Reaching over and squeezing my forearm, she smiles. "I'm so happy for you."

Sadie reached out to me a few weeks ago asking if I had any interest in taking on some more writing work. Apparently the spotlight partnership with Cooper was such a success that Spark the Flame received a record amount of donations this year and even more interest from the community. The growth will be great for the program and the kids that it benefits, but it means a lot more work for everyone's favorite lady boss.

My role, which Levi insists he did not put me up for, will involve writing the articles and captions for all of the advertisements, as well as interviewing the participants and everyone involved. It's not enough for me to quit writing *Kiss and Tell*, but it will take a big chunk of work off of Sadie and allow me to stop working at The Gilded Pub. It will also get my feet wet with doing some real journalism and keep me around my favorite coach a little more.

A whistle calls the players back onto the ice, and Cooper taps me to watch, bringing me back to the moment. Levi's hands fall behind his back as he clasps them together in his usual stance. Petrov skates across from the King's center and the ref drops the puck between them, the clock beginning its descent down from the last sixty seconds.

As soon as it touches the ice, Petrov pushes the puck between his opponent's skates and moves around him, taking control of it on the other side of his body. Drew takes off for the net and slides around it, tapping his stick in front of their goalie.

"Oh my God," Coop says eagerly.

"Language," I shout, my eyes flashing to the time on the jumbotron above us.

*40 seconds...*

Petrov lifts his stick, and I gasp. "Oh my God."

*37...*

Brooke grabs hold of me, and I lunge for Cooper, all three of us out of our seats and leaning practically over the glass.

*30...*

In a perfect pass, the puck's sent to Drew, and with no delay or hesitation, he taps it toward the net.

*25...*

The goalie leans, but he's a split-second too late, and the puck crosses the goal line with twenty seconds left.

Goal.

Game over.

The Flames win the Cup.

The horn sounds and the three of us—along with the rest of the arena—start jumping and screaming. The players on the ice immediately lunge for Drew, while the others hop the boards and start throwing their equipment. Gloves, helmets, and even sticks start flying in all directions from the bench, and hats, cups, and shoes are tossed from the stands.

After hugging Cooper, I step forward slightly, my son and my best friend still celebrating behind me. I look up to see Levi smacking the boys' helmets, then clapping Erik and Gavin on the back. As he strides down the bench, he looks over his shoulder. Seeing me, his face glows like I've never seen before. This is quite possibly the greatest moment of his life, and it's not lost on me that it took until we made eye contact for him to fully light up about it.

We used to have so many walls up, him and I. It's how we survived, but it's also what kept us alone. I think we both thought that keeping others out was the easiest way to be happy, the best way to keep us focused on our first true loves, and the safest way to save ourselves from getting hurt again. But the truth is, doing that left both of us miserable in our own ways.

It's true, love is hard. It's hard to find, and it's even harder to keep. It takes someone special showing up for you to trust in it and to *keep* showing up even when things are tough or inconvenient to fully lean in.

But love is also beautiful. It's patient and forgiving, and with the right person, it's unconditional.

I think all of us have barriers that we put up to help keep ourselves separated from the world that can break us. We would be crazy not to be at least a little bit cautious. But the person you're meant to be with will tear down those walls without you even realizing it because your heart will still feel just as protected.

Turning to me, Levi winks and mouths the words "I love you." Grinning from ear to ear, I do the same.

He keeps his focus on me as I lean forward, placing only my fingertips on the clear barrier in front of me. Levi turns his lips in and chuckles, his dimple in plain sight. Stepping over a stick, he mirrors my movement and matches his hand to mine on the glass above the boards between us—the one and only wall still dividing us.

Fishing yet another piece of confetti from my hair, I wait in Levi's office. Once the ice settled down a bit, all of the team's families and partners, including me, Brooke, and Cooper, were led down to Levi and the rest of the players to celebrate together. Champagne was sprayed, pictures were taken, and they performed a little ceremony for the Flames with the Cup. There was cheering and laughing and of course, confetti—lots and lots of confetti.

Seeing Levi in all of his well-deserved glory was everything. He has worked so hard to get here, and to see it pay off was such an honor. The pride in his eyes when he looked at his team was one similar to how a parent may look at their baby after seeing them reach one of those monumental milestones. It was the perfect reminder of how much this means.

He and I have come so far since the first time I was here in this office. We have both stopped holding onto the past and started realizing that we're deserving of love. We've learned not only to trust each other but to also trust ourselves, and that we can handle anything that life throws at us—as long as we do it together.

These last few months have been some of the best in my life. Of course things have come up that have put hockey first. He was traveling on the same weekend as Cooper's last game, and the holidays were cut short because of his schedule. But none of that seemed to matter as much as I thought it would when all of this started. Not once have I felt lonely with Levi, even when I'm alone.

"You're here."

My favorite voice echoes off the walls of the office, and I whip my head around to see Levi in joggers and an NHL Champions t-shirt. He has a towel wrapped around his neck and one lock of his still damp hair has fallen onto his forehead. He looks so light—as if he could float right out of this room—and my eyes and smile both grow wide as I take him in.

"That's a good look on you," I say, walking toward him. He throws his towel over his head, and it lands on my shoulders.

"You flirting with me, Bennett?" he asks, yanking me closer.

Wrapping my arms around his waist, I dip my hands under his shirt and drag my nails down his lower back. "Oh, I'm definitely flirting with you. You're a Cup winning coach now, aren't you?"

"I am," he says, raising his brows. "Got the t-shirt to prove it."

"I'm so proud of you," I whisper, hugging him tightly.

Levi leans into me, mint and apple flooding my senses. Purring into my ear, he grabs me from under my thighs, and I squeal as he carries me back to his desk.

"Oh, please tell me you're about to make my dream come true," I say softly to myself as he drops gentle kisses along the side of my neck.

The memory of my first sex-dream with Levi flashes to the front of my mind, and the thought alone is enough to excite me. Levi's teeth graze the soft skin above my collarbone as he smiles into me, probably guessing at what I'm trying to say.

"Well, you'll have to tell me more about *that* later," he laughs. "But I can tell you I'm hopefully about to make *my* dream come true."

"Mmm," I moan, sitting back on the edge of such a familiar desk.

Over my shirt, Levi continues his trail of kisses down the front of my chest until he reaches the spot right above my jeans. He pulls me to stand and drops to his knees. I gasp and look down at him, his face falling into the most genuine grin.

I extend my arm for his cheek, but he ducks his head first, lifting his one leg and reaching for the hem of his pants.

"Wait, what are you—"

My voice fades away as he pulls out a gold diamond ring from inside his sock. "Bennett."

"Montgomery," I say out of habit. He chuckles and my hand flies to my mouth.

"From the moment I met you in that terrible vest..."

"You love that vest," I quip breathlessly. He looks at me blankly before snorting a laugh. "Sorry, keep going."

"From the moment I met you in that terrible vest, which I have since grown to love, I knew you were special. You're fierce and independent and you have the best, worst attitude I've ever seen in a woman." My mouth drops open and my brow creases deeply. "Yep. That. Right there." He points up at me, and we both start chuckling before he continues.

"You challenge me and you encourage me, but most of all, you make me feel so unconditionally loved. All of this," he says, gesturing to his office. "The money, the fame, the status, the Cups—all of it means nothing to me compared to you. And I know we won't always be perfect. We'll share losses and injuries and take bad calls. But I don't want perfect. I want us—win or lose."

Taking a deep breath, he holds out the ring so I can see it more clearly. It's a studded band with one giant diamond and one little gold jewel off to the side.

"Like a spark of a flame," I say, touching the yellow.

"Or the spot in your eye that feels like home."

Standing, Levi takes my hand. "Alex Bennett, will you marry me and make this the best day of my life?"

"But you just won the Cup," I laugh.

He brushes away a single tear that falls down my cheek. "But I still need you."

Nodding, I grab his face in my palms.

"I'm gonna need you to say it, baby."

"Yes," I say, kissing him hard.

He melts into me, wrapping me up, then speaks without pulling away. "Good girl."

# The End

# The Playlist

1. U & Me – Kyle Hume

2. Before You – Benson Boone

3. Better For You – Max McNown

4. The Blue – Gracie Abrams

5. Little Bit Better – Caleb Hearn & ROSIE

6. Heaven – Niall Horan

7. To The Men That Love Women After Heartbreak – Kelsea Ballerini

8. More Than A Feeling – Declan J Donovan

9. Think I'm Gonna Love You – Michael Leah & Caleb Hearn

10. Stargazing – Myles Smith

# Acknowledgements

First and foremost—to my husband and my girls, thank you. You have stuck by every trial and tribulation of this journey, and I wouldn't be starting a whole new series (can you believe it??) if it wasn't for your constant encouragement. Tyler, thank you for helping me so much with this one specifically. I know I asked you a million questions, but I was hell-bent on writing a hockey romance filled with actual hockey. And who better to ask than the real-life coach. I'm sorry I didn't add your name to the cover...

To the rest of my family, specifically Mom—thank you for showing up. From coming to events, to helping with my website, to babysitting my little noodles, you guys are always there in the background cheering me on. With our huge family I could be here all day naming specific instances, but please know that I remember every single one.

To Stef—thank you for being here for literally everything. For making my business your business, for believing in me when I didn't believe in myself, and for celebrating my wins as your own. You yapped your way into my life, and now I can't picture it without you. You're the kind of friend I always prayed for, and all of this quite literally would have never happened if it weren't for you. I can't wait to buy our island.

To Kelli, who started out as my bookie and is now a real life bestie—I don't know what made this *take me or leave me* girl bang down your walls to be my friend, but I'm so grateful that I did. I'm not sure I'd ever be able to write another book without you by my side. You're always there to talk something through, finish my thought, or tell me to stop overthinking. I hope when we're eighty and writing our hundredth dark romance together that we still share a brain.

To Lindsey—thank you for always being a safe space for me to complain or celebrate or bounce off ideas. Your steady support and unwavering encouragement are something that has truly kept be going. Thank you for always having my back even in rooms I'm not in. I don't think you realize how great of a friend you are by just being you. Mostly, thank you for creating Tate. Damn, that (fictional) man...

To Chris—where would I be for the last decade without you? You have gone above and beyond for me and my family and are a huge reason why I am even able to continue writing. Our friendship has been one of the biggest constants throughout the last almost ten years of my life, and I am so thankful for it. Neither of us are ones to get mushy, but you, your loyalty, your support, and your trouble-making antics mean so much to me. Now go write your own book!

Finally, to my beta team, street team, and YOU, the readers—thank you for being here! I am blown away every single day that people actually care about my work. Without you guys, none of this would even matter. *You* are the ones who are changing *my* little corner of the world.

# About The Author

Cassandra Moll is a hockey wife and girl mom to three little ladies who are the inspiration behind her imprint name - *Three Bows Books*. When she's not chasing them around, Cassandra loves to be outside, lift weights, and read. After falling back in love with books, and hearing other authors' stories, she was inspired to finally write her own. Cassandra's books are filled with love and angst and sprinkled with banter that keeps you coming back for more.

For more information on Cassandra and her books, please visit cassandramoll.com.

Made in the USA
Middletown, DE
13 May 2025

75386377R00209